ALEX THURSTAN KRAY
is a young musician and composer, as well as an
aspiring novelist. Bi-lingual English–French, he lives
in Devon most of the year and travels to far-off
places when the mood takes him.
Power Failure is his first book.

Alex Thurstan Kray

POWER FAILURE

The Thriller Club
T.001

 Aspire Publishing

An Aspire Publication

First published in Great Britain 1998

ISBN 1 902035 00 3

Printed and bound in Great Britain by
Caledonian International Book Manufacturing Ltd, Glasgow

Typeset in Palatino by Kestrel Data, Exeter, Devon.

Cover design by Ian Hughes

Aspire Publishing – a division of XcentreX Ltd.

AUTHOR'S NOTE

Some mention is made of members of Government past and present and future. No offence is intended. All other characters and events are fictitious.

The island of Sgeir Varlish does not exist, although similar ones do off the west coast of Scotland, as does a similar lighthouse elsewhere in the British Isles. Nearby islands named in the story do exist.

Prologue

Just two days after I slipped him a thousand pounds in crisp twenties Eric Bottomley went and made a mess on the pavement.

It was a soft, sunny late September morning, officially autumn though you'd never have guessed it. The sort of morning that makes up for a dozen wet, windy antecedents. The sort of morning too, that knocks years off your age and kicks your cares and woes into touch. Poor old Bottomley's cares and woes were clearly immune to the weather's wiles, and he emphasised as much by taking a running jump through a window of the London Hilton Restaurant, which happens to be about thirty floors above street level.

RIP, Eric Bottomley.

I got there an hour after the event. I left the Bentley – a silver Mulsanne Turbo, registration VYV 99 – on a double yellow line behind a flashing ambulance. My windscreen pass made me immune from harassment by traffic wardens. The immediate area had been cordoned off and blue uniforms abounded. Also numerous was the *de rigueur* ghoul contingent; one such sight-seer was busy with a camera. Souvenir snaps for the family album.

The press was about, though not yet in force: Bill Myers from the *Mail* and Dicky Devlin from *Today* were the journalistic clan's only representatives. The rest of the vultures were sure to be along for the feast; it wasn't every day a trade union vice-president took the high dive.

I exchanged nods with Devlin, flashed my DTI pass at PC308, who was guarding a corner of the roped-off area. He looked about sixteen, with a crop of pimples on cheeks and chin.

As I bent under the rope, a uniformed Inspector, red of hue and brimming with establishmentism, came charging across and ordered me to get the hell out of it. So I flashed my magic pass at him too. He stared at it, started to bluster, then subsided behind a grimace of resignation.

'Do you want to take a closer look, Mr Fletcher?' he asked, as deferential as could be, stepping back and drawing me into the inner circle of CID and police lab experts.

I didn't particularly but felt I should, and it was just as well I have a cast-iron stomach for Eric Bottomley's remains under the white polythene sheet were not pretty to behold. He'd burst open like a dropped bag of flour: his clothes had mercifully contained the worst of it, but his head was a squashed, shapeless stump in a congealing, blood-marbled placenta. He must have landed on it – a true header.

'All we heard was that he'd had an accident,' I said, almost apologetically.

'What's the DTI's interest?'

'Can't say yet. Just a matter of keeping our records up-to-date, I suppose. They don't tell me anything.' I adopted a whining tone, in the manner of the office dogsbody forever landed with the unpleasant jobs nobody else want to touch.

Two ambulance men set about wrapping up the remains for the ride to the mortuary. A kind of sigh arose from the ghouls; they were already dispersing. The show was over.

'I'll be off then,' I said to the Inspector. He was issuing orders to a portly sergeant and didn't hear, so I tapped him on the arm. 'I'll be off,' I repeated. 'Thanks for your help.'

'My pleasure, Mr . . . er . . .' Already he'd forgotten my name.

I left them to their grisly work and, since I no longer felt like putting in a stint at the office, I piloted the Bentley down Park Lane, jousted with the dodgems on the Hyde Park Corner roundabout, and shot away along Knightsbridge, homeward bound.

Home – and I use the term in the sense of the place where I sleep most nights – was set in sixteen acres of Buckinghamshire countryside, close to Beaconsfield. Of those sixteen acres, four were officially classified ancient woodlands and therefore theoretically saw- and axe-proof; six-and-a-bit were leased to a neigh- bouring dairy farm, and the rest were a mixture of cultivated gardens, high hedges, many of them trimmed into fancy shapes, a spinney or two, an apple orchard, and an oval, heated swimming pool. Plus the house, a Regency palace with walls in grey-white stucco and along the front an enormous portico of seven fat, fluted columns. Within were nine bedrooms and more antiques than pass through Sotheby's hands in a month. The whole ensemble gloried in the title of 'Kingscourt'. George IV was rumoured to have enter- tained a succession of mistresses there, before and during his reign, and the place hadn't stopped preen- ing itself since.

'Kingscourt' was also home for a number of live-in servants – usually seven – and above all for my rich bitch wife, Julia, younger daughter of the 8th Baron Rosthwaite, peer of the realm. When Julia was thirteen, she and her sister and her two older brothers had jointly inherited the estate of an emigré uncle, an estate then valued at several million pounds, much of it in cash and gilt-edged securities. Shrewdly invested by the Baron on behalf of his offspring, this inheritance had mushroomed beyond recognition and now gener- ated an income for Julia that made mine look like a social security hand-out.

From time to time the house was also occupied by our incorrigibly spoiled, mother-doting son, Gavin; eleven years old and presently boarding at Harrow School. *The* Harrow School. He and I, sad to say, had little in common.

Julia loved Kingscourt. I loathed it. Regrettably there were other bad vibes between her and me and of late these had been in the ascendancy.

So there I was: lousy father, shaky marriage. Now, courtesy of Eric Bottomley's suicide, the less-than-pure atmosphere at Kingscourt was about to receive a further dose of poison gas.

I almost forgot: the day Eric Bottomley died was also the day a rising young star in the trade union Hollywood, name of David Yeo, was appointed to the executive of the Power Engineers Union. The occasion made negligible impact outside the Brothers and Comrades hierarchy. In fact you could say it went off like the proverbial damp squib.

Its ultimate impact on me, on my marriage, and on the entire nation was, however, thermonuclear.

At ten o'clock on Saturday morning, twelve days after Bottomley hit the pavement and headlines, I was summoned to the Home Office.

When the summons came I was in the study, my favourite retreat and the only room in that mausoleum of a house that fitted the epithet 'cosy'. It was a long, narrow room at the rear, with a view out towards the wood. The four tall windows gave ample natural light and a log fire was kept burning in the vast grate from autumn to spring. It was the room's smell that endeared me to it most of all: a smell of woodsmoke from the fire, of furniture polish, and of old books.

The phone had shrilled and so slow was I to answer it that Simba, the Burmese cat, a svelte brown extension to the head-rest of my well-stuffed armchair – my thinking chair – opened a tawny eye and fixed me balefully with it.

It was the Principal Private Secretary to Her Majesty's Secretary of State for Home Affairs. Although I had met the man around various conference tables, this call to my home broke new ground.

Would I grace the Home Office with my presence immediately, was how he put it, in his exquisitely modulated voice.

'It's Saturday,' I said in nominal protest.

'It's urgent,' he countered, and fifteen minutes later, dressed in my City pinstripes, I was trundling the Bentley out of the garage and down the meandering drive. Nobody asked where I was going; Julia was away for the weekend, and I couldn't ever be bothered to buzz Willoughby, the butler.

London was hell as always. I shuffled and braked and lane-hopped across half of it to Queen Anne's Gate, SW1, and was entering the shadow of the modern monolith that now houses the Home Office a few minutes before midday. I flourished my pass and the uniformed lackey in the kiosk condescended to raise the barrier to admit me to the underground car park. It being a Saturday, I had an unusually wide choice of parking bays so I cheekily nosed the Bentley into the reserved section next to *his* Daimler. Two spaces along was a 3.5 Vanden Plas Rover that also looked familiar. State perks both.

The lift hissed me up to the ground floor. It stops there automatically. I got out and signed the book.

'Dunno what's going on,' the security guard-cum-receptionist grumbled. 'You're the fourth today. His nibs is upstairs.'

'Really?' I left him mumbling away and rode up to more heavenly levels where I was met by the Minister's secretary: his name was Disley, his nickname 'Drizzly,' and nicknames don't come any apter.

'A word of warning, Fletcher,' he said, his jaundiced

11

complexion even more jaundiced than usual under the hairless dome of his head. 'Sparks have been flying in there, I can tell you.' He licked his lips wetly, a habit that made me shudder. 'Your commissar is closeted with him.'

In Disley-speak a 'commissar' was any member of the Cabinet below the rank of Prime Minister.

'What's up then?' I asked as we tramped along the corridor, our feet thudding on the thin, utility carpet.

'As if I would tell you even if I knew. It's not my place to give previews.'

Pompous twit.

The Home Secretary's office possessed two doors: one leading directly into the corridor, the other into Disley's adjoining office. I was shown in via the latter, the tradesmen's entrance.

As ministerial offices go, the Home Secretary's bordered on the austere. Large, yes, and with panelling to all points of the compass. Otherwise it was strictly functional. Even the tepid-beige wall-to-wall carpet was barely deeper than that in the corridor.

And there they sat. The Home Secretary behind a desk a shade smaller than the deck of an aircraft carrier; the Secretary for Trade and Industry – my boss and dubbed Old Nick by the less well-disposed towards him – on the far side of the rectangular table abutting on to the desk. Nobody spoke. A firing squad ambience obtained. Should I request a last cigarette?

'Good morning, gentlemen,' I said with the utmost civility. The replies were inaudible, though to be fair Old Nick did dredge up a languid salute.

The Home Secretary, greyest of grey politicians, was reputed to be a man of action, aggression even; tough, gritty, no-nonsense. Traits belied by the bland features that even the cartoonists were hard-pressed to caricature.

'You know Vyvyan Fletcher, don't you, David?' Old Nick said, doing a fly-whisk movement with his wrist.

'We have met, yes.' A smile was switched on and off, as if to economise on consumption of energy. 'So nice to see you again.'

He didn't offer to shake hands. I was waved to a seat opposite Old Nick. Empty cups reposed before both of them, but nobody suggested tea or coffee. Or prussic acid.

I crossed my legs. I laced my fingers across my waistcoat. I waited.

'Sorry to break up your weekend, Fletcher,' Old Nick murmured. 'We thought it best to get the matter settled right away. No sense in dilly-dallying, eh?'

I still waited. I hadn't a clue what he was babbling about.

'It's about this Bottomley business.' The Home Secretary peered at a sheet of typewritten paper on his desk blotter. 'Eric Bottomley. Have you read the police report?'

'Yes, Home Secretary.'

There was silence. I was obviously expected to elaborate, so I added, 'It's inconclusive.'

The Home Secretary smiled. 'I concur in your assessment. Unfortunately, the incident poses a problem . . . a question, rather.'

I politely raised enquiring eyebrows.

'Yes,' he said. 'The question of responsibility. At whose door do we lay Bottomley's death? Hmm?'

'You're forgetting my terms of reference, Home Secretary.' I glanced at Old Nick. A nerve was jumping above his cheekbone. His gaze was fixed on the Home Secretary. 'I only make recommendations. I have no executive powers. You're talking to the wrong man if you're looking for reassurance.'

The Home Secretary tilted back in his chair, nose twitching like a petulant rabbit's. 'All right, Fletcher. It doesn't really matter anyway. Nicholas and I . . . er, the *Minister* and I, that is, are agreed that the whole business has got out of hand, gone too far. To go further

13

would be, at best, politically imprudent, and at worst, illegal.'

Behind him I could see the plane trees in Birdcage Walk. The green of their foliage was no longer rich but dull and, in places, yellowing. Mellow yellow. Winter was coming for the trees and, I fancied, for me.

The Home Secretary had fallen silent. Old Nick stepped into the breach.

'What the Home Secretary, is trying to say, Vee . . .' He leaned across the table, resting on an elbow, 'is that we're shutting up shop . . . your shop. As of now.' The rancour in his voice was unconcealed and it wasn't directed at me. So the decision hadn't been unanimous.

'I see.' I wasn't quite sure how to react.

Old Nick ploughed manfully on, though with clearly increasing discomfort.

'Which means . . .' he said hesitantly, 'er . . . which is to say . . .'

'Which means,' the Home Secretary intervened brusquely, 'that your employment with the Department is herewith terminated.' For a politician especially, this must rank as the ultimate in plain-speaking.

'I see,' I said again, but now a note of asperity was creeping in. 'You're chucking me out of the Civil Service altogether then – have I got it right? Making me the scapegoat.'

This affront to his integrity left Old Nick floundering for words, and it was again the task of the Home Secretary to wield the cudgel.

'Yes to the first; no to the second. We are *not* making you the scapegoat.'

'The hell you aren't!' I was trembling too, but from suppressed fury. 'You're not writing me off as easily as that. I can just visualise your report.' I adopted a pompous voice: 'The operative was considered to have exceeded his authority and acted against the interests of the State. Accordingly he was severely reprimanded

14

and dismissed from the Service. Not to be re-engaged without ministerial approval. Is that the size of it?' I aimed an accusing finger, wishing it were a gun. 'No, you bloody well don't, Mister Home Secretary. You're not going to treat me like one of your nine-to-five arse crawlers!'

I jumped to my feet, anger getting the better of me.

The Home Secretary battled with his own temper. 'Who said we were going to treat you like a . . . er . . . treat you shabbily.' He made a soothing gesture. 'Sit down, man, sit down. Let's discuss the matter rationally, for heaven's sake.'

I would sooner have walked out and left them to suffer torments, wondering what my next vengeful move might be. Instead, catching a whiff of a golden handshake, I did as he asked and sat, slowly and resentfully, still glowering and putting on the air of a man who can't be bought. Not cheaply, at any rate.

'Now then, old chap.' The Home Secretary was back to wearing his conciliatory hat. 'Let's talk terms. The decision to dispense with your section and your services is irrevocable, there must be no mistake about that. However, we naturally wish to soften the blow. Consequently, there will be a sweetener, shall we call it, in appreciation of your sterling services. Normally you could have expected some more overt form of recognition as well – an OBE, or even a knighthood. All kinds of people are knighted these days. As it is . . .' His attitude implied regret. 'As it is, you'll have to settle for being an unsung hero.'

'You're so kind.'

He detected the sourness. The sun dimmed.

'Look here, Fletcher . . . you know damn well my hands are tied.' Classic fall-back position for flustered politicians. Pass the buck to Downing Street.

'I understand, Home Secretary,' I said, biting my tongue.

He picked up a silver propelling pencil, and fiddled

with it. His fingernails were quite badly chewed, I noticed. A penalty of high office.

'Vee . . .' This came from Old Nick. Now the crisis was over he would want to make a contribution. 'Vee, your services to the Government . . . to the country . . . have been of inestimable value. But no one . . . *no one* . . . must ever know.'

No one must ever know.

No one must ever know, for instance, how the steel-workers were destroyed once and for all as a force on the industrial stage; how the miners' union was pro-pelled into an unconstitutional strike and thereafter split asunder; how Michael Edwardes was able to transform the bolshy, lemming-minded BL shop floor into a model of industrial relations. The printers' union, the dockers, the teachers, the GCHQ, the railwaymen . . . all taken on. All beaten.

The list of scalps was long, and went back to the beginning of the decade when the Tories under Margaret Thatcher launched their campaign against the unions. It was a tale of subterfuge and subversion, provocation and intimidation; of lies and scandal and blackmail. Of careers ruined, marriages broken, loyalties betrayed. Of people hurt.

And now, finally, of a life ended.

Oh, yes, mine was a slimy profession.

'. . . and I'm sure you'll find something to suit your special, ah . . . talents,' the Home Secretary was saying.

'Yes. Yes, I could always apply for a job with the TUC.'

He froze. 'That's not funny, Fletcher.'

'It wasn't meant to be.' I met his hard stare, matching flint with flint. I uncrossed my legs, got up. 'Fair enough, Home Secretary, you've made your point. The times they are a-changing. The unions have been re-educated, the laws tightened up; no need for my unsubtle methods any more. For what it's worth, I think you're wrong. We've won a few battles, but the real war's hardly begun. You'll see – it will all blow up in your faces one of these days. When it does . . . I'll be there. I'm not petty-minded. It might cost you a bit more, that's all. And don't worry . . .' This to my boss . . . *ex*-boss. 'I'll be good. You don't have to throw Official Secrets at me.'

'I should jolly well think not,' the Home Secretary said, slightly mollified. 'I'm glad you're taking a reasonable line, old chap. No need for us to fall out amongst ourselves, is there? We are all on the same side, after all, striving for the same goals. It's simply a question of adapting to changing circumstances. New policies are being developed . . . new tactics . . .'

'Yeah, yeah. Save it for the uninitiated.' At the door I turned. 'Anyway, give my love to the Iron Lady. For what my opinion is worth, I don't think it'll be long before she joins me in the dole queue.' I let them absorb that, which they did, spongelike, and not a murmur of dissent did pass their lips. 'Do you?'

Julia didn't return home until just before midnight on Monday, so I held off breaking the bad news until the next morning. Her reaction was a predictably aggrieved, 'So you'll be expecting me to fund your beer and cigarettes from now on.'

'No, my angel,' I said, keeping a tight rein on my temper. 'I gave up those particular vices when I married you – or hadn't you noticed? It's champagne and cigars these days.'

As an attempt at whimsy it fell flat. I crunched into toast and marmalade and studied her as I chewed. At thirty-five she was still striking, still vividly beautiful, the first fine crazing of wrinkles merely giving depth to her beauty. Thick raven hair, casually waved and worn shoulder-length; huge, deep-socketed eyes in a pale, almost bloodless oval face. Good figure too: plump breasts, slim waist, just the hint of a tummy – she'd had it since carrying Gavin and hadn't been able to lose it. Slightly below medium height, which made her just right for my own inch-under-six-feet. In appearance we could have passed for brother and sister. In temperament . . . let's just say there were differences.

Twelve years' matrimony lay behind us. When we married I was twenty-three, she was two years younger – and I suppose our still being together was in itself a measure of fidelity, though on the whole we trod separate paths. Apart from the sex, which was truly sensational, our relationship might best be described as that of two people sharing the same habitation. It was my belief that Julia tolerated me out of habit, that she no longer had any feelings for me beyond the most superficial affection. I wished I could say the same, but the hell of it was I still loved her – selfish, self-centred cow though she was. Over the years our marriage had been soured by her wealth compared to my near-poverty. Not that I didn't contribute to the family pot: £25,000 a year plus generous expenses did more than just keep me in champagne and cigars. Trouble was, I lived beyond it. Life's luxuries had become everyday essentials – the Bentley, for example. Now, with no job, notwithstanding the year's tax-free salary I had been promised as a farewell gift, I would be wholly dependent on Julia's charity. It was not a propsect I relished.

'Well, you needn't think I'm going to pay your gambling bills,' she said bluntly, dusting crumbs from the front of her housecoat. She wasn't dressed – some of her habits were quite slovenly – and without make-up her features seemed somehow . . . incomplete. Still lovely, but like an unfinished portrait awaiting the final strokes of the artist's brush.

'A thousand a year is hardly going to break the bank,' I protested, then cursed as my toast crumbled, showering débris over and beyond the plate.

'Nevertheless . . .'

'You know, Julia, my precious, you can be such a

bitch when you really put your mind to it. Or maybe it comes quite naturally.'

She smiled, sweetness mixed with savagery. 'And you, my darling, would in ages past have been described as a bounder and a cad. If you didn't fuck so beautifully . . .'

'I know – you'd cast me adrift without a penny.' I wiped my mouth on a pristine napkin. 'Speaking of fucking . . .'

I rose and dragged her off her chair. She let out a startled squeal but didn't resist. Julia never ever resisted.

I unzipped her housecoat, pulling it down over those creamy shoulders. She had nothing on underneath and smelled faintly of last night's perfume, faintly of sweat. Her breasts popped out, all soft and quivery.

'The servants . . .' she murmured. She was panting. Literally panting.

'You'd love it if they came in,' I said and there was a snarl in my voice.

Not for the first time I gave it to her across the table. A fast, furious screw to the accompaniment of gasps (hers) and grunts (mine). Whatever else was wrong with our marriage, the physical side was a knockout. When I came, it was some kind of carnal earthquake. Her gasps became shouts and her legs shot up to scissor my neck as we photo-finished to a roaring finale. The servants – well-disciplined lot that they were – stayed below stairs, observing a church-mouse silence. Ears cocked upwards too, I didn't doubt. Servants being servants were bound to know that breakfast à la Fletcher consisted of more than just kippers and toast.

Julia flopped back across the table, her body bent almost at right angles to her legs, her hair mixed up in the toast rack, her pubis jutting at me.

'God, that was good,' she breathed. 'In fact it was bloody sensational.' She propped herself up on an

19

elbow to look at me. 'It always is with you, dammit!'

The 'dammit' summed it up. Ours was a fuck-hate relationship: a compatibility of the flesh – on her side, at any rate.

'By the way,' I said, hoisting up my trousers, 'we're dining with Charlotte and Honry tonight. You've nothing else planned, I hope.'

Sigh of resignation. 'No . . . nothing important. I suppose Honry wants you to do something for him. It must be a year since we were last honoured and then it was only because he wanted you to spy out that French vineyard he was thinking of buying.'

'Honry' was the family nickname of Julia's second cousin, the Honourable Henry Tiverton, third son of the Viscount Tiverton, and loaded to his baby-smooth gills with lucre, like the rest of Julia's relatives. Money clung to that family the way barnacles cling to a ship's keel. Sour grapes? You bet!

'Better make yourself decent,' I said, not caring whether she did or she didn't.

'I suppose so.' But she didn't move.

'Of course, if Willoughby comes in you can always offer him a piece of the action while you're still in a come-and-get-it position. Shame to waste it.'

She roared with laughter; she had the laugh of a barmaid. I grinned and watched her breasts jiggle.

'You're so *coarse*, Vee. So deliciously coarse.'

'That's me.' I was suddenly hungry. I rescued a cold slice of toast from the overturned rack and buttered it. Julia stayed sprawled amidst our breakfast, legs splayed, pubic hair damp and spiky around the glistening pink gash. 'You and me were two of a kind.'

I
POWER HUNGRY

Chapter One

Honry's town pad was in Knightsbridge, a terraced Regency house just off Belgrave Square. Millionaire country.

He came to the door in person, though he kept a permanent domestic staff of two.

'Julia, darling!' he exclaimed and was all over her in his flamboyant yet innocuous way. To me, he said, 'How's the security business?'

We shook hands.

'Could be more secure.' I punned, brushing errant locks of hair from my forehead.

Honry's wife, Charlotte, popped out of the dining room and planted welcoming kisses on cheeks and mouths, relieving Julia of her stole. She was in her late forties, tall and thin with a face that was a Picasso of angles: unusual yet quite pretty apart from a too grand nose. Her hair was her best feature: very thick, very straight, a rich chestnut colour. This evening it was piled in elaborate coils.

There were no other guests. Over dinner we talked banalities and never once touched on business or politics. Unusual, bordering on unheard of. It made me suspicious about Honry's motives.

After dinner, in the time-honoured tradition of the gentry, we retired to his den on the ground floor, a room stuffed with Victoriana, a million books and assorted Parker & Hale hunting rifles. Our wives were left to natter on over a rather superb chocolate liqueur that Honry imported in caseloads from Holland. As a matter of fact, Julia took rather amiss at this segregation, but in someone else's house she could hardly raise a stink over it. That would come later.

Honry settled us both with brandy and cigars, then paced about for a bit. Twice he went to the window, drew back the drapes and peered out. From where I sat, the full moon was visible, bright and sharp-etched.

'Could be a touch of frost tonight,' Honry murmured after his second reconnaissance.

'Honry,' I said, swishing brandy around the balloon glass. 'Do sit down, there's a good fellow. Get it off your chest. If you want me to give another vineyard the once-over, I shan't mind. Rather fancy a trip to *la belle France*.'

He stared at me, a smile plucking at the corners of his mouth. 'It's not that, old boy. I was just trying to decide on my opening gambit.'

Honry was a tall man, certainly over six feet and very slim with it. A man of graceful, well-oiled movements. A handsome man too, despite the retreating, prematurely-grey hairline. The rather weak mouth with its long top lip was more than redeemed by the bristling, military moustache and a jawline of Desperate Dan proportions. Actually he could be very forceful indeed when the occasion demanded.

He had a habit of running a finger along the inside of his collar as if it were too tight. Usually he did it when under pressure or flustered. He was doing it now.

'Come on Honry,' I urged and blew cigar smoke at him. 'Let's have it.'

'Right-ho, old top.' He imbibed a good half of his brandy in a single gulp that made his Adam's apple bounce like a ping-pong ball. 'Here it is then . . .'

It took him less than two minutes to open his can of maggots. When it was clear that the can was empty and there was nothing more to come, I tapped a cylinder of ash from my half-Corona and said simply: 'You can't possibly be serious.'

Not to put too find a point on it, I thought he was off his well-groomed rocker.

He made a pretence of wiping spittle from his eye. 'Don't splutter, old boy. It's so unbecoming. And I am serious – never more so.' His long face dropped. 'It's a matter of supreme national importance, perhaps, ultimately, the safety of the realm.'

'Safety of the realm?' I repeated blankly and laughed. 'Crap!'

'I say, old boy . . .'

'Well, rot then,' I amended. 'Anyway, I have a business to run.'

'Rot to that, too. You have a perfectly good right-hand man . . . what's the chap's name?'

'Vosper.'

'That's it. On the tip of my tongue.' He toyed with his glass, peering inside as if he expected to see his future there. 'You're what . . . forty-two, forty-three?'

'Forty-three next February.'

'Forty-three,' he said wistfully. He was about ten years my senior and obviously feeling insecure about it.

'Look, Honry, I've been away too long. All my connections, my information sources . . . they don't exist any more.'

He inspected fingernails that were as immaculate as the rest of him.

'Not an insurmountable problem.'

'Just forget it, will you? I'm not in the market. I'm making a living and I enjoy being my own boss.'

He sighed, heavily and artificially. 'I suppose having a wife with a seven-figure bank balance must incline one towards a free-wheeling existence.'

Free-*loading* was what he really meant, I suspected, and I shifted uncomfortably. I didn't enjoy being kicked in the crotch, even figuratively.

'You don't still bear a grudge, do you?' he asked. 'Against the Department, I mean.'

'Because they fired me?' My laugh was more of a humourless bark. 'Ten years is a lot of water under a lot of bridge. None of the crowd who were responsible are around any more, so who's to bear a grudge against? Certainly not your new socialist masters.'

'They don't like to be referred to as masters,' Honry said primly.

I well remembered the new PM's maiden address in Parliament after his landslide election. Servants, not masters, of the people. Fine words. And for once the Government had tried to live up to them.

'This is an excellent brandy, Honry, old chap,' I said, not because I cared less about his booze, but to open up new vistas for discussion. Politics and politicians bored me witless.

Instead of handing me the expected rebuke he picked up the TV set remote control and pointed it at the widescreen Sony in its rosewood cabinet.

'There's an item on tonight's news I want you to watch.'

'You're either too late or too early.' The ornate pendulum clock over the fireplace shown a few minutes to eleven.

'I taped it.' His left hand held a second remote. The screen was blue as he rewound the cassette, cigar clenched in his teeth.

'Ah.' A grunt of satisfaction preceded the opening bars of the BBC's Nine O'Clock News.

We polished off our brandies and Honey organised healthy refills before sinking into the other armchair. In silence we sat through a multiple pile-up on the M6, a particularly gruesome rape and murder, some political sleaze, and a protest against some by-pass or other. I was beginning to get restless when a report came on about the Post Office. Suddenly Honry was on the edge of his seat, cigar forgotten, brandy forgotten, nose twitching like that of a mouse on the cheese trail.

'. . . an exploratory meeting today at the Post Office headquarters,' so the spiel ran, 'between the leaders of the communication workers union and Mr Bernard Eames, Director General-designate of the Post Office.'

'The talks lasted about ninety minutes. Afterwards the union issued a statement expressing satisfaction with the progress made and the belief that a better understanding would be achieved than had been the case under previous Governments, under Margaret Thatcher and John Major. The union is optimistic about the prospects for agreement on all major issues at tomorrow's meeting with a reduction . . . '

'In other words a complete surrender by the Post Office,' Honry grunted.

'. . . Mr Eames confirmed that a degree of rapport had emerged, but would not comment on the union claims of probable agreement on pay and working hours.'

There followed a typical interview with some lesser union baron in the midst of a pack of braying supporters.

'So what else is new?' I sneered at Honry, as the performance was concluded.

'Wait!' he hissed; he was riveted to the screen.

'. . . the official inauguration ceremony today of the newly-formed Amalgamated Union of Energy and Water Engineers – or AUEWE – Mr David Yeo, the union's president, prophesied a new dawn for his members and the trade union movement in general, with marked improvements in pay and conditions. The amalgamation of the power engineers, the electrical and gas workers, and the water workers, said Mr Yeo, will make for unprecedented bargaining strength and will virtually guarantee his members a much higher standard of living. Mr Yeo was interviewed at a press conference after the ceremony at Power Base, the union's new headquarters in Chiswell Lane.'

Not much joy there for the Government, I reflected as we flashed over to Power Base and a crowded scene in a large room, in which a dais faced several rows of seats, occupied to the last one. Yeo was on stage, surrounded by his cronies – the executive members of the union council, most likely. I recognised two or three of them, including the general secretary, former leader of the now absorbed electrical workers' union. They all seemed to be talking at once and at the tops of their voices. Elation does that to some people.

'Mr Yeo . . . Mr Yeo!' The cry for attention came from all corners of the room. The BBC's interviewer succeeded in detaching the great man from a rival by dint of a more stentorian voice.

'How will you conduct the negotiations with the electricity and gas companies next week?' The interviewer was young and bald, and bore a remarkable resemblance to the leader of the Tory Party. 'Will you negotiate with them separately, or combine the two?'

Yeo stared straight into the camera and his expression alone gave me and a few million others a hint of what lay in store. His eyes were like chips of broken glass, cold and calculating. Their message was a double-barrelled death ray.

I had never met the man. During my stint as union buster he had been too low down the ladder to merit scrutiny, only surfacing when I submerged, as it were. After a decade away from the world of labour relations, my knowledge of all but the top echelon of trade unionists was scanty. In his mid-forties by the look of him, apparently tall and broad of shoulder. Physically personable: a thatch of fair hair, thick and wavy and of Prime Ministerial length. Nose wide, nostrils flared, mouth a giveaway slit. There was something of the ladykiller about him; women would find him attractive, I guessed.

He was speaking to the interviewer in measured, accentless phrases, picking his words with care.

'. . . hope to conclude a single agreement for the two industries. Let me emphasise though, it is not our intention to . . . confront either the employers or the Government. We have no quarrel with either.' Reasonable so far. No red rags in that statement. 'But we do intend to secure justice for our members and recognition of their real status as contributors to the economy. In the past they have been subordinated to the . . . to certain other industries and this must . . . this *will* change. Other workers will have to acknowledge the pre-eminence of the AUEWE. Without us the country would come to an immediate standstill. It follows therefore, that our members deserve the highest rewards.'

Groans rose from the other armchair.

'I knew it, I knew it!' Honry wailed.

Now I was hissing at him to shut up. Yeo had me hooked.

The interviewer, a youngish, eager-beaver type, had drawn closer to Yeo, thrusting his mike at him as if offering a lollipop to lick.

'You're really saying that you're prepared to sacrifice the rest of the union movement on your altar.' This accusation from the interviewer barely ruffled Yeo's millpond exterior.

'No, *you're* saying it.'

Well-fielded, I mouthed.

'Can you give me some idea of the percentage increase you will be seeking at the pay talks, Mr Yeo?'

Yeo chuckled, but the humour didn't go above his lips.

'You wouldn't expect me to bare my cupboard in advance, would you?'

The interviewer clearly would, but he didn't pursue it. He contented himself with an ingratiating titter, then asked: 'What line will you take with regard to an increase in the work force in the electricity and gas supply industries? This has been reported as forming a major plank in your strategy.'

'Has it indeed?' Yeo rearranged the lapels of his sober suit, straightened an already-immaculate tie. 'Well . . . I am on record as wanting to see the work week reduced – and soon – down to thirty-five hours and the inevitable shortfall in output made up by massive recruitment. This, in turn, will mean enhanced training facilities since the apprenticeship scheme has been allowed to atrophy as a result of government cuts and couldn't begin to handle the new intake.'

To give Eager Beaver his due, he knew precisely when to pounce.

'And what would this "intake" amount to, Mr Yeo? How many extra workers do you envisage a need for?'

A small hesitation, marshalling the syntax. 'I would rather not put a definitive figure on it – it tends to restrict one's room for manoeuvre, you know?' The mouth curved upwards, still not touching the eyes: they were like a shark's, I decided. Soul-less. Predatory. 'However, it would certainly not be less than fifty thousand in the short term; ultimately, a great deal more.'

Behind Yeo, union executives nodded vigorously. Eager Beaver's nod was slower, pensive.

'That would indeed make a useful dent in the unemployment statistics,' he said. 'How would you answer those who accuse you of wanting to put an arm-lock on the Government?'

'I would say this: we are a responsible union and we will act responsibly in so far as our members' wishes and objectives are not compromised.'

'Could you perhaps . . . ?'

'I'm sorry.' Yeo sliced through Eager Beaver's next question with cultivated courtesy. 'I really can't give you any more time. If you'll excuse me . . .'

Eager Beaver wasn't easily put off. 'There is just one . . .' But Yeo pushed past him, not roughly but firmly, and the executive fell in behind him like a train of railway trucks as he descended from the dais.

Back to Broadcasting House and the newscaster.

'Speaking in Parliament today, Mr Hague, leader of . . .'

Honry punched the remote control on his chair arm and I was left staring at my reflection in a blank screen.

'Well?' Honry said.

I yawned ostentatiously. 'If you insist on having an opinion – it sounded like standard union rhetoric from a jumped-up demagogue anxious to see his name in lights. To be enshrined for posterity on the union movement's roll of honour alongside Appelgarth, Mann, and Nye Bevin.'

Honry didn't hide his disappointment. 'Is that all?'

I knocked back what was left of my brandy. Pondered.

'Broken down, the words said nothing that hasn't been said before. Better assembled perhaps, better presented – he's a sight more articulate than some of his brethren. Otherwise, if you discount that business about the fifty-thousand recruits it wasn't all that dramatic.' I angled a glance his way. His face was intense, his colour high as if he had been drinking heavily, which he hadn't.

'However . . .' I let the word hang in the air; he almost peed his pants in his impatience for me to continue. 'Nobody has come on quite that strong, been quite so openly demanding and so subtly threatening before. Not even Scargill in his day. And anyway, he was anything but subtle.'

'So?'

'So . . . it's not what he says, it's who he is; it's the man himself who disturbs me.'

'Aaah!' It was a sound of fulfilment. The Honourable Henry Tiverton sat back in his chair, smoothing his moustache with thumb and forefinger. The cat that got the cream wasn't in it.

'That's what you wanted me to say,' I reproached him.

He just looked.

'Okay, Honry, I begin to understand the problem. The Government is running scared of Mr Yeo and all his works: the AEW . . . hell, why did they have to make it so complicated? You can't even make an acronym of it, like ASLEF or NALGO.'

Honry reached down and regulated the control of the ceramic-log gas fire; the ghostly dance of the flames died a little.

'The Government *is* scared. Not scared-frightened, but scared-wary. They are convinced – and with justification, in my view – that they have much more to fear from the man than the machine he controls. He's clever, ruthless, and has persona. You should see him manipulate an audience. I guarantee he'll be the union movement's standard bearer in no time at all.'

'Not if the TUC can help it. They don't approve of demagogic union leaders.' I fingered my chin. 'I must say I'm not well-acquainted with Friend Yeo. He's a bit of a Johnny-Come-Lately.'

The pendulum clock chimed the half hour. I had a sense of travelling back in time, to the era of strife and class politics; of squabbling, bullying, and sectarian warfare that had served only to drag the country and its people, most of whom wanted no truck with any of it, deeper into the mire of decline and fall. First Thatcher, then Major, had stripped the unions of their power to disrupt and dislocate. Now, with the Socialists back in the driving seat and the so-called honeymoon period behind them the old union Kraken was stirring in the deep.

If Britain's future prosperity were to revolve around the actions of men like David Yeo, we were in for a thin time.

'Returning to the nub of our discussion.' Honry spoke through a swirl of cigar smoke. 'Will you do it?'

I played with the dewlap of skin under my jaw. It seemed to me I was developing a bit of flab in that quarter. In my forties, it was to be expected. Now I felt depressed as well as tired.

'Let me get it quite straight what's involved,' I said, shaking off the doldrums. 'You want me to infiltrate the union.'

Furrows grew on his aristocratic brow. 'Did I say *that*? I think you must have misheard me, old top. Whether or not you decide to infiltrate the AUEWE as a means of delivering the goods will be up to you; personally, I doubt the need. But that isn't the object of the exercise.'

'What is the . . . er . . . object of the exercise then? Since I'm such a dummy you'd better explain it to me again – in kindergarten language.'

His gaze was so earnest it troubled me.

'What we really want is for you to infiltrate *him*. We want you to infiltrate Yeo himself.'

In bed that night I talked over Honry's extraordinary proposition with Julia.

'Have you decided what to do?' she asked at the end of it. Her hand strayed over my groin, quite abstractedly. Groins exerted a strong pull on Julia.

'I've decided to sleep on it,' I said and rolled over to do just that.

But Julia had other plans for me.

Afterwards, drained in body but not in mind, I was no longer inclined to sleep on the evening's events. As Julia's breathing settled down to a steady rhythm and faded into the background like the throb of distant traffic, I lay wide awake with my fingers interlocked behind my neck – my favourite thinking position. The Fletcher sensor was stimulated on two counts. Count One – the Government wanted me back in the fold. My cue for a hollow laugh. But let that lie for now, to concentrate on Count Two – David Yeo.

Now there was a man of great potential, be it for good or evil. A man, in certain circumstances, to cultivate, also to beware of. Whenever he had looked directly into the camera it was as if he had been looking at me, and me alone. As if he were issuing a challenge, saying here I am, about to make a shambles of this United Kingdom. With my army of stout-hearted but easily manipulated British blokes who, if I say so, will pull switches, turn off taps, and disconnect pipelines, I can bring the Dark Ages back to this country. Maybe I can even start a revolution.

The words I was putting into Yeo's mouth had no basis in fact, and I was startled by them. But the conviction that these were his true sentiments, his true intentions, was rock-solid. In vain I tried to dislodge it, to sneer it away as the product of an over-active imagination.

Ultimately, at some small hour in the morning, fatigue stilled the bees that buzzed around inside my skull. My last waking resolve was to forget all about Yeo. It was none of my business. I was retired – remember?

Yet somewhere between the advent of sleep and next morning's belated awakening to the rasp of a chain saw from the direction of the orchard, the instinctive urge to make it my business, to bring the juggernaut to a shuddering stop, had hardened into obligation. Single-handed, I, Vyvyan Fletcher, latter-day St George, would slay the Dragon Yeo and save the nation. Subject to negotiation of a satisfactory fee.

Chapter Two

Latterly, during my term of employment at the DTI, I had had at my disposal, round the clock, a Special Branch Detective Inspector called Mike Hutton. A tough competent policeman whose regard for the niceties of law was at best marginal. We never became pally, but had built up a professional solidarity of sorts plus a certain mutual respect – albeit a mite grudging on his side.

From Honry I had elicited the number of Hutton's current direct line. But when I tried to contact him on it, some eight days after my session with Honry, an officious female intercepted and in spitting razor-blades voice demanded to know who I was, where was I calling from, and did I change my underpants daily. I gave her my vital statistics. She ordered me to wait and left me listening to the sound of my own breathing in the mouthpiece.

When, after an interminable wait, she got back to me, it was only to bark: 'We'll call you!'

She hung up without even saying goodbye.

I stared at the whining receiver, my feelings mixed. Did all this mysterious nonsense mean I was not to be accepted back into the fold after all. It was one thing for the politicians to decided to enlist me, quite something else for the security services to lower the drawbridge and invite me into their fortress. Viewed dispassionately, such precautions were only sensible. I'd left the Government Club and could no longer expect to enjoy the benefits of membership.

Except that *they* were serenading *me* to sort out another mess. One that portended to be too smelly, too fraught with political scandal, for any government department to be linked directly to it.

Twisted reasoning? Maybe.

The phone trilled before I came to any conclusions. I snatched it up.

'Hutton,' my caller announced.

'Ah, hello, Inspector,' I said breezily, as if it were only yesterday I had last used his services. 'Sorry to trouble you, but I need a meet.'

'Just like that?' No hints of welcome back to the fold. 'And it's Chief Inspector, now.'

'Sorry. Congratulations. About the meeting . . .'

'What gives you the right to demand meetings?' he snapped. 'Jesus, it must be eight years since you quit the DTI.'

'Call it a personal favour then.' I said, nettled by his attitude.

His grunt was not encouraging. Nonetheless he agreed to meet me for a pie and pint at The Anglers, a pub in Richmond.

It was one of those rare autumn days when, but for pavements ankle-deep in leaves, it might have been Spring. After a week of heavy rain it was more than welcome. I got to The Anglers ahead of Mike, parked the car in a cul-de-sac and my behind on a bench in the pretty garden at the back of the pub, overlooking the river where a pair of ducks sculled in lazy circles. The sun was low and platinum-brilliant; I could have used sunglasses. Behind me, in the Tap Room, a juke box pumped out some dirge, all throbbing guitars and a metronome beat. What Mike saw in the place beat me, but it had always been his favorite venue. Maybe he owned it.

Ten minutes after the hour he rolled up in a white Mondeo, blemished with dried mud. No apologies for his lateness. Proving he didn't need to kowtow to me any more. Not that he ever had.

His handshake was half-hearted.

'How are you, Mike?'

He made a face. 'Mustn't grumble.'

He had a boxy figure with the thick neck of a weight-lifter. Medium height, broad, hands big enough to paddle a canoe with; fair hair, very straight and held in place with hair cream. He was a year or two my senior, though a good deal more frayed at the edges, with the air of a weary bloodhound.

I fetched drinks for both of us: Watneys for him, G & T for me.

'Keeping the crime rate down to manageable proportions?' I asked as he swallowed half the contents of his pint pot.

He made another face, sardonic this time. 'Like hell.' He was not given to verbosity.

'Still on special duties?'

He looked me in the eye at last. 'Yes, but not your kind. Speaking of which I was told you were running a private security outfit. What's this all about?'

'The security outfit runs itself. This is about more of the mixture as before. Only private enterprise.'

His eyebrows ascended in disbelief.

'Private enterprise? You on a crusade?'

'Don't make me laugh; I'm no do-gooder. I mean I'm being employed privately.' Wrong tense, since I hadn't yet accepted Honry's commission, but hopefully he wouldn't have checked.

He poured the other half down his long-suffering gullet and belched. His eyes swivelled towards a group of teenage girls, debouching from the pub, glasses in one hand, heaped plates in the other, chattering gaily. For all the notice they took of us we might as well have been plastic gnomes.

'I need information,' I said, 'from your box of tricks.'

'Do you now? You don't want much, do you?'

The 'box of tricks' referred to was the criminal

37

records computer at New Scotland Yard. It contained data not only on conventional criminals, but also on known and suspected political agitators, subversives, and terrorists – past, present, and simmering.

'Can do?' I asked.

'Who's the subject?'

'Have another beer,' I said instead of answering. I wanted him as sweet as Watneys could make him before I told all.

When I got back with his beer and my top-up he was mulling over the girls who were seated at the next table. He had separated from his wife just before I was outed from the DTI. Maybe he was on the lookout for a replacement, though this bunch was about a generation too late.

'Who's the subject?' he repeated as I handed him the glass.

I partook generously of my G & T. Here goes. 'David Yeo.'

He didn't even blink. 'And the purpose of the exercise?'

This was the tricky part.

'I can't tell you.' He shot me a hard, come-off-it glance. 'Not yet,' I added. 'It's still exploratory. You'll have to take it on trust.'

A small cabin cruiser bumbled past, labouring against the current. A fishing line trailed unattended from its stern, collecting river weed but not much else.

The sun was dazzling me so I turned my chair through ninety degrees.

'Well?' I said.

'About Yeo . . . what gives you the idea he's on record?'

He was stalling, determined not to make it easy for me. I tried a fresh tack.

'What do you think of him – Yeo?'

'Think of him? I don't think of him at all. I don't play politics, you know that.'

'Fine – then play patriotism!' I said, angry now.

My outburst took him aback.

'No need to get stroppy, Vee. You know I can't afford to take sides the way you do. The police have to be apolitical. We just provide a service for the powers-that-be, whoever they may be.'

'Good. Give me service then.'

He reached inside his raincoat pocket, and drew out a brown envelope. He dipped in it and scattered a handful of bread crumbs on the water, near the edge where they wouldn't be swept away by the current. The ducks quacked their appreciation and a second pair emerged from nowhere and hydroplaned over to where the action was.

'What's going on?' Mike demanded abruptly.

'How do you mean?'

'I mean . . .' His jaw stuck out pugnaciously, 'you're supposed to be off the payroll. Yesterday, I had a call from the Commissioner himself and he said that if you contacted me I was to be . . . helpful. No questions asked. So . . . what's going on?'

Inexplicably I wanted to laugh. Even before I had agreed to do it, strings were being pulled to smooth my path.

'So why don't you do as you're fucking-well told? Be helpful. Ask no questions.'

He twitched. I wouldn't have put it past him to hit me.

'Let's walk,' he said and downed his second pint in a single, prodigious draught. That thick neck evidently contained a throat like a drain.

We walked across the blue-painted iron footbridge that spans the Thames here and down the narrow island in the middle of the river towards the weir, where we stopped. Transformed by the recent rains into a miniature Niagara, the weir gave off a sustained roar, the water descending in a glacial rush and setting up a chain of crystalline explosions. Beyond, all was white foam and swirling vortices and spray drifting like early morning mist.

'Water fascinates me,' Mike said absently. 'The sheer power of it. Like here, or a waterfall. Or sometimes just the action of the tide – like at Perranporth. You know Perranporth?'

'Can't say I do.'

'It's a small town in Cornwall. When I was much younger I used to go land-yacht racing there. The beach is flat as a bowling green and there are some unusual currents that cause the tide to come in quickly – and I do mean quickly. It can cover several hundred yards in a matter of minutes. It's easy to get cut off.' He had his hands in his pockets and was standing there in a relaxed slouch, every inch the down-at-heel cop. 'Commissioner or no Commissioner, I want to know what you're up to.'

The switch of subject caught me wrong-footed. My instinctive reaction was to bluster, a tactic that would have got me nowhere with Mike Hutton. So, shrugging, I said, 'I've been asked to check him out. To see if he's clean.' It sounded better than 'I've been asked to dredge up dirt on him'. 'That's as much as I can tell you without betraying confidences. Trust me, Mike.'

He gnawed at a fingernail like a squirrel attacking an acorn. Spat shreds towards the river. 'Again I ask you: why should you think we have a file on Yeo? On the other hand . . . we might have one on you.'

I didn't doubt it. 'Stop pissing around, Mike. We both know who you've got files on. Do you really want me to arrange a telephone call from the Home Secretary to the Commissioner?'

I was bluffing. Telling tales out of school wasn't my style.

'Bastard,' he said without heat.

A middle-aged woman in furs and boots passed us with an object in tow that looked like a small rug with feet, but might, stretching the imagination, have had canine origins. I waited until she was out of earshot then asked: 'Is it yes or no?'

After a long simmer he said, with a lop-sided grin, 'I can see I'm not going to get any more out of you, you tight-lipped shit-stirrer. Meet me at the Yard tomorrow at ten.'

He shoved a two-fingered adieu under my nose and stalked off back towards the bridge, leaving me alone on the island with only the thunder of the weir for company.

From Richmond I drove to High Wycombe, and dropped in at the office. VEEFLETCH SECURITIES was more of a hobby to keep me out of mischief than a serious moneymaking business. Peter Vosper, who ran it for me, neither needed nor wished for my participation. I had made him a director, handed him a ten per cent stake in the company, and for most of the time, I left him to it.

'Nothing to report,' he said cheerfully, when I stuck my nose through his door. 'We're still making money.'

I had noticed. He produced monthly P & L and cash flow statements, mainly for my benefit.

We chewed over a couple of contracts he was trying to win, drank some coffee from his ever bubbling percolator, and after an hour I left him to his devices. Obligations discharged for this month. Now I was free to get into mischief.

Not every Tom, Dick and Harry is allowed through the bullet-proof glass front door of New Scotland Yard and only a small proportion of those who are get to set foot inside Criminal Records, which is part of the Yard's Technical Support Division. My previous visits there could be counted in single digits.

In these push-button days the hub of Criminal Records is a computer: jealously-guarded and held by the Law in deity-like awe. Without it their job would be infinitely more difficult, nay impossible, so they were fond of telling me. Yet as recently as three decades ago computerised records were only a twinkle in some progressive commissioner's eye. Up until now I had diplomatically forborne to point this out.

Mike, as a senior Special Branch officer, had security clearance for just about every recess of the computer's electronic archives and the material to which he was privy included the Interpol Databank – the records of all known criminals worldwide, updated daily. This plenitude of information was inputted onto the computers internal disk and copied onto CDs which in turn were stored in a fireproof library, next door to the computer room. The CDs were many in number, but then it's a big subject. The criminal fraternity is hydra-headed and ever on the increase.

Mike collected me from the Security Desk on the ground floor, a corridor's length away from the computer centre. The centre itself was unoccupied apart from a chubby, shirt-sleeved man with unruly hair, sitting before a monitor in an adjoining, glass-panelled office. As Mike and I entered, the man swivelled round in his chair. He greeted Mike casually before switching his gaze to me.

Mike did the introductions. 'Vee Fletcher – Detective Inspector Ivan Smithson.

'Mr Fletcher,' Smithson acknowledged with a tight smile.

'Inspector.'

'Mr Fletcher has temporary clearance.' Mike confirmed in a voice that implied disapproval.

'What can I do for you?' Smithson was swivelling his chair from side to side, looking from Mike to me.

'I want the works on David Yeo,' Mike said shortly. 'In print.'

'Ho, ho,' Smithson said, which might have meant anything. 'What's he done?'

'You watch the news, don't you?' Mike said irritably.

Smithson made a placatory gesture. 'Okay, okay. Coming right up. Bring your card.'

Mike went and stood by Smithson and produced a plastic card, like a credit card except that it was all white. This he fed into a slot at the front of the monitor and tapped out a five-character sequence on the keyboard. Numerals leapt onto the white screen, a whole string of hieroglyphics. The card was returned. Mike pocketed it and rejoined me and we sat down to watch the show, which opened to Smithson playing scales across the keyboard with the loving dexterity of a concert pianist. More digits flowed forth. I was too far away to decipher them.

Mike lit an untipped cigarette and stared straight ahead. I twiddled my thumbs. Studied a poster behind Smithson's desk warning against careless talk and the consequences to your career in the Metropolitan Police of a flapping mouth. It was pure Big Brother.

The printer beside Smithson hiccupped into life, a frenzied chatter, spewing out words faster than a machine gun spews bullets. The top edge of the print-out sheet, alternating green-and-white horizontal stripes, climbed upwards from the depths of the machine in a succession of jerks as each line of data was printed.

After a good five minutes of this the printer paused. Maybe it was tired. Smithson did his concert pianist act again. This was followed by a *brrrrp* from the printer, and the sheet, now a yard or more in length, jerked upwards several times before coming to a standstill. Silence was restored.

Mike and Smithson arrived at the printer together. I stayed put; I was a guest here. They gave the print-out a practised once-over. An occasional grunt from Mike punctuated this exercise while Smithson tapped his teeth with a pencil. Their faces were as bland as a whitewashed wall.

'Okay, is it?' I said, mildly irritated by all this heavy pondering. 'Ink's not smudged?'

'Ha, ha,' Mike said softly, and unsmilingly. Then he leaned over the printer and ripped off the sheet along its perforated crease. 'Thanks, Ivan. Buy you a pint after school.'

'You're on.'

Apparently we were leaving. I headed a goodbye at Smithson and followed Mike out, down the corridor, up nine floors in the lift. His office was on the Dacre Street side of the building with a crick-neck view out over my late place of employment, the uninspiring Department of Trade and Industry, towards Westminster Abbey and Big Ben, newly encased in scaffolding, forbidding silhouettes against forbidding skies.

The only luxury Mike allowed himself in his utilitarian cubicle was a coat stand. I hung my raincoat next to his fawn 'detective special' trench coat without waiting to be asked; I'd have had to wait forever. Just as I was subsiding into the steel-and-plastic seating in front of his desk a knock came to the frosted-glass panel and a head popped around the edge.

'Ah . . . you're back, chief,' the head said. It was young and bearded. 'Fancy a cuppa?'

'Don't mind if I do.'

'Me too,' I said. The head sought Mike's okay, got it and withdrew.

Mike spread the print-out across his desk for me to read. 'Help yourself.'

As was my wont I first did a fast, superficial scan, focusing on the non-intrinsic points and skipping the obviously mundane. Then I went back to the beginning and repeated the exercise only much more thoroughly. I was jolted by the MOST SECRET rating that preceded the text: in triplicate too, for dyslexia sufferers.

Below, it ran:

SUBJECT: YEO/DAVID JOHN
SEX: M
ETHIC GRP: WH CAUC
NATIONALITY: BRIT/ENG [B] ENG [B]/[AD –
                  RPU]

The 'Nationality' bit signified that both parents were of British-English stock by birth, as distinct from British-Scottish or British-Welsh.

Date of birth, place of birth, height, weight, place of residence, passport number, waffle, waffle. I stifled a yawn. Most of this was old hat to me. Since my talk with Honry I had been swotting up non-stop on Master Yeo. There was the odd revelation: he had been a full-time official for the Power Engineers' Union ever since leaving York University, where he'd gained a First with Honours in Industrial Economics (coincidentally we'd read the same subject though I'd gone to Bath and hadn't rated Honours or First): the revelation was that he'd quit the union for eighteen months when he was twenty-seven, to establish a union of his own in the electronics industry. The venture had foundered through lack of funds and a certain amount of opposition from the Electricians, then also cultivating the industry. He battled – bloody hard, if you read between the lines – and lost. Lost the battle but gained in stature. According to the printout he'd won a lot of respect amongst leading unionists. He returned to the Power Engineers and it was by no means an ignominious scuttle: recognising his talents no doubt, they not only took him back but promoted him to Area Organiser. For someone still well short of his thirtieth birthday this was quite an accolade.

I moved on to his immediate family. Wife: Carol, aged forty-two. I skipped much of her background. York University too; presumably that was where they'd met, though he would have been in his final year while she was still a freshman. They had married when she was twenty-one and he twenty-three. First child, a daughter, Rowena, was born a full fifteen months later. Nothing juicy there for me to sink my scandal-mongering fangs into. Second child, another daughter, Regina, now sixteen. Third and last of the dynasty, a son, christened Roger. The three 'Rs'. An academic bunch, I bet.

Considerable guff on Daddy Yeo's recent career, specifically since his elevation to the union executive. None of it explained why he had been appointed President of the new amalgamated set-up over the heads of more exalted and conceivably more worthy personages. Was it to avoid unseemly public squabbles between the obvious contenders? For an official of the second rank, whatever his talents, to be given the top job ahead of his 'betters' is unusual in the intensely hierarchical trade union movement. Was he then no more than a figurehead? A crownless king? A *puppet*? Hamstrung by a constitution that forbade him to so much as fart without the say-so of the executive. Stranger things have happened in union history.

And did it matter for my purposes?

I sucked my teeth over it. Mike was no help, still browsing over his papers. I was about to bounce a few theories off him when a tiny buzzer was triggered off inside my brain. I had missed something. Somewhere in those soulless lines of print was an aberration. A wrong note. My pulse beat accelerated and the adrenalin got up off its hankers and creaked into motion. These were normal Fletcher reactions to a discovery and as pointers were as reliable as a compass needle.

Mike must have scented the vibes because he looked up. 'Found something, Sherlock?'

Now I felt foolish. 'Ye-e-es. That is, yes, but I'm not sure what it is yet.'

'One of your flashes?'

It wasn't a sneer. He was remembering when we had

worked together and my 'flashes' as he termed them, had often sparked off a solution to a tough problem.

'Wait.'

Again I waded through the verbiage. Name, sex, nationality . . . oh, where, tell me where . . . education (primary), education (secondary) . . . stop! Back three, four lines to nationality. British-English (B) – English (B)/(AD)(RPU). There it was! (AD). I rested my finger on it. It meant nothing to me so I asked Mike to translate.

'Anno Domini,' he cracked and jokes from him were such a rarity I almost fell off the chair.

'Seriously. It's under 'Nationality.' After it comes R-P-U.'

'A-D stands for adopted. R-P-U, real parents unknown.'

Adopted. *Adopted*. Now that was a revelation. The sole quirk in an otherwise depressingly normal and respectable life history. Was it a key? Was it *the* key? Would it unlock a treasure chest of muck for the raking? It was a long shot and fraught with hazard. Any attempt to make capital out of the circumstances of his birth and early childhood would backfire as sure as the Bottomley payoff that was the catalyst of my downfall had backfired.

Still . . . it was a lead. It would do for openers.

I skimmed the print-out for the parental details. Found them half-way down.

'I don't suppose I'll be allowed to take this away,' I said, rustling the print-out at Mike.

'Hardly, with that security rating. You know the rules.'

I took out a pen and my pocket diary and noted the names and address of Yeo's adoptive parents. They were in their late sixties, the woman older by almost a year, and had two children of their own, both quite a bit younger than Yeo. I also noted the names and addresses of various other people who had figured prominently in Yeo's life, such as his tutor at York, and the now-retired General Secretary of the Power Engineers' union, who had initially recruited him; yes, the information really was that extensive.

'Do we know anything about the adoption?'

Mike finished igniting a cigarette before replying around it.

'If it's not there, we don't know about it. Like you, I haven't made a study of Yeo. He was strictly second-echelon until the amalgamation.' He exhaled smoke at the wall; to judge from the discolouration there it was his favourite aiming point. 'Queer, that. His elevation from an ordinary member of the executive to top dog.'

'Rare but not unknown. You should read up on union history. Something similar happened when the TGWU was formed. Also . . . the amalgamation of four unions, none of which was entirely dominant, is probably a unique event – certainly since the war. So it's hard to draw comparisons.'

Mike cleared his throat, a wet crackle, mildly disgusting. 'So what now?'

'What now is that I make a few enquiries.'

'Uh-huh. Just remember you're on your own, won't you? Unofficial. For your own good, stick to making enquiries, not waves.'

He saw me to the door. There I faced him – him with his remote, lifeless expression. Mike the Mask. When it came to inscrutability, the Chinese weren't in the same league.

'You don't like me very much, do you, Mike?'

'No.' The bluntness of it shocked me.

Now I'd gone this far I had to press on, though I already regretted asking.

'Why not?'

'You really want to know?' He saw that I did and obliged me. 'It's what you are, what you represent I can't stomach: a rich woman's parasite. Idle hands looking for mischief to occupy them. To you, the DTI job – if you can call it a job – was just fun and games. Oh sure, you believed it had to be done. I even think you genuinely wanted to do your bit for Britain, make a contribution. All very noble and patriotic. But it never really *meant* much to you, did it? You never felt it inside, in your guts – here!' He pounded his midriff. 'It was just a paid hobby. Just a bit of a giggle. Because of you, a man died. A poor, frightened stooge who needed a few quid and who was gullible enough to let you sweet-talk him into forgetting his loyalties and his principles. The way I see it you're only one step up from a common villain; the difference is that a villain doesn't pretend to be a paragon.'

It was stronger, more vicious than I had bargained for. It hurt.

'Is that the lot?' I said quietly, masochistic to the last.

'You want more? Believe me, I could give it to you.'

I belted my raincoat mechanically. 'Bottomley happened a long time ago and I can't undo it. As for the rest: parasite looking for kicks I may have been, but I didn't have to slum to give my life meaning, and I still don't. Don't you think that if all I wanted was a bit of a giggle, as you put it, I should be out there playing the playboy, screwing every wench in sight, and stuffing myself full of chemicals? There's no shortage of diversions for a man with a fat wallet.' I was making no impression: his facial muscles were locked tight. He was as still, as passionless as a tombstone. 'Instead I chose to contrinute in a way that my financial independence – or dependence, if you like – allowed me to. Now I'm back to do more of the same for the same motives, and if that sticks in your windpipe, Chief Inspector Hutton, you can choke on it!'

The stone didn't even crack.

'Fuck off, Fletcher.'

'I'm going, I'm going. But if I need any more of your measly help, I shan't be too proud to come back.'

He slammed the door on me.

Chapter Three

Yeo's parents lived in Sheffield, a city of half-a-million inhabitants and once proud heart of the steel industry. Once busy, bustling, and prosperous, with a reputation that encircled the globe.

Now, partly due to the recession of the early nineties, partly due to leftwing dogma pursued by its Council in the seventies and eighties, resulting in the levy of usurious rates on industry and individual alike, great chunks of it had been reduced to a seedy wasteland. Where, not so long ago, mighty blast furnaces roared and forge hammers thundered, sending out tremors over a quarter mile radius, were now to be found dead factories, piles of rubble like bomb sights, and empty, echoing streets. Nobody had ever minded the noise and the grime; it brought money and, much, much more important, it brought purpose.

Now it was all gone, probably for good, and the pathetic developments of terraced houses that were gradually filling in the bare patches, were no substitute.

I went there via the M1 (was there ever another route?) and it was a little after three in the afternoon when I rounded the corner into Athol Road, a long cul-de-sac in the suburb of Attercliffe, to the north of the city centre. I'd forsaken lunch, which hadn't improved my humour, but which may have been all to the good; Julia had recently berated me for putting on weight – 'Getting tubby, aren't we?' was how she actually phrased it, although at twelve stone and five feet eleven, I wasn't more than a few pounds over the top. Women always exaggerate.

Like all the houses in Athol Road, number 48 was a semi-detached Victorian property with basement, bay window on the ground and first floors, an attic dormer window in the roof, and intricate, wooden gable ends. The brickwork, presumably once red, had been laminated with a century of factory outpourings and was now uniformly dark bronze. Not unattractive – you could say it added character. The peeling green and cream paintwork of the window frames and the front door with its stained-glass porthole told a different tale, however – neglect.

There was a driveway but no gate. Two cars: a Ford Cortina embellished with rust, and a metallic-blue H-registration Honda Accord. I parked my shiny three-months old Bentley Continental behind them in the driveway. Presumptuous of me, but Bentleys and city streets don't mix.

It was cold and trying to rain. Slipping into my blazer (I habitually drove in shirt-sleeves), I mounted the five steps to the tiny, recessed porch where I ran a comb through my hair and made minor adjustments to tie and cuffs. First impressions count, and never more so than when your credentials are phoney.

I prodded the illuminated, plastic bell-push and set off a musical fanfare within, immediately followed by an hysterical yapping. While I waited, expelling white breath, a train rumbled past nearby, clanking over points. It was invisible from where I stood; the tall houses shut out the surrounding area as effectively as a prison wall. Sheffield has many such streets.

The dog was still yip-yipping away. No other sound of habitation. My finger was poised for another prod when the door opened with a squeal and there before me was a young woman – a girl, I should say, for she was in the eighteen to twenty-one age range, at a guess. Tall-ish, slim-ish, and as far as you could tell

51

under the long, baggy sweater and faded jeans, she had the customary rounded areas front and back. Nicely-shaped face too, on a long but not over-long neck, with features that individually might have been presentable, but collectively didn't amount to much. The greatest disservice to her looks was done by a pair of large, round glasses, lightly tinted blue, and the mid-brown hair scraped back into a bun at the nape of her neck. A few, escaping strands hung down over her cheeks. On the credit side, her smile was pleasant. Teeth slightly crooked but white as a TV announcer's.

'Good afternoon, miss,' I said, assuming my best travelling salesman manner.

She said, 'Hello' so naturally and unself-consciously that I took an immediate liking to her. The smile stayed in place; it even reached her eyes. She was the sort of girl who makes up for what she lacks in glamour with a friendly, outgoing personality.

'Can I help you?' she said.

I handed her a card from my special collection. It gave my real name, but described me simply as a 'Journalist.' Freelance by implication.

'Mr Fletcher.' Still smiling away, still friendly. No hint of animosity towards a representative of the despised *paparazzi*. So far, so good.

'I'd like to see Mr and Mrs Yeo, if that's possible,' I said with all the humility I could muster. 'It's for a newspaper article about their son, David.' I named a rag of suitable political orientation. 'Are you a member of the family, by any chance?'

'I'm Mr Yeo's daughter – David Yeo, that is.'

So this was Miss Rowena, was it? Just twenty years old, I recalled from Mike Hutton's print-out; university student, family rebel. I looked at her now with new interest. Still not my type, though I wasn't averse to the occasional extra-marital activity when the need or the desire arose. She might just be worth cultivating for smut of a different hue: The Truth About David Yeo.

Always supposing there was such a Truth. Some people really did live clean, smut-free lives, and David Yeo was beginning to shape up as one of these.

'You'd better come in,' Rowena Yeo said, moving aside.

I stepped inside, into a gloomy entrance hall, warmed by central-heating. Took in a straight flight of stairs off to the right, a passage off left with doors at intervals. From behind the nearest came a scratching and a whimpering. Man's best friend chafing to be allowed to greet me. No thanks.

Rowena showed me into a sitting room where a modern gas fire burned in an old-fashioned, tiled fireplace. The room was crammed with furniture – crossing it was like tackling an army obstacle course. A vast, rolltop bureau in a corner of the room was open and littered with papers, as was a sizeable area of the surrounding carpet.

'Sorry about the mess.' Rowena waved an unconcerned hand. 'I'm working on a thesis.'

'Oh, really? On what?'

'Oh . . . the negative effect of modern unionism on freedom of choice. Of jobs, that is.'

Christ. I bet her old man would be chuffed about that. In his eyes, criticism of the union movement would rate as sedition. At her invitation I sat down in a plasticky armchair and just about had room to extend my legs without touching an identical chair opposite. Rowena went away and came back in less than a minute with a big, paunchy man in his sixties. This would be Yeo's adoptive father – officially sixty-eight but with his ruddy complexion and full complement of pepper-and-salt hair, looking a good bit younger. Rowena introduced him as 'my Gramps'. Hands were wrung: he had the grip of a bear. Rowena left us to get acquainted.

'Good of you to see me, Mr Yeo,' I said and meant it. Being there under a false flag didn't mean I was any less appreciative.

53

He was holding my card by its edges and looking dubious.

'What can I do for you, Mr Fletcher?'

We both sat. I perched on the edge of my chair and offered him my most earnest look.

'It's about your son David. Now he's become a national figure overnight, the public wants to know all about him.' I threw in a deprecatory smirk. 'It's par for the course. And to be candid, most of our readers are only interested in scandal. In my column though, I stay well away from that kind of material and simply try to present a balanced portrait. Not an out-and-out eulogy, you understand, but whatever a person's flaws, to bring out his or essential goodness. Nobody has led an entirely blameless life and you don't get to the top without stepping on the odd toe. What I try and do is present these less . . . er . . . complimentary ingredients in their true perspective. Do you follow?'

Yeo Senior pursed his lips. 'I'm not sure David would want me talking to the press behind his back.'

Rowena returned just then in the company of a round, rosy-cheeked woman in a shapeless brown dress and with curlers in her frizzy grey hair. Yeo's mum. More introductions were made. She was clearly uncomfortable in my presence. Everybody sat, Rowena and Mum next to each other on the settee.

'Mr Fletcher is doing an article on David,' Yeo Senior explained in a loud voice that implied she was hard of hearing. 'I said he might not agree with us talking to a reporter.'

Mum mumbled something I didn't catch.

Rowena, bless her, piped up: 'Let Mr Fletcher ask his questions, Gramps. You don't have to answer them if you don't want to.'

I beamed her an appreciative glance. 'That's quite right.'

'Well . . .' The uncertainty was receding, resistance

was crumbling. 'All right then - ask your questions and . . . well, we'll see.'

I led off with a succession of trivial, undemanding items concerned with his son's early childhood schooldays. The height of non-sensationalism. As we trudged across this deadly dull terrain that wouldn't have added a single copy to the circulation figures of the rag I purported to represent, Yeo Senior relaxed to the point where he was inserting the occasional amusing anecdote of his own free will.

As we talked, dusk settled on the street outside. A car buzzed past now and again. Even less frequently, the head and shoulders of a passer-by showed above the privet hedge. Athol Road was a regular backwater.

Rowena kept glancing at me, eyes huge, shadowy pools behind the tinted specs. Without them she might have been passably pretty. She didn't contribute much to the interview. Mum even less; correction, Mum zero.

When we reached what I judged to be the point of maximum rapport and the old fellow was at his most malleable, I sprang my mean, nasty little trap.

'Going back to the beginning - the *real* beginning . . .' I consulted my pretend-reporter's notebook, 'where exactly was David born?'

'Born?' Yeo Senior's voice had a tremor in it. Mum actually blinked. Her mouth opened and for a cliff-hanging moment she seemed about to break her vow of silence.

I was smiling at them. A seductive, beguiling smile. The hiss of the gas fire was suddenly audible.

'Dad was adopted.' Rowena spoke quietly, evenly. 'It's no secret.'

No, indeed.

'Nor is it anything to be ashamed of,' I agreed, jotting industriously.

Yeo showed relief at the shifting of the onus of responsibility from his shoulders to his grand-daughter's. Mum clicked her false teeth and settled more deeply into the settee. Her eyelids began to sag.

'Yes,' Yeo Senior said, recovering well. 'He was just four months-old when we had him. Wasn't he, Mum?'

Rumble from Mum.

I jotted some more. 'Do you know who his real parents are . . . were?'

That question produced an unexpected response, though not from Yeo Senior and even less from his blob of a wife; it was in front of Rowena that a defensive wall sprang up. Rowena who stiffened, became . . . watchful, uneasy.

'No . . . we never knew,' Yeo Senior was saying. 'And we never asked. Best not to know, eh, luv?' This to Mum, who made a movement with her head that might have signalled agreement. Either that or she was nodding off. Asleep she was probably livelier.

Him, I instinctively believed. Believed he – they – hadn't known the identity of Yeo's real parents and still didn't. Miss Rowena, now, was another matter. Maybe her reaction had been born out of concern that the subject might distress her grandparents. Maybe. Unsentimental, suspicious bastard that I am, I doubted it.

If I were a real news-hound I might have worried at it, rooted out the cause of her unease. Instead I pressed on to less controversial topics. It would keep. It was enough that there existed a secret of sorts.

Night had fallen by the time I wrapped the session up, trotting out voluble thanks and sundry smarm. I declined a cup of tea, bade farewells to Mr and Mrs, and Rowena did escort duty to the front door.

'I suppose you'll be talking to a lot of people,' she said, her hand resting on the knob of the Yale lock. 'About Dad, I mean.'

'Quite a lot. Actually . . .' I hesitated and in part at least it was a genuine hesitation. Pumping Yeo's parents was one thing, pumping his daughter was to walk a tightrope over a swampful of alligators. Fathers were notoriously protective towards daughters. What the hell? I took the plunge. 'Actually, I wouldn't mind interviewing *you*. Get the daughter angle . . . you know. I hadn't planned to, but since you're here . . . Could we make an appointment? I can stay overnight – or perhaps you're leaving this evening?' It all rang a bit false, over-eager. Made me sound like a dirty old man on the make.

She took it in her stride well enough though.

'No, I'll be here until the weekend.' In the feeble light of the hall her eyes were dark, veiled cavities. Esoteric. Some unseen, unfelt force was drawing me to her. It wasn't sexual – not recognisably. It wasn't anything I could hang a tag on. It just . . . was.

Disturbed and irritated, I shook the feeling off.

She was quite close to me and the smell of her perfume percolated my senses. It was a nice smell, not at all overpowering. She was probably a nice girl. She didn't deserve to have a cad (as Julia rated me) and a parasite (per Mike Hutton) like me fouling up her life.

'Well then?' I said, since she still hadn't given me an answer.

'An interview? Possibly. But not here. I'll phone you if it's yes – one day next week.' She hauled the heavy door open. 'If you're interested, Dad's speaking here tonight – in Sheffield.'

I was passing over the threshold as she spoke; I pulled up, pivoted slowly. 'I certainly would be interested. Where exactly?'

'It's nothing special, you understand. Just an inaugural meeting at the Yorkshire area HQ. I shall be going. You could come with me, if you like.' She looked past me at the Bentley, and grinned mischeviously. 'Better not to go in that anyway. If the comrades saw it they'd probably chuck a petrol bomb over it. Journalists must earn more than I thought,' she added pointedly.

I let that crack evaporate in the chill air that was

drifting in through the open door. We arranged that I should phone her from my hotel – when I had a hotel to phone from – and that she would collect me at seven.

'It's very kind of you, Miss Yeo,' I said.'

'Most people call me Rowen. Without the "a".'

'Fair enough.'

'What do people call you, other than Mr Fletcher?'

'Names, mostly.'

'See you later then, Names,' she riposted, matching quip with quip and eased me politely out into the sub-arctic Sheffield evening.

I tracked down four-star accommodation that went by the name of Hallam Tower Hotel, twenty or so floors of what qualifies as opulence this far north of the Mason-Watford line. I showered and I shaved and generally prettied myself up; I'd had the foresight to pack a holdall before setting off and the sports jacket and cords I'd brought to relax in would set about the right note for a union meeting. Open collar obligatory, of course.

My chauffeuse arrived just after I had put the receiver down on a typically tiresome conversation with Julia, who had accepted a last-minute invitation for us to attend a party this evening. Now the stupid bitch would go solo, would undoubtedly get tight as she extolled the non-virtues of her inconsiderate spouse, and undoubtedly pick up some smooth, virile stud, at least fifteen years her junior, and spend the night being fucked frontways, backways, and inside-out. And none of it would be a new experience.

Bitch!

In a foul temper I descended to the reception lobby to be met by Rowen, looking very fetching in beige leather boots and a green, knee-length wool dress under a mid-thigh belted coat. Shame about the specs and the hair-do.

My churlishness bounced off her, leaving no dents; she was as sunny as I was black. During the drive out to Hillsborough, she chattered light-heartedly, a veritable babbling brook, and finally eroded away my gloom.

The union area HQ was a thirties-style single-storey building with a flat roof, partly modernised with aluminium-framed windows and door. It had once been a toolmaking factory, Rowen explained as she manipulated the Honda into a tight corner on an adjacent lot, already near chock-a-block with parked cars. The company had gone bust in the mid-eighties and the premises were acquired dirt-cheap by the Electricians' Union as was.

Security was lax-to-non-existent. Rowen had a union card of some sort and succinctly passed me off to a grizzled Yorkshireman at the door as 'my cousin'. He replied with what sounded like 'Aw-rate, luv,' and then we were in: my Trojan Horse to Rowen's Helen.

The assembly room, about the size of a squash court, was nearly full and already hazed with smoke. At a rough estimate, some two hundred souls were packed in there, seated in ranks facing a low dais on which stood a table with five chairs in a line behind it. On the table was an old-fashioned microphone on a short stand and a glass water jug ringed by tumblers.

It was going to be standing room only for late-comers. Yeo was clearly quite a crowd-puller: most local union meetings do well to attract a tenth of this evening's attendance. Rowen pointed out a couple of unoccupied seats three rows from the front and we made haste in their direction, beating by a short whisker a cloth-capped merchant who was carrying too much beer-belly to match our pace. He was a good loser: 'Cunt!' he said (he had the decency to keep it singular) and accompanied it with a certain gesture – in case I was deaf or led a sheltered life.

On the very front row, by the centre aisle, was a

black-haired woman, mannishly and datedly dressed in a trouser costume. Apart from her, Rowen was the only woman present. It was strictly a stag's night out.

'We seem to have caused a stir,' Rowen whispered.

She was right. Heads had turned, mutterings were exchanged. Next to me was a fat, bald man who smelled of pipe tobacco: he kept flicking sidelong glances at me. It was the same on Rowen's side. I began to feel uncomfortable. It was as if they knew I was here as a spy and saboteur.

We were saved from further scrutiny by the entrance right of Yeo and associates: four nonentities and one working man's totem. I studied Yeo anew and my earlier impressions were reinforced: this was a dangerous man. Combine brains with ruthlessness, add ability as a public speaker, mix well with a dash of persona and you have a recipe for social change on a grand scale. Hitler, possessed of the same talents, had conquered most of Europe. Yeo's policies were different from Hitler's but the rest was kith and kin.

The first half-hour was given over to an introductory speech by the Area Organiser, Ken Childs. I wrote notes, mostly meaningless, for appearances' sake and to help me stay awake. After Childs came a sharp, rabble-rousing harangue from Terry Cubbins, one of the union's better-known personalities and a National Organiser, one step below Executive status. He would have travelled up with Yeo; union chiefs never travel alone.

So far nothing extreme had been mooted. Cubbins rounded off his address with a vote of thanks to the local membership for their contribution to the merger of the four unions, and some cliché-riddled blather on the changes to be wrought within the energy and water industries. All strictly routine. The stuff of somnolence.

Then it was the turn of the Star of the Show. He stood, a solid pillar of a man, and the hall stood with

60

him. Even me. I could hardly stay seated and hope to remain inconspicuous, so I joined in the acclaim.

Yeo, acknowledging the ovation with clasped, raised hands, caught sight of Rowen, mouthed a greeting which she returned with an unobtrusive finger-waggle. His gaze shifted to me and the tiniest crease formed at the bridge of his nose. For a panic-stricken instant I thought he had twigged me, though common-sense denied it. We had never met. My face, so far as I was aware, had never appeared in print during my time with the DTI. To any trade unionists who had crossed my path in those days I had been a minor official, a civil servant. The very select few who had known the truth had all been 'double agents,' serving two pay-masters. Exchanging information for hard currency.

Eric Bottomley, deceased, had been such a person.

That disturbingly piercing gaze moved on along the row and some of my tension dissolved. I was reminded again of my isolation. If anyone tumbled me, a roughing up was the least I could expect.

Yeo plunged into his speech.

It began moderately enough: more tributes, only at a national level now, followed by a dissertation on the great and glorious past of the four amalgamated unions and on the union movement as a whole from the time when the Friendly Societies, which provided mutual insurance for their members against sickness and old age, were accorded legal status. That had happened way way back towards the end of the eighteenth century and is generally considered to have been the launching pad that led to the creation, in 1829, of the first 'real' union, the Grand Union of the Operative Spinners of Great Britain and Ireland. In the event, not so grand as its title implied: it folded up two years later after an unsuccessful strike.

The history lesson led into the expected partisan sermon. Government beware, was the ringing battle cry – the unions are coming! Rampant approval was shown at this point: whistling, stamping, clapping. I contributed virtuously. Rowen, strangely, was luke-warm in her support.

'Clearly,' Yeo said, his amplified voice crackling, 'with the press here . . .' he let his eyes fall on Miss Trouser Suit in the front row, 'I will not be able to speak to you with absolute candour. We don't want to worry the legally-elected representatives of the people, do we? To conclude, therefore, I would like to send this message to the Government and the long-suffering British public: we do not recognise the right of government to take away a man's job which means that we do not recognise their right to conceive and pursue policies which bring about that end. We intend to make a stand. Any further reductions in the establishments of the electricity, gas, and water companies will be halted. And not merely halted, but *reversed*. We will ensure that, through reductions in working hours, more people are recruited into our industries. By so doing, we will set the pace for the whole employment scene in this country.'

This was more of the same garbage I had listened to at Honry's. It was no more moving for a second ear-bashing, though Yeo in the flesh was undoubtedly a powerful speaker. He looked mean and purposeful. The flinty eyes were narrowed and glinted like gun-metal in sunlight. His jaw was thrust out, hands expressively mobile. The image was deliberately tough-guy and his audience loved it. They didn't just drink up his performance, they wallowed in it.

Yeo had broken off to slake his thirst. The merest peek at his notes and away he galloped again.

'Be assured, brothers, in our primary purpose of expanding employment within our industries we shall succeed. But the struggle doesn't end there. The day will come – *must* come – when our forces will combine with other forces to forge an omnipotent lever to thrust in the cracks that are now appearing everywhere in the plinth of so-called democratic government, whatever its political stance. With this lever we will open up these cracks; we'll demolish the foundations and bring the whole festering edifice crashing to earth, and government as we know it will disintegrate.'

Yeo drew a shaky breath while his words sank in. Chairs creaked, somebody coughed nervously. Hell-fire and brimstone invectives were wasted here. All this audience wanted was a good wage, enough for life's necessities, plus a modest surplus to fund the colour TV licence, a few evenings a week at the local, and if the statistics are to be believed, a moderately heavy tobacco consumption. The British working classes tend, on the whole, to be an undemanding lot.

Yeo turned a page of his notes. 'The present Government poses as our allies yet pursues policies every bit as unsocialist as its predecessors. At least with them we knew how we stood—' Laughter – 'and how to respond. The present crowd use placatory words and do Tory deeds. It smiles as it wields the knife. It simply will not do and we will not stand for it. Up until now it is doubtful whether any single union had the clout to defeat the Government. By themselves, even the electricians probably couldn't do it. The Government would scrape up enough scabs among the dissidents and the armed forces to keep the generators turning. But now, brothers . . .' He crashed a fist on the table; the mike jumped, fizzled through the speakers, 'together, we have the muscle to bend them to our will. To bend, then to break. We will snap them like a dead twig. Together we will be unstoppable. *Unstoppable.*' Feedback distorted the thundered superlative, but it didn't lessen the impact. The whole hall was mesmerised. Me along with the rest, it has to be said, though my mesmerism was born of disquiet not adulation. He had me convinced he wasn't just talking for love of his own voice. He was telling us, telling the world, what his strategy would be. And it was this very openness that was so menacing.

The Area Organiser, Childs, poured more water to lubricate his master's lungs. Yeo nodded gratefully and partook.

'It need not happen, of course,' he said, on resuming, and restraint was back in his voice. 'There need be no battles, no war. Some wars are won at the conference table; by all means let this be one of them. We shall present our demands and they must respond as they see fit. They will protest, but they will have to listen. They will resist, but – ultimately - they will have to surrender!' Again the thumped table; an empty glass toppled over. 'If this Government is as spineless at heart as I believe it to be, we shall achieve all our objectives without strife or sacrifice. And so that there should be no misunderstanding, I do mean *all* our objectives. There will be no compromises, no cobbled-up deals, no half-measures. And especially no arbitration. It will be all or nothing, I promise you. But if they determine to confront us by offering less than we seek, then I tell you, brothers . . .' he leaned forward across the table, fingers spread, supporting his weight; peering out across the hall, 'we will rewrite the constitution of this country – in blood if necessary!'

If the paean had been enthusiastic before it was downright hysterical now. Yeo sat down to cheering and manic clapping, palpably relaxing now, the hardliner crust softening to let real pleasure show through. Again, to my surprise, Rowen did not join in the ovation. As a rule, left-wing parents spawn left-wing progeny. Must probe, I decided. My feeling that she was the chink in Yeo's armour was growing by the minute.

I became conscious of Yeo's eyes on me. The frown was more than ever apparent and as I returned his stare he bent to whisper to the National Organiser, who immediately glanced across at me. I tried to look nonchalant. All around people were filing out, no doubt heading for the licensed bar I had noticed by the entrance.

'Will you run me back?' I said to Rowen. I was anxious to be up and away. 'Or would you prefer I took a taxi. I don't mind.'

'Wouldn't you like to meet Dad?'

'Not tonight, thanks.' Not with his own private army to hand.

She was knotting the belt around her slim waist. She didn't have a bad little figure. If it weren't for the glasses and the scraped-back hair . . .

'Okay. I'll just say hello. See you outside in a couple of minutes.'

'Right.' We shuffled to the end of our row and split up. Yeo was still watching me. The National Organiser had disappeared. Organising a reception committee for one gate-crasher? I'm no coward but the odds frankly frightened me.

Then suddenly I was out in the sharp, frost-tinted night air, unaccosted, unmolested, with men ahead, behind and on either side and all of them supremely uninterested in my doings. The height of normality. Still I remained convinced that Yeo meant to put the boot in, and I hung around Rowan's Honda, psyched up to take on all-comers. I was rehearsing my favourite defensive tactic – the boot in the crotch – when Rowas showed up.

'What on earth are you doing?' she exclaimed, hovering between amusement and concern.

'Oh . . . er . . . just limbering up for a match on Saturday,' said I, who hadn't kicked a ball for amusement in nearly twenty years. For good measure I performed a few more theatrical flicks with the foot.

I was so relieved to get away from there with no broken bones I didn't even mind the odd looks she kept darting at me during the drive back to the hotel.

Chapter Four

Rooftops. As far as the eye could see, extending into the drizzle-laden mist. Grey slate tiles, slick and glazed with rain. Smoke rising in aimless tendrils from fifty-thousand chimney pots, merging with the drab October sky. Here and there a high-rise block, sometimes a cluster of them, unreal and out-of-time, as if dumped there in a hurry in the hope that they would take root. In spite of their outward modernity they failed to disperse the ambience of decay and depression and poverty that clung to the city of Sheffield.

That's how it struck me from my eyrie up on the twelfth floor of the Hallam Tower Hotel. Put bluntly, I didn't much go for the place.

My mind dwelt also on Yeo. That had been some diatribe last night. For inflammatory content it licked his TV performance into oblivion. Re-write the constitution indeed! That would raise the temperature in Downing Street. I chuckled at my reflection in the bathroom mirror as I mowed the night's growth away.

In truth though, it was no laughing matter. Yeo wasn't a comedy act. If he was minded to, he could inflict great hardship and havoc on the country and the populace, and personally I no longer doubted either his ability or his will to do just that. Any regime less ludicrously democratic than ours would now quietly remove him from circulation for incitement to revolution. Yet what do our worthy leaders do? Hire me to exhume juicy tit-bits from Yeo's past. For their sakes I hoped there were some to exhume. Portents so far were not encouraging.

From Yeo, logically, thoughts shifted to Rowen. Interesting girl. No, wrong adjective: *intriguing* girl. Superficially plain yet with such a lively personality and so self-confident, she compelled attention. We had parted on friendly, Christian-name terms, and she had promised to phone me when she returned home (to Enfield), probably some time next week. I would take her out to dinner, I decided. Somewhere grand like the top floor restaurant at the Hilton in Park Lane.

Then I remembered Eric Bottomley, shuddered, and struck out the Hilton forever.

Buzz at the door. My reflection looked puzzled. Callers at 8.30 am? I hadn't ordered breakfast in my room. *Buzzzzz.* Longer, more peremptory. I splashed water over my now baby-smooth chin and, naked to the waist, went grudgingly to answer it. Hoping for a pretty chambermaid in short skirt and black stockings.

What I got was not a chambermaid on my doorstep but three scruffily-dressed youngish men who grabbed my arms and hustled me back into my room in quick tempo. The whole operation was so slick and well-coordinated it never occurred to me to resist.

'What is this?' I demanded, a cry of outrage that terminated in a startled gasp as I was flung into the chair beside the writing table. The leader of the pack – middle height, brown hair cropped to skinhead length, pasty features – came to stand over me.

'Fletcher?' he said and his voice was almost a wheeze. His chums, also crop-headed, one blond, the other dark, took up flanking positions. They were big bastards. '*Vyvyan* Fletcher?' the leader said and sniggered. 'We know all about you, Vyvyan.' He pronounced my name mincingly.

If this bunch were who I suspected they were, I was in deep trouble. I'd had run-ins with union stormtroopers in the past and had once been badly mauled.

My balls contracted involuntarily at the prospect of a repeat dose of steel toe-caps in the groin.

'Who are you?' I injected a modicum of artificial terror into my voice to pad out the real terror.

'No, Vyvyan – who are *you*?' A finger prodded my chest. 'And what were you doing at that meeting last night? Conning that silly bitch – oughter be ashamed of yourself.' His face homed in. It wasn't pretty and his teeth were a lost cause. I hoped my distaste wasn't obvious.

'I'm a journalist.' I contrived an exaggerated whimper. 'I was just doing my job.'

'You're a journalist like I'm Mary Poppins' mum.' He glanced round at his grinning cronies. 'We don't believe that shit for a minute, do we, cobbers?'

Confirmation from the cobbers.

'Let me prove it,' I squawked. A dribble of sweat was sliding down my temple. Nothing artificial about that.

'Prove it? How, you stupid prick?'

'Papers.' I indicated my brief case on the bed.

'Don't feed me that pap.'

'Aw, Dev, gie 'im a chance,' the blond crop-head said. ''E might be tellin t'truth for all tha knows.'

'Don't kid yourself, old luv.' Dev straightened up. 'But okay – I'm a reasonable man. Prove you're from the press and I might let you you off with a broken leg or two.'

There was a click and a four-inch shaft of steel – Sheffield Steel, surely – shot out of Dev's hand. Flick knives are illegal, was my first, inconsequential thought. Then so is assault. Such offences and worse would be all in a day's routine to this bunch.

They let me stagger across to the bed. Dev didn't move, but signalled Blondie to stick with me. That was Blondie's tough luck because that put him right in the firing line.

Inside the lid of my so ordinary-looking brief case was a hidden compartment, with a spring-loaded flap

that opened at the touch of a button. I raised the lid
with a natural briskness, using my body to block
Blondie's view of the interior. My finger found the
button, jabbed, and the knife – flat rubber handle, flat,
wide blade with the cutting edges of a cut-throat razor
and the point of a Zulu assegai – was in my hand. It
was designed for throwing, but was equally at home in
a close-quarters contest.

A single sideways slash was enough to disable
Blondie: the blade went through sleeve and bicep and
barely checked. He screamed, falling away, clutching
his arm. Dev shouted, a meaningless noise, and was
starting towards me when I reversed the knife and
threw, aiming for his right shoulder – I wanted him
deactivated, not dead. The tearing sound as it
skewered him in exactly the intended spot had musical
qualities for me beyond any classical symphony. His
own knife thumped to the carpet.

'Get 'im!' he commanded the third member of the
party through clamped teeth. With obvious reluctance
Yobbo number 3 moved forward, but by then I had the
second knife, twin of the one protruding from Dev's
shoulder, free of the compartment. A threatening
twitch of the unblooded blade galvanised all three into
motion – in a race to the door. The uninjured yobbo
beat Dev by a couple of lengths; Blondie was last,
moaning and groaning and clutching his arm. His
sleeve was sodden with blood.

Then it was all over; as swift and as sudden as that.
One minute knives and blood and shouting, the next
just me in the middle of the floor, shirtless, a knife in
my fist, the door wide open. Sounds of panicky descent
– curses, thudding feet – reached me. I shut the door.
Incredible that this had all taken place in daylight in a
respectable four-star hotel, with occupied rooms to the
left, to the right, above and below!

I was sorry to lose the knife. I'd had them both since
my days in the Intelligence Corps. They had been

bosom companions throughout three tours of duty in Northern Ireland, and had never, until now, been deployed in anger.

Reaction set in. My body began to tremble and the tremble became a shake until I was an uncontrollable, quivering jelly: teeth chattering, hands jiggling and dancing. I dropped the knife. Cursed loudly and volubly. Reeled to the valise stand, to my suitcase. Unscrewing the cap of the hip flask was a major challenge and when I finally got the thing off, it shot across the room to God knows where. I upended the flask and let Cognac glug freely down my throat. This subdued the worst of the shakes and I fell across the bed, where I stayed, the Cognac soothing my stomach, for quite some time. I skipped the planned hearty breakfast; I had no appetite for food.

But I had acquired a hunger of a different kind.

Before this attack I had still been in two minds whether to accept the commission to discredit Yeo, notwithstanding the real danger he posed to the State. Other considerations apart, I had doubted the existence of any sins deadly enough to topple him.

Now . . . now I was first and foremost angry. I was angrier than angry. I was in a white hot, boiling fury.

And beneath the fury, in the cooler, analytical zone, I was professionally gratified. Gratified because the attack proved that Yeo, or somebody close to him, was nervous. Implying that his past was not so bland as it seemed and that I was not to root around in it in search of impurities.

Nevertheless, David John Yeo, I aim to finish what I've started; aim to smash you and your destructive ideology. You'll be the revolutionary-that-never-was. A year from now people won't even remember your name.

That's *my* promise to you.

*   *   *

On Wednesday I lunched with Honry at his club – Chalfont's in Pont Street, SW1. Tall, multi-paned windows, dark-panelled walls dotted with portraits of former exalted members, leather armchairs complete with snoozing octogenarians. Another world.

We had *truite menunière* with celery and creamed potatoes. To wash it down, a bottle of Chablis' 82, a wine of fragrant bouquet coupled with a dryness that bordered on acidity.

I'd told Honry the tale of my visit to Sheffield, omitting the dust-up at the Hallam Tower primarily because he was sure to over-react and throw panic switches left, right and centre. Consequently the main topic was Yeo's speech, reported verbatim in the national press. The Government, as Honry expressed it, was 'saying nowt'. Hoping the problem would wither away in the fullness of time.

'But as you and I well know, dear boy,' Honry murmured between appreciative mouthfuls of Chablis, 'friend Yeo is not the withering kind. Ignoring him will not make him go away. Quite the reverse.'

A waiter wafted up alongside with less commotion than a dandelion spore making a touch-down.

'Everything to your satisfaction, gentlemen?'

We made suitably eulogistic grunts. Our glasses were topped up, thereby draining the bottle. The waiter arched enquiring eyebrows.

'No more plonk for me,' Honry said. 'I've got a report to write on that Dunlop business. I'll need a clear head.'

I likewise passed. We ordered desserts: fresh fruit salad for me, Black Forest gâteau for the glutton opposite, coffee and liqueurs to follow.

'What Dunlop business?' I asked when we were alone again.

'What? Oh, I keep forgetting – you're not with the Department any more.' He tapped the side of his nose, and winked. 'Hush-hush, I'm afraid, old boy. Here's a tip though . . . buy now.'

'I already have,' I said drily. 'You're not the only tipster I know.'

'You'll be a rich man a month from now. But enough of the stock market – we have the State of the Nation to consider. You've had a chance to size up the enemy. Will you take him on or will you not?'

'In principle . . . yes; putting it crudely, there's nothing I'd like better than to fix that bastard.'

Honry beamed, reached across and grasped my arm. 'Good man!'

'Don't get carried away, Honry,' I cautioned. 'I said, "in principle". My preliminary investigations into Yeo's life history haven't been over-fruitful. *Prima facie*, his track record looks purer than boiled water. I've two possible . . . call them "angles" . . . which give me cause for hope.'

'Care to elaborate?'

'As a matter of fact, I don't.'

Honry exchanged 'Good afternoons' with a bent old man who was shuffling past with the aid of a brace of knobbled sticks.

'Marquis of Newbury,' Honry said *sotto voce* as the ancient trundled on into the adjacent reading room. 'Ninety if he's a day. Six sons all waiting for him to turn his jolly old toes up. Not to mention fourteen grandsons and a dozen or so great-grandsons. And Lord knows how many girls in the family.'

'Remarkable,' I said.

'*Revenons à nos moutons*, as our Gallic brethren would have it – you agree then? You'll accept the job?'

'There's the question of my fee to be settled before aught else, dear Honry, dear Honry.'

'Your . . .' He donned a bemused air; he was rather good at it. 'Well, I should think we'll put you back on the payroll for the duration. You'll get the going rate for a senior, with perhaps a modest bonus at the end of it.

I gave a soft laugh. 'Think again. Add a few thoughts.'

'Oh.' He looked nonplussed, then hurt. 'I say . . . you're not going to play hard to get, are you, dear boy? Because it won't work, you know. Our lords and masters won't stand for any nonsense.'

'*Your* lords and masters,' I corrected. 'But fear not, Honry. I accept your offer of employment. My rate for the job is £50,000 now, and the same again on completion. And those figures are non-negotiable.'

Our in Pont Street a car horn blasted and another responded. Honry, by whom peace and tranquillity were highly prized, radiated waves of displeasure.

'Where do they think they are – Paris?' Then he focused shrewd eyes on me. '£50,000 in advance? Done. Plus an equivalent sum on *successful* completion. No cure, no pay.'

His swift capitulation was instructive. He – they – had been prepared for just such a demand. Had been prepared for it and had agreed to pay it. It said a lot for the Government's concern over Yeo.

'No cure, no pay,' I agreed and we clinked glasses laughingly.

'Welcome back aboard, Vee. You'll get the first instalment tomorrow, in cash, delivered to Kingscourt by special messenger. Be sure to be there between eleven and midday.'

They were well-organised. The machinery was already in being, tuned-up, lubricated, and all ready to roll. Naive of me to suppose it might have been otherwise.

'As for expenses . . . ' In speaking of expenses, Honry was not referring to travel allowances and suchlike, but bribes and what were termed within the department "specialist fees", of which the less said the better. 'The budget is provisionally fixed at £100,000. All, if spent, to be accounted for to the last penny.' He fixed a stern, schoolmasterish gaze on me; you would have thought he was entrusting me with the crown jewels. 'A bank account will be set up for you to draw on as necessary.

No more than £5,000 per transaction and a limit of £15,000 per week, other than at my discretion.'

Such munificence. My usual budget was £10,000 – total. Still more evidence of a government with its knickers in a twist.

'Subject,' Honry added, 'to ratification at the committee meeting on Friday week.'

'Committee meeting? What . . . ?'

Honry silenced me with a glare seconds before our desserts arrived. My fresh fruit salad included raspberries and mangoes. On occasions such as this I was glad and grateful to be living the life of 'the other half'.

'Your coffee will be served in five minutes, gentlemen,' the waiter intoned before making an elegant withdrawal.

I spooned fruit, chewed. 'Now . . .' I said through it to Honry, whose Black Forest gâteau was piled so high he had to peer round it to see me. 'What committee? What meeting?'

'You didn't think this business would be entrusted to just you and me, did you, dear boy?' Honry's spoon flashed and the gâteau shrank rapidly. 'No, there's to be a committee to which you – and I – will report. To discuss and agree strategy and tactics, to receive and debate your reports, and to generally monitor progress. You will be answerable to it, not to me. I shall serve as the committee's executive, its mouthpiece, if you prefer.'

'Can you really see me on a committee, Honry?'

'The Earl of Deverill will occupy the Chair,' Honry name-dropped, as if I hadn't spoken. 'And the peerage will be further represented by Viscount Stambourne. The rest of the committee will be made up of gurus from the Home office, the DoE, the Energy Department, the MoD, the Treasury, and the DTI – the last mentioned being Yours Truly. Nine in all, including your worthy self.'

'And all good men and true,' I said with resignation.

Inside I was writhing. A committee, for God's sake! The decision-making process reduced to the pace of the slowest thinker, or the most cautious, or the most obstructive. Two lords, six bureaucrats, and me. It was a prospect to cause flutters in the stoutest of hearts.

Empty dessert dishes were exchanged for empty coffee cups. Coffee, steaming, black, aromatic, was poured. We both sniffed in appreciation.

'The first session will settle your terms of reference . . .'

'After they've settled the seating arrangements,' I interrupted cynically.

'There'll be none of that nonsense.' Honry was uncharacteristically sharp. 'The fundamental aim – to discredit Yeo – is one to which all departments are fully committed – even the Treasury. Whilst speed is acknowledged to be of the essence, it doesn't mean we're going to rush helter-skelter into any old lunatic scheme. The Minister's edict to me was not merely to find the man for the job, but to oversee and scrutinise his activities at every stage so that he doesn't get carried away by enthusiasm. Know what I mean, old top? The Cabinet is in an absolute blue funk, Mossy especially . . .'

'Mossy?'

He chortled discreetly. 'Of course, you wouldn't know. Mossy from M-O-S, for Man of Straw.'

'Oh.'

'Where was I? Oh, yes . . . the Cabinet is collectively terrified of Yeo – with the exception of Lionel, as you'd expect. At the same time they're terrified of stopping him by any method that doesn't smell of political roses.'

Mossy, Lionel – the Civil Service penchant for nick-naming their masters was obviously as alive as ever. I wondered how the PM would feel about being tagged after a professional dancer. But then leading the country did call for nimble footwork, I supposed . . .

I made soothing noises and offered solace in the form of a Cadre Noir Imperiales Havana cigar, two of which I had stuck in my pocket for the occasion.

'This meeting,' I said, cropping the rounded end off my cigar. 'Friday next, did you say? Got a time and a place?'

'2.30 pm. Finch Lane, off Threadneedle Street.'

A cruising waiter lit our cigars and swept away the discarded tubes. The club restaurant was beginning to empty; several waiters bustled about clearing away dishes, eerily soundless.

'Any particular building?' I asked. 'Or shall I go from door to door until a familiar face appears?'

'Don't be flippant. We'll go together. Meet me at the DTI half-an-hour before and don't be late. Lord Deverill is an absolute martinet on punctuality.'

We made smoke signals and for the next few minutes were content to luxuriate in the taste and aroma of the world's finest cigar.

'My main worry is,' I eventually said, 'that we're going to get so bogged down in blather at these meetings of yours that no decisions will ever be made. Committees leave me cold, Honry; in fact they leave me frostbitten. We're in a race – and Yeo's already away from the starting gate.'

'You're referring to the meeting between Yeo's crowd and the electricity and gas suppliers, I suppose. Yes, I realise it's today.' Honry brushed ash off the tablecloth. 'I share your worry, Vee, my dear fellow. There will assuredly be those on the committee to whom prudence and circumspection will be paramount. Having said that, I reiterate that they are all behind the project one hundred per cent. There isn't a man among 'em that doesn't see Yeo as a menace to society; as the spearhead of a new wave of union *panzers* set to blitzkrieg democracy into oblivion.'

'To coin a phrase,' I said, grinning.

He smirked back at me. 'Not bad for an ad-lib, was

it? No, my dear chap, take my word for it – there will be no dissenters.' The smirk widened. 'Who do you think selected the committee?'

'I might have known.' I raised my liqueur to him. 'Your health, Machiavelli.'

Our business thus satisfactorily transacted, I let myself relax physically and mentally and surveyed my quaint and regal surroundings. Crystal chandeliers suspended from high, vaulted ceilings; the wall panels stained dark with age and smoke; the beautifully-crafted Regency furniture. On a more mundane note, the silver-plated cutlery bearing the club crest, the candlesticks to match, the dazzling table linen, and above all the waiters who were seen but seldom heard, moving with such spectral grace that the very air was undisturbed by their passing.

This and other institutional symbols of Empire and tradition were under siege. The people were on the march, the ruthless leading the uniformed. Down Pall Mall they would tramp one fine morning, to the beat of the drums of revolution. To the cheers and the clamour of the proletariat. To the singing and the banner waving and the hopes and expectations of a New and Better Deal.

It was, as I saw it, an inexorable process towards an inevitable ending. Stopping Yeo wouldn't stop the process. It might retard it a little, until another Yeo arose to take up the cudgel and the day came when nobody in authority had the nerve, or the wit, or the will to challenge him.

Meanwhile . . . meanwhils there was me, the Government's secret weapon. God help us.

Julia was in a mood that evening. Snapping and snarling over dinner, slamming off upstairs having barely touched her food. Leaving me to dine on in splendid isolation. Lord of the Manor.

Huh.

An hour passed before she made her customary stealthy descent. I was in the sitting-room by then, preparing for the forthcoming committee meeting, assembling my disjointed notes on Yeo, deciding how much of what I knew I was prepared to disclose. As it turned out, most of the material I preferred to keep to myself was of a speculative nature and possibly quite valueless.

Hands came around from behind to cover my eyes.

'Guess who?' Julia's voice said with a self-conscious giggle.

'Come in, darling.' I tried not to sigh. The pattern was so familiar. Now she would gush with apology and want to be screwed. Here, in the sitting-room.

She came around the armchair. She was wearing skin-tight black satin trousers that picked out every muscle and tendon and the lack of undergarment. Her blouse was gossamer-light, outlining the nipples and dark areolae of her breasts. Julia's come-ons were never subtle.

'If Willoughby saw you in that, the poor old bugger would have a seizure.' I bent forward and kissed her, and papers fluttered from my lap. She tasted good, smelled even better.

I wrinkled my nose. 'New perfume?'

'Yes. I went on a spree today. I bought some earrings at Cartier. Like them?' She pulled her hair back from her ears. A tiny stone twinkled in a miniature golden Tudor Rose setting. I was glad I hadn't had to fork out for them.

I made suitable murmurings.

'I'm sorry about my bad behaviour.' She hung her head and I instantly forgave her. 'It's just that . . . I get so *sick* of people at times. They can be so bitchy.'

Which translated as 'one of my friends has been gossiping about me.'

I kissed the tip of her aquiline nose. 'Forget

them. Forget the world.' I gave her a quick hug. 'I love you.'

If only she would say it back to me, even as a reflex action. It was years since she had. Usually she covered up by flinging her arms around me, and in this respect tonight was no different. She kissed me, her mouth loose and wet, tongue squirming between my teeth, hot and abrasive. Her hand covered my crotch, kneading.

It tested my will-power, but I heaved her off. 'I want to watch the news.'

'The news?' She looked understandably blank. 'You want to watch the *news*.'

I stood up. 'It's important. To do with the job for Honry.' I had kept her abreast of developments.

Slightly dishevelled, more than slightly flabbergasted, she flopped back on to her lovely bottom. 'I must say, you're full of surprises, Vee. That's the first time you've ever turned down a fuck to watch he news. Jesus Christ!'

'Leave him out of this.' Which made me sound priggish. 'It's important, I tell you.'

I tapped buttons on the remote control box and a commercial for the new Rover burst across the screen. The accompanying jingle bounced discords off my eardrums.

To the blare of the ITN news theme – for bombast the BBC can't touch it – I prepared drinks. Julia stayed on the floor in front of the armchair, cross-legged and pouting, and looking about thirty. Thanks to a some expensive facial sculpting and several sessions of liposuction.

Scotch and a meagre splash of soda for me, Cockburn's port for Julia. I resumed my seat. Julia used one hand to hold her glass, the other to fondle my leg and adjacent zones. It spoiled my concentration, but I let her get on with it. Thankful that she was willing to settle for half a loaf.

Yeo had grabbed today's headlines. The proceedings opened with a resumé of the talks at the National Power head office in Queen Victoria Street.

'The power generators and the supply companies unanimously rejected Mr Yeo's pay and recruitment plan,' the male newsreader informed us. 'There will, however, be further talks in ten days' time. Mr Yeo said that he hoped the next meeting would be more fruitful. Andrew Whitehead was at the National Power offices when the talks broke up at half-past four this afternoon.'

Flash to the scene of the talks: a spokesman for the employers caught in mid-sentence. '. . . demands were unreasonable and, in the present economic climate, unrealistic. Nonetheless, the atmosphere remained amicable throughout and the attitude of the union was constructive, if a shade unbending.'

'Do you hold out much hope of an early settlement?' the reporter, Whitehead, asked.

The spokesman hesitated. Dying to say, 'Not a hope,' but he was stuck with his script, which didn't provide for personal opinions.

'It's too soon to say. We are not . . . optimistic. The cost of meeting their claim in full would be staggering and would have to be passed on to the consumer of course . . .'

Of course. Poor, long-suffering, unprotesting consumer.

'Snivelling bureaucratic worm,' Julia fumed. 'As long as we have gutless toadies like him in positions of authority, how can we hope to prosper as a nation? At least this Yeo person, from what I've seen and heard of him, has some fire in his belly. Imagine him running the country.'

I shuddered inside and out. 'If he ever made PM, I'd be on the next flight to Tierra del Fuego.'

'Tierra del what . . . ?'

'Shhh – here's your hero.'

Yeo had just blossomed before the camera lens to be accosted by Whitehead.

'From your point of view, Mr Yeo, was the meeting a success?' was Whitehead's opening shot after the barest of greetings.

Yeo – a great man getting greater day by day – looked into the camera. It was a technique he came to develop, that of talking directly to the viewer rather than the interviewer. Forever selling himself to the masses.

'No,' he said shortly. No pussyfooting around. 'We failed to reach agreement on any of the three major issues.'

'I see. Those would be pay, a reduction in the working week, and a major increase in the work force.'

'Essentially.' Yeo smiled and it was almost disarming. If you were gullible enough you might even grow to love him. Julia sat entranced, no longer stroking my leg. 'These are early days,' Yeo was saying. 'We meet again on the 12th.' A crush of faces hove up behind him, the Union General Secretary among them. The reporter immediately cornered him, perhaps hoping for a slightly softer stance from the former Electricians' leader.

'Have you anything to add to Mr Yeo's statement, sir?'

The General Secretary exchanged glances with Yeo. 'I think he's said it all.' His tone was neutral, giving nothing away of his real attitude. No reason to suppose he and Yeo were at loggerheads over any of the issues though.

'Do you not feel that a twenty-five per cent increase coupled with a thirty-five hour week is somewhat . . . er . . . excessive?' Whitehead asked him.

The General Secretary snorted. 'It's value for money we're talking about. Our members are worth every penny of what we're asking. *And . . .*' a wagging finger here, 'and we'll be creating more jobs – ten thousand at least this year, even more next year if our proposals are accepted.'

A big, big, 'if', chum.

Yeo thrust his head in front of the camera again, startling his colleague and the reporter. 'And they *will* be accepted – take my word for it. Because the alternative is chaos!'

End of commercial.

'Well!' Julia said, which summed up both our reactions to this outburst.

On that note the interview ended and we were transported to the forecourt of the DTI HQ where the Minister, pale, harassed, hair tossing in the wind, was delivering a political homily on the iniquitous 'black-mailing' stance of the AUEWE. His parting comment, that moves were afoot to deal with the potential confrontation, unsettled me a touch. If it was meant as an oblique reference to my one-man show, it was a breach of security I didn't need.

'What a difference,' Julia remarked from down there on the floor. 'Yeo looks and sounds like a man with a purpose, no matter that he stands for all I detest. Whereas Whatsisname is so obviously all bluff and bluster. Put them in the ring together and it would be like pitting a heavyweight against a flyweight.'

I switched off the set. 'You're well-informed about the art of pugilism, my love. But, yes, I tend to agree with your assessment.' I guzzled Scotch. 'Yeo impresses you then?'

'As a man who knows what he wants and isn't afraid to go after it.'

'And what about me? If I got in the ring with him – would I be a flyweight too?'

She turned her head slowly. Fixed her magnificent dark eyes on me.

'I don't know, Vee. I honestly don't know. You tell me you're going after him, whatever that might mean.

There's no one better equipped to do the job, that much I grant you. But . . . be careful, that's all.' Julia showing concern? Amazing! If it comes to a showdown between you and him, he's the kind who'll fight dirty.'

'Let him. It's a game two can play, and the Government's resources will outlast his. But the key to fixing him is surprise. His weakness is that he doesn't yet know war has already been declared and by the time he wises up, it'll be all over.'

Brave words, but to fight a war you need weapons and my armoury as yet boasted not so much as a bent pea-shooter.

Chapter Five

Incognito was now the rule.

The Hallam Tower dust-up had swept away all complacency: in pursuance of the next phase of my enquiries, I donned false moustache, glasses, and substituted Midlands accent for Home Counties, rounding off the physical transformation with a false identity – that of 'Mel Forsythe of *Ventura* magazine'. Although *Ventura* was a bogus publication it boasted a phone number which, when activated, gave the appropriate response.

Even so, a thin enough disguise with which to a-questioning go.

I left on Saturday morning at nine-thirty. Julia was still abed after a late night dinner party. I hadn't even kissed her goodbye; that custom was long gone like most of our marriage vows. Today though, it didn't matter quite so much. With £50,000 in freshly-minted banknotes reposing in a Barclay's safe-deposit vault, I had taken a giant step towards financial independence. Towards becoming a man of means in my own right. I entertained vague hopes that such status would magically remove the abrasion from my relationship with Julia and restore lost caring and mutual respect.

You can always hope, can't you?'

Up the M1. Rain, mist, drizzle, fog, in that sequence, before breaking out into brittle-bright sunshine around the Leicester Forest Service Area. Using the Bentley's bulk and power to bludgeon other motorists out of the third lane. By midday I was passing Sheffield and at one o'clock precisely sitting down to a cold lunch at the White Swan Hotel in York, home town of a retired university lecturer named Edgar Stopps.

Stopps lived just off the A1036 Scarborough road, next door to a golf course, in a pretentious suburb of mock-Georgian detached houses and sundry other once-fashionable imitations. Nice enough if you don't mind paste copies.

A lady answered the door – his wife, I supposed. Seventy or more, elegant and courteous, and speaking with the tiniest French inflexion. Stopps was out. No, he hadn't forgotten his appointment with me, but he *had* forgotten he was committed to take part in a cycle endurance test (at seventy-three!) to raise money for a sports centre. Would I be so kind as to meet him at the Poacher's Arms, a pub a mile or so along the Scarborough road. So sorry to cause inconvenience. She really was quite, quite charming. I felt I should kiss her hand but my English reserve held firm.

Onward to the Poacher's Arms, in whose vast car park were gathered a number of people, from toddlers upwards. As I swapped snug interior for chill outdoors – a lousy trade – a bunched-up troupe of cyclists came around a bend further up the road, passing what I took to be a course marshal, and entering the long straight stretch that ran along the front of the pub. I watched them approach, aware that I was in a minority – most of the other spectators had eyes only for the Bentley.

The cyclists crossed the line, their track suits-of-many-colours the only bright spot on a cheerless landscape. They were all, I now perceived, elderly and all looking disgustingly fit for their ages.

An obliging spectator pointed Stopps out to me. I went forthwith and barged into the circle of riders, now dismounted and swigging from their plastic bottles. Stopps, grey-haired, diminutive, bespectacled, was given to much gesticulation: as I homed in on him he nearly floored me with an expressively outflung arm.

'Mr Stopps, I believe,' I said, laughing away his apology. 'I'm Forsythe, *Ventura* magazine.' I dished out a card. The other riders melted complaisantly away.

'Nice to meet you, Mr Forsythe.' He dabbed the sheen of perspiration from his forehead. 'Sorry about the mix-up – entirely my fault. I seem to be getting forgetful these days. Do you mind if I get rid of this before we talk?' 'This' being the bike, a super-light French Motobecane: £2000-worth of boneshaker, at a guess.

'Let's go over there.' He led me to a corner of the car park occupied by a newish Citroën Xantia. French bike, French car, probably-French wife. Edgar Stopps had a distinct Gallic bias.

'Did you win?' I asked as he pulled a padded anorak from the car boot.

'Win? It wasn't that kind of race. It was an endurance run: we set off at nine and had to cover sixty miles in six hours. Without stopping.'

'And?'

'Did we do it, you mean?' He gave a chuckle of triumph. 'Five hours seventeen minutes. Subject to confirmation. And not one of us under sixty-five.'

'Bloody good show,' I said with sincerity.

'Now then, Mr Forsythe—' Dry-washing his hands vigorously, 'how can I help you? About a story you're doing on David Yeo, you said.'

'Correct. Er . . .' I glanced around meaningly, 'is there somewhere more conducive to a chat we can go? I really need about half-an-hour.'

He inclined his head towards the pub. 'Come on. We'll talk inside. The landlord's a friend of mine – he might even break the law for us if we ask him nicely.'

Which was how we came to be installed in the 'Snug' with an illicit glass of lager apiece.

Stopps drank and tongued froth from his top lip.

'David Yeo.' He nodded reflectively. 'Man of the moment.'

'Tell me about him. Academically brilliant, I gather.'

A nostalgic glow lit up Stopp's lined features. 'A near-genius. And I'm not exaggerating. If he was so minded he could . . . he could achieve almost anything. Without extending himself at all. I've followed his career with interest; I keep tabs on all my high-flying ex-students. For a while I thought David was going to disappoint me, remain a behind-the-scenes man.' He clucked at his own lack of faith. 'But then he always was a dark horse. He would keep his head down for months on end, then suddenly, when you'd almost forgotten his existence, he would surface with a dazzling paper that left his contemporaries floundering. Amazing . . . amazing. Now, of course, he's coming into his own, bent on moulding society to his own vision of it. And he'll succeed, mark my words, Mr Forsythe, he'll succeed.'

I proffered a cigar which he accepted with frank appreciation. We puffed smoke and made a fug in the Snug. Somewhere in the building a telephone shrilled. Nobody hurried to answer it.

Stopps had given me the glimmerings of an insight into Yeo. But there was no substance in it and sweet FA to the man's detriment. I probed deeper. I prodded and pushed and as the disclosures remained bland and dishearteningly short on scandal, my tactics became rougher, more provocative. In courtroom parlance I 'led my witness'. Stopps, initially benign, took exception to my bullying and after a blatant near-slander of his former student, leapt to his feet. His glasses glinted with fury, his face was flushed.

'That's enough, Mr Forsythe,' he rapped; he was breathing hard through his nose. 'It's perfectly obvious you're bent on vilifying David. I take it this . . . this magazine you work for is one of those that trawl the gutter for their material.' As I started to protest he crashed the base of his glass on the table. 'Hear me out! I may be old but I'm not yet senile. You've been pumping me for malicious gossip on David and don't deny it. Now let me put you straight on two counts, Mr Forsythe: first, you've come to the wrong man. I don't tell tales about anyone. Second – and more to the point – there's *nothing to tell tales about*. David Yeo's behaviour during his stay at York University was exemplary – above reproach. And to the best of my knowledge and belief it's been that way ever since. You may abhor his policies – I don't entirely sympathise with them myself, if it comes to that – but you're on the wrong track. He's not *News of the World* fodder and if you're cooking up some sort of smear campaign you've picked the wrong subject. Not to mention doing him an injustice. If you want to attack him, attack his policies. Do it the *clean* way. Out in the open.'

If only I could, old man, I thought wistfully, if only I could. But there were no Queensberry rules in politics. Hammering unions publicly over the folly of their deeds in the hope of stirring up rebellion among the rank-and-file simply did not work. Union membership, broadly speaking, espoused the policies of the union hierarchy and either dismissed all criticism or remained ignorant of it. The result was a head-in-the-sand solidarity, unreasoning, often unreasonable.

'Sorry you feel like that.' I saw no sense in debating the issue with Stopps. Integrity and loyalty make a tiresomely shatter-proof combination.

I thanked him for his co-operation.

'If you're an honest man you'll write an honest article,' he said, calmer now, but still disapproving. 'It's no more than he deserves.'

'Remember what happened to the Prince in *Beauty And The Beast*?'

'*Beauty And The Beast*?' Out and out mystification.

'Read it. Your precious David Yeo has gone the same way. And somebody's got to do something about it.'

I left him in the Snug wearing an unfathomable expression. An innocent abroad. A lost lamb in a world of big bad wolves.

It transpired over the following week that Yeo's conduct during his forty-odd years on the planet had been an example to we lesser, frailer mortals. Everyone I interviewed said as much, if not quite in those same words. Fellow students at York, girlfriends including one he became engaged to and subsequently disengaged from, former next-door neighbours, former team-mates from the amateur football club for which he played in his early twenties; in all I talked to twenty-three people and although some bore grudges and were now estranged from him, none was able or willing to give me bullets to fire. Personality quirks, little eccentricities, individualistic behaviour – these were not ammunition I could use.

Dawned the day of the committee meeting I had exhausted all lines of enquiry but one. And I was no further forward than at the outset.

I was also coming round to the view that Yeo really was as near a living saint as any member of the human race could ever hope – or wish – to be.

Honry and I travelled by taxi from the DTI to Finch Lane. To a building as unremarkable in that most institutional part of the City of London as a back-to-back terrace house in Salford.

I left him to pay – he had the Treasury to draw on. I followed a pair of be-jeaned behinds up a flight of narrow steps and lusted mildly. At the top I waited for Honry. It was five minutes to two on Friday, 30th October. A chill but sunny afternoon, the sky an anaemic blue, unblemished but for a couple of criss-crossing vapour trails.

We went up two floors in a lift that might have been the prototype of all lifts. They seem to be obligatory in

London's older buildings, as if to replace them with fast, modern, roomy lifts would be to deny our heritage. Same goes for the central heating and the plumbing.

The corridor into which the lift wearily expelled us was quiet. No blue-jeaned bums hereabouts – this was pin-stripe country. Committee country. Speaking of committees, I wasn't looking forward to participating in this one.

Understatement. I was dreading it.

Then we were squeezing through half a double door into the torture chamber itself, a typical City boardroom. More of those ubiquitous wall panels, the floor space between them filled with well-trodden but impeccable-quality carpet. The celing was up in the stratosphere, with masses of that convoluted plasterwork that is the hallmark of 18th-century decor. Tall rectangular windows, four in all, with floor-length drapes in some heavy, faded material. Through one of the windows you could see part of the northern end of that fattest of all financial fat cats, the Bank of England.

At a long table with semi-circular ends were seated seven men: three along each side and one at the head – the Chairman. There were also two vacant chairs. I guessed that Honry and I had arrived last by design rather than circumstance.

Seven faces were directed my way. Curious, quizzical faces. What species of creature was it that had once bribed and blackmailed and intimidated in the name of HM Government? they must have been wondering. It was like looking into a battery of searchlights.

No introductions were made, not immediately. Honry directed me to a vacant chair, parked himself opposite. Gave me a reassuring nod. Opened his briefcase and dumped papers in front of him. I had no papers. I never used notes when speaking. All I had was a slim pocket book in which I would record matters of substance arising out of the meeting. If any.

'Good afternoon, Honry,' a voice boomed. 'And good afternoon, Mr Fletcher.' Hearing my name startled me.

The speaker was the Chairman. The Fifth Earl of Deverill. Active in the House of Lords, active in the City: directorships by the score. Married, two daughters. Scion of respectability. Aristocrat of aristocrats. Sixty-six years old. Rich. Reputedly a heavy drinker. Most of this stuff came from 'Who's Who'. I had never met the man.

He was a well-chosen Chairman. Power and influence sat astride his shoulders and reached out down the table on invisible tentacles. He seemed to tower over the rest, yet I estimated him to be only slightly above medium height. Square face, bloodless lips, grey eyes – where had I seen those eyes before? Nose convex and big. Jug-handle ears. A mass of white hair like icing on a Christmas cake.

The ensemble was not pretty. Nor was it forgettable.

Honry had slipped me a scrap of paper. On it were written the names of the seven and their positions around the table. A typically thoughtful gesture on Honry's part.

I placed my hands flat on the table top. It was walnut, polished to mirror brilliance. The faces of the men opposite were reflected in it.

'Gentlemen,' Honry said said at last, 'may I introduce Vyvyan Fletcher.'

The magnificent seven responded with an assortment of mumbles and grunts. Nothing that remotely resembled 'How do you do?' or 'Glad you could make it,' passed their lips. I felt like a snake at a mongoose convention.

'Vee – I don't believe you know Lord Deverill, our Chairman.'

'My lord,' I said in sepulchral tones and my voice boomeranged from walls and ceiling. The room had the acoustics of a tunnel.

A grave inclination of the white-maned head.

'On your right,' Honry continued, addressing me, 'and starting with the gentleman next to you: Mr Terence Rigg, Department of Employment,' round and dumpy with a fringe of hair: Friar Tuck in modern dress; 'Doctor Maxwell Jennings from the Treasury,' Mr Purse-Strings: slender as a young girl and debonair as they come; 'Sir Malcolm d'Abo, Home Office,' nodding acquaintance: small and slightly satanic of feature, dressed by Savile Row; 'and continuing anti-clockwise: Viscount Stambourne,' The House of Lords was well-represented: Stambourne was petite, more so than even d'Abo, with curly hair, once brown, now predominantly pewter. Oblong rimless glasses rested on the tip of his nose. Fabulously wealthy, I'd heard; 'Mr David Wainwright, Department of Energy,' ugly-attractive, sweeping handlebar moustache. We'd met. 'Goronwy Rees, Department . . . ah . . . MoD . . .' On behalf of the undercover mob. Looked to be tallish with shoulders built for breaking down doors. A face like a used car: battered and sagging. Somebody, sometime, had taken a dislike to it. It happens in his line of trade.

A well-shuffled deck, our committee. Ages, if I was any judge, ranged from mid-forties – d'Abo, Rees – to the sixties of the two peers. What qualified them to serve on the committee was unclear. A common denominator would surely be the desire to do Yeo down. This wasn't a debating society; argument for its own sake wasn't on the agenda. I hoped, I hoped.

'. . . there you have it,' Honry was quietly burbling. 'The Committee for Operation Strikeback.'

'Strikeback?'

'Apt, don't you think? They strike, we strike back.'

Incredible. 'Code names are not supposed to give away the nature of the operation.'

'Precisely my view,' d'Abo murmured.

'Let's get on, shall we?' Lord Deverill sounded testy. 'All this talk of code names . . .'

'But, my lord . . .' Honry demurred, 'we have to call the operation *something*. We can't simply . . .'

'Hangman.'

The word left an empty void in its wake. Everybody looked at Goronwy Rees.

'Hangman,' he repeated without expression. 'That's what we're going to do to the bastard, isn't it? Hang him?'

'I say.' Honry's protest was a feeble effort.

'Figuratively speaking, you mean,' Deverill said, then did a swift traverse of all present. 'Why not? Operation Hangman. All agreed? Good. Note that, will you, Secretary?'

Honry, as Secretary and taker of minutes, meekly noted.

'Now let's get on.' Deverill was already setting the seal on his chairmanship, letting us all know who was boss. Some of my worries began to fade. 'We are here to settle on a course of action against one David Yeo, President of the Amalgamated Union of Energy and Water Engineers. In specific terms, our brief is to expose such unsavoury aspects of his past and present activities as may be used to discredit him in the eyes of his union and the nation as a whole, and thereby reduce if not eliminate his power and credibility; ideally, to bring about his removal from the post of union president.'

So far, no dissenters.

'How this information is to be . . . unearthed, shall we say, has not been decided, except that Mr Fletcher here has been recruited as consultant for the duration. For the benefit of those by whom Mr Fletcher's work has gone unnoticed, I will simply say that he spent some years at the DTI as their Industrial Relations Adviser and was instrumental in resolving many union disputes. His methods are, I am told, a shade . . . unorthodox, but his success rate is remarkably high.' He fixed his granite gaze on me. 'Haven't committed any slanders, have I?'

'Not yet, my lord.'

He grinned roguishly and I warmed to him.

'Mr Fletcher left the DTI some years ago but will be employed on a freelance basis in this instance. However, since his methods will largely determine the outcome of Operation . . . Hangman . . . I think it is only fair and reasonable that the Committee as a whole be told something of his background and qualifications beyond his rather nebulous record at the DTI.'

Again, no dissenters. Unless you counted me, and who did?

'You are forty-two years old.' He was reading from a sheaf of papers in a buff folder that I recognised as from the DTI personnel archives. 'Born in Lewes, Sussex, an only child. Initially educated at Cheam Public School, whence you were expelled after three years – at the age of twelve – for . . .' He peered at me from under his bushy eyebrows. '. . . infamous behaviour. On to Sevenoaks School, in Kent, who were apparently in ignorance of your expulsion. You lasted a further three years there, then left suddenly. No reason given – or none that appears in your file. Your father evidently despaired of English schools at this point and sent you to stay with his brother – your uncle – in New Zealand, where you attended the . . .' he consulted the papers, 'Rotorua Technical High School, a co-educational establishment. There, it seems, apart from a hushed-up pregnancy rumour, you generally behaved, and stayed the course through to the age of eighteen, when you returned home to read Industrial Economics at Bath University. Quite how you qualified for a place at an English university is not explained here. Anyway, you surprised your family by obtaining a respectable degree, then surprised them even more by signing on as an officer cadet in the Army Signals Corps. After you were commissioned you transferred to the Intelligence Corps and three tours of duty in Northern Ireland followed. An exciting time for you: wounded once,

94

beaten up by the provos, awarded a going, and by the age of twenty-five you had attained the rank of Captain. A star performer indeed. Not long afterwards though you resigned your commission . . . something about an unexplained incident in the Irish Republic . . .' he turned a page, 'in which three known terrorists seem to have been . . . ah . . . kneecapped.' The old boy was actually beaming. 'What a dreadful shame.'

'Dreadful,' Stambourne agreed, in false lament. Even Rees' junkyard features registered approval. I started to relax. Maybe I was among kindred spirits after all.

Deverill resumed the story of my life.

'After the army you became a security consultant for a major industrial group. There you came into contact with trade unions for the first time and became – "fascinated" is the word used here – fascinated by the growth of their power. You went on a course in industrial relations, gained two or three promotions, and were finally appointed Industrial Relations Director. Nothing controversial in your private life during that period other than the failure of your father's insurance brokering company which seems . . . ah . . . to have prompted him and your mother to join his brother in New Zealand. Some sort of moonlight flit, I gather.'

'I had no connection with my father's business interests,' I pointed out and at once felt disloyal.

'Oh . . . quite. There's no suggestion you had; this is just background material. To give us a flavour, if you like. Now then . . .' eyes down again, 'yes, I think this is pertinent: the man-days lost by your employer through stoppages were running at over twenty-thousand annually at the time you joined the group. In the subsequent four years the figures were 3,800, 212, none, and 17 respectively.' He shook his head wonderingly. 'And this, gentlemen, is a group with twenty-three thousand employees. It's not recorded here how you achieved this miracle and I won't ask.

Suffice it to say that your doings came to the attention of the DTI; Henry is a cousin of Mr Fletcher's wife,' Deverill said for the benefit of the other committee members, 'and he and Mr Fletcher were acquainted socially. Very soon afterwards you joined the DTI and stayed there until September 1989 when, as a matter of political expediency, your function was declared obsolete.'

'What about Mr Fletcher's achievements at the DTI?' Rigg piped up, North country accented. 'Does he claim credit for the big reduction in days lost through strikes during the eighties?'

This evoked a few sardonic chuckles.

Deverill, absolutely straight-faced, said: 'About as much credit as you would claim for solving unemployment, I should think, Terence.' And the chuckles turned to laughter; even Rigg joined in.

'But in answer to your question,' Deverill went on, 'I have to tell you that Mr Fletcher's work at the DTI was and is classified. Even *I* am not privy to it, and I won't embarrass Henry by asking him if he is. However, I do have it on fairly reliable authority that a number of major industrial disputes were thwarted and several unions well and truly emasculated in the years following his recruitment. You must search your memories, gentlemen, and decide for yourselves which particular triumphs might be laid at the door of our friend here.'

All eyes swivelled towards me. The curiosity was overlaid with grudging respect now, and in a couple of cases even mild trepidation.

'Now I think we have aired enough of Mr Fletcher's linen. Are there any questions before I let him step down from the dock?'

'I have one.' It was Wainwright who spoke, tugging diffidently at his flamboyant facial growth. 'While you were with the DTI, did you ever break the law in pursuit of your duties?'

Which was one hell of a question. Uneasy, I turned to Honry. 'Is this an inquisition, Honry?'

'Most certainly not.' Honry was suitably nettled on my behalf. To Wainwright, he said: 'Mr Fletcher is a specialist in the field of union law and activism. He was employed to get results. His methods were essentially his own affair but were tacitly approved by the Home Office. Will that do, David?'

Wainwright looked smug. I rather feared Honry had supplied the answer he sought.

'I simply wanted to know what we would be expected to countenance . . . to *tacitly* approve.'

'And you're still none the wiser,' Deverill snapped. 'If that's all then . . .'

It was all.

'Mr Fletcher.' Deverill extended a hand, transferring the floor to me. 'We would like to hear your proposals, and any other pearls of wisdom you see fit to cast before us.'

'My lord.' I pulled up my chair and scanned the eight worthies who sat there in judgement like a jury at a murder trial: Deverill, eager, tense; Stambourne, cynical; d'Abo likewise, though less overtly. Rees had an air of professional interest, waiting to trip me up; Rigg, Jennings, Wainwright were all variously on tenterhooks: these three were the most likely to shy away from any whiff of irregularity. As for Honry . . . Honry was himself: cool as a sea breeze, unflappable as an old bloodhound.

'Over the last week or so I have been investigating David Yeo,' I began. 'I have talked to members of his immediate family, I have talked to his University professor, to his friends and his ex-friends, male and female. I have tried to extract from them anything at all that might reflect badly on him.' I looked at Deverill: he was literally on the edge of his chair.

'Yes . . . yes,' he said, only seconds into my pause.

'I have failed to expose a single item of smut or

scandal, gentlemen.' My voice was flat, revealing nothing of my disappointment. 'David Yeo would appear to be as pure as a maiden aunt. Sure, I found instances of wild behaviour dating back to his teens, the odd jilted girlfriend with a diehard grudge, a neighbour here and there who didn't get on with him. But not a thing I could use. Even *Private Eye* magazine would give him up as a bad job.'

Deverill glowered. 'Nobody is that pure. Dig deeper.'

'I've already hit solid rock, my lord.' Not strictly true, but being naturally cagey I made it a rule never to lay all my cards on the table.

'Does this mean . . . ?' Jennings voice tailed off.

'. . . we must let Yeo do his worst without lifting a finger?' Stambourne completed, harsh in his incredulity.

'No, it doesn't.' Goronwy Rees beat me to it. 'Mr Fletcher was just scene-setting. Getting us all in the right frame of mind. Now he's going to ring up the curtain.'

'Curtain?' Deverill growled. Metaphors were wasted on him.

'He's going to tell us what we must do.'

'You're so perceptive, Mr Rees,' I said, in a tone that was just this side of sarcastic. Then, to the committee as a whole: 'The directive from Honry, sorry . . . Henry . . . was to dig up dirt. We didn't discuss whether the dirt was to be real or whether it was to be manufactured.'

I let the last word drop in their midst like a mortar bomb; let it take root on their faces and seep into their minds. The reactions ranged from Deverill's grunt of satisfaction to Jenning's open bewilderment.

'Manufactured, you say?' This from Stambourne. 'Would you care to elaborate, Mr Fletcher?'

'Certainly.' This drew a nod of encouragement from Deverill, who was in no doubt at all as to my meaning. 'Real dirt is the ideal. Being true, it can't be disproved and any action for libel or slander is bound to fail – ask Jonathan Aitkin or Neil Hamilton. *Manufactured* dirt on the other hand, is largely or totally false and consequently open to rebuttal. Worse than that, if disproved it will backfire on its creator and his sponsors. The outcome would then be the opposite of that desired: the victim, having been proved innocent and the dirt proved false, would actually gain in stature. His detractors would be shown to be no better than criminals.'

A tremor travelled around the table. It was a fearful prospect for respectable men to contemplate. Only Deverill and Rees took it in their strides, displaying only nonchalance while the rest all but wet their pants.

'All of which means,' I said, bent on hammering my point home, 'that any move to manifacture a smear on Yeo will put all of us and perhaps even the Government at risk.'

Deverill and Stambourne conferred in an undertone.

'What's your view on this, Rees?' d'Abo said in his easy, authorititive manner.

A tiny shrug from the Welshman. 'Professionally I can't fault Mr Fletcher's appreciation. If the man is to be discredited and no genuine material exists – and I'm prepared to accept Fletcher's assurance on this – then synthetic material is the only answer. My department feels that Yeo would best be dealt with by more . . . positive methods . . .'

'Yes, so we understand,' Jennings said, mouth primly downturned. 'We have all read your recommendations. Fortunately, we are not yet in the business of arranging accidents to our own citizens, however distasteful we may find their politics.'

Deverill rapped the table for order. 'Gentlemen . . . I would like Mr Fletcher to tell us more. What, precisely, have you in mind?'

'The nature of the dirt, you mean, my lord? Nothing specific as yet, except that it must be "quality" dirt. Meaning it must stick – for the reasons I've already given you. Before I can conceive a plan, much less carry it out, I need your and the committee's say-so. This also raises the question of the job specification: am I to simply devise, or devise and implement?'

'I don't follow.' Deverill placed a long cigarette precisely in the centre of his mouth.

'Do you simply want me to concoct a scheme for discrediting Yeo and hand it over to the committee for execution? Or am I to see it through from start to finish?'

The furrows cleared from his lordship's brow and he smiled faintly.

'For a hundred thousand pounds I think we would require the full service, Mr Fletcher. A to Z. Yeo delivered, bound hand and foot, to the slaughter.'

'In that case,' d'Abo said, 'would it not be a good idea for us to toss a few suggestions into the ring for Mr Fletcher to mull over? Since we are gathered here, it seems a pity to waste the opportunity – especially if his own ideas are still inchoate.' He was toying with the gold watch chain slung across his immaculately-waistcoated midriff. A cool, calculating customer.

Deverill grunted. 'That all right with you, Fletcher? We don't want to limit your room for manoeuvre.'

'Nor do you want to pay out good taxpayers' money then do the job yourselves.' The steely eyes wrinkled with amusement. 'But, no, I've no objection. I'd welcome suggestions.'

'Very well.' Deverill expelled a plume of expensive smoke into the space between the opposing ranks of the committee. 'The floor is now open, gentlemen. What has Mr Yeo been up to?'

'Well . . .' Rigg, hesitant, reluctant to be first away from the grid. 'Could we prove he isn't English?'

'Make him a Russian, you mean?'

'Rather a Frenchman,' some wag suggested to loud laughter and a spate of applause.

'A capitalist?' someone else ventured.

'With a Swiss numbered account and a villa on the Côte d'Azur.'

Another round of laughter.

'A homosexual?'

'Who cares about queers these days?'

'A drug addict?'

'A child abuser.' From Rees. This had some merit and was kicked back and forth.

'Photos are easy to fake.'

'Where do we get the child from?'

We dropped it.

'Make him a traitor?' Rigg proposed.

Silence briefly fell.

'A traitor?' Deverill rubbed his chin as if checking the state of his beard. 'You mean a traitor to his country? To Britain?'

Rigg shrugged with one shoulder. 'I don't know. I hadn't really thought it through. This is just a brain-storming session, isn't it?'

'Wait a minute,' I said abruptly. Rigg had planted a tiny seed and it was germinating fast. 'A traitor, yes, but not to his country. Why not a traitor to his union?'

Only Deverill immediately caught on to the possibilities. 'By God, Fletcher! That's the answer. Let him betray his own members.' He drew on his cigarette, face lit up, animated . . . excited. 'How would you go about it?'

It was unreasonable of him to expect me to cook up some scheme on the spur of the moment and I told him so. He was unabashed.

'Then sharpen your plotter's pencil and go to work on it.' He prodded his cigarette at me. 'Spend what you need to, within the parameters laid down by Henry, but don't delay; above all, don't delay. Have you read the transcript of that speech Yeo made in Sheffield last week?'

'Better than that – I was there.'

'Were you indeed?' A glimmer of surprise. 'You get

around, don't you? So, anyway, you know what manner of animal we're up against. Understand this, Fletcher – Yeo is to be stopped. One way or another. And that's official.'

'Message received.'

'And understood, I trust.' Deverill grinned then, a savage, twisted snarl that gave him the look of a wolf. 'I want his name to stink higher than a Bombay sewer. I want him cast out of his union, out of society, out of the country even, if it can be done. I want him crucified on a cross so high they'll be able to see him all the way from Beijing!'

His voice had become rasping and his eyes were pinpricks to bright, stabbing light, hot and glowing. I stared at him. Everybody was staring at him.

'I want him *destroyed*!'

Chapter Six

Guy Fawkes Day dawned crisp and clear, and perfect bonfire conditions were forecast for the evening. After breakfast Julia and I went riding; we kept a pair of stallions at stables on Farnham Common. Mine, a roan of sixteen hands, was a powerful, tireless beast, seven years old, named Pagan, and I'd had him since he was a foal. Julia's was slightly smaller, three years younger, and infinitely more temperamental. Much like her. His name was Soldier Boy, usually just 'Boy'.

We rode across the downs towards Cookham, crossing a couple of minor roads and going on as far as the river where we dismounted and, leaving the horses to graze by a well-galloped bridle path, strolled across a slippery wooden footbridge and up a gentle slope covered with gorse bushes. It was a spot we visited often.

'I've been thinking about your . . . your *thing* with Yeo,' Julia announced after we'd been walking for a few minutes. 'Whatever you do, however you tackle it, you're going to be right out on the slenderest of limbs. The Government distanced itself from you once before by firing you – and that was a *Conservative* government. Imagine what this crowd would do to you if you cock it up. It's all part of the same plot, I'm sure.'

'What plot?'

'Don't be so dim. Why do you think you're being paid in used fivers under the table. If it all goes wrong the link between you and the Government would be jolly hard to prove.'

'The used fivers, as you call them, were actually

straight from the Royal Mint, and in any case they were at my insistence.'

'At his insistence, the man says.' Julia gave an unladylike snort. 'You can be very gullible at times, darling.'

'It doesn't really matter anyway. I wanted the job. It needs to be done.'

I also badly wanted a hundred thousand smackers.

Julia was in particularly fetching shape this morning. Her colour was high from our canter in the frosty air, and although her lustrous dark hair was tucked away under a white headscarf, a few strands had escaped and lay coiled across her cheeks. Hacking jacket and jodhpurs suited her too.

'They'll abandon you at the first hint of a setback,' she warned and as we breasted the slope she stopped and turned to me. 'So will your committee of lords and gentlemen. Even Cousin Honry.'

I reached out and stroked her cheek with the backs of my fingers. I loved her as much as ever, but in spite of her professed anxiety it was strictly one-way traffic. From an unimpeachable source I'd learned that she'd spent Tuesday afternoon and evening, when she was supposed to be respectively shopping and dining with an old (female) friend, shacked up in a central London hotel with a notorious stud-cum-rising pop singer. Twenty if he was a day. I hadn't confronted her with it. Didn't intend to. It wasn't a new experience. And I had my own trail of infidelities, so who was I to crib?

'Your concern touches me,' I said.

The view from our elevated position was of rolling downs flecked with isolated trees and coppices, and away to the east the dark woods of Burnham Beeches. Most of the trees apart from the oaks were now bare of leaves; they clawed at the sky, black and ugly, stripped down to meet the assault of winter. Although sunny, it was still cold, the frost lingering on the ground in patches where the sun hadn't reached it.

Julia was prowling, slashing at clumps of gorse with her riding crop, scuffing her toes in the dirt. 'If you do it . . .' She faltered.

I folded my arms. Something was brewing and I had a hunch it wouldn't be to my liking.

'If you do it,' she began again, taking a gulping breath, 'and you get caught . . . arrested . . . whatever – it'll be the finish between us. You know that.'

'Yes.' I *had* known, if only in my subconscious. Having it confirmed didn't hurt. Much. Julia's family were not pro-Fletcher. They would never stand for any scandal if I was at the root of it. They would form a square against me and Julia would be expected to join them, to choose blood before marital ties. And she would do exactly that. When the only bond in a marriage is coital, it doesn't take much of a tug to sever it.

'You don't seem put out by the prospect.' She stood before me, one knee bent, fist on rounded hip, crop tapping glossy riding boot. Made to order for the front cover of *Vogue* magazine.

'Let's just say I'm as familiar with the rules as you are.'

'Well then?'

'Well then, I'm still going to do it.' I took her arms, dragged her to me. 'Don't write me off just yet, sweetheart. If I thought I was going to fall down on the job I wouldn't touch it with the flagpole on your dear daddy's lawn. All you've done is given me an extra incentive to stay out of the jug.'

I crushed my mouth against hers viciously, teeth gouging lips, tongues fencing. Her body hardened against mine, loins thrust forward in physical wanting.

There, on that knoll, under the cold November sky we made frantic, furious love.

Or to be strictly accurate, I did. Julia simply fucked

*　　　*　　　*

That night Yeo again enlivened the TV screens across the land: in the fourth in a series of live interviews with up-and-coming personalities and their family, entitled 'Live at Home.' As implied by the title, the interviews took place in the subject's own house. No editing. I had missed all the previous transmissions, but was told the formula made for amusing and occasionally sensational viewing. I watched alone. Julia was in the tub.

The intro was short and unmemorable. We moved quickly to the street outside Yeo's house in Enfield, a solid des res: stone facade, leaded cottage-style windows, double garage, behind a low hedge, a willow tree in need of pruning, some soggy pampas grass, a Grecian urn in the centre of a decorative paved terrace. The camera closed in, focusing on the front door, a windowless affair done up in mediaeval format, with fancy hinges and studs. It opened to the interviewer's rat-a-tat on the knocker. I half-expected a knight in clanking armour, but no, 'twas only Yeo forsooth, a rare, dazzling grin of welcome switched on for the viewing millions.

We were conducted through a wide hall into a sit-
ng room, full of traditional dark-stained furniture and
ssian-covered walls. Lots of pictures and books; wall
ts in the form of imitation flaming torches; a set of
ed swords over the high stone fireplace where
lazed. Magazines scattered on a long coffee table
liberately haphazard arrangement. A true pot-
taste and vulgarity.
in an easy-chair with carved wooden arms,
eo – Carol. From the Yard print-out I knew
rty-two and a diabetic. Pouter pigeon chest,
r figure lost in a billowy caftan dress. Mid-
t attractively short in soft waves, framing
e whose best asset was a pair of slightly
yes. In her computer CV she was
ghly-sexed.' How a computer came

by that piece of intelligence was food for lurid speculation.

The camera slid to a curved settee and introduced us to the Yeo kids: Rowen, of course, in her undergraduate's attire, still with her tinted specs, still too severely packaged for her free-spirit disposition. Seeing her reminded me she hadn't phoned as promised.

Next to Rowen, Roger, aged eleven. Any resemblance to Daddy was purely non-existent. Another spectacles-wearer: National Health frames set in freckles. Gingerish hair. Superman motif on the blue sweat shirt. Jeans. Just an ordinary kid.

Younger daughter Regina was in altogether another category. Sweet sixteen and I bet she'd been kissed plenty, what with her blonde hair, which she wore long and done up in tight ringlets. She had her mother's face and eyes, only prettier. She had me wishing years off my age.

The limelight was restored to Yeo as he folded his tall frame into a second easy-chair opposite his wife. Relaxed, casually put together in open-neck shirt and maroon V-beck pullover with a leaping panther motif left of centre. The presentation was that of an ordinary, average family man. Everybody's next-door neighbour.

The interviewer sat beside him and the interrogation got under way.

It began as an attempt to depict Yeo as moderate, modest, and upstanding, and it worked to perfection. It almost converted me. Early in the proceedings Yeo produced a pipe, a curved-stem affair with a knobby bowl. Now for sheer, clean-living respectability a pipe-puffer rates even higher than a non-smoker. Harold Wilson used the device during his spells as PM and succeeded in keeping his penchant for Havana cigars out of the public eye.

It was only a half-hour transmission and the interviewer had to work fast to get all his questions out and give all members of the family a say. Time was two-thirds up before any topics other than of a humdrum, domestic hue were aired.

Turning to Carol Yeo, the interviewer said: 'Mrs Yeo, your husband has been variously described in the press as – and I quote – "democracy's sworn enemy", "a red rag to the Government bull", "Stalin's English son", to mention some of the milder sobriquets. Does this name calling upset you?'

'Absolutely not.' She smiled as she said it and if she was merely putting on a brave front it didn't show on my screen. 'The *Tory* press were bound to throw brick-bats: the actual words they choose are unimportant. Most thinking people, whatever the colour of their politics, recognise empty invective when they read or hear it, and will laugh it off. Rhetoric doesn't only flow from David.'

Bravo, I mouthed.

'So you think your husband should ignore all the . . . er . . . vituperation?'

'I do. Most certainly.' Said with a fond look at hubby; she was quite the doting wife. 'He is doing what he believes is best for his members. He is spearheading a new era in trade unionism and I'm right behind him.'

The interviewer was momentarily wrong-footed by her unequivocal reply. 'Well . . . well, that's . . . certainly a positive stance you're taking, Mrs Yeo,' he said and his voice was shaded with admiration.

'That doesn't mean we all feel the same.' This came from off-camera and was immediately followed by a sharp 'Rowen!', also off-camera. The camera panned with almost indecent haste, settled on the offending Miss. Here was controversy, here was drama in prospect: a renegade in the camp. I would have given a lot for a glimpse of Daddy's mush, but in the television crew's eagerness to get a fix on Rowen, he was overlooked.

She hadn't expanded on her remark. On the screen she appeared as a demure, butter-wouldn't-melt young lady. The last person to propel excreta at Daddy's fan.

The interviewer, a lizard snapping up an unwary fly, stammering in his haste, said: 'You don't share your father's political views, Miss Yeo?'

Rowen glanced across the room. I could visualise Yeo's frantic signals, warning her against rocking the boat of his downbeat image. She wasn't cowed.

'I don't want to seem disloyal,' she said coolly, 'so I'll simply say we don't see eye-to-eye on politics in general and trade unions in particular.'

'Why should they?' A defensive cry from Carol Yeo. 'This is a family not a commissars' training camp. If I didn't agree with David's ideology he wouldn't force it on me willy-nilly. In fact . . .' the fondness illuminated her face again, 'knowing him, he would insist I stuck to my own beliefs, no matter how much they diverged from his. The same applies to Rowen.' No fondness for wilful, wayward Rowen. 'She's an individual. If she chose to vote National Front we'd respect her right to do so.'

'And me,' Regina said assertively. The camera swivelled. 'I've got opinions too. Not that politics and unions interest me very much.'

No, with her it would be boys. Rowen was the thinking daughter; Regina stood for glamour.

The interviewer switched to son Roger.

'What about you, Roger?'

The boy reddened, grinned idiotically as boys of his age are wont to do. 'Er . . .'

'Are you interested in trade unionism?' the interviewer said encouragingly.

Roger shook his head.

'Football is all he's interested in,' Yeo interposed. 'Football and model aeroplanes.'

The camera had flicked briefly to Yeo, but was now back on the boy.

'It all seems daft to me,' he declared suddenly. 'All these strikes.'

A roar of laughter from Yeo.

'I won't comment on that,' the interviewer wisely said, though he too was showing amusement.

'Everyone's afraid of my father,' Rowen complained. 'If they knew his secret they wouldn't be.'

I sat up with a jerk.

'His . . . secret?' The interviewer sounded apprehensive.

'Yes. Would you like to hear about it?'

I was bolt upright, ears pricked. The camera was on Yeo: he was thunderstruck and . . . yes, the flint in his eyes was shot with unease.

'Well . . . would you?' Rowen demanded of the interviewer.

'I . . . in principle, yes. Provided it's not too . . . er . . . personal.'

Rowen grinned and it was of pure devilment. 'You can decide after I've told you what it is. I'm sure all your viewers – how many are there . . . thirteen million? – I'm sure they'd all *love* to know.'

My God, the hussy was actually going to do my job for me!

'Rowen!' Yeo spoke sharply.

But Rowen wasn't in the market for fatherly censorship. She was having far too much fun.

'It's this . . .'

'Perhaps after all . . .' the interviewer croaked, in dread of some unspeakable exposé, his nerve crumbling to dust.

I was balanced on the edge of my seat.

'. . . he plays with toy trains in his spare time,' Rowen said with such a delicious chuckle that the whole room was instantly convulsed.

The funny side of it was lost on me in my relief. Yeo was not after all to be denounced before the television cameras. Fletcher's thunder (not to mention his fee) was not about to be stolen. Yet Rowen's revelation, or rather the run-up to it, had served to bolster my belief that there existed another secret, infinitely more damaging that a juvenile hobby. Why else, before she revealed its true nature, had Yeo reacted as he did: fearful, close to panic.

As a result of what I had just seen and heard I decided on a last do or die effort to dig up authentic as distinct from manufactured dirt on Yeo. I decided to tackle Rowen head-on.

To telephone Rowen at home would have been less than discreet so I wrote to her c/o University of London to request a meeting. She rang me two days later and rather brusquely consented to meet me on her free afternoon, next Tuesday. The former friendliness was missing; she even addressed me as 'Mr Fletcher'.

After hanging up I puzzled over it. Her near-hostility might imply that my journalistic cover had been exposed for the sham it was. If so, why see me at all?

The mystery was still unsolved when I turned up for our appointment at two o'clock on a damp, misty afternoon in Regent's Park, which was her choice, not mine. There, as soon as the initial terse greetings were done with, she enlightened me.

'I hope you weren't put to any inconvenience coming here,' she said to the tinkle of icicles, 'because all I want to say to you is – you are a turd!'

I'd soaked up worse insults. Blotting paper had nothing on me.

'Passing myself off as a journalist, you mean?'

My admitting it straight out upset her calculations. She would have expected bluster, protest, if not outright denial.

'I'm sorry for the deception,' I said, and from a personal angle my regret was real. I took her arm. 'Shall we walk for a while – it's not the best of days for a stand-up slanging match. All that heats up is the air.'

She didn't pull away. We stared at each other for a full minute, her eyes enormous behind the round lenses. Her hair was tucked out of sight under a headscarf and her plainess was painful. What was it about her that exercised such a pull on me?

'Do you always find it so easy to manipulate women?' she said as she fell into reluctant step beside me.

'I don't find anything easy these days. Women least of all.'

A male jogger loomed out of the mist, chugging towards us at scarcely more than a walking pace, his red track suit a vivid scar on the grey backcloth. He went past with sawing breath: middle-aged, flabby, face slack and sweaty. A clear case of kill or cure.

'My father calls you a Government gigolo,' Rowen said.

'He's a perceptive man.' I looked sideways at her, but her attention was firmly fixed anywhere but on me.

'He also says you're not all you pretend to be.' She dipped inside her handbag, came up with a pack of cigarettes.

'No thanks,' I said when she offered them. I lit hers and she dragged down smoke with obvious appreciation. It seemed somehow out of character, her smoking. Too hedonistic.

'If I'm not what I pretend to be, what am I really?'

'That, I think, is what he would very much like to know.'

It was worrying that my front was so transparent, so soon after my return to the ranks of the Civil Service, though perhaps it was inevitable.

'Your father has a persecution complex,' I said lamely.

'Be that as it may, I think the way you tricked my grandparents, not to mention me, was despicable. You obviously intended to maintain the deception today, if I'd been dumb enough to fall for it.'

'Obviously. I do what I have to do to earn a living.

112

Part of my job is to gather information on union activities. All inoffensive stuff, I assure you. There's no ulterior motive.'

She slowed, looking down at her booted feet. 'It's not your motives I object to, it's your methods.'

'Look, Rowen.' We finally came to a stop by the bandstand, a ghostly relic of another age. I held her by the shoulders and deep down in the pit of my stomach something uncoiled. I put it from me firmly, reminding myself she was only half my age, and said: 'I watched you on television the other night, and it was quite a performance. You had me fooled right up to your dénouement. But it was . . . ' I broke off; she was trembling. 'What's wrong. Are you cold?'

'Cold?' She laughed, but it was shaky, mirthless. 'No, I'm not cold. Far from it.' I didn't try to analyse the suspected double-entendre. 'Far from it,' she repeated and gave another shudder, looking round at the greyness: the outline of the bare trees and the terraced buildings along Prince Albert Road, blurred and softened by the most. A woman passed us, pushing a pram of Cadillac styling and proportions, cooing away to the tiny, unseen occupant.

'What were you going to say?' Rowen asked. 'You were talking about the TV thing.'

'Ah . . . yes. I was intrigued by your father's reaction when you mentioned his "secret". The secret he thought you meant wasn't the one you told us all about, was it? There's another tucked away somewhere in his past. He knows you know it and so do I.'

She had nerve enough and to spare to face me down. 'And if there is, Mr Fletcher – do you really imagine I would tell you? Of all people. A government *snoop!*' She almost spat the word. 'You expect me to tell tales about my own father?'

That would have been too much to expect. I had expected – no, hoped – to trick the information out of her. Trickery was my *métier*.

'You don't agree with his politics – you said so publicly. I thought maybe *your* political conscience . . .'

'Political conscience!' Now she positively blazed. I stepped back. I'd once been belted by a woman and, take it from me, the weaker sex is a pure misnomer.

'What about moral conscience?' she snapped. 'What about loyalty? Hey? I don't suppose such codes of behaviour figure in your nasty, smelly, sneaky world, *Mister* Fletcher.'

She certainly had a feel for adjectives. And I didn't dispute any of them: my world was exactly as she described it.

'You're wrong, Rowen. They do figure. But the only way to do this job is to shut out all emotion and all instincts, all likes and dislikes. When I'm working I'm an automaton: they wind me up, point me in a particular direction, and off I go. Programmed only to get results because, in this game, results are all that count.' I felt bitter and the look I gave her probably reflected that bitterness. She was cooling off fast, a glimmer of understanding peeping through like sunlight from behind a cloud. 'I do it for my country and the people who live in it. Hell, I do it for the likes of you!'

It wasn't pretence. It wasn't histrionics. It was me, being true to myself, for I was genuinely angered by Rowen's contempt. Forestalling any counter-argument I turned and marched off down the path. Where it led I hadn't a clue and to be truthful I didn't really care.

Having drawn a blank with Rowen I fell back on my own inventiveness. Over the next four weeks I drafted numerous schemes and consulted numerous 'specialists' whose services might be required in their execution. In due course I whittled down my portfolio of options to a short-list of three. Further consultation begot further whittling – down to a final, ultimate master plan.

During the latter part of my military career I had

been fortunate to have attached to me a Sergeant Sloan, known as 'Bull' on account of his taurus-like physique. He was a cipher expert and a judo black belt, and had stayed on in Int Corps after I departed for pastures civilian, moving into the electronics field in which he duly became something of a virtuoso. On regaining his liberty, after a full twenty-two years in uniform, he went to work for a video tape manufacturer in London, just as the boom in that industry started to take off. It was there, while making enquiries into allegations of union bullying of the firm's moderate work-force, that I had rediscovered him. That was back in '86, and we had kept in touch socially ever since.

Now I had need of him – professionally.

I drove across London to his flat in Lewisham on a frosty Wednesday evening. The traffic was unusually light. I respected all speed limits, jumped no lights, and generally behaved towards other road users as a gentleman should. I also mulled over my plan as I drove, ironing out the odd wrinkle. It wasn't a perfect plan, nor yet perfected, and it would call for an interrogation technique of such finesse and subtlety that I was still unsure of my ability to pull it off. And this even though in Int Corps I had practised and refined such techniques to the point where many of the themes developed by me were subsequently to appear in training manuals.

Bull's flat was in a renovated tenement just off Lewisham High Street. I beat the lights at the bottom of Loampit Hill and found a niche large enough to accommodate the Bentley's eighteen feet, a few doors down from Bull's. It was a respectable enough district as this part of London goes and the night was cold enough to deter all but the hardiest of car thieves, otherwise I might have sought a more secure haven.

Bull was expecting me. His wife, small and skinny as he was big and brawny, let me in. She was a timid creature and invariably greeted me with a jink of head and body that was almost a curtsy. Bull said it was because I was married to a nobleman's daughter. I assumed he was joking.

Though physically the pair had little in common, they were temperamentally well-matched. No children, no other family, and God knew how they spent their leisure time, yet they seemed content. In that respect, I envied them.

Bull was in what he liked to call his study, though it was really only a sitting-room with a desk and a vintage Anglepoise light. His handshake was warm and knuckle-crunching firm. He looked pleased to see me.

'It's been a while, Vee,' he said in his Norfolk brogue as we lowered bottoms into chairs on opposite sides of the desk. 'Scotch?'

'Why not? It's a cold night.'

The door was closed; Bull's wife was in the kitchen making washing-up noises with the dinner plates. I loosened my tie, Bull loosened his belt and unbuttoned the top of his trousers, then drew a bottle and two glasses out of his desk drawer. Poured generously.

'Here's to you,' he proposed.

'Likewise you,' and we drank. Also generously.

Bull Sloan was a solidly-built man, over six feet tall and correspondingly wide, and none of it was flab. Square-faced, incongruously rosy cheeks – the bulbous cheeks of a glass-blower even down to the network of broken blood vessels; a slight cast in the left of his piggy blue eyes. He would be about fifty-five.

Less visible, except when he walked, was the stainless steel foot, the legacy of a brush with an anti-personnel mine in Northern Ireland only months short of his demob. Likewise not on show were his skills in armed and unarmed combat and his utter dependability. All in all, a formidable ally. Or adversary.

He set his glass down on the desk. Picked his nose

with a forefinger. Some of his habits were best not dwelt upon.

'A job, you said, Vee – a *special* job.' He always got straight down to business.

'Ten thousand pounds.' Talking money before all else was my way of stimulating immediate interest.

'Ten . . . *thousand*? That's special, all right. How do I earn it?'

'I'll need you for upwards of four weeks, possibly even as long as three months, and even that I can't guarantee as an outside limit.'

He blew out air in a tight hiss, like a punctured tyre. 'Up to three months? Difficult . . . difficult. My job . . .' The bull head shook dubiously.

'Ten thousand, Bull,' I said, just in case he'd overlooked a nought. 'Plus a bonus of, say, £500 for every week after the first four, and £1000 a week if it goes beyond three months.' You mad, free-spending fool, Fletcher.

His eyes were bright and calculating as he sipped Scotch and did silent sums.

'I suppose I could ask for dispensation to visit my brother in Australia.'

'Have you got a brother in Australia? I didn't know that.'

He grinned then. 'Don't be so fucking dim.' He explored deeper within his long-suffering nasal cavity, discovered unmentionable delights. How he disposed of them was not apparent.

'This job . . . where and when, for openers?'

'The where . . . somewhere remote. A Scottish island, probably. I've a list of possibilities and I'll be checking them out between now and the end of the year. As for when . . . book your Australian trip for mid-January.'

'H'mm. Any special skills involved?'

'Your video expertise. I shall want you to set up a camera-recorder where it can't be seen, capable of

117

operating continuously for up to four hours at a stretch.'

'You planning to make an epic blue movie?'

I wished to God I was: more fun, less risk.

'Will you be there?' he asked then, topping up our glasses.

'Most of the time.'

'Anyone else be there? Can you cook? 'Cos I can't.'

'At a pinch I could keep us from starvation, though I wouldn't much fancy weeks on end of pre-packed, pre-cooked pap. So . . . yes, there will be someone else. Certain other . . . ah . . . functions may be necessary, so it'll be a woman.'

'A woman, eh? A cosy threesome.'

'Plus the subject.'

'The subject? Ah-*hah*.' He was quick on the uptake. He ran stumpy fingers through his already-dishevelled brown hair through which pink scalp glimmered.

'Now you've worked it out. I'll give you the full scenario. Afterwards, I'll want a yes or a no from you. Like right away.'

'If you say so.'

I emptied my glass, refused a refill in deference to the breathalyser laws, and briefed him on my scheme for Yeo's destruction.

Chapter Seven

The week before Christmas I flew Air-UK to Aberdeen where resided a man called Robert Sellar, owner of Heli-Link, a helicopter taxi service plying the well-flown stretch of air space between Scotland's east coast and the oil rigs. Legend has it there's a fortune to be picked up in these parts.

Sellar's HQ was at wet, wind-battered Aberdeen Airport, the only man-made structure within a ten-mile radius of the city that isn't built of granite. He had two rooms in a block adjoining the terminal: an outer office the size of a telephone kiosk complete with perforce the thinnest secretary in the northern hemisphere, and the owner's suite, palatial enough to accommodate some sticks of miniaturised futniture and two people standing to attention. Heli-Link was clearly comitted to keeping overheads down around vanishing point.

Sellar the man was burly, red-headed, freckled, and as Scottish as a sporran. A year or two older than me, I estimated, and with more lines and wrinkles running through the freckles than his age merited; flying choppers over the North Sea for a living would hardly be a prescription for eternal youth.

'You're a wee bit early, Mr Fletcher,' he said as he waved me to a seat. 'But there's no harm in that.'

He was affable and obliging. Yes, he could fly me to and around the Western Isles and, yes, he would pilot the machine personally and, yes, like the recommendation said, he would guarantee absolute secrecy. The last-mentioned was what distinguished Heli-Link from its contemporaries.

And what was the cost of all these special services? Why, a paltry £3000 on top of his standard hourly charge of £500. In cash.

Within the hour we were aloft and hammering westward over rugged grey countryside. The helicopter was a French built Aérospatiale in red and white paintwork, and in contrast to his cheeseparing of the office fixtures and fittings, Sellar had been positively spendthrift when it came to the airborne hardware. The Aérospatiale was all-electronic, almost a flying computer; the radar equipment wouldn't have disgraced a jumbo. Occupying pride of place was a moving video map of the topography below and up to fifty miles in any direction, even country lanes being plotted. The A96 Aberdeen-Inverness trunk road cut a wriggling, arterial swathe across the screen and when, for my benefit, Sellar zoomed the antenna, individual vehicles could be seen travelling along it.

We flew in a straight line across the Grampians and the southern tip of Loch Ness, arriving over the Island of Skye in under an hour. A change of course to WSW and another ten minutes flying brought us to my first objective, the island of Eilean nan Each, a sombre black hunk of rock, protruding from the sea like the snout of a submarine monster, sheer and glossy on all sides.

We circled it three times. No flat surfaces, therefore nowhere to put down. I crossed it off my list.

Sellar threw me an enquiring glance. 'No good?'

'No. Next stop Flodda-Chu . . . Chuain.' I had trouble pronouncing it. '57°26 north, 4°30 west.'

The clamour of the engine increased and we were pulled forward at an airspeed approaching 200 knots. Rain splattered against the curved windscreen, but was mostly swept aside by the airflow, the single long wiper easily coping with the residue. It was only early afternoon, yet already darkness was encroaching. This far north with the shortest day imminent, night would fall a little after three.

'We have about an hour, hour-and-a-half of daylight left,' Sellar said as we left no-go Flodda-Chuain behind. 'We'll have to land at Stornoway, and spend the night there.' Taking my consent as read, he radioed Stornoway Airport and alerted them to our intended visit. I was startled to hear him ask the controller to book us hotel rooms.

'He's my brother-in-law,' he explained afterwards.

On to Eilean Troddar, which turned out to be a repeat of Eilean nan Each only longer and with two peaks not unlike the spires of the Dom Cathedral in Cologne. Another blank.

Sellar nodded philosophically, waggled the control stick and flew us on across and through the greyness. He pointed out a dark gash down at four o'clock – a crude-oil carrier forging stolidly through the heaving seas, a quarter of a million tons deadweight or more. Then the murk gobbled her up and she was gone, mirage-like.

Two more islets were inspected and rejected before total black-out put a stop to operations. Flying on instruments, we beat it to Stornoway where Sellar's brother-in-law, now off-duty, was waiting to run us down to the Broad Bay Hotel. Fortunately I'd thought to transfer my overnight bag from the Bentley.

The hotel was homely, with tiny, spotless rooms and a bar done out like the Captain's cabin of an 18th-century man-o'-war. It was packed from the moment it opened: seamen of all shapes and sizes and nationalities, a handful of transitory pilots like migrating birds stopping off for a breather, a drilling crew en-route to their rig – a truly multi-national meeting point. We drank a fiery and unbranded Scotch from a keg beneath the bar and sang – hummed in my case – old Gaelic fishing songs. No women entered the bar.

Once during that evening of such simple pleasures

my thoughts wandered to Rowen. Funny how that girl kept popping up inside my head. It wasn't as if I fancied her. It wasn't as if she was fanciable. Nice personality; strong willed, intelligent, vivacious, but with a sexual attraction rating well down below the pass mark.

Next morning, in brighter if blustery conditions, we flew out beyond the Isle of Lewis to the Flannan Isles. Thirty miles out into the Atalantic, and from there to Greenland is a wilderness of uninterrupted water. It was a wasted flight. So back to Lewis to search along its western coastline, then down the eastern side of the two isles of Uist. Islets a-plenty here, but it wasn't until two in the afternoon, while munching our hotel-packed cheese-and-tomato sandwiches and with Sellar beginning to fret about the fuel gauge, that we found it.

Sgeir Varlish.

Superficially little different from most of those we'd already checked out, except that it had a flat, comparatively smooth area on its western side, exposed to the prevailing weather but otherwise the landing pad we needed. Another feature was the disused lighthouse, on a promontory adjoining the flat area.

According to the map the island measured some three hundred yards from tip to tip by two hundred and twenty across the middle. Its highest point was a shade below two hundred feet. A manageable piece of real estate. Set it down in the Med or the South Seas and you'd have instant paradise.

The sun had broken through and pale shafts of light streamed on the island's rocky sides, highlighting the vertical folds and fissures, and bouncing off the stark tube of the lighthouse.

'Know anything about it?' I asked Sellar as we went into orbit around it, the cabin tilting at forty-five degrees and the sunlight traversing from right to left.

'Only what I see. Is the lighthouse important?'

'Any structure would be useful if it can be occupied. Can we go a bit lower?'

'No problem.'

In dropping below the level of the island's summit I was able to form an impression of its profile: it resembled a British Army helmet but with an extension like a short raked funnel on the dome, off-centre. A frill of rocks encircled it, constantly lashed by waves. I saw no natural harbours, which was all to the good, tending to discourage boat-borne callers.

We came around the southern headland and the lighthouse reared up, dead ahead. The structure was more or less intact though the lantern was gone, swept away by some freak wave. Chances were the inside was a mildewed, fetid mess, but if the shell was sound it might be made fit for habitation. With resources, i.e. money, nothing was impossible.

And there too was our ready-made landing pad: a wide shelf, flat as a flight deck and polished to a gloss by wave action. The lighthouse stood at the edge of it.

I indicated the spot to Sellar. 'You can put her down there, I should think.'

'Maybe.' He wasn't quite ready to commit himself. Allowance had to be made for the sweep of the main rotor, which increased the total length of the helicopter by as much as a quarter. The wind strength and direction were other factors he would have to take into account.

Sellar juggled with control and pitch sticks and we decelerated to a stationery hover over the flat ground, close to and on a level with the deformed top of the lighthouse. Every detail of its tiara of rusty, tangled metal – all that remained of the lantern – was laid bare by the sun, and so close were we I could even make out the gaps between the interlocking blocks used in the construction of the tower itself. Once white, these were now shades of grey-smeared-brownish-green. On this, the seaward facing side there was but one tiny window right at the top and the whole edifice had a gaunt, forsaken look. Difficult to imagine as home.

We descended. I looked down over the edge of the rock shelf on which the lighthouse stood, a vertical drop of some thirty or forty feet to the sea, a sea that beat and battered at the land as if to destroy it: the most mindless, most destructive vandal of all. Then the cliff edge rose up and shut it out as we came to earth, in a touchdown of dragonfly delicacy.

'Nice one,' I complimented, and Sellar projected a quick grin at me as he cut the engine.

The din over our heads ceased and suddenly all was quiet. Now I could hear the cries of the gulls as they performed their wonderful aerobatics along the cliff face. The wind too was audible. A mournful resonance through the now-motionless rotor blades and so cold that condensation was already forming on the perspex panels.

'It'll be a mite chilly out there, I'm thinking,' Sellar remarked. He got up and rummaged behind his seat, producing a quilted, fur-lined parka fit for an Arctic explorer, with a hood, elastic cuffs, and draw strings everywhere. By contrast I, in my suede car coat and flat cap, was supremely ill-prepared for the rigours of mid-winter in the Western Isles.

'You want to stay inside?' Sellar's grin was a blatant challenge.

'No point coming this far to let you hog all the excitement.' I unstrapped, turned up my collar, and was out in the frost-laden air before he was. I pulled on my gloves, compared them disparagingly with his mittens. Then, because it was too cold to hang aboug, I set off resolutely towards the lighthouse.

'Come on, sissy,' I called over my shoulder to Sellar.

Now the full force of the wind was buffeting me and whereas in Stornoway that morning it had been scarcely more than a stiff if glacial breeze, here it was strong enough to propel me across the fifty yards of smooth, flat rock that looked slippery but wasn't, at a fast stagger.

By the time I made the foot of the lighthouse I was chilled through. I sheltered behind the great, drum-like base that formed the foundations and watched Sellar saunter across, his cheeks glowing pink but otherwise unaffected by the icy daggers coming *en-masse* off the sea.

'You planning to set up home here, mister?' he said on reaching me.

'In a manner of speaking.' I tilted my head back to gaze up the side of the tower. Seen from ground level it was huge, yet from base to apex was probably less than eighty feet. The walls, built with stones that interlocked like pieces of a jigsaw puzzle, were as solid as if carved from the rock itself, and a century or more of storms and several decades of neglect had made little imprint on them beyond discoloration. The whole structure was probably good for another century.

Iron rungs, rust-covered but still sturdy, were set in the side of the base, leading up to a door, also iron and rust-covered, but fortunately ajar otherwise shifting it would have been a job for a team of wreckers with a ten-foot crowbar.

Up the rungs, testing each one before putting my full weight on it. Sellar, sensible man, let me climb to the very top of the base before starting his ascent. But then he was carrying a few more pounds than me.

He was panting slightly as he came over the ledge. 'This is my first tour round a superannuated lighthouse,' he said and his breath came in white bursts, 'and it'll be my last.'

I nodded, not daring to speak for fear my teeth would chatter; it was *so* cold. Together we examined the door. It was rusted solid on its massive hinges and there wasn't quite enough space for a man to squeeze through. Sellar gave me an enquiring look and I nodded again. We took hold of the edge of the door and shoved. It creaked, moved an inch. We repeated the exercise and gained another inch. A third, mighty heave, a groan of real agony from those long-seized hinges, and we had a gap wide enough for even Sellar to pass through, Eskimo outfit and all.

Inside all was dark and dismal and smelly: it reeked of the depths of the ocean; of damp and decay and the presence of men long dead. I'm not superstitious, but stepping over that threshold gave me as bad an attack of the heebies as I'd had since I was a kid, seeing ghosts in every dark corner. It was as if there were a misanthropic force at large, waiting to pounce.

Sellar made a noise of distaste. 'You'll never get planning permission.' His voice ricocheted from wall to wall.

'Pessimist.'

Sellar had brought a small flashlight: its beam flickered over a circular, central pillar, thick as a telegraph pole, with an iron staircase spiralling upwards around it. Beyond, walls black with slime and sleek with ice. The floor was part-frozen, part-slush. Melting ice on the ceiling filled the place with spatterings as from a thousand dripping taps.

'It might be better upstairs,' I growled, my heart in my boots. Perhaps it was beyond restitution after all.

I relieved Sellar of his flashlight and plodded up the staircase. More rust here, but it was only surface oxidization; underneath, the metal was sound. Sellar plodded behind me, muttering about crazy Sassenachs and mad dogs. I let him get it out of his system; I had views about Scotsmen too.

The first floor was – or had been – a store room and also held the oil storage tank – fuel for the lantern. It was also agreeably free from damp; in comparison with downstairs, that is. There was a sheen of moisture on the walls, but the floor and ceiling were pretty dry.

'Better, huh?' Sellar wheezed.

'Much.' I opened a steel store cupboard that was virtually rust-free. Inside it smelled vaguely of dead sea-weed, but was otherwise okay, useable even. The oil tanks had also fared well, though I wouldn't be needing them.

There were no windows on this floor and but for the skirl of wind around the tower all was silent. Like the inside of a tomb.

'It's a wee bittie spooky,' Sellar said and laughed, a nervous snigger.

I directed the thin beam on him. 'I'll let you hold my hand if you're frightened.'

The Scots are great ones for their goblins and kelpies. The place made my flesh tingle too, though I wasn't about to admit it.

'Coming up?'

He grunted at that. 'You've got the bloody torch, have ye not?' Which was a sort of answer.

So we toiled up the second spiral and discovered light – in the shape of a small, rectangular window, salt-encrusted almost to the point of opacity, and orientated towards the island's centre. The glass, divided into eight tiny panes, was miraculously intact, though two panes were starred. I switched off the light. We were in a kitchen-cum-living room. The cooking range – an AGA – and cupboard were still in-situ and a table and four upright chairs were stacked in a corner. Under a rotting dust sheet I uncovered a pair of armchairs, slightly mildewed but serviceable.

'This would be where the keepers spent most of their leisure time,' I said, half-thinking aloud.

'Aye, and they're welcome to it.' Curiously Sellar now seemed to be feeling the cold more than me; he was shivering and had a bluish pallor. Perhaps excitement was keeping me warm, for excited is what I was. My initial misgivings were gone. The lighthouse was a goer, I was convinced of it. If the rooms above were as dry as the kitchen, making them habitable was a matter of installing a few powerful heaters, followed by a good scrub down and a lick of paint.

I crossed to the window and used my sleeve to rub a hole in the internal grime. The glass remained stubbornly opaque for the reason that most of the muck was external. Okay, so no room with a view.

The next floor up was the dormitory, again with a window to landward. Two iron-framed, double-decker bunk beds, two steel wardrobes, a bathroom leading off. All very serviceable, though no water flowed from the taps and the loo was . . . well, primitive was the word that sprang to mind and that's being charitable. As for the smell – the less said of it the sweeter.

Finally we came to the top floor, immediately below the lantern platform. This was the service room and had small windows front and back, both undamaged. Here were spares for the lantern and maintenance equipment. A work bench, made-to-measure to fit the curve of the wall, a lathe, a winch, twin grinding-wheels; it was a mircocosmic machine shop.

'Above here's the great outdoors, I'm thinking,' Sellar said. He was huddled inside his parka, mittened hands tucked under his armpits. The only part of him on display was a freckled circle containing eyes, nose and mouth.

I studied the ceiling reflectively. It was sound and watertight, despite the loss of the lantern above. The spiral staircase continued on up to it, ending in a steel trapdoor. I went up and gave it a once-over: it was secured by a single flat bolt, which must have been kept well-greased for it was only lightly rusted and moved freely. The trapdoor itself was another proposition altogether. Pushing upwards produced a gentle rain of red oxide and thirty-years old dirt but no movement.

'Give me a hand, will you?' I called down to Sellar, who was engrossed in the lathe.

'Poor wee Sassenach,' he said with a sneering grin

and came unhurriedly up the stairs. 'I'll bet the big lads used to kick sand in your face when you were a spalpeen.'

'You push there . . . ' I stationed him below a corner of the trapdoor. 'When I say . . . now!'

We heaved and the trapdoor gave a crack and shot upwards but not far enough, dropping back into place with a clang that made my ears ring. Second time round we got it right and there above us was a square of blue sky and a wind that shrieked like a tribe of demented Apaches on the warpath: a bedlam of noise that momentarily blunted all constructive thought. Warily I poked my head out. And saw why the wind sounded so: the wreckage of the lantern – a monkey-puzzle of twisted bars and tubes wrought into grotesque loops and whorls – was an inanimate orchestra of woodwind and brass. They were all there: piping clarinet and deep-throated bassoon, rousing trumpet and regal horn. Together they made music to roast in hell by. If ever Satan needed a signature tune he need look no further.

'What's that bloody racket?' Sellar wanted to know.

'Wind blowing through the wreckage,' I said shortly and against my better judgement, scrambled up into what had once been the inside of the lantern. A black petrel perched on the platform wall shot me a startled glance before launching into space, uttering cries of alarm.

The outlook was spectacular, I'll say that. Sea and islands and the sun flooding the scene with pale light. Sea birds of all shapes and species, wheeling and crying, resentful of this intrusion into their sanctuary. Away to the east, in the sound between the island of Vatersay and the sinister hump of Sandray, a sailing boat was beating against the wind.

Sellar jack-in-a-boxed up beside me. 'What a racket! I've never heard the likes of it.'

'You Scots have no ear for music, that's your trouble.

Otherwise you'd never try to pass bagpipes off as a musical instrument.'

But he wasn't exaggerating; the din was truly hideous, beyond description. It rose and fell with the wind's changing velocity, from deep rumble to agonized squeal with all the intermediate variations. And talk about cold! The wind simply knifed through clothes as if they were fishnet.

'Your knees are knocking,' Sellar observed, and they were too.

The sun, sinking towards the horizon, was full in his face and he squinted, shielding his eyes to look at me.

'Well then, Mr Sassenach from the big city, is this what you want? Is this your blue heaven?'

A gull cruised past my head, was tossed by a gust and dropped out of sight below the parapet. Then the wind howled, raising a shrill descant from the jumbled metal and it might almost have been a warning.

But I wasn't in the market for such nonsense. Let the spooks and the devils do their damnedest.

So I said: 'It's perfect.'

And indeed it was – the perfect prison.

Back at Aberdeen Airport that evening I paid Sellar off in £50 notes.

'I'll have another job for you in the New Year.'

'Oh, aye?' He stuffed the money uncounted into the pocket of his parka. 'And what would that be?'

'Flying people and equipment to Sgeir Varlish.'

He corrected my lousy pronunciation then said: 'Who and what . . . and why?'

'You'll be paid not to care.' It was hot in the office so I undid my coat.

'A dram for the road?' He had the bottle out of a filing cabinet and was pouring a tot apiece even as I answered. It went down like hot oil, scorching my tonsils and injecting instant fire into my bloodstream. The bottle bore no label.

'Not bad,' I said in a whisper, when my vocal chords had recovered from the shock.

Sellar guffawed. 'Not bad, he says.' His glass was empty. 'So what are you offering, Mr Mystery Man? What price my services and my silence?'

'Your costs, plus twenty thousand for up to a maximum of five round trips.' I was spending Treasury money like I owned the Royal Mint.

'Jesus.' Then after a moment's reflection: 'It can't be legal.'

More firewater was slopped into our glasses and thence down our hatches.

'It is and it isn't. Let's just say it's sanctioned at high level, but that it will technically be an offence. How's that?'

'As an explanation it's garbage, but it'll have to do, I suppose. I'll take the money and see no evil.' He lowered his broad beam into his wooden swivel-armchair and contemplated me with the sharp blue eyes that had pound signs for pupils.

'Kidding apart, who told you about me? You must have known I'm not fussy about how I make a crust or else you'd never have come up with a proposition like that.'

'Who told me? A little bird, who else?'

He cackled. Drank. 'A little *Whitehall* bird.' He named the right name. I contrived inscrutability.

'Never mind,' he said, a good-natured growl. 'About the job: what, in detail, will be required of me?'

'All gaps will be filled in when the time comes. Talking practicalities though – in future, unless it's dark or foggy, I want you always to approach the island from the sea and at wavetop height. Keep the hill between you and the mainland. And if there are any boats about, move on until they've gone, even if it means cancelling a landing. Is that clear?'

A nod would always be as good as a wink to a man like Sellar. 'You're saying you don't want anyone to know you're using the island.'

'Correct. And don't you forget it.'

'Me?' Wide-eyed innocence. 'I'm the original elephant. Care to tell me when this will happen?'

'Just make sure your secretary always knows where to contact you between now and the end of January.'

'Will do. Anything else?'

'No . . . except that I'm paying for silence and I expect to get it. Keep your mouth shut tighter than a nun's fanny, Robert Sellar, or else . . .'

'Or else what, mister?' He rocked forward, hands bunched, eyebrows drawn in. Even seated, he posed a threatening figure.

'Or else one of these days somebody might cancel your pilot's licence. Or slap a tax evasion writ on you. Or nationalise you.' I shrugged. 'Who can predict these things? Civil servants are a funny lot.'

He rumbled deep in his throat. 'You've made your point, mister. Anyway, I'm no blabbermouth, as our mutual friend has obviously told you.'

'I never suggested you were. Shall we seal the contract with a lethal dose of your vintage meths?'

Chapter Eight

Came the festive season, I set aside my machinations and resolved to take a breather from Master David Yeo over Christmas and the New Year. It proved surprisingly easy to exorcise his spectre for the duration – a duration spent at the Rosthwaite family seat in the Cotswolds. Gavin was with us, of course, and I tried hard, really hard, to build bridges between us. As I had tried so often before. He was seventeen now, and the void that separated us grew deeper and wider with his every birthday.

'What is it between you and me, Gavin?' I said with unaccustomed bluntness on the afternoon of the day after Boxing Day. We were in the library, just the two of us before a mountain of blazing spitting logs. 'Why don't we hit it off?'

'I don't know, Dad,' he said, wretched and uncomfortable. 'I just feel as though you're . . . as though you're a stranger. Or maybe it's me; maybe I'm the stranger.'

No, you're at home here with the Rosthwaites, my son, I said to myself. At home among the silver spoons. Me, I was just a fellow-passenger, a freeloader. Therein lay the barrier.

Ever wished you could go back to the beginning and have another throw of the dice?

New Year's Day maintained the prevailing trend of frost and sun, the early shroud of mist clearing by mid-morning. We went in convoy – 'we' being the Baron and Baroness, most of their offspring and their offspring's offspring – to Cheltenham Races. Honry and Charlotte had joined our happy throng, having driven over for the New Year's Eve booze-up; Honry had been agitating for a chat with me ever since, but so far I had managed to avoid him. Today was the last day of my sabbatical from Yeo and as such was inviolate.

That was to reckon without Honry's natural persistence.

The course teemed with racegoers, West Country gentry unconcernedly rubbing shoulders with local bumpkins, and in the crush Honry – blast him – succeeded in detaching me from Julia and the rest to pin me to the rail the very instant they came under starter's orders for the 3.05 Malvern Novices' Hurdle. I had twenty-five each way on Chipped Metal at 5-1.

'Must we discuss it here and now, Honry?' I grumbled. 'Why can't it wait until we get back home on Friday? Come round to dinner both of you, if you like.'

'Kind of you. I accept anyway. In the interim I want something to feed the lords and the masters tomorrow morning.'

'Tell them I've got a plan. Won't that do?'

'You know better than that,' Honry reproved. 'Mossy is asking for feedback too, and he will certainly expect chapter and verse, down to the last semicolon. You're spending the good taxpayer's money – what are they getting for it?'

'I haven't worked it out in detail. Your boss will have to wring his hands for a bit longer.'

The field was off, fourteen horses in all, the jockey's bright silks contrasting with the drab greys and browns of their mounts. They went into the first bend in a bunch but for a couple of early stragglers, one of which was Fletcher's Choice. I sighed. I should have stuck to knockout whist.

Meanwhile, Honry kept on at me.

'Put it like this,' I said in the end, keeping the binoculars trained on the pack as they negotiated the third jump. 'I know how; I know where. I've got my team together. All that's left to settle is the date.'

A horse fell at the fourth jump. Not my Chipped Metal though, he was still going like a good 'un and what did it matter that he was last? It's effort that counts, some headmaster or other once told me in reprimand.

Two more horses went down at the sixth. At this rate Chipped Metal was still in with a chance.

'Actually,' I said, 'there is a small service you could render: I need a cook-and-bottle-washer, with commando training. A twenty-five year old female weight-lifter with big knockers will do admirably.'

'Weight-lifter?' Honry's wrinkles of bewilderment were manifold. 'Big knockers? What's it all about, old boy?'

'All will be revealed on Friday. Seriously, though, Honry, I would like you to track down a reliable, capable, and – if possible – personable young woman to join the Hangman team. There must be one or two such animals within the depths of Whitehall. Ask Gonorrhea Rees. The MoD has quite a few female operatives, doesn't it? What about Miss Moneypenny?'

'Moneypenny?' The wrinkles multiplied.

'Forget it,' I sighed. 'You've obviously never been near a Bond movie, much less read the books.'

'Ah . . . that Moneypenny. But look, let's stick to the real world, Vee. Why must this bottle-washer person be a woman?'

The penultimate jump and my fancy, still lying ultimate, went flying in a confusion of legs. I lowered my binoculars resignedly.

'I've just blown fifty quid.'

'Julia will be pleased,' Honry said with unaccustomed nastiness. 'Now answer my question – why a woman?'

I slid the binoculars back into their case and gave him my undivided attention. 'Because Brother Yeo may need softening up and I'm not talking about lead-filled hoses bouncing on his cranium. Savvy?'

'I . . . think so. You're planning to . . . er . . . seduce him into spilling the beans?'

'No, Honry,' I said patiently, 'I'm not planning that at all. The woman . . . girl . . . will be a contingency, no more than that. Hopefully I won't have to resort to such wiles, in which case she may come in handy for entertaining the troops.'

Honry blinked.

'Which means,' I said remorselessly, 'that I don't want some dusty spinster from the Records Department. I want looks, sparkling personality, good figure, intelligence, discretion . . .'

'And a *cordon bleu* nymphomaniac to boot!' He was grinning broadly.

I gaped. 'Honry, you never cease to amaze me. I didn't think big words like nymphomaniac were in your vocabulary.'

'Never judge a book . . .' he murmured. 'She . . . this Superwoman . . . a weight-lifter you said. Any significance in that?'

'Some. I'd prefer someone who's has training in unarmed combat and can use a gun.'

'A gun, eh? Will she need one?'

'Hopefully not. But I'll expect her to pack one along with her Tampax.'

The surviving horses were into the final furlong and the crowd surged forward to the rail. Men and beasts pounded past on the frozen track, the former urging the latter with voice and whip and briefly all was shouts and snorts and rasping lungs. I pulled my scarf up around my ears and watched a photo-finish between the favourite and a 33-1 no-hoper. It looked to me as though the favourite had the edge and sure enough large chunks of crowd were now surging in the opposite direction, towards the bookies and the tote.

As the space around us opened up, Honry said: 'Friday then. Come to the office at nine. I'll set up another committee meeting too – for next week, if I can rope everybody in.'

'You do that.'

Honry was silent for a moment, and for a change. The winner was announced and it was no surprise. A bad result for the bookies.

'How would you like a weekend in Brussels?' Honry said over the dying crackle of the loudspeaker.

I stared. 'What? With you? Honry!' I fluttered my eyelashes. 'This is so sudden. I hardly know what to say.'

'Footling idiot,' he said ruefully. 'I mean you and Julia. Charlotte will be coming.'

'Tell me more.' I watched the favourite being led off to the winner's enclosure, hemmed in by well-wishers and arse-crawlers. The sound of clapping reached us across the heads of the throng. I thought I saw Julia with Gavin, and waved. No answering wave. I felt deflated. Silly, really; it probably wasn't them at all.

'On 10th and 11th January there's going to be a convention of leading Euro trade unions in Brussels. On the agenda, amongst other earth-shattering topics, is a programme of concerted action to reduce unemployment within the EC.'

'It sounds like an excuse for a binge and a crack at the Brussels fleshpots.'

Not that, in my experience, the Brussels fleshpots merited the effort.

'Well, I'm going.'

Stunned, I said: 'To the *convention*?'

'Good lord, no. They'd never let me within a mile of the place. No, I'm going to the reception. Ostensibly as a bona-fide representative of Her Majesty's Government.'

'The devil you are. And you really could wangle an invitation for me and Julia?'

'Nothing simpler, my dear chap. I'll just make you an aide-de-camp for the evening.' Honry smoothed his moustache. 'I think you should come. Most of the leading lights from our dearly beloved TUC will be in attendance. And Yeo. You could . . . er . . . engage the enemy at close quarters.'

'What a cunning, conniving cove you are, Honry.'

He blushed faintly. Took a much-folded sheet of pale green paper from the pocket of his hairy tweed coat.

'What's this?' I asked as, without explanation, he passed it over.

'The convention agenda.'

'Christ.' I unfolded it. 'So the old spy network still functions, eh?'

'Why not? You set it up to be self-perpetuating.'

'Nice to be acknowledged.' I nipped my rising bitterness in the bud, scanned the crumpled sheet.

'Item four is the nasty.'

I read and my scalp prickled.

' "Formula for disruption – initiation of an action programme to force increases in public expenditure with the object of creating unemployment," ' I read aloud from the agenda. ' "Speakers . . ." ' I caught Honry's eye. ' "Speakers . . . for the UK, David Yeo, President of the AUEWE." Admit it Honry, they couldn't have chosen a better man.'

'Whose side are you on?' Honey snapped, scowl converting instantly back to smile as a passing middle-aged couple called a greeting.

'Clerk of the Course,' he side-mouthed to me.

The rest of the agenda was fairly innocuous in comparison with Item 4. A possible exception was Item 7, which was a proposal to form a permanent European equivalent of the TUC, to co-ordinate union action along the lines of Item 4.

'The unions represented are almost all hard left,' I observed. 'Had you noticed? Yeo's lot, the transport workers, the car workers, the printers. the seamen; and look at the French contingent – miners, car workers again . . . they're about as left as they come.' I moved on down the lengthy roll call. 'The Italians are turning out in strength. I wonder if the Mafia will be there. They're a union, aren't they? The Unione Sicilione.' I mimicked an Italian accent. 'More to the point,' Honry said quietly, 'are *you* going?'

I considered. 'No reason why not, Honry, old dear. So long as you pick up the tab.'

His mouth twisted. 'Always preoccupied with money. Anyone would think you were hard up.'

Just then Julia strolled up, arm tucked inside her father's. She looked ravishing, snuggled inside her furs and matching hat, and wearing hopelessly impractical high-heel boots. Her colour was also high: pink cheeks, pink nose, dark eyes that sparkled.

The Baron, big and pseudo-hearty, barked at us: 'Come on, you two – don't be so damned con-spiratorial. We're all going for a noggin to get the circulation moving. Damned nippy, what?'

'What are you up to, anyway?' Julia asked and when no answer came forth, sniffed. 'Plotting again, I sup-pose.'

I kissed her cheek. Detached her from Daddy, who didn't take kindly to the severance.

'Planning a little holiday for us, my sweet, as a matter of fact.'

'Oh, goody. Where? The Canaries are lovely in the winter.'

Discreet mirth from Honry. The Baron merely glow-ered.

'No . . . er . . . not the Canaries. Brussels.'

'Brussels!' Julia searched my face. 'You're not serious.' She swung round. 'Did you hear that, Daddy? Vee wants to whisk me away to Brussels.'

The Baron humphed.

'It's partly business,' I explained. 'It's Brussels or no-where.'

Brussels or nowhere! Who was I kidding? If Julia wanted to take off to places distant she'd do it – with or without my acquiescence.

'Okay, darling,' she said cheerfully. 'I'm in a good mood. Let's go to Brussels.'

Honry beamed. The Baron humphed longer and louder. I stamped my freezing feet.

'That's settled then,' Honry said.

So we all went off to the Arkle Room to hob-nob with the Chosen Few.

And when the last race was run and a cold, dank dusk descended upon us, we drove back in our four-vehicle convoy to the stately Rosthwaite home. Back to the fag-end of Christmas; to the gay decorations of coloured streamers and tinsel, to the holly and wilting mistletoe, to the Christmas Tree as high as the average house, shedding needles like a bad case of dandruff. Back to the remnants of that marvellous, convivial festive spirit. The season of peace and goodwill to all men was almost over.

Sham peace, sham goodwill.

Sham people, including me.

Correction: especially me. I was the biggest sham of all.

The news on Monday was out-and-out lousy. Even the glamorous newsreader couldn't dress it up any different.

'Talks were finally broken off today,' she informed the nation, 'between the electricity and gas supply companies and the AUEWE, with none of the union's claims settled. A spokesman for the employers said that a generous counter-offer had been put forward which went much of the way towards satisfying union demands and that the offer was final. Although the existing pay agreement runs out at the end of February no further meetings are planned for the time being. Mr Yeo was not available for comment . . .' She suddenly pulled up in mid-bulletin, changing tack with professional ease to announce: 'A short statement has just come in from the AUEWE press office, the essence of which is that the employers have been given until Monday 1st February to respond to the union's claim. It is also reported that failure to meet the union's terms in full will lead to an immediate strike call.'

So there it was. The Final Demand. In default of settlement, it would be war.

I would have liked to sit quietly and mull over Yeo's ultimatum, consider its impact on my timetable. But in the next room were eight dinner guests, and my pretended call of nature was already well into extra time. So I switched off and sneaked back like a schoolboy returning from a midnight raid on the pantry, making my re-entry just as liqueurs were being served. Julia's quick frown hinted at retribution.

Oh well.

II
POWER PLAY

Chapter Nine

We touched down in Brussels on a cloudy, not-quite-raining Friday afternoon, checked in at the Royal Windsor in Rue Duquesnoy and dined out that evening at Le Cygogne, an elegant restaurant which basks in some sort of reflected glory from the tavern next door where, back around 1850, Marx and Engels used to meet to dream their revolutionary dreams. There was nothing left-wing about the restautant's prices though – they were strictly for the plutocracy.

Saturday was the second day of the trade union convention. Since the reception was not due to start until 8.00 pm, we had the best part of the day to kill and Brussels being a city that neither Julia nor I had ever visited socially, we embarked on a sight-see by taxi. Which, if extravagant, must rate as the least arduous way of doing it ever devised by man.

We went first to the Grand Place, the true hub of the city. The flower market was open and I bought Julia an orchid, which made her giggle self-consciously and then go strangely quiet. Then it was on to the antique shop in the Place du Grand Sablon where we acquired a tiny wood-carving of a Flemish peasant woman dating from the mid-eighteenth century. It wasn't cheap.

No tour of Brussels is complete – so the taxi driver claimed – unless it takes in the Cathedral of St Michael: a pile of Gothic architecture with baroque stained-glass windows and tapestries. Julia was impressed to the point of reverence, despite her agnostic leanings. A Gordian knot of paradoxes, that was Julia.

Our final call that busy morning was the Atomium, at the Parc des Expositions. A 200,000 million times magnification of an ion crystal molecule made up as a building for the 1958 World Fair. In the top 'atom' is a luxury restaurant which also happens to offer a rather splendid view of the city and it was there that we broke for lunch, joining a veritable United Nations assembly of other diners. Each table had a miniature national flag flying from a foot-tall flagpole with a weighted base, and no two flags were alike as far as I could see. Then along came ours: the Stars and Stripes forever. We burst out laughing.

Our afternoon was slower-paced and limited to an hour at the Museum of Ancient Art, which is jam-packed with Flemish masters, including Rubens, Brueghel, and van der Weyden. Not my scene, though I could recognise the work of genius when confronted with it.

Back at the hotel we made love, and in a tender, undemonstrative way that was as alien to our natures (Julia's especially) as plain-speaking to a politician's. Yet it was a satisfying emotional act; so much so that I dared to hope it signalled a new beginning between us. Hoped but doubted. More likely Julia was too worn out by our jaunt to muster up energy for swinging from the chandeliers or standing upside down in the shower.

Sometime after six, while Julia was in the shower – alone and right side up – and I was sorting out my DJ, the phone chirped. It was Honry, calling to let me know that he and Charlotte were likewise installed.

'Actually, old boy, I'm quite done in,' he said and he really did sound dispirited. 'We had an all-night do at the office to discuss this blasted convention and its likely outcome.'

'And got nowhere, I imagine.'

Chuckle. 'You're so astute, dear boy. As a lesson in the art of hypothesis though, it was second-to-none.'

We were to meet in the lobby at 7.45 pm. Honry had already ordered a taxi to take us to the Europa Hotel, where the reception was to be held.

'See you then,' I said and hung up.

Julia had bought a new dress for this as for every occasion: crushed crimson velvet, ankle length, and tighter-than-tight around the backside. Tarty, some would say. But then that was Julia: a rich, high-born trollop. Still, there was no denying that the colour suited her alabaster complexion.

For jewellery she wore a simple string of pearls with matching ear-rings. £5000 worth of simple.

She paraded for inspection. Past forty or not, she would have every man in the place lusting for her.

'You're looking mighty handsome tonight,' I said, taking her in my arms.

'And you, sir, are looking quite, quite beautiful.' She touched my nose with a gloved forefinger, a somehow patronizing gesture that irritated me.

I picked up her mink stole and draped it around her shoulders. Kissed the nape of her neck. Wished we were staying in.

In the foyer we teamed up with Honry and Charlotte as arranged. Our taxi was already waiting: inside it was crematorium-hot and stank of BO. It was, thankfully, only a short haul to the Europa; breathing through the mouth is not a practice I care to indulge in for lengthy periods.

We were deposited before the Europa's canopied entrance on the stroke of eight.

'Am I supposed to be incognito or what?' I whispered to Honry as we passed through the automatic sliding doors. 'One or two of the old timers in the British lot might remember me from way back.'

'You're here as my PA this evening, and that's official. You're on the guest list and I've got your invitation card. Nobody is going to argue with those credentials.' He glanced sharply at me as if a thought had occurred to him. 'Your cover's not blown, is it?'

'One can never be hundred per cent sure,' I hedged. I still hadn't told him about the dust-up with Yeo's thugs in Sheffield, nor about Rowen's disclosures.

'Then stop worrying, my dear chap.' Honry accosted a braided commissionaire. '*Où se trouve la réception des syndicats?*' he rattled off, with barely a trace of accent.

'*Au deuxième étage, monsieur.*' The commissionaire pointed. '*Voilà les ascenseurs.*'

'Never knew you could parley the lingo, Honry,' Julia said. She herself was fluent in French and Italian.

'Honry can do everything, dear,' Charlotte said with a blown-up sigh. 'I thought that was common knowledge.'

Honry declined to rise to the barb and, nose held aloft, led us all across the reception lounge to the lifts where a number of other evening-dressed people were standing. I recognised a Permanent Under-Secretary, a nodding acquaintance, and duly nodded.

On the second floor we ran into our only security check. A commissionaire, more heavily braided than his chum downstairs and presumably therefore of senior rank, demanded to see our invitations. Honry dealt him four white, gilt-embossed cards, and we were cleared to enter.

The room chosen for the reception was vast, but even at that was crowded to capacity. It was going to be a binge to remember. I'll say this for the unions: they don't mind raiding the kitty in times of need.

'How many of these are union people?' I asked Honry as we stood on the fringe, having deposited our coats and scarves with the slim, pretty, but unfortunately male, cloakroom attendant.

'About half, I should say, including wives, relatives, and direct hangers-on. The rest'll be from various governments and embassies, a sprinkling of favoured industrialists *à la* Alan Sugar, and friends of friends.

Oh, and the press – hoping for a scandal or a revolution.'

'Perhaps we should oblige.'

Our wives emerged from the powder room and we sallied forth. This part of the room was all bar and floor space, and most of those present were gathered here, standing in groups, invariably with drinks in hand. Yattering. Waiters circulated, balancing trays. Beyond lay the dining area. Over and between heads I saw long tables, each with twenty or so place settings, and at the far end a single table arranged broadside on to the rest. For the dignitaries. *Genus homo unione.* I felt my mouth turn down of its own free will.

A familiar face bee-lined towards us, wreathed in smoke from a pipe that was as much as part of it as his nose. Ernie Tigwell, member of the Steelworkers' executive. If I had ever had any friends at all in the union movement during my previous stint as a Government snoop, he was it. Like all his brethren he had believed me to be a PR Officer. Had he ever suspected my real function he would have torn up his membership card rather than be seen on the same side of the street as me.

''Allo, Vee,' he said with such genuine warmth that I had a rare twinge of guilt over the deception I perforce practised on him and other so-called decent unionists.

We shook hands warmly. He had met Julia before though I doubted she'd remember. Diplomatic when the occasion demanded, she covered up well.

'So nice to see you again,' she said, glowing all over him. From that moment he would have forgiven her any sin in the book.

'And Lord and Lady Tiverton,' Tigwell said, somewhat less benignly. The aristocracy in concept and in fact were the bitterest of the unions' bitter pills. Tigwell always addressed Honry as 'lord', a distinction to which he was not entitled.

'How are you, old chap?' Honry, conversely, used

149

the same style of address for everyone. Charlotte just smiled wanly. She was not at east with hoi-polloi.

Tigwell was sixty-ish, short and circular of face and body – a golf ball on a football. In his dinner jacket he resembled an overfed penguin. A bouquet of pipe smoke clung to him as always. The image was authentic muck-and-brass.

"Ow are things, lad?' he enquired of me in his broad Rotherhamese. 'We am't seen much of thee lately.'

'In retirement, Ernie. The previous lot put me out to grass. We were over-manned.'

His small eyes widened.

'Over-manned. You mean they made you redundant?' When I nodded, he whistled. 'Ee, lad, I am sorry. You should've 'ad t'strength of t'unions around thee. Still, from wot I 'ear, your wife . . .' He remembered that Julia, although engaged in conversation was within earshot, and clammed up fast.

'Quite right, Ernie. I'm not on the breadline yet. Tell me . . .' I indicated the still-growing multitude, 'who's here I might know?'

'Oh, everybody who counts.' Tigwell grabbed a waiter. And I do mean grabbed. "Ere, let's get thee and t'missus a drink.'

I ordered gin-and-tonics for us both, looked around for Honry, but he and Charlotte had been cornered by a tall, bald character in tinted glasses so I left them to fend for themselves.

'Who, specifically?' I said to Tigwell as he freed the waiter.

'Well . . . there's Bill Morris, o'course, and Bickerstaffe of UNISON; Ken Jackson is 'ere, and Bloody Davies, flashing 'is OBE as usual. Oh, and young Bob Crow, still trying to make a name for hisself. Who else now . . . ? Oh, Jimmy Napp, David Yeo . . .' Tigwell nudged me in the ribs, cackled. 'All the big guns are out. Wouldn't you like to spike 'em, Vee.' He cackled again, eyes almost disappearing into his cheeks.

'Not any more. Like I told you, Ernie, I'm finished with all that.'

Julia docked alongside me. 'Finished with all what?'

'The unions. Since my retirement.' I relieved the returning waiter of two brimming glasses.

"Allo – there's King Arthur,' Tigwell said, punctuating with a snort.

Julia's brow creased. 'King Arthur? Has he brought his round table with him?'

'Scargill,' I said out of the corner of my mouth as the balding, now much discredited of the Hard Left swept down on us, a few surviving sycophants hanging on to his every inflammatory slogan. He spotted me, slowed. I saluted him with my glass.'

'Fletcher,' he said, and the entourage to a man turned to look me over. 'I thought all Mrs Thatcher's poodles had gone into tax exile.'

Ho-ho.

'You haven't met my wife, have you, Arthur?'

Julia showed her teeth. I'll be charitable and call it a smile.

The miner's leader was deadpan as he said: 'Howdy do, Mrs Fletcher. Do accept my condolences.'

With that display of charm and wit he bustled off, the smirking retinue of middle-aged groupies drawn along in his slipstream.

'He's a card, all right,' Tigwell observed with nervous jocularity.

'Isn't he?' Julia agreed, her irony undisguised. 'Where's his wife?'

I pointed with my glass to a buxom woman in her early forties holding court with a trio of thick-necked delegates.

As yet, no sign of God, alias Yeo. Probably perfecting his walk-on-water trick.

Some unseen MC called us to order and in the ensuing quiet invited us in French to take our seats for dinner. He repeated the request in a variety of other languages, of which I understood only English.

With the aid of a master-plan by the door we pinpointed our places, battled through the scrimmage to table number 17, about half-way down the room, by the right-hand wall. On our right Honry and Charlotte, on our left a M. Robert le Duc whoever he might be. Opposite turned out to be a German diplomat and a Belgian Eurocrat with their spouses. All spoke English after a fashion, and the cross-talk during the inclined-to-stodginess six-course meal had a distinctly mongrel flavour.

Still I hadn't caught sight of Yeo. I noticed, with a degree of satisfaction, that he hadn't rated a seat at the top table. That, it seemed, was reserved for TUC and equivalent chairmen. Our own John Monks was there, to the left of the Burgomaster of Brussels, chain of office and all.

Feeding time was followed by speaking time. The Burgomaster rambled at length in alternate English and French on the need for European nations and by implication European Trade Unions to work together and set an example to the less-developed world, drone-drone. You hear the same idealistic garbage, dressed up differently, on television every day of the week. The audience claps loudly, 'hear-hears' vociferously, and goes home to get on with more practical matters.

John Monks was next in line. He dished up more of the same without the duplication in French. The more prominent among his Continental counterparts also had their say. The surrounding boredom grew and grew and grew until, at last, sometime after eleven, we were set free. The surge to the bar and the adjacent ballroom where a band was warming up, beat any First-day Sale stampede.

The band kicked off with the Waltz of the Toreadors, a long-standing favourite of mine and Julia's. For a while we danced, she and I, her body hot in its slippery crimson sheath, her breasts undulating excitingly in their negligible support, her pelvis bumping mine. In the art of tease and titillation Julia was unsurpassed and for her a crowded dance floor was as good a place as any. Eyes aflame with wickedness she would grind her pubis into my groin, a pestle to a mortar, then skip away, shaking her hips and breasts at me. If only her father could have seen her.

When I could stand it no longer I sought out Honry and Charlotte and did a straight wife-swap. Julia was laughing delightedly as Honry whisked her away.

By comparison Charlotte was docile and undemanding. We danced a waltz or two, fox-trotted, even jived. She was in the mood to prattle and I let her get on with it, interjecting the odd 'M'mm' and 'Uh-huh' for form's sake.

Later, all danced-out and deserted by both my partners, I bought a drink and rested my elbows on the bar next to a young couple who were attempting to climb inside each other. They weren't aware of me. Or of anybody. I sighed. Out of envy? Probably . . . probably.

While I was soaking my sorrows in double-malt Honry came hurrying past, eyes fixed on the exit. I caught his arm, swung him round.

'Have a drink, Honry. You look all hot and bothered.'

'Taken short, old top. Must find the loo.'

'How about finding Yeo? The man I came here to meet. Remember?'

He hesitated. 'Yes . . . quite. It *was* all laid on. But now . . . I'm not really sure what to do . . .' His voice tapered off unhappily.

'What's up? You're not a happy Honry, are you?'

'Oh, I suppose you'll find out sooner or later. Fact is, I can't pin the blighter down. For the last thirty minutes he's been dancing with Julia and now they've both disappeared.'

*   *   *

Honry had accelerated away in search of relief and I was back to playing gooseberry to the wrestling couple. Oh, lonesome me. Another drink made me feel lonelier still. What should I do? Go hunting for Julia, demand she be restored to me unsullied by Marxist hands? What ignominy!

Have another drink instead. Drink and think – it even made poetry. More Scotch went down my throat and a female voice went 'Hello, Vyvyan,' in my left ear, the use of my despised given name with all its androgynous connotations causing me, as always, to mentally cringe.

I pivoted round, a mechanical smile already hoisted. 'Hello . . .' The greeting died on my tongue like champagne fizz. The voice had been that of Rowen Yeo, but the girl before me – a slender, vivid creature in a black evening dress cut so low that the tops of her breasts were showing – was like no Rowen I recalled.

I tried again. 'Hello, Rowen.' It came out creaky and hoarse. 'I didn't know you were here.'

'Nor I you.'

The biggest transformation was facial. Gone were the glasses; the eyes now were revealed in all their velvet-brown hugeness. And they were beautiful. God, *she* was beautiful! All over. The hair hung long and straight and she wore a narrow grey headband that, with her dark colouring, gave her the look of an Indian maiden. She could share my teepee any time.

'You look . . . different,' I managed to say, understating madly. I was fumbling for words like a spotty teenager. Reminded myself she was barely out of *her* teens.

'Is that different-good or different-yuk?' she said coquettishly. She was clutching a glass of dark liquid and as she raised it to her mouth she peeped over the rim of the glass at me, eyelids at half-mast.

'Good, definitely good.' I was almost stammering. 'You look abso-bloody-lutely ravishing.'

She reddened, bit her lip, then settled for a grin.

'Can you see okay without the specs?'

'Contact lenses,' she said cheerfully and unself-consciously. 'Worn them for years, though I mostly leave them out in the daytime.'

'I hardly recognised you.' I plonked my empty glass on the bar top. 'Let's dance,' I said and plonked her glass too. Masterful stuff.

She didn't demur and came into my arms as smoothly and as easily as if she'd been doing it for years.

'You dance well,' she remarked presently.

I returned the compliment. Held her closer and she didn't fight it.

'When we last met,' she murmured as we shuffled to a slow waltz, 'that day in Regent's Park . . . I said some cruel things. I . . . I'm sorry. I didn't mean them.'

'Yes, you did. And you were more right than wrong.' My fingertips explored the bumps of her spine, slipped lower to rest just north of her bottom, an inch or so closer to that part of her anatomy than would normally be considered proper. She didn't seem to mind. Her own grip tightened on my shoulder. She was making all the right responses.

The General Secretary of our beloved teachers' union twirled past, catching us a sideways swipe. He was in the clutches of a statuesque, centrefold blonde, a good head taller than him and no way was she his Mrs. He looked at me the same way I was looking at him, ie knowingly. Then his beaky nose was back blonde-nuzzling and the false smile turned back up to full wattage, and away they spun.

'Vyvyan . . .' Rowen began.

'Call me Vee. Everybody does.'

'Vee?' She said it again, weighing it. 'Vee . . . yes, well, it's easy to get your tongue round.'

'You were going to say?'

155

She angled her face away. 'I was going to ask you something.'

'So . . . ask.'

'I'm not sure if I should.'

What was cooking in that sharp little brain? I wondered for a moment if Yeo had planted her on me – a beautiful union mole. Not such a wild impossibility really. Surely, though, he wouldn't use his own daughter as a spy.

Surely.

'Ask,' I repeated.

Now she looked me straight in the eyes and it was pretty devastating; I was fancying her like I'd just discovered what the opposite sex was all about.

'Take me for a drive,' she said.

I smothered my surprise, mock-bowed. 'Your every wish . . . '

Which was how I came to be in the back seat of a Mercedes taxi with a girl half my age who also happened to be the daughter of the man I was being paid to ruin. Mid-winter madness. All else was set aside: Julia, Yeo, my reason for being here in Brussels . . .

'We just want to cruise,' I instructed the driver, who was fluent in English.

'Cruise, eh? Like the missile.' And he chortled at his own *esprit*.

'Skip the comedy and drive – and no speeding. The lady wants to see Brussels by night.'

And if he swallowed that, he'd swallow anything.

We filtered into the scurrying Brussels traffic, thick on the ground as flies on a cowpat. I'd heard tell that Belgian drivers are the world's worst, so I kept my eyes off the zipping traffic and on my fetching companion.

We swept past the Parc de Brussels and turned left into Rue Royal, which led down to the Palais de Justice, all done up with fairy lights. In the square before the Palais we did some complicated and possibly illegal manoeuvring and back-tracked along a parallel route to the Palais du Roi – the King's Palace. Thence to the true heart of the city, the Grand Place and l'Ilot Sacré – the sacred Isle – which is not an isle at all except insofar as it stands as a sanctuary of tradition and culture, resisting all attempts at development. More power to its elbow.

All this I learned from our friendly driver who – obligingly or irritatingly, depending on your priorities – kept up a desultory travelogue.

Between the flashes of commentary we managed an infrequent sentence of our own, mostly superficial chat. Not until we were speeding down the wide Boulevard Leopold II, bound for the Parc Elisabeth and the Basilique Nationale – thank you for that information, driver – did I shift the conversation into a higher gear.

'What would your father say if he saw us?' It was a thought spoken aloud.

She turned her head towards me, the first time she'd really looked at me since we boarded the taxi.

'I'm twenty years old, Vee. That makes me officially an adult. What the hell does it matter what he thinks?'

Spoken like a true rebel. Impulsively I swayed across and kissed her on the lips. I lingered there for a matter of seconds only. It was not a lover's kiss, nor was it fraternal. Somewhere between the two: ambiguous, like my feelings for her.

'Do that again,' she said quietly, after a tiny silence. 'Please.'

The driver was watching us in the mirror. The stream of travelogue had temporarily dried up.

'*Attention la route!*' I said sharply.

I pulled Rowen to me and kissed her again. I meant the formula to be as before, but she took charge. A hand on the back of my neck was enough to hold me there, mouth-to-mouth resuscitating like fury. Her lips were mobile, eel-like, wriggling; moist, sensuous, seductive. I tasted her and smelled her and the taste and the smell were powerful stimulants both. God knows how long we remained like that, but when I came up for air we were at the Basilique. The road encircled it and the driver, enthusing over the Basilique's undoubted architectural virtues, took us around it twice.

'Stupendous,' I said, to satisfy national pride, which prompted him to do a third circuit before darting off along yet another brilliantly-lit thoroughfare. My disorientation was now complete, and in every possible sense.

Rowen sat with her head lolling against the back of the seat, her profile sharp against the sodium street lighting. It was a truly marvellous profile, I decided, and understood now why her presence had stayed with me since that first meeting in Sheffield: subconsciously, I supposed, I had all along seen through the glasses, the scraped-back hair, the unflattering clothes. Seen them for the trappings they were. Recognized the beauty that lurked behind them.

But Yeo's daughter, for Christ's sake! What was I thinking of?

'Vee,' she said. Her eyes were closed.

'I'm here,' I said, mostly wishing I wasn't.

'I haven't stopped thinking about you since the day we met.'

I might have said the same. Instead, I said: 'Well, stop thinking about me from her on in, Rowen. There's no future in it. I know it's a cliché, but either you're too young, or I'm too old.'

In spite of the attraction she held for me I was trying to do the decent thing. It wasn't often decency played a part in my conduct, and even now I was more motivated by fear than morality. Fear of Yeo – not physically, but professionally. I wanted no complications to louse up my plan. I needed the money.

I instructed the driver to return to the hotel.

I must have been mad, I decided, to sneak off with Yeo's daughter. Mad or drunk. Whichever, I was now wholly sane and sober. And as cold inside as a deep freeze.

Then Rowen's hand, warm and small, was clutching mine and – damn it! – I was clutching back. Sanity began to crumble all over again.

'You can't fool me, Vee. You feel the same. I can tell.' Her voice was fierce, possessive.

No, I didn't. I was attracted to her, strongly attracted, but it went no deeper than that.

'Shut up,' I said, gruffly. 'Whatever I feel, it's point-less.'

A wailing, flashing car ripped past, displaced air slamming the side of our taxi. We wobbled, our driver cursed: '*Espèces de salauds*,' and other worse insults.

'Go back to school, Rowen. Forget all this nonsense.'

Naively perhaps, I never thought of that as an insult. But suddenly we weren't holding hands any more; hers came out of the darkness and glanced off my jaw – a badly aimed slap. Only then did it occur to me I might have given offence. It wasn't much of a slap – I'd suffered a lot worse – but it told me a lot about Rowen.

She didn't speak again and neither did I. We sat out the rest of the short return drive inside our own private Arctic circles. Even our driver shut up, which shows how serious it was.

We pulled into the hotel forecourt and Rowen was out and away before the wheels stopped rolling. In such a public place I didn't dare call her back. I paid off the driver, tipped generously, and got a sympathetic shrug.

'Maybe next time,' he said, misunderstanding the reason for the slap.

I grunted bad-temperedly and went into the hotel. The digital clock in Reception said 12:43, which meant we had been away an hour. Long enough to be missed.

Rowen was nowhere around. Headstrong girl. An affair with her would be like riding a roller-coaster: all ups and downs. Who needed it? I had quite enough on my plate for the present, both sexually (if not emotionally) and professionally, without such distractions.

But in my heart of hearts I knew it wasn't over. That tonight had been only the curtain-raiser and the main act was yet to come. It had the whiff of inevitability about it.

So it was in a pensive and slightly confused state that I wandered into a small lounge just off the reception lobby with the intention of relaxing over a pot of strong black coffee. And there, finally, came face to face with my destiny.

Chapter Ten

Around a circular, glass-topped coffee table were seated three people: Julia, Honry . . . and David Yeo. Yeo was talking. Rapidly, volubly. Unlike his stage performances, this one was economic of gesture: no flailing arms, no demonstrative fingers.

Unnoticed, I stood there and simply observed. Julia and Honry both seemed in a state of entrancement, though Honry's earnest look was surely put-on, jollying the great man along in the hope of gleaning the odd useful snippet here and there. As for Julia . . . her rapt attention held more than mere admiration for Yeo's words, even had her politics been in tune with his, which they emphatically weren't. There was a luminosity about her that I hadn't seen since the early days of our marriage. I recognised the symptoms; all too well I recognised them: Julia had the 'hots' for Yeo. They didn't happen often, these sudden passions – about once a year on average. But when they did, they were unmistakeable, and the usual cure was to fix up an impromptu trip abroad for us both. Or let it run its course. Only neither alternative was viable in this case.

What a hoot. Julia and Yeo, Rowen and me. An eternal quadrangle.

As I moved forward into the room all three of them glanced up simultaneously. Their reactions were interestingly varied, from Julia's guilty start, through Honry's cheerful hail, to the glint of battle that appeared in Yeo's chilly grey eyes.

'D'you know Vee Fletcher, Mr Yeo?' Honry said in

that relaxed, so-natural manner of his.

'Only by reputation.' Yeo stood up slowly for the ritual introduction. We crunched each other's knuckles and pretended it didn't hurt.

'I was hoping to be able to meet you tonight,' I said smarmily, flexing my pulped fingers.

'Where've you been, darling?' Julia asked. As if she really cared. 'We've been looking everywhere for you?'

I longed to tell them and watch the shock register.

'Out.' I grinned. 'Over-indulgence. I needed to clear my head.'

Banal, but what the hell? Yeo's nostril twitched; clean-living paragons like him never over-indulged.

'Had a good convention, Mr Yeo?' I enquired, dropping my coat across the back of a lounge chair and dumping my haunches in another.

'You're with the DTI, aren't you?' he said, apparently ignoring my enquiry.

'Used to be, long ago. Now I'm in security.'

He pursed his thin lips; they didn't purse well. 'All right – you *were* with the DTI. Maybe I'd still better watch what I say. I don't have many supporters at Whitehall.'

'Is that a fact? So you don't want your world domination plans leaked just yet?'

'Actually, I'll settle for Britain-domination.'

Up until then I had been ahead on points in the verbal ping-pong. At a stroke he had levelled the score, drawn ahead even.

You had to admire his directness too.

'So you intend to take us all over,' Julia said, showing little concern at the prospect.

'Naturally.' The thin lips smiled at her and I read into that smile a message that probably existed only in my fantasies. Julia read the same message though and responded as Julia was designed to respond, displaying all her wares: eyes, teeth, breasts . . . all marketable commodities. *Her* message was unmistakeable.

162

'Mr Yeo does not speak with forked tongue, eh?' I said bitchily. 'A no-bullshit union leader: we say exactly what we mean and we do exactly what we say. Refreshing if nothing else.'

A waiter glided into the lounge and took our order for a round of coffee. As he left, a bevy of giggling, overdressed females and DJ-attired, cigar-toting men old enough to be their grandfathers, passed by the doorway. I thought I recognised Davies of USDAW. Serve him right if the press were lurking in Reception.

'Do you disapprove of plain speech?' Yeo asked.

'On the contrary. I'm delighted to hear you tell people just what you intend to do. It's the parts you keep back that bother me.'

The instant the words left my lips I wished them unsaid. Honry's wince reached me across the table. I was doing it all wrong: baiting Yeo when I should be staying strictly neutral. Letting my hostility hang out. It was not professional.

But I couldn't help it.

Julia was fidgety with excitement, scenting bloodshed. Her idea of the ultimate visual entertainment was a world-class boxing match: the giving and taking of punishment by two well-muscled males. Invariably, while watching, she became sexually aroused. A verbal bout would be less stimulating, but better than none at all, especially if she imagined we were scrapping over her.

'What *do* I keep back?' Yeo was relaxed behind a slightly supercilious smile. Content, for now, to let me set the pace.

'Your master plan.' I made it deliberately flippant. 'Enslavement of the masses, elimination of the upper classes. The same as all your contemporaries past and present – only more so.'

I expected him to laugh, to join in the joke I was belatedly trying to put across in the hope of averting open warfare.

Instead of laughing, his face set like concrete and I was treated to a hard, intimidatory stare that might have bothered me had I not been so sure that the sands of his power and glory were fast running out.

'You may joke, Mr Fletcher. But the British Constitution – unwritten as it is – would enable me to do just that, should I be so minded. The whole democratic process in the UK is so flabby and complacent that I could smash the Government and the infrastructure of the country just by snapping my fingers.'

That bit of braggadocio roused even Honry to objection. 'That's rather strong, Mr Yeo,' he reproved.

'You wouldn't do that to poor little me, would you?' Julia said, feigning hurt.

'I'd exempt you, naturally.' He spoke so disarmingly no offence could possibly be taken. 'I'd make you an honorary member of the party.'

'And will you snap your fingers?' I said, genuinely curious to know.

Wisely, he refused that jump. Bombast was replaced by slyness.

'You're avidly following our talks with the electricity and gas suppliers, I'm sure. If they don't see sense, we'll have to impose sense on them. Otherwise, why talk at all? Why have a union?'

Why, indeed, was my private amen.

'So you *will* snap your fingers?' I was set on hanving an answer, aggro or no.

Julia was glancing from one to the other of us, excited as a child on Christmas morning. Anticipating the KO.

Yeo almost rose to it. He badly wanted to flaunt his power before us – we, the so-called ruling caste he held in such contempt. He yearned to rub our noses in prophecies of nemesis.

But after an internal struggle that had him squirming in his seat, he simply said: 'Wait and see.'

Then the waiter arrived with fresh coffee, and

Honry, shaky with relief as at a cataclysm averted, rushed to channel the flow of debate into calmer tributaries. And thus set a pattern which lasted until around two o'clock when a yawning Charlotte wandered in and broke up the party: Yeo to return to the dance floor, we four to organise a taxi back to the Royal Windsor.

Outside it was snowing, small powdery flakes like flour. The pavement was already lightly coated. En route to the hotel we passed a gritting vehicle at work.

Our suite was on the fourth floor at the side of the building overlooking a large church – the Chapelle de la Madeline, and while Julia was performing her usual lengthy, laborious ablutions, I stood in idle contemplation of this particular House of God now, under its silver anointment, assuming a fairy-tale aspect.

'Where did you go tonight, Vee?' Julia had come up behind me. She had removed her make-up and was wearing a white bath robe.

'Oh . . . I just walked. Down to the roundabout by the museum.'

'Liar.' No heat, just a flat accusation of such certitude that denial would have been pointless.

'So I'm a liar.' I was too tired to argue.

'You went out with a girl. You were seen.'

I shrugged.

'Who was she, Vee?'

I thanked my stars she didn't know. 'A girl. Nobody.' Sorry, Rowen.

Julia unpinned her hair, shook the long, coal-black tresses so that they lay across her shoulders.

'Did you fuck her?'

I swung on her, goaded at last into a reaction. As she meant me to be.

'Christ, Julia! Is your mind on rails, or what? I like a screw as much as the next man, but my life doesn't bloody well revolve around it!' She was wearing her cool, arrogant veneer; it infuriated me beyond measure.

'And where, my goody-goody wife, were *you* while I was out? Dancing with Yeo! Of all people. My God, Julia, I've turned enough blind eyes to your indiscretions, but Yeo . . . ! Couldn't you find anyone else? Anyone at all, even the fucking barman, rather than Yeo. It's not as if you don't know what's going on.'

Her jaw set stubbornly. 'You don't tell me whom I may or may not dance with. At least it was in the open; I didn't sneak off with him. Anyway . . .' She moved away, found cigarettes on the dressing table and lit up. 'Anyway, I like him.' Her tone was subdued, slightly puzzled. 'In spite of all the rotten things he stands for, I actually like the man. He made me laugh.'

'Okay, okay, let's cool it. Let's leave it at that. Just don't go off on one of your wild affairs. Not with Yeo.'

'Whatever you say, darling.' She undid the cord of her robe, let it fall open. Needless to say she was naked underneath. She shook her breasts at me. Those blancmange breasts with their brown nipples, big as fingertips. The robe lay around her ankles. Her pubic hair was fluffed up and sticking out in tufts; she sometimes shaved the immediate area around her labia to emphasise them. So it was now, the pink folds livid in their nest of black curls.

Down in the pit of my stomach the tom-toms began to pound their age-old message. My body flushed with heat, my pulse accelerated like a dragstrip racer, and then I was past the point of no return; past the point when bodily need becomes omnipotent and the psyche has no option but to do its bidding.

And Julia, once aroused, was unstoppable. Against every instinct that mattered a damn, I let her seduce me into providing the services she craved.

What made me angry most of all was that I enjoyed it every bit as much as she did.

During our absence it had also snowed in England. Not, alack, crisp, sparkling snow, the kind that crunches and crackles underfoot and throws up a glare that sears your eyeballs. No, this was *English* snow: wet, slushy, more grey than white, and lying under skies that forever presaged more helpings of the unwholesome stuff.

The morning after our return to Kingscourt, Honry phoned to give notice that the next committee meeting had been fixed for the day after tomorrow. This was shorter notice than I'd expected; I at once dug out my master plan and spent the morning rounding off corners and generally tidying it up.

Over lunch Willoughby brought tidings of a second call: Lord Deverill, no less. I left my meal to take it. Conditioned by upbringing and an opportunistic streak to jump when the high-and-mighty say 'jump'. You never can tell when you might need a friend in high places.

He was terse and to the point. Would I meet him at his country house tomorrow? Say 3.00 pm? No problem, my lord. Yours to command, my lord. Grovel, grovel.

Julia was impressed.

'Maybe he wants to offer you a job.'

I snorted into my soup, making waves. 'As what? Head bootlicker? Anyway, I don't need a job, thanks very much. No, I'd say he wants a preview of my plan before Wednesday's meeting. His lordship likes to be out in front of the rest of the field, if I'm any judge of character.

I was only partly right.

The Deverill residence was near Faringdon, in Oxfordshire, about an hour by car, though I allowed a little more than that in case the snow delayed me. The skies had cleared that Thursday morning and under its white garniture the countryside was transformed. Along the road between Henley and Wallingford I even passed a group of would-be skiers, creating a piste on a hillside.

I had timed my journey well. It was five minutes to the hour when I came upon the start of the six-foot high wall that formed the boundary of the estate. I followed it as far as a pillared entrance, left the road and swept past a well-kept gatehouse. From there to the house itself was a good half-mile, mostly through woods of pine and spruce, giving way to oak, horse chestnut, and beech before the sudden emergence to an amphitheatre of lawns and geometric hedgerows. To my left I glimpsed a snow-bound tennis court, netless and forlorn.

Deverill met me at the foot of some steps leading up to a balustrade along the front of the house. *House*, did I say? Kingscourt, placed alongside it, might easily have been mistaken for a potting shed. Interesting to note that some of the upper, second-floor windows were frosted over, which suggested that even the resources of lucre-laden earls were not infinite. The cost of heating the place must have been horrendous.

Deverill was well wrapped-up in a short suede coat, deerstalker cap, and various heat-retaining accessories.

'It's such a nice day I thought we might walk,' he said.

'Certainly; a good idea.' Luckily I carried a pair of Wellington boots in the Bentley. I pulled them on and we set off towards another wood, lying beyond the house, our feet bruising the virgin snow.

'I'll tell you why I asked you to come and see me,' he said, before we had taken a dozen paces. 'It's about tomorrow's session: I'd like to know in advance what you're going to propose.

So maybe I was clairvoyant.

'No reason why not, my lord. But I shan't just be making proposals tomorrow; the plan's already in motion.'

'Is that a fact? You don't let grass grow under your feet, do you?'

'It has been said. Let me tell you something, Lord

Deverill: I'm opposed to this committee. I'm opposed to all and sundry committees. Debate retards the decision-making process and slows down the action. You can't afford to sit around arguing pros and cons while Yeo and his merry union men prepare to make war on the State.' I let my words sink in, then ventured, 'He won't let grass grow under his feet, you know.'

Deverill's leonine head bobbed. 'You don't have to tell me that. I'm probably a darn sight better-informed about Yeo than you are.'

'I'll take your word for that. Just as long as you understand – it's either my way or not at all. Unless you hire someone else to do the job. In which case, I wish you – and him – luck.'

He made no comment so I gave him the bones of my plan, keeping to the method only, and leaving out the when and the where and the names of my accomplices. By the time I had finished we were among the outlying trees of the wood. The snow lay only thinly on the ground here and a path led into the wood proper, just wide enough for two to walk side by side.

When it became apparent I had nothing more to say, Deverill released a heavy grunt.

'That's it then.' No clue in the tone as to approval or otherwise.

'Some loose ends still, but – yes, that's the essence of it.'

'Mmm.'

We trudged on, passing a frozen-over stream. A large black bird fluttered through the treetops, squawking.

'Jackdaw,' Deverill said absently. 'Wood's full of 'em.' Then: 'You'll have informed Tiverton, I suppose.'

'Yes. He's happy with it.'

'Is he now, is he now?'

We came to a place where the trees grew more sparingly and the snow in consequence was deeper. Bird and animal prints criss-crossed it.

Deverill stopped, obliging me to do the same.

'Fletcher, I can't really advise on the merits of your proposals,' he said sombrely. 'It sounds over-complicated; full of imponderables and uncertain in outcome, though if you do pull it off it would appear to be leakproof.' He looked searchingly at me. 'And it must *be* leakproof, my friend. Yeo must be deactivated – permanently.'

Recalling the virulence of his discourse on Yeo, I said: 'Don't think I'm prying, my lord, but I can't help feeling you're so against Yeo for reasons other than – or should I say additional to – Queen and Country.'

A fast double-blink was the only outward sign that I was right on target.

'How d'you mean?' He was ultra-casual.

'If you truly need to ask, then I'm wrong.' I squared up to him. 'But if I'm right . . . well, it might help if you take me into your confidence. Might help both of us.'

He grinned then, grudgingly. 'You weren't in Int Corps for the fun of it, were you? All right . . . there is, as you suspect, more to it than a desire to prevent strife. And, as you may also have guessed, it's personal – personal-financial, that is.'

The 'financial' bit was unexpected. I waited for him to explain and when he didn't I fired off a prompt.

'Personal-financial?'

A sigh, heavy and visceral.

'How shall I describe it – without seeming preoccupied with profit and wealth?'

He had no need to worry; it was a preoccupation we shared.

'You must know that I have a great many business interests,' he said, a lengthy pause later. 'I own several small manufacturing companies outright, and hold equity stakes in other, larger concerns. Electricity – gas – water.' He ticked them off on his fingers. 'These are the arteries of industry. If they dry up, industry comes to a stop. And the AUEWE controls all three.'

'Your anxiety is understandable. What it boils down to is that, if the strike goes ahead, your business interests will suffer and your shares will take a hammering. But it's not calamitous; it will only be temporary. I've a good few shares myself, so I'm not entirely immune from the effects.'

'It's not that simple,' he said, irritation just below the surface. 'What's temporary for one man may be permanent for another. I . . . I . . . damn it, Fletcher, I'm on the rack – don't you understand? My resources are stretched so thin that any setback at all will mean certain insolvency. Let me explain: at the end of last year I put money into a new process for a super-tough plastic, a guaranteed winner once it comes on the market. Unfortunately, as often happens in these cases, the development costs have gone way, way over budget.' He glanced sharply at me. 'And I'm not talking about penny numbers, but tens of millions. Most of the funds came from external sources – I exhausted my own long ago – and the vultures are hovering, just watching for the slightest stumble, the slightest sign of uncertainty . . . A strike, *any* strike, let alone the sort of disruption Yeo could cause, would finish me. This estate, the house and everything in it . . .' The broad frame slumped, seeming to diminish in stature.

You could even feel sympathy for a multi-millionaire aristocrat, I discovered. yet, while accepting the account of his troubles for what it was, I had a hunch there were other forces at play within the man. Although I wanted, quite badly, to extract them I held off. Under gentle pressure he had already hung out much of his dirty washing; to demand more would be to invite resentment, and to no useful purpose.

'So you see,' now his grin was wry, 'there are some big bets riding on you.'

He needed reassurance, was close to begging for it. So, reassurance being cheap, I supplied it.

'Trust me.' I hoped I didn't sound condescending. 'I'll give you his head on a silver platter.'

The eyes sighted on me like a pair of 20mm cannon as he said: 'You know, I do believe you will.' He rested a benign hand on my shoulder, gripped firmly. 'I really do believe you will. Come on – let's walk back. Come and meet Lady Deverill. I expect you could use something to thaw out your circulation, too.'

We returned to the house by a different route. He talked a lot, I became 'Vee', he, 'Michael'. Other than at committee meetings, he qualified with a chuckle.

Michael. Desperate hunter of a dangerous prey. Both of them imbued with the killer instinct. Two men who would let nothing stand in their way: the power of wealth, title, and influence versus the power of the big stick.

It was set to be a battle of the giants. And what was I but piggy in the middle. How did that nursery rhyme go?

> Piggy on the railway, picking up stones
> Along came an engine and broke poor Piggy's bones
> 'Oh!' said Piggy. 'That's not fair.'
> 'Oh!' said the engine driver. 'I don't care!'

Chapter Eleven

In the interests of security a different venue had been selected for the second meeting of the Operation Hangman committee, specifically a small country house on the edge of the village of Biggin Hill, quite close to the RAF airfield of battle of Britain fame. Honry drove us there in an unremarkable Ministry Vauxhall.

The meeting room was smaller and lower of ceiling than at Finch Lane and the table slightly shorter with squared-off rather than rounded ends. The seating arrangements, however, remained as-you-were.

Flexing his chairman's muscles almost as soon as the chairs ceased to scrape on the wooden block floor and without any preamble whatsoever, Deverill asked me to unveil my plan.

It took about a quarter of an hour to repeat in somewhat greater detail what I had already revealed to Deverill the day before. I gave it to them flat – no dressing up, no watering down. No kidding either about the prospects for success: 60–40 in favour was my rating, which prompted Rees, openly sneering, to observe: 'I could improve on those odds.'

'We're well aware of that, Mr Rees,' Deverill said tartly. 'Unfortunately, your particular brand of solution has already been rejected by a higher authority than ours.'

'Too final,' Rees said, grinning without humour.

'Just so.'

'Success or failure pivots on my ability to get Yeo to

speak the right words,' I explained. 'He has to denounce himself. It's the only sure way, outside of our MoD friend's final solution, to smash his power and persona. We have to expose him to his colleagues and members in his true colours.' My gaze roved over the stolid faces of the committee. 'It's an exercise in iconoclasm.

'Experience has proved that we can't expect results from ordinary smear tactics. Take Scargill: the miners went on strike, effectively on his say-so. In spite of his obvious determination to have a strike on any issue at all no matter how spurious; in spite of his refusal to hold a nationwide ballot; in spite of the withholding of strike pay from his members; in spite of his secret liaison with Ghadaffi and his trips to Moscow; in spite of his condoning – and some would say inciting – violence, and his refusal to make concessions or meet the Coal Board half-way. All these seeming weak points in Scargill's credibility were splattered across the Tory press. They wrung every drop of vilification out of them, and the Government had a right to expect that the strikers would come to resent being manipulated for such blatantly political reasons. But, no. As a propoganda exercise it was a dead loss. The miners just didn't care. They gave Scargill blind obedience throughout, and the charisma, mystique almost, of the man was barely touched. Even when the strike disintegrated he was still a hero, still 'King' Arthur. Why? Because the Government, the press, and the NCB combined hadn't been able to shake his stance that he was doing it all for the good of the mining industry, that he was fighting for its future, and therefore for the future of the miners and the mining communities. He had made the miners believe that they were the vanguard of a working-class revolution.'

'You're presumably drawing a comparison between Scargill and Yeo,' D'abo said, reaching for the carafe of water in the centre of the table. 'If I've read you correctly, you're saying that tactics which failed against Scargill would also fail against Yeo. Presumably the converse argument holds equally good.'

'Clearly. Just supposing we were able to show Bill Morris or John Yeo on TV admitting . . . actually telling the world they were simply using their members to achieve political gain and person aggrandisement. That in reality they despised their sheep-like mentality. And that the damage inflicted on their industries and the harm done to innocent people, especially the elderly, was not "regrettable", nor even merely irrelevant, but desirable. And that they personally *didn't care*.' Several mouths around the table hung open. 'Suppose we got them to actually crow over misery and suffering and even death, because the more people suffered and died the more readily their demands would be met and the quicker would be the progress towards the social upheaval they yearn for, now that a more malleable – meaning weaker – regime is back in power.'

'That's . . . quite a supposition,' Stambourne said slowly.

Rees cleared his throat sardonically. 'You don't actually specify how Yeo might be induced to commit professional suicide. More importantly, how he might be induced to do so willingly, so that it won't appear on video as if he's screaming out a confession from some M15 torture chamber. It can't be done. Come down out of the clouds, Fletcher.'

'Don't be hasty, Goronwy,' Honry jumped in before I could riposte on my own account. 'Vee isn't stupid. He must have some wheeze up his sleeve.' He flicked anxious eyes in my direction. 'You have, haven't you, Vee?'

'Not exactly a wheeze. But nor am I relying on a crystal ball or prayers to Allah. My experience in interrogation techniques, acquired during my stint with Int Corps, is a key factor, I'm sure you all appreciate. Added to which, Yeo won't be aware he's being video'd, so he'll be more inclined to talk freely; especially after being cooped up in solitary for a week or more. Take it from me, gentlemen, he'll sing long and sweet. Then there's the editing.'

'Editing?' This came from two or three different corners.

'Of course,' Rees muttered, twiddling a propelling pencil in his stubby fingers. 'Adapt the answers to the questions and vice-versa.' Then, more loudly, to the whole assembly: 'It might work, you know; it just might – if friend Fletcher here really does know his stuff.'

'Don't worry on that score,' I said.

A timid knock at the door put a stop to all chinwag. At Deverill's bellowed 'Yes!' a small, wrinkled, and probably male personage entered to propose refreshments for 'your lordships'. We stipulated a mixed bag of teas and coffees and sent it away. Outside, I noticed during this diversion, an evil mass of low cloud was forming, and here and there a scrap of white spiralled lazily to earth.

Deverill rubbed the palms of his hands together briskly. 'If everybody's satisfied, I move we put a seal of approval on Mr Fletcher's scheme and let him get cracking. I understand he's already made some . . . er . . . arrangements, not to mention blowing large sums of money. Is that correct, Mr Secretary?'

Honry nodded. 'Yes, my lord. We decided that the committee's approval must be anticipated . . .'

'Pre-empted, you mean,' Rees, beside him, murmured.

'Anticipated,' Honry repeated firmly, 'and the necessary preparations set in motion.'

Wainwright shifted restlessly. 'The outcome of the project concerns me less than the moral angle, it has to be said. Strongly as I oppose Yeo, it doesn't seem right to . . . to incriminate him for pursuing policies he presumably believes in. It's like fighting crime with crime.'

'I must say I incline to the same view.' Thus spake Jennings, whom I had previously marked down as the most liberal of the bunch and therefore a likely opponent.

'It's not on,' Wainwright said, encouraged by Jenning's support. 'It's simply not on. It's . . . it's un-British.'

'Un-British, you say,' I scoffed. 'You do realise, don't you, that if Yeo and the rest get their wish, we'll all be un-British a few years from now?

'Are we supposed to stand back and let this man Yeo ruin the country and millions of lives in the process because we're too squeamish to hit back? Nobody's asking you to get dirt under your fingernails, Wainwright, nor you, Jennings. Just carry on fiddling like all the other Civil Services Neros. Pretend the Yeos and the Scargills don't exist. Observe the rules of democracy no matter what the cost. Do you really believe that because the USSR went democratic the world would be rid of demagogues?' I laughed, a harsh, jarring discord. 'What Thatcher achieved can be undone in the amount of time it takes a strong union to rally its members to strike. We've seen signs of it already . . . it all started within weeks of the election, with the BA cabin crew dispute. As we now know that was the tip of the iceberg. The union bandwagon is on another roll, and the huge increase in membership over the past twelve months testifies to its new popularity.'

'Union power is back in fashion and democracy won't survive in such a climate unless the people to whom its entrusted are prepared, exceptionally, to take *un-democratic* action in its defence.' Somebody stirred. A chair creaked. 'All right . . . so it's a contradiction. So it goes against the grain, against all you believe in and what the hell did we fight Hitler for if only to resort to his methods.' I thumped my fist on the table. 'Wake up, gentlemen. This is reality we're up against. And the reality is Yeo and Morris, Saddam Hussein and the

Ayatollahs . . . Democracy in its purest form is an ideal. An impossible dream – like the one Martin Luther King dreamed before someone woke him up with a bullet!'

Heads nodded sagely.

'Let the dreamers have their dreams,' I said, 'and let the rest of us make do with what we've got and try to keep it functioning.' I was almost pleading now. 'That means defeating the wreckers, and Yeo is potentially the biggest wrecker since Scargill. He may even be our ultimate test. If we fail that test the nation will deserve the strife, the chaos, and the possibly bloody revolution he threatens to impose.'

As I drew breath to wind up in my diatribe, there came once more the timid tap at the door, and in trundled a trolley load of refreshment: two large pots, an assortment of china, a heaped plate of biscuits. Gourmand fare by Civil Service standards. The asexual creature bowed and bobbed and scurried from the room.

Forestalling the rush to the trough, I said in summation: 'As I see it there are three alternative courses of action open to us. One . . .' I checked it off on my finger, 'we can call his bluff; let him do his worst. Two . . . we can negotiate a settlement, which will mean giving him most of what he wants, and thereby betray the other 99.5% of the population. Or, three . . . we can do what we were charged to do . . . stop him.'

Now Deverill threw his hat into the ring.

'I don't believe there's a man in the room would support either of the first two alternatives,' he said, coldly. 'As for the third, it really boils down to the method, and I thought we'd already agreed that Yeo is to be defamed and that such defamation would have little basis in fact. Why, then, resurrect the morality issue?' He glared from Wainwright to Jennings and they wilted like water-starved flowers.

I silently praised Deverill.

'For the record,' I resumed, 'I won't be a party to any

half-hearted compromises. Remember Yeo is a very, very intelligent man; his former tutor rates him a near-genius. Outsmarting him won't be a walkover – the fit-up has to stick: it has to be water-tight, air-tight, and lawyer-tight. The scheme I've put forward is the only one I'm prepared to guarantee will meet these criteria. It may not succeed – I've given my assessment of the odds – but whether it does or it doesn't, Yeo won't be able to prove the Government had anything to do with it. Nobody but me will be breaking any laws.'

Talk of breaking laws brought forth an uneasy cough here and there. Feet shuffled under the table.

'I move we give Fletcher the go-ahead without further debate,' the usually taciturn Stambourne said, and d'Abo immediately seconded the motion.

'A show of hands,' Deverill suggested. 'All those in favour?'

Hands rose; Wainwright's tentatively, Jennings even more so and last of all.

'Carried unanimously. And just as well considering the amount of good taxpayers' money our friend here has already squandered.' Deverill's good humour bordered on the extravagant. 'Shall we celebrate with a cup of ministry swamp juice, gentlemen? Now, who's going to be mother?'

Cups clattered amid the murmur of voices. Relief was in the air. The proceedings were over, the dirt not so much swept under the carpet as piled up around me like a rubbish tip. I had been given my rubber stamp, my carte blanche to do as I would. The committee could now scamper back to their thoroughly respectable pursuits and wipe me and Yeo and the whole smelly business from their phoney consciences.

It left just a single, solitary, and for me crucial loose end. I said as much to the committee.

Deverill paused in the act of raising his cup. 'What might that be, Fletcher?' Nobody else displayed much interest.

'My immunity.' I snapped a ginger biscuit in two. 'Yeo will see and recognise me.'

'Wear a disguise,' Rigg suggested.

'I've considered it. The trouble with disguises is that they need regular and expert maintenance and absolute consistency, which is difficult to achieve over a long period. Especially if, as in this case, you're facing the same person day-in, day-out, across a table. Apart from that, there's always a chance he'll recognise my voice. No, I don't think a disguise is the answer.'

'What is then?' Stambourne demanded.

'Either the police will have to be fixed or I want an unshakeable alibi. And I mean unshakeable.'

At this point Honry became engrossed in his minute-taking, avoiding the gaze I let wander his way. So Julia's warning had been well-founded. Honry was as prepared to sacrifice me to the common good as any other Government lackey.

The suggestion of legal tinkering gave Wainwright and Jennings renewed fits of the horrors. Not for them this talk of police complicity and false testimony. To them Britain was still great with a small 'g', the home of honourable gentlemen and good sports, the spiritual leader of a decadent world. The Yeos and the Scargills were a breed apart and beyond comprehension.

'Suborn the police!' Jennings cried, clucking and spluttering. 'Out of the question!'

'You'll get your immunity,' Deverill's voice was a scalpel and the incision he made across Jennings' bluster was a masterpiece of surgery. 'Henry, I'll leave you to arrange it with the Minister.'

Honry gave off a sickly whinny. It wasn't a commission he would relish. Asking the man who is, in effect, at the head of Britain's police force to countenance a wholly illicit cover-up.

I crunched ginger biscuit. Around me others did the same, wearing frowns of varying intensity. Only Deverill appeared unconcerned.

Refreshments over, the meeting was formally concluded. Briefcases were snapped open, papers deposited within. Goodbyes bounced back and forth. None were directed my way; I was suddenly a pariah. Then Deverill was at my side, patting me on the shoulder, shaking my hand warmly.

'Until next time, Vee. Which will be after the event, I imagine. And . . .' He hesitated. 'Keep in touch, anyway, eh?'

'Michael,' I acknowledged, and watched him go, a broad, upright figure, capped with white like snow on a mountain summit. An interesting man. A useful patron. Keep in touch? Yes, I might just do that, Lord Deverill.

'Have you tracked down my nympho housekeeper yet?' I enquired of Honry as we let ourselves out of the room, the last to leave.

'It's in hand, dear boy. Rest assured.'

'Well don't dilly-dally, dear boy. I'll need her next week to help my . . . er . . . specialist (Bull would like that) set up the holiday home. And I'll need her for an indefinite period.'

'When's actual D-Day?' Honry's voice had fallen to a whisper.'

I held his arm, drew him conspiratorially close. 'The 6th of June, 1944,' I hissed back and, suppressing the laughter that bubbled up inside me, went on and out into a white-speckled world.

At eight pm on Thursday, 14th January, the AUEWE gave one hour's advance warning of their intention to cut electricity supplies to the region served by South Western Electricity plc, between nine and ten pm. This pronouncement sparked off some frantic backstage pleading by SWEB, which deflected Yeo from his course by not so much as a single degree.

The consequences of this act were hard to assess with accuracy. The news next morning was full of it, naturally, and reported an estimated near-doubling of road accidents during those sixty minutes, owing to lack of traffic lights and street lighting. Accidents in the home had also risen: in Totnes a man was electrocuted when the current was restored as he searched unwittingly for the cause of the cut; in an Exeter hospital a young woman died when her life support machine packed up and the reserve generator also failed. In the village of Branscombe a young couple blew themselves to bits improvising a gas heater. And so on.

After a while I got depressed listening to one lurid tale after another and switched off the radio.

It had been a telling demonstration. The point had been well-made, the muscles well-flexed. David Yeo was omnipotent and able and willing to cause death by his actions.

Question: when in present-day Britain is a murder not a murder? Answer: when committed in furtherance of an industrial dispute.

Sick.

'You're watching a lot of TV these days,' Julia complained as I switched on the six o'clock news some twenty hours after the big black-out. 'You know we're going out tonight.'

'I haven't forgotten.' I wasn't much looking forward to dinner at the Twelveses, not this night or any other night. Deirdre Twelves was a close friend of Julia's and the biggest gossip in West Kensington, if not in the capital. As if that were not enough of a disincentive, her husband, thirty years her senior, was both bore and boor.

The news still focused on the power cut and its consequences and I sat through it in a smouldering rage. I may not have been long on morals, but I had a highly-tuned social conscience, and Yeo's *coup de main* turned my stomach.

After a ten-minute catalogue of tragedy came the

inevitable interview. There was a Department of Energy spokesman who waffled and fudged, a SWEB official who was angrily and refreshingly outspoken, and an AUEWE executive who couldn't have been less forthcoming if his lips had been stitched together. Nor was he visibly contrite over the suffering caused by the switch-off.

An emergency meeting had been called at National Power HQ, the newsreader intoned, to discuss measures for countering further lightning walk-outs. It was also announced that the talks between employers and union would resume on Monday instead of at the end of the week. The power suppliers and the electricity companies were running scared and who could blame them?

'Isn't it incredible how the impossible always becomes possible after a few deaths?' I said, punching the OFF button with unnecessary force.

Julia didn't comment, which surprised me. Usually she was every bit as vociferous as I in condemning union bully tactics.

'It doesn't upset you then?' I snapped, stirred by my own fury to pursue the issue, to make her speak out.

'What do you think?' she almost snarled back. 'Am I supposed to break down and dissolve into tears to prove how upset I am?' She had been leafing through a magazine; now she tossed it aside. 'Aren't you going to put a stop to it anyway? Won't your marvellous, magnificent plan free us from David Yeo for once and for all?'

I pushed a stray lock of hair out of my eyes, mooched up and down a while before replying.

'If all goes well, yes, I'll stop him. But that alone won't guarantee we'll live happily ever after. There's a new sickness gaining ground here and it's malignant. Hack of one tumour and another will grow in its place. You wait and see. With or without Yeo, it's going to get worse.'

She stood up abruptly, tall in spiky-heeled shoes and narrow black slacks. 'If you really believe that why the bloody hell are you so set on going through with it?' And she whirled away, out of the room, slamming the door so hard that the chandelier light tinkled musically and the two-year-old studio portrait of Julia and Gavin and myself fell off the wall to hit the floor face-down with a crunch of breaking glass.

Chapter Twelve

Of necessity I had pulled into a petrol station in Enfield, less than thirty miles from home but no longer able to resist the red warning light that had been burning accusingly from the dash panel for the best part of an hour.

I was the only customer. I unhitched the pistol and squirted a small fortune of Super Premium Unleaded into the Bentley's bottomless tanks.

Enfield. Middle-class country. Solicitors, bank managers, even a few stockbrokers. And David Yeo. How did a Marxist trade union baron fit in with such pillars of capitalism?

I had neither hope nor expectation of a chance meeting with the man himself. All I desired was to resume my journey and beat the traffic that would shortly be spilling onto London's roads, homeward bound.

The bill paid – painlessly with my VISA Goldcard – I was set to plunge back into the warm womb of the Bentley when a metallic-blue Honda Accord charged aggressively onto the forecourt, braked showily, and there was Rowen Yeo beep-beeping at me for all she was worth. Too late for me to affect not to have seen her.

She wound down her window. 'Hello, Vee!' she called out and so cheerily I couldn't help but feel a surge of pleasure.

With her was sister Regina. Whom I had thought of as pretty, but who in reality was no prettier than the Rowen I had kissed in Brussels. Rowen's image today, I noticed, was back to serious undergraduate but less the specs, which was something. A real Cinderella, this girl.

'Hello, Cinders,' I said as she got out, boots landing in a pile of blackened slush.

She made a face. 'Ugh!' Then, straightening up, said: 'And what do you mean – Cinders? Sounds like dead ashes.'

'Or hot coals,' I countered, and the inference wasn't wasted on her.

'Like to meet Reggie?' she said hurriedly and swept a hand towards her sister, who was coming around the front of the car to join us, openly curious, sensing more than just a casual acquaintanceship. I hoped she could keep a secret.

'Reggie? I wouldn't stand for that if I were you,' I grinned and winked at little sis, who responded in like manner and with compound interest. 'But hi, anyway.'

'Hi, yourself . . . Vee, is it?' A total absence of shyness. 'I've heard a little bit about you.' She flicked her fingers at Rowen. 'I'll get on, Rowen. I've got to pick up my stuff from the cleaners.' She grinned again, impishly. 'I'll walk home from here.'

Tactful too.

'Okay,' Rowen said off-handedly.

'Bye, Vee,' Regina said and trudged off through the slush.

Rowen showed her slightly-crooked teeth in a wide smile. 'It's super to see you again, it really is.' All was forgiven, it seemed. Though the contretemps in Brussels hadn't troubled me, I was glad.

'Whatever are you doing in Enfield?' No trace of suspicion. Just a natural enquiry.

'Just passing through.'

She hooked her arm through mine. For her, that too was natural. I was coming to know her better and the more I knew the more I liked. It wasn't love – I loved

Julia, for all the heartache that entailed. It wasn't even infatuation. But whatever it was, its grip on me grew tighter with every meeting.

'Buy me a coffee?' she suggested, indicating a well-lit coffee bar across the busy road. It looked warm and inviting with its steamed-up windows.

'The least I can do,' I said into her smiling, happy face.

'You're so *forward*,' she giggled. 'Are you the same with your other girlfriends?' Her hands flew to her mouth as if she'd uttered some dreadful blasphemy. 'I . . . I didn't mean . . .' she stammered, the easy poise disintegrating.

'To imply you're my girl friend? I'm too old for girl friends, Rowen, and I'm married. Married men only have mistresses. You applying?'

That subdued her, but then we had to separate to transfer our cars to the other side of the road, and when we met up again in the coffee bar car park all her natural bounce was back in place.

Our exchanges remained light until we were settled at a plastic table, amidst plastic decor, drinking plastic coffee – and that's flattering it.

'About Brussels . . .' she began, but faltered and resorted to frenetic stirring of her sugarless coffee.

'Me first: I'm sorry I said what I did. Put it down to senile dementia. I'm just not used to girls your age.'

'Age, age,' she grumbled. 'All I ever hear is age. You're what – forty-two? I actually prefer mature men, so you can't scare me off with that one.'

'Give me time and I'll figure out another way.'

She made an impatient gesture. 'Save your brains.'

It was hot in the coffee bar and steamy as a jungle swamp, and we had both discarded our coats. She had on a jumper with a huge rolled-over collar that she kept ducking her chin inside. With minimal make up she looked even younger than she was. Serving only to make me feel older.

'Vee . . .' Fingers plucked at my sleeve. 'Vee . . . do you like me at all?'

'Like you?' I said guardedly. 'What a silly question. Yes, I like you, Rowen.'

A sight too much, I might have gone on to say.

'Then . . . I shouldn't ask this, but I'm going to. You probably won't agree, because of this age taboo you're so sensitive about.' She had ducked the lower part of her face into the roll-neck and her voice was muffled. 'Can we . . . see each other?'

There it was then. Gift-wrapped and on a plate, my very own teenage paramour. I could have feigned puzzlement, acted dumb: *'See each other? We already do, don't we?'* It wasn't my style.

'You mean as lovers?' Forthright Fletcher.

Her eyes widened to almost perfect circles. 'Oh.'

A pregnant, scruffily-dressed woman, laden with shopping, was hauling two yelling kids – twins, one of either sex and aged about three – past us down the aisle. The boy suddenly wriggled free with a whoop of triumph and dived under our table. Rowen started laughing behind her hand and set me off.

The child's mother made a silent appeal and I hauled the little blighter out from behind my legs. He fought a determined rearguard action, but my battalions were bigger than his.

'Don't wanna go!' he bawled and other customers turned to stare at me as if I were molesting the kid.

'I'm sorry, old chap, but when the boss says you've gotta go, then you gotta go. No use fighting it.'

Galahad that I am, I found myself helping the woman to the door. Once there I took pity on her (she had a bus to wait for) and used my cellphone to summon up a taxi. I then waited with her until it showed up, holding on to her still rebellious infant, and paid off the driver in advance, based on his estimate of the fare plus his tip.

To me it was an infinitesimally tiny act of kindness. To her it was probably the highlight of the week.

Her face lit up in gratitude.

'Thanks ever so, ever so,' she said in Cockney-ese. Then, poised to enter the cab, asked my name.

'Fletcher.'

'No, your first name.'

'Most people call me Vee.'

'Vee? That's a funny name.' A quick nervous smile and she and her kids and the taxi were gone.

Rowen gave me a soft look when I returned to my seat. 'That was kind.'

Strangely saddened by the incident. I gazed out of the window, out past our reflections. Nightfall was veiling the sky, merging with the silhouetted rooftops into uniform blue-black.

'Kindness . . .' The word wasn't at ease on my tongue. 'The price of a taxi ride? Kindness means nothing unless giving it calls for sacrifice. If a millionaire donates £100 to charity, is he being kind, or bribing his conscience?'

'You're a selective misanthropist.'

'What's that in English?' I quipped. But as character assessments go, she wasn't far out.

I sampled the lukewarm dregs of the coffee. Shuddered at the taste.

Rowen said: 'The answer to your question, by the way, is yes. I do mean as lovers.'

I had all but forgotten the subject under discussion. It came back to me with the rude impact of a clout around the ear.

'You don't know what you're saying,' I protested feebly. 'I'm no prude; I've had affairs and will probably go on having them until I run out of stamina. But even discounting the age difference, you're too . . . too . . .'

'Don't you dare say "nice",' she hissed. 'You don't know me.'

'Okay, so you're a scheming bitch. But why me, especially? Why not the boy next door, or some kid at the university?'

Honourable conduct had never been my strong point, but to embark – deliberately – on an affair with a girl whose father I was about to abduct and subsequently ruin called for a special brand of immorality.

'Why you? That's easy. I love you.' She said it several times over in a voice that became progressively more weepy. 'I can't help it,' she said finally, blinking ten-to-the-dozen.

Oh, God. Get out of that, Houdini.

'Well, I don't love you,' I said crossly, an instinctive rejoinder, hoping to shake her out of it. All it did was to unleash a waterfall of tears.

I glanced around, expecting all eyes to be on me. First a child-batterer, now a heartless lover. But no, the good old British Public was staying true to form and minding its own business.

'Don't cry . . . please don't cry. Here . . .' I passed her a handkerchief and she patted her damp face, gingerly, as if she were dusting a piece of priceless china. The tears streamed on.

'Pathetic, aren't I?' she said and blew her nose demurely. 'I tried not to. Honest. You can't say I've chased after you.'

True. All our meetings had been either fortuitous or at my instigation.

She sagged in her seat, ageing about five years while I watched. 'It's no use though,' she snuffled into the handkerchief. 'I love you and that's that. I don't seem to care about anything else; even my studies have gone to pot lately.'

'Now that you mustn't allow to happen,' I said, concerned and vaguely conscience-ridden. I took her hands in mine, squeezed them. 'Not on my account.'

She sniffed, blew her nose again. 'I don't care. Don't turn me away, Vee. I'll do anything . . . anything. I . . .

I'll even tell you what you want to know, if you like.'

The tears sparkled in her eyes, crystal-like. Again I experienced that twist in the gut, that hot, burning sensation down low where all primeval urges originate.

Then it dawned on me, with the groping realisation of a man coming awake: I had just been offered the goods on Yeo.

'You mean . . .' I nearly choked over the words.

'You want to know about my father, don't you?' She was calm now, her gaze level and calculating. 'His darkest secret? Isn't that what you want?'

I just looked. My vocal chords were paralysed.

'*Isn't* it?'

I felt ashamed, sick at heart. To have so swiftly and absolutely corrupted the girl that she was ready to denounce her own father. Why wasn't I throwing my cap in the air or dancing a jig on the table? Because, came the answer, self-seeking parasite though I was, it bothered me more than I would have dreamed possible that a girl like Rowen should think me capable of striking such a bargain.

She clutched my arm. 'Well?'

I shook myself free of my grim reverie and of her grasp. 'Rowen . . . I want to see you again. And not just for a cosy chat over a cup of coffee.' Seeing the lights go on inside her, seeing misery become joy, did me a power of good. 'We'll go away for a weekend – get to know each other. Then, if we still like each other enough . . .'

I let her figure out the rest.

'Oh, Vee.' She kissed my hand, telling all around, if they cared, that she was mine and I, hers. A man across the aisle stopped loading sugar cubes into his coffee to gawp. I grinned sheepishly at him.

'As for your father: I don't want to know anything. Not from you, Rowen. I don't want you touched by this . . . this project of mine. Whatever we do, whatever happens between us, must be separate from what happens between me and your father. Understood?'

She understood.

'When?' she breathed, and I was touched by her fervour, her direct simplicity. Touched and disturbed. So much intensity – enough to devour a man.

'Our weekend? Soon. Next week, probably. Give me a number where we can talk freely.'

While she scribbled on the back of a 'Boots' receipt I went to the cash desk to be ripped off to the tune of £3.40. I was tempted to write a cheque in protest.

'Made your first million yet?' I enquired of the doughy woman behind the till. She responded with a blank stare and sixty pence change. Her 'thank you' was of the unspoken variety.

Driving home with Julia from a charity concert around midnight, I tuned the radio into a late night news programme to be told that talks between the employers and the AUEWE had ended inconclusively an hour earlier. No agreement reached or in sight. The two sides were to re-convene in the morning.

'It's a reprieve at least.' I was voicing my thoughts aloud.

'From what?' The tip of Julia's cigarette described an orange arc in the darkness.

'The beginning of the end. For the likes of you and me, that is.'

A sharp, unconvincing laugh. 'Such drama! It's just another passing crisis – God knows, the country ought to be used to them by now. It'll fizzle out, you'll see.' She snuggled into her furs, staring ahead along the straight, narrow road, bordered by trees that flared whitely in the headlights. 'You'll see,' she repeated, an empty, parrot-like assertion that carried not an ounce of conviction.

Chapter Thirteen

'Thar she blows,' Robert Sellar called out over the helicopter's clatter.

We three in the passenger seats broke off from our last-minute conference to look out across the island-splattered sea to the helmet profile of Sgeir Varlish. A more austere and unwelcoming slab of real estate would be hard to imagine.

It was a windless, brooding day. Mild for the time of year and the northerly latitude, the sea a sheet of crumpled foil, made silvery by the bars of sunlight that radiated from behind yellow-fringed clouds. There was a frigid, impassive beauty about it, I supposed.

'Could be we took a wrong turn coming out of Aberdeen,' Bull Sloan suggested hopefully. In his olive-green, padded flak jacket and old army beret he was Sergeant Sloan of Int Corps reincarnated.

'Sorry, Bull. That's home for the next few weeks.' Or months.

'It's not so bad,' said the third member of my task force.

Bull's head and mine rotated as if linked, to contemplate Fiona Morris. Scots-born, creamy-complexioned redhead of thirty-two. Unmarried, a long-serving MoD employee, and possible – no, make that probable – MI5 operative; they never actually did tell me. And wouldn't, even had I asked outright.

She was nothing spectacular in the looks department, though her athletic-bordering-on-muscular figure was no hardship to dwell upon. Normally I didn't go much on the iron-pumping, transexual type, but if the deprivation became intolerable, would I say no? I would not. Honry, on reflection, had chosen rather well.

'I once spent a week on Spitzbergen as part of a NATO survival course,' Fiona went on. 'No shelter at all – not even a tent, and the temperature below freezing twenty-four hours out of twenty-four. Existing on a diet of raw shellfish and seaweed. After an experience like that, a soggy lighthouse on a soggy rock sounds like a bed of clover.'

Bull and I were staring at her with new respect. I was the first to find my voice. 'That must have sorted out the women from the girls. What were you training for? A journey to the centre of the earth?'

'Training *for*?' She seemed amused by the idea. 'In those days we didn't train for anything. We just trained full stop. And non-stop. It was designed to make us fit, purely and simply. Nobody actually expected us to face such conditions in the course of our work.'

The island loomed up. Because we were flying only feet above sea level an abrupt climb was required to clear the cliffs. We were at the very top of this climb, lining up for the landing, when a vicious downdraught caught the chopper, sucking it into a sideways, downwards spin.

Sellar cursed and fought the controls. 'Come back here, you cocksucking scrapheap!' he bellowed, and we all sat rigid with anxiety as his great frame heaved and contorted. Above us the rotors shrieked at maximum revs and still we tumbled from the sky; the sea was suddenly terrifyingly close.

Even as I braced myself against the impact, equilibrium returned, the noise fell away to its usual shattering roar and we were side-slipping evenly down to our landing pad as if the incident were standard descent procedure.

'Sorry about that.' Sellar sounded calm and at ease. 'You do get some awfu' funny air currents in this part of the world.'

'Next time you get the urge to loop the loop,' I said in his ear, 'let us know beforehand and we'll get out and walk.'

He laughed and put us down soft and light as a falling leaf. The engine stopped, the rotors slowed, and we three wrapped up, zipped up, and generally prepared for the great outdoors.

'I'll stay inside, if you don't mind,' Sellar said.

'We'll be an hour or more.'

'If I get lonely I'll come looking for you, don't worry.'

The lighthouse, with its spooky air, had put the wind up him, I decided, and patted him on the shoulder before following Fiona and Bull out through the hatch.

It was almost exactly one o'clock in the afternoon and although far from cold by Scottish winter standards the outside temperature was low enough to bring me out in a fit of the shivers. To keep warm we set about unloading our gear right away, or at least Bull and I did. Fiona conveniently wandered off 'for a pee'.

Our inventory of equipment and supplies would not have disgraced a polar expedition: radio transmitter, two small generators, fuel for same, food and drink for a month, waterproof goose-down sleeping bags, thermal clothing, butane gas heaters and lamps plus spare cylinders weighing a ton; only the kitchen sink was missing.

Fiona reappeared, zipping up her jeans, and between the four of us – Sellar relented and offered to help – we shifted the gear to the base of the lighthouse in a matter of minutes. Neither Fiona nor Bull commented further on the desolation of the place. Shocked into speechlessness most likely, at the prospect of a month or more on what was little more than an Atlantic breakwater, with only the gulls and each other for company.

Until, that is, I returned with our guest of honour, and then we would be four.

Not until the last of the stores had been transported to the lighthouse and Sellar, still declining to enter, was trudging back to his beloved whirlybird, did Bull let his feelings hang out.

'How about a pay rise – like 100%?' he said, and Fiona, the least breathless from our exertions, glanced sharply at him. She, of course, would be on a fixed salary plus possibly the miserly 'hazardous duties' allowance. If she learned the size of Bull's pay packet there'd be rumblings on a Vesuvial scale.

'Fiona's not complaining,' I pointed out, praying she wouldn't promptly make a liar of me. By way of tipping Bull off to let it drop, I added: 'All she'll get is a bare monthly stipend. No special bonus. No overtime. No compensation for having to suffer your snivelling and whining.'

He caught my drift, nodded in acknowledgement, and hefted the radio on his back. 'Let's get on with it then. I want to be settled in before dark. Toasting my toes in front of a hot stove and the telly.'

'Fat chance,' Fiona snorted, picking up a heavy gas heater with less effort than most of us expend picking up a teapot. With her ski-booted foot she tapped the carton containing a portable Hitachi TV. 'You'll get fuck-all reception on that toy out here.'

Bull and I swapped glances. Fiona's profanities, trotted out so casually and without breaking the rhythm of the lilting, middle-class Midlothian accent, had not yet ceased to shock us. I'm old-fashioned. I prefer women to be ladylike: soft and genteel and just a wee bit submissive. Fiona wasn't like any of those things at all. Fiona and soft, genteel, submissive women had about as much in common as tequila has with milk.

'We'll get fuck-all anything if we stand around here all day,' Bull said with some asperity and limped through the doorway, hauling two gas cylinders. I selected a third cylinder and the camping stove and followed him, panting, up the winding staircase to the third floor. Ultimately all floors from the second up would be made habitable: additional equipment, including more powerful generators, was to be flown in by Sellar over the next few days for this purpose.

What with the cost of materials and all the to-ing and fro-ing, my £100,000 budget was already under strain. Sellar's fees alone, inflated by the guaranteed secrecy premium, would account for more than a third of it. If the spending went on at the same prodigal rate I would be knocking on Honry's door, cap in hand, before another week was out. The resultant huffing and puffing would be painful, but the money would be found. In for a penny . . .

It took six more round trips apiece to lug all the stuff up to the third floor, then while Fiona and I sifted through it, Bull got busy on a much-needed gas heater. It became operational minutes later with a *pop*, quickly settling down to a steady, muffled hiss. A second heater followed suit, then a couple of gas lamps to augment the meagre natural light filtering through the tiny apology for a window.

Getting shipshape proved easier than expected. The furniture was all of the lightweight camping variety: loosen a wing-nut here, extend a bracket there, and miraculously beds, chairs, and tables sprang up. Instant home.

'Ah . . . coffee!' Fiona exclaimed, flourishing a giant-size jar of instant. 'Anybody like?'

Bull grunted an affirmative without lifting his head from the radio transmitter.

'Might as well get some practice in making it,' I said. 'I've a feeling you'll be needing a lot.'

'When will the rest of the gear arrive, did you say?'

I left off rummaging through a carton marked MISC, full of books and magazines on keeping fit.

'Sellar will be back tomorrow afternoon, and again on Friday morning. After that by arrangement.'

'And then we'll have what . . . ten days to fix the place up?'

'At least ten: maybe twelve.'

It was warming up fast in the living room and Fiona stripped off her bulky windcheater. Underneath she had on a tight sweater which showed off her impressive biceps and small, rubbery breasts. Muscles apart, her figure was generally good: lean, slim-waisted with a backside that curved agreeably in profile. If – when – the need arose, I wouldn't have to pretend. Always supposing she was receptive to a bit of slap 'n' tickle. It wasn't in the contract.

'What's it like upstairs?' Bull asked as he placed the transmitter carefully on a picnic table and centralised it.

'Come and look. Fiona?'

'Later, thanks.'

Bull and I took to the spiral staircase once more, ascending to the fourth floor, the dormitory. There he proceeded to poke around in all the nooks and crannies.

'Hardly any damp,' he declared, reversing out from beneath a bunk bed. 'Incredible.'

'Oh, I don't know. These walls are pretty thick.'

He nodded. 'More than two metres at the base, tapering to maybe half-a-metre at the top. They're thicker at the front too, where they face the sea.' He reached up and scraped a fingernail across the low ceiling. Tiny particles pattered down. 'I've been reading up on lighthouses; it's a fascinating subject. Did you know the first lighthouse ever was built in 280 BC in Egypt, and that it lasted for over fifteen hundred years, and even then it took an earthquake to demolish it?'

'Let's skip the history lesson.'

'A thousand apologies, guv.' He was grinning, teeth discoloured in the half-light.

'Skip the hyperbole too. Let's go up.'

His inspection of the fifth floor was more thorough still.

'So this is to be his cell,' he mused aloud, feeling around the window. 'I'll fix some bars across here when the welding gear arrives. A cell ought to look like a cell, don't you think? This window needs a lockable screen as well – come to that, all the windows will need screening at night time, unless you don't mind advertising our presence.'

'Smart thinking. I'd overlooked that danger.'

Bull bent over the lathe, picked at the flaking, pale green paintwork. 'Coventry Machine Tools Company,' he read aloud. 'I bet some museum'd like this. Might even be worth a bob or two.'

'Looks like scrap iron to me. You're welcome to it.'

'They must have brought it up in bits and assembled it here in this room.' He moved away from the lathe, roamed some more, the artificial foot dragging slightly. 'I'll have to put up a false wall to hide the video camera. Split the room in two with a partition. That way I'll have plenty of working space.'

'A partition? It had better be solid. We don't want our guest getting curious and ripping it down to see what's behind. That, my erstwhile friend, would be a disaster of the first order.'

He was quite offended. 'Do I look like a simpleton? If I build a wall to make a prison, it won't be a wall you can tear down with your hands, by God. Just so long as Sellar can bring me the materials. And just so long as you don't let Yeo smuggle any jelly in here.'

We both laughed then in easy camaraderie. Now that the show was actually on the road Bull was relaxed and matter-of-fact about its bizarre nature. Now it was just a job; a job and a challenge to his technical ingenuity. Even the wages would be forgotten. He would slave, non-stop if need be, to ensure we were in business on the day. I didn't even need to ask for his assurance.

'Any more rooms above here?' he said as he examined the electric motor of a small grinding wheel.

'Viewing platform that's all. There was a lantern but it's long gone.'

He spun the wheel; it rotated raspingly. 'Bearings buggered,' he observed with a down-turned mouth and came to help raise the trapdoor.

Whereas on my first visit the day had been bright and vivid, the setting made benign by blue skies above it, today was sombre, the intermittent sunshine of the early afternoon having been replaced by stacked, slate grey clouds that bore down on land and water both, like a crushing weight. At least, there being no wind, the lantern orchestra was silent.

The sea resembled liquified lead, and the random blotches of spume, a white pox. Restless, saturnine, forbidding. Earth's final frontier. It inspired dark, romantic dreams in me. Watching it was to feel puny and insignificant. It was not my element. I was in awe of it.

I shivered. Faced landward, what little landward there was. The centre of the island being higher than the lighthouse, no seascape was visible in this direction. Only the raw, scarred rocks and cliffs, and the ever-present gulls riding the air currents, wings at full span, orange feet streaming behind. Their overlapping shrieks had become background noise, like the chant of a crowd at a football match.

Bull was gulping in ozone, greedily as will a man who lives in the polluted confines of a city. Especially a man who has travelled and known the wide open spaces of the world.

'This is quite a place,' he said and there was a catch in his voice. 'Quite a place.'

'You like solitude?' I asked curiously.

'Depends. The solitude of an island like this, or a lonely moor, or a dark forest – yes; provided I've someone to share it with. Someone who appreciates it as much as I do. But solitude in the sense of loneliness? No thanks.'

A murmur of breeze stirred his hair, lifting the long, wispy strands so carefully arranged across his naked scalp.

'I couldn't have stayed here alone, Vee, I don't mind telling you. Not for ten thousand, not for a hundred thousand. I'd go barmy.'

'Good job we've got Miss World to look after you then. Just think of the fun you'll have together in your spare time: shot-putting competitions, tossing the caber, wrestling . . . on second thoughts I'd skip the wrestling. Can't afford to have you injured.'

A black-and-white sea-bird cruised by in a shallow dive to the sea, passing so close you could pick out the individual feathers along the trailing edge of its wings.

Bull watched it too and his expression was wistful. Then as the bird dropped from sight below the cliff edge he swung round and wordlessly climbed over the wreckage to the trapdoor.

Exposure to nature in its most primordial form has that effect on some people.

I took a last look round, shivered again. Solitude? Bull could have it and welcome. Give me bright lights and bustle any time.

In London the snow, apart from irregular cones of slush on the pavements, was just a memory, and the temperature almost Spring-like.

From Gatwick I cabbed it to the City to attend a debriefing meeting with Honry; debriefings were a cross to be endured by all Government employees, even private enterprisers like myself. They were as much to monitor expenditure as progress, and as a taxpayer I could but applaud the concern to obtain value for money.

Apropos of expenditure I was expecting a rocket. But

then what were budgets for it not for breaking? As a DTI colleague once blithely put it.

Honry's office was on the fourth floor of the totally uninteresting and rather shabby Trade and Industry building in Victoria Street. He met me himself in Reception. It was an odd feeling, being escorted inside my former place of work, where not long ago I came and went at will, but those are the rules. Outsiders never, but never, wander freely within governmental walls.

'Tea, old boy?' he enquired, the very instant we entered his office.

A 'yes' froze on my lips. I stopped short and stared at Mike Hutton, whose square, solid frame filled a chair by Honry's desk.

'Hello, Mike,' I said neutrally, recalling in minute detail our last meeting.

Vee.' Economic of speech as ever.

Honry, perhaps sensing acrimony, countered it with a gushing 'That'll be three teas then.' He sounded like a waitress.

While Honry was phoning our order through, I took the only vacant chair, a shaky, straight-back job, and stared at a large, framed photograph of the Queen – the full length study by Beaton – that hung behind Honry. I pondered Hutton's presence, but contemplation of majesty enlightened me not at all.

'Let's get on with it, shall we?' I said a trifle curtly, as Honry ended his call. 'Miss Morris and I met up at the . . .'

Honry lifted a languid hand. 'Not now, old boy, if you wouldn't mind; the de-briefing can wait. Chief Inspector Hutton is here on a different errand.'

I glowered. 'What "errand" might that be?'

'To discuss your immunity from arrest, naturally.' The reply came from Hutton. I continued to glare at Honry.

'Your alibi,' Honry murmured. 'Or don't you need one any more?'

My surprise was total. I had supposed the alibi would come from persons of substance, whose testimonies would be beyond impeachment; that I would be set down in a distant land, far removed from the scene of the crime, with such documentary proof – airline tickets, passport visas with entry and exit stamps – of my presence there as would satisfy the most incredulous of police bloodhounds.

Now here was Honry talking about alibis in front of the meanest, most hard-boiled cop ever to wield a truncheon. And a cop, to boot, who hated me like poison.

'It may seem a silly question, but what has Mike Hutton to do with my alibi?'

Honry smirked. He was about to drop a bombshell; the signals were unmistakeable. 'He is it. He's your alibi.'

Again I was completely floored.

'Him? My alibi?' Not a very original remark, but my brain had deflated from the shock.

Hutton said: 'In Special Branch we often have to bend the rules in the national interest.' He crossed his legs; the toe-cap of his right shoe was scuffed. Kicking tin cans – or heads? 'This *is* in the national interest, isn't it, Vee?'

'You decide for yourself. Or ask him.'

"Him" looked aggrieved. 'Why so hostile, my dear chap? What could be more cast-iron than an alibi from a senior police officer, who just happens to be on holiday in Sicily the same time as you?'

'Sicily! Visiting his Godfather, is he?' I said nastily. 'If I must spell it out for you – I don't trust him.'

'Don't trust me!' Hutton gasped.

'Don't trust him!' Honry was equally disbelieving. 'That's ridiculous. Next thing you'll be saying you don't trust me.'

'I don't,' I snarled. 'You're only concerned with keeping your own nose clean.'

Honry was slow to take offence. 'This isn't like you, Vee.'

'Not like me, eh? I suppose you think I'm paranoiac. Okay, so humour me. Give me somebody I can trust. Has Hutton told you how he feels about me? Has he?' Honry broke off from stabbing his blotter with an engraved paper knife. 'Too damn right he hasn't. I'll tell you this – sooner than rely on the likes of him for an alibi I'd call the whole bloody shooting match off!' I realised I was shouting. By a feat of will-power I brought my choler under control, and when I spoke again I was as composed as a priest hearing confession. 'Anyway, what's so special about Sicily?'

Honry made a dismissive movement. 'Why not Sicily? It has to be somewhere. And we have certain . . . ah . . . interests in an hotel at a holiday resort on the island which will do admirably for your *séjour*. But . . . it doesn't have to be Sicily, if you're agin it. *You* choose.'

I waved the issue aside as of no consequence. Then a telephone buzzed, a muffled, unbroken whirr that didn't come from any of the three handsets on the desk.

'Excuse me.' Honry opened a drawer and lifted from it a black receiver. 'Yes, sir?'

He listened at some length. Twice he did his trick with a finger along the inside of his collar.

'Agreed, Minister.' His eyes were on me. 'Quite. Unfortunately we've run into a minor hitch. He's not prepared to accept the gentleman concerned and has even expressed doubts about the Department.'

From the earpiece came a Donald Duck gabble.

'That might help, Minister. We're too committed now to change horses. One moment, if you please.' He thrust the receiver at me. 'He wants to speak to you.'

I shuffled my chair forward. 'Yes?' I said into the mouthpiece, deliberately curt.

'Fletcher – how are you? And how are things going

up there above the Arctic Circle, hey?' Chuckle-chuckle.

'According to plan.'

'Excellent, excellent.' I pictured the false, thin-lipped smile, the twinkling bespectacled eyes – the eyes of a cobra. 'Now what seems to be the difficulty? You've asked for certain . . . ah, insurance, and you're getting it. Doesn't that take care of everything?' Chuckle.

'Regrettably not.'

'Perhaps you'd . . .'

'Now *listen*,' I interrupted and derived a lot of satisfaction from the indrawn breath at the other end of the line. Honry went white. 'First, the price has just gone up: I want double. I repeat, double the agreed figure, of which a further £50,000 in advance.' A sound like a distant explosion greeted this demand. Chuckles were of the past. Honry was blinking away fit to rupture his eyelids. 'I also want four eminently respect-able witnesses to my . . . holiday in Sicily and I want their post-dated statements prepared, signed *and* sworn, and deposited with me by Monday next.' I glanced at Hutton; his mouth was twisted in a rueful grin. 'And if I don't get an unconditional acceptance within twenty-four hours – say by mid-day tomorrow – the deal is off!'

I tossed the receiver back to Honry, who fielded it badly: it hit the desk top with a crash.

I felt good. Bloody marvellous, in fact. A cigar to celebrate. I lit up, ear half-tuned to Honry's balm-laden patter: 'Certainly, Minister, I quite understand . . . no, no, out of the question . . . quite so . . . must be prag-matic.'

'Tell him expenses are going to go over budget as well,' I said, raising my voice.

Honry frowned at my lack of etiquette. 'You heard that, did you, sir?' More Donald Duck from the phone. 'Right-oh . . . jolly good. I'll check with you first thing tomorrow morning.'

Back went the receiver into the drawer. Slam went the drawer. Glare went Honry. A man of even temper, he wasn't often outwardly displeased; now he positively seethed.

'Vee . . . ' he began; he was holding the paper knife like a dagger.

'Don't say anything you might regret, dear second-cousin-in-law. Just a phone call tomorrow morning will do, with a simple yes or no.'

Honry was purple. Never had I seen him so worked up.

Nearby Big Ben launched into its hourly repertoire, tinny-sounding through the double-glazing. It was beginning to rain, little droplets exploding against the glass, blurring the outline of the river and the buildings of Southwark beyond.

'When's the snatch?' Hutton asked. This haggling over money was of no concern to him.

'Ask me another.'

'I will. We'll need some dates for your alibi – whether or not I personally get involved.'

'That's right,' Honry put in snappishly. 'Can't provide statements without dates.'

'I'll supply dates for the alibi. And sometime within these dates I'll do the job. Fair enough?' I blew an irreverent smoke ring at Honry, followed it with an ingenuous smile. Neither were well-received. He tugged furiously at his collar.

I flicked through my pocket diary.

'The alibi is to run from . . . Saturday, the day after tomorrow, until . . . let's say for fifteen days.'

Hutton pounced. 'Then it's Saturday.' Honry was canted across his desk, rancour forgotten in his thirst for enlightenment.

'Maybe, maybe not.' I mashed my cigar in the ash tray made from the sawn-off base of a shell case. 'Stop fishing – it makes me nervous. I'm going now.' I stood. 'Talk to you tomorrow, Honry. And give this message to whom it may concern, will you? – sink or swim, we do it together.' I winked cheerfully. 'Togetherness is the key word. Get it?'

'See you in Sicily,' Hutton said drily. 'I'll be there, even if you won't.' Unlike Honry he wasn't in the least upset over my hard-nosed approach. But then he was just a cop, thick-skinned and thick-skulled as they come.

'Vee!' Sternly, from Honry. 'We haven't finished yet.'

'You mean the debriefing? Do it without me.'

I opened the door on a thin, severely-dressed woman of about fifty, supporting a tray on which reposed three mis-matched cups and the ritual plate of Ministry biscuits.

'How thoughtful,' I said to the woman, lightening her load to the extent of one biscuit. 'And how typically long-winded. I'm afraid I must fly. Keep the tea warm for my next visit; I'm sure I shan't be able to tell the difference.' I patted her arm, bit into my biscuit, and steamed off through Honry's secretary's office and away from the world I used to be a part of; a world that now suddenly and for no good reason turned my stomach.

They could have stopped me. Even the innocuous DTI has its heavy mob. But they didn't.

And the next day, well before noon, I got my phone call and my acceptance.

Chapter Fourteen

The Dirty Weekend.

I have a theory about it, which is this: though it must assuredly have been conceived by a Casanova (if not *the* Casanova), it has since been discreetly hyped up by the hotel trade acting in concert, for that least romantic of all motives – profit. Why do I utter this slander? Because at the Inter-Continental Hotel in Paris, whither I whisked Rowen Yeo on a drab Friday afternoon – the Friday afternoon following the morning of Honry's phone call with its clenched-teeth acceptance of my demands – every other couple comprised a middle-aged-upwards male with a twenty-five-and-downwards female. The *crème de la crème* of this Sugar Daddy set was a frail, wrinkled walnut of a retired English General – or at any rate the hotel staff all accorded him the rank – who was forever in the company of a *pair* of little darlings, hanging on to his arms like grapnels. You could speculate for a million years on what they got up to after lights out and still get it a hundred per cent wrong.

I had chosen Paris for the Fletcher version of the Dirty Weekend partly for its (some say *passé*) romantic image, partly for its proximity. As for the rip-off prices – well, Julia could afford it. And speaking of my nearest-and-dearest, she believed (or did she?) I was here to meet Henri Meylon, top official of the French steelworkers' union, for some palm greasing in connection with the Yeo affair. Meylon and Yeo were fallen-out friends, though as far as I knew the Frenchman was no more open to bribery than President Jacques Chirac.

The details of our two night-stay at the Inter-Continental are not for the setting down in writing. Rowen was not a virgin – I'd have been amazed if she was – nor was she up to Julia's standard of skill with hand and all the orifices. But she made up for these shortcomings with a super-abundance of enthusiasm and a flair for originality.

What's more, she didn't just copulate, she made love, and the boot, in consequence, was now on the other foot: it was for *me* that the act was purely physical, inspired only by my attraction to her face and body. It was I who now viewed from Julia's perspective. All the same, I tried to show tenderness. I believe I succeeded.

So the bed bit was good. We spend many happy, energetic hours there, descending at lunch-time to the fading splendour of the restaurant with its matchless cuisine and high waiter-customer ratio that guaranteed no delays between courses.

If I had any complaint at all about my rather lovely and vivacious companion it was over the frequency of her avowals of love: 'I love you so much I feel dizzy'; 'I never thought I'd ever be so much in love – I feel as if I'm glowing all over like a light bulb. *Am* I glowing all over?'; 'Love me just a tenth as much as I love you and I'll be the happiest woman in the world!'

If I'd reciprocated her feelings, all well and good. Who can say I wouldn't have waxed equally lyrical on the subject? Yet in spite of it all, in spite of the girl being mine for the asking, in spite of the crumbling state of my marriage, my love for Julia remained as staunch as ever.

God *damn* it.

Sunday afternoon, before flying back to London, we rode to the top of Eiffel Tower. To me heights are just heights. But I don't commend the experience to vertigo sufferers. It may be the lattice-work construction and the illusion of standing on nothing of real substance that distinguishes the tower from conventional tall structures, but I gather it's common for visitors to be taken quite ill on stepping out of the lift onto the top platform. Happily, Rowen showed no signs of giddiness and the weekend was thus rounded off in a very agreeable fashion.

From the tower we went by taxi to Charles de Gaulle *Aérogare* no 1, and even with an only averagely-demented driver made it in under thirty minutes. Rowen kept her eyes shut for much of the ride.

In the curved bar we drank coffee and gazed westward through the floor-to-ceiling windows upon a yellowing sky that depicted in relief the uninteresting terrain with its *zones industrielles.*

Our hands were clasped. Rowen's felt small and very hot. Like a child's.

'I love you,' she whispered, almost as soon as we sat down. 'I'm round-the-bend crazy about you.'

Here we go again.

'I'm a lucky man,' I said evasively.

She snuggled up close to me and the collar of her coat rubbed against my cheek.

'Can we do this again soon?'

'Honey . . .' This wasn't the right place for home truths. Fortunately I had a genuine get-out. 'The fact is, I have to go away for a few weeks. Out of the country.'

She battled with disappointment, didn't quite win. 'Where to exactly?'

'Er . . . Sicily exactly.' I felt faintly idiotic. Why hadn't they chosen Gstaad? Or the Canaries? Nobody who is anybody goes to Sicily. In January.

Rowen was of like opinion.

'Sicily! There's nothing in Sicily except Mount Etna and the Mafia. What on earth do you want to go there for? And in January!'

Wasn't that just what I'd been asking myself?

'It's Julia. She always insists on a winter holiday in

the sun; to chase away post-Xmas depression, as she calls it.'

Well-invented, Fletcher.

Rowen was silent for a moment; a rare, almost unheard-of occurence.

'Will you phone me?'

'Sure,' I said easily. In a month she'd have forgotten me.

Our flight was announced and we trooped off with the other cattle.

'How would you like to go to Sicily, my pet?' I said to Julia after breakfast on Monday morning. We were in the study; she was sifting through her mail, I was settling various bills, including my bookie's. A painful exercise.

'Sicily? In January?'

Now where had I heard that before?

'Warmer than London in January.' Outside it was grey and blustery. A day for staying indoors. A day for planning holidays in Sicily.

'Don't be asinine.' Julia was reading a letter as she spoke. It didn't make her any less scathing. 'We've loads of engagements over the next few weeks.'

'I'll have to be away anyway,' I persisted.

'Where?' Still reading. The message hadn't got through.

'Just . . . away.'

Now she raised her head.

'Your "thing"?' Lately she always referred to it as my 'thing.' It was meant to sound disparaging, I suppose.

I didn't need to confirm it. Her face darkened.

'So you're still going ahead with it.' The bitterness was unexpected.

'Haven't you listened to anything I've said these past eight weeks?'

'Haven't you listened to anything *I've* said? You

must be mad. And it's . . . it's cowardly. Can't you fight out in the open?'

More familiar sentiments. Not trusting my temper I walked to the window. The elms behind the summer house, ragged survivors of the disease that had come close to eliminating the species from the land, were bending before the wind, their uppermost branches whipping. Under the summerhouse veranda, Bob, our young gardener-handyman, was at work replacing a section of rotting floorboards: the structure was over eighty years old.

'Will you go to Sicily?' I said.

'Alone, you mean?'

'Regrettably. It's very important, Julia – to me personally. Part of my . . . er . . . protection.'

That unbent her a little. 'For how long?'

When I told her she burst out laughing.

'Don't be ridiculous. What am I going to do in Sicily for three weeks? On my own.'

'You'll think of something. And you won't be on your own for long, if I know you.'

'No, I won't, because I'm not going. You change *your* plans.'

And though I persuaded and cajoled and even seduced, she remained obdurate.

Fortunately, though it would have slightly strengthened my alibi, I didn't absolutely have to have her there to keep my spiritual self company. None of our relatives and close friends would find it remarkable if I took off on a bachelor odyssey abroad.

Which says a lot for the state of our marriage.

Honry came round with a parcel. He was inclined towards excessive mateyness, presumably in the hope of healing the breach opened up during the meeting at his office.

I rejected the olive branch. His devotion to the Establishment, coupled with Julia's warning, had cooled my liking for him, though the parcel was more than welcome. I didn't count the contents there and then, though I did give the phoney statements a thorough going-over. They looked bona-fide enough; all the 'witnesses' were known to me personally. All pyramids of respectability.

All prepared to lie under oath.

'Don't miss the news tonight,' Honry said on leaving.

It was an unnecessary reminder. Today's talks between the electricity and gas companies and Yeo's union were expected to be decisive – one way or another.

Jaw-jaw was still in progress when I tuned in at six o'clock. Better than war-war as Churchill once rhymingly put it. The newsreader passed lightly over the topic. No news is also bad bews.

Three hours later, the BBC's version had nothing new to impart. I left the set on anyway and did some homework on union history in preparation for my dialogue with Yeo. Then, ten minutes into the programme came the dramatic announcement that the talks had just been concluded, and we were whisked over to the National Power headquarters where one Terence Pettigrew, the Beeb's man-on-the-spot, awaited us.

Even swathed in scarf, woolly hat and gloves, Pettigrew was clearly feeling the cold. His pink cheeks blazed from the screen like a pair of brake lights and his breath was a perpetual mist.

'Just a few minutes ago the final round of talks between the electricity and gas suppliers and the AUEWE – talks that have lasted on and off for eight weeks – came to an end. It is understood that, despite new concessions from the employers, the union has not seen fit to moderate its stance, the main elements of which are a thirty-five hour week, twenty-five per cent pay increase for all employees, and a recruitment drive aimed at attracting ten thousand workers – mostly apprentices the industries don't need – over the next twelve months.' Pettigrew darted a glance over his shoulder at the well-lit National Power building entrance. 'We hope to have a word with representatives from both sides, especially Mr Yeo, President of the AUEWE, to find out just what this failure to reach agreement means for the rest of us.'

We found out almost immediately as Pettigrew hooked Sir Robert Hemmingway-Blythe, deputy head of British Gas.

'Sir Robert!' Pettigrew hailed and the tall, spare baronet coasted into the BBC's embrace with good-natured resignation.

'Hello, Terence,' he said around a weary smile.

'Would you care to fill us in on the outcome of today's meeting, Sir Robert?'

'Yes . . . well . . . as you've probably heard already we won't be raiding our champagne cellars tonight, unless to drown our sorrows. Put simply, we haven't been able to meet any of the union's demands. What we have done is to make a damn good compromise offer which would give them double the going rate for settlements in the public sector.'

'And . . . ?'

'And they've rejected it. Flatly rejected it.' Hemmingway-Blythe's incredulity revealed the innocence of him and his fellow-negotiators; revealed also their poor perception of the motives of the man on the other side of the table. 'They insist on having the lot. They weren't negotiations, not as I interpret the word. That man . . . Yeo . . . he's . . .'

Pettigrew was instantly alert, sensing four-inch headlines. 'Yes, Sir Robert?'

'Never mind.' Hemingway-Blythe turned up his collar against the polar airstream. 'Now if you'll excuse me, Terence . . .'

But Pettigrew, openly disappointed at the baronet's reticence, wasn't quite ready to call it quits.

'Just one more question, if I may, Sir Robert,' he said, and Hemingway-Blythe was too much of a gentleman to refuse.

'What,' Pettigrew said, 'does the union intend to do?'

'The union?' Hemingway-Blythe went blank. 'Do? You ought really to ask them, you know. As I understand it, there's to be an emergency meeting of the executive later in the week and a recommendation made that all members in the three industires – electricity, gas, and water – be called out on strike from Monday next.'

Overnight, the money markets on the other side of the world marked the pound down an average of seven cents against the US dollar; in Hong Kong it slipped ten cents. The slide continued the next day in London, Paris, Zürich and elsewhere. The all-share index tumbled over a hundred points during the day: some companies were nearly wiped out. A full-blown crisis of confidence was in the making.

I got in touch with my and Julia's stockbroker and unloaded some especially volatile holdings, around £30,000-worth in all.

'Where shall I place it?' he asked in a wringing-hands voice.

'Sit on it until you hear from me.'

A message arrived from Sgeir Varlish on Friday, via the RN base at Holy Loch and thence to the Ministry of Defence and thence to Honry. It read, after de-coding: *Holiday home ready for guest. Love Fiona*

The 'Love' was unofficial. The rest was the signal for Operation Hangman to swing into action.

My response was even more succinct: *Small hours Sunday*.

No sender's name. The fewer clues I left for the inevitable subsequent investigation-stroke-cover-up, the more secure I'd feel.

Then I phoned a Birmingham number. Got a Birmingham voice.

'Richardson,' I announced. My *nom-de-guerre*.

'Evening, boss. We were expecting to hear from you this week. Seeing what's been happening, like.'

This was a man I had used during my previous tenure at the DTI, and had remained loosely in touch with since. You never knew when you might need a man with no nerves and no scruples.

'Saturday,' I said. 'He'll be at Power Base all day.'

'Then it's to be Plan B.' There was glee in the words; he relished his well-paid work. 'Er . . . now don't forget the crinkle, will you, boss?'

'You look after your end, I'll look after mine.'

He was laughing as I hung up. Even his laugh had a Midlands inflexion.

At five past seven on a dry, sub-zero Saturday evening, I was sitting in a hired and much-abused Rover 400, parked in a muddy lay-by a few miles north of St Albans, listening to a scratchy Simon and Garfunkel cassette that had come with the car. Sitting, listening, and twitching like a junkey on a cold turkey cure. Two hours I had been there with the tension building up inside me, ankle deep in fingernail chewings, the adrenalin anti-freezing my bloodstream.

Headlights twinkled in the inadequate mirror: full beam, a white explosion, blinding as a magnesium flare. I tensed anew for the ninety-ninth time. The glare expanded, filling the mirror, and then with a *swoosh* that rocked the car on its springs a large removal van swayed past at an impossible speed. Dis-interestedly I watched the tail lights – a pair of feeble glow-worms – recede then extinguish abruptly as the van rounded the next bend.

I wound down the window to change the air and for something to do. "*Hello darkness, my old friend,*" sang S and G, and set me off brooding about Julia. Our goodbyes had been perfunctory, cold even. From the moment I announced my impending departure for 'Sicily' she had been strangely subdued. Still wouldn't change her mind about going though. If her abstraction was on my account, because she was worried about me, then I was truly gratified. But that explanation didn't gell with the loveless parting.

Where, oh, where did I make my big mistake, Julia? Was it in marrying out of my class? Perhaps we should have just lived together and done without the pomp and ceremony. Or was it because I tried too hard and a shade too obviously to ingratiate myself with your family? Until I realised I was trying to do the equivalent of climbing Everest with my ankles bound, and thereafter switched to the other extreme – that of indifference dotted with insolence, which likewise had no measurable effect. Would it, I wondered, help my cause if I used the capital I was in the process of amassing (courtesy of HM Government) to buy myself a title? Then I remembered the Baron's words during a rare fireside chat: "Nobility is a birthright. It can't be created or manufactured. I don't approve of Life Peerages."

He would approve a damn sight less of my laying down cash for one, like a membership fee.

A car, low, white, Lotus genre, snarled past Londonwards. The crackle of its engine had scarcely faded when headlights blinked in the mirror: dipped headlights that went to full beam, back to dip, and again to full beam. This was it!

A dark saloon drove past slowly, nearside winker flashing. A Sierra, J registration. It pulled in about twenty yards ahead of me, braked to a stop. I sat still, scarecrow rigid, heart going bumpety-bump. It had to be them. The Sierra's engine was still running, throwing out a pennant of exhaust smoke, rose tinted in the flush of the rear lights. A door opened and a burly figure emerged.

I poked my head out of the window. A sliver of light stabbed at me and I instinctively raised my hand.

'Evening, Mr Richardson.' The light snapped off. 'Sorry about that. Had to be sure it was you, like.'

'That's all right. Chadwick, isn't it?' They were alike, him and his partner, who was also his cousin. In the dark, you couldn't tell them apart.

'Yeh.'

He stood motionless, a yard or so from the car, a square, chunky figure, menacing in the darkness.

I waited. Sat on my impatience. Wouldn't do to be overanxious in front of the hired help.

'Want to see chummy?' he said presently.

'Lead on,' I said, sliding out.

'If a car comes turn your back on it. Nothing like headlights for picking out every wrinkle on your mush.'

Which was a precaution that would never have occurred to me, for all my experience in doings devious. In the world of real crime I was still a neophyte.

Chadwick's cousin, Briggs, was behind the wheel of the Sierra. He twisted round to glance a nod off me as Chadwick opened the rear hatch. On the floor of the boot, lying sideways and hunched up, was a man in a light grey suit. His head was shrouded in a black hood and his wrists and ankles had been handcuffed.

'Take a butchers,' Chadwick invited.

I leaned over the huddled form and the sickly aroma of chloroform rose in my nostrils.

'Car coming,' Briggs called out, and a thrust from behind propelled me on to my knees. The hatch slammed and Chadwick was down there with me, his breath fanning the back of my neck. The layby was suddenly bright as a strip-club stage, the hire car spotlighted – metallic green paintwork, reflective number plate (thankfully false), and all. Then, with equal suddenness, it was dark again, as with a curtain drawn across a lighted window, and the dying note of a high-revving engine sounded the all-clear.

'No damage, I hope, boss.' Chadwick straightened up and I with him. 'Can't stand on ceremony in an emergency.'

'No.' I wiped mud off my trousers. 'No, indeed.'

Up went the hatch again and I turned my attention back to Yeo, tugged ineffectually at the black hood.

'Here, let me.' Chadwick eased me aside. 'It's tied at the throat.'

The hood was off in seconds. Chadwick flicked the torch on, played the beam on the fleece of blond hair and the slit of a mouth. Just long enough – it was Yeo all right. There was dried blood under his nose, but he was otherwise in good nick.

The torch went off and blackness closed in, relieved only by the car lights. A tiny breath of wind whispered through the trees at the roadside. I felt shivery – simultaneously hot and cold, and it was nothing to do with the weather. Jubilation was the name of my fever: the bastard was mine at last!

'There's blood on his face,' I remarked, to show I wasn't going to be fobbed off with sub-standard merchandise.

'It wasn't a bleeding walk-over, you know. He put up a bit of a struggle. And he had his minder with him – a right wanker, that, and no mistake. Soon sorted him, though.'

My stomach fluttered.

'You didn't . . . kill him.'

'The minder? No way. It wasn't in the contract. No, we just showed him the shooters and while he was working out what time of day it was, Dave put him to sleep.' He whickered, tapped the side of his head. 'Got small brains, you know, these minders. Like dinosaurs.'

'Just make sure the goods don't suffer any more damage while they're in your care.'

Teeth glinted.

'You're the boss, boss.'

In the woods nearby an owl hoo-hooed, accentuating the isolation of the place: the nearest house was a mile or more away, and the chances of a cruising police car happening on the scene were remote. Nevertheless, we had set a two-minute limit on this part of the programme and owing to the unplanned passing car were already running late.

'Let's move,' I said and we parted with crisp farewells.

While I was still squelching back to my car the Sierra made off like a formula one racer leaving the grid. I let it get clear away before following. No sense in travelling in convoy. If they *were* nobbled, best I was nowhere in the neighbourhood.

Through the village of Wadesmill I poddled, my driving deceptively relaxed, speed limits scrupulously observed. The route led along country roads in the main, bypassing all conurbations and, except where unavoidable, all trunk roads. The possibility of an accident was ever-present in my mind. In Chadwick's and Briggs' too, for a certainty. Until Yeo was handed over, they carried all the risk.

On a straight-ish section of the road east of Biggleswade I lapsed into more reminiscence, to dwell not upon the lost cause of my darling wife, but on Rowen, and the dwelling was not disagreeable. Unusually, the affair had left no aftertaste of regret, except on her behalf. For me it had been no more than a pleasant diversion and she merited better. I had phoned her that very morning, ostensibly from Heathrow Airport, ostensibly about to board a 737 to Sicily, and even though forewarned of my departure, her distress had cut deep into my conscience. Matters were not helped by my refusal to give her the name of the hotel, though I was genuinely booked at the Mazzarò in Taormina-Mazzarò (breathtaking views out across the Strait of Messina towards the toe of Italy's boot – so ran the blurb) where I was to remain an invisible guest until 15th February. By then, whether or not I was finished and done with Yeo, my alibi for the fortnight following his disappearance would be set in concrete.

I pictured Rowen as she had been for the greater part of our weekend in Paris – in a state of partial or total *déshabillement*. A body sleek and sinuous as spilled oil, with small breasts of exquisite symmetry and prominent nipples like pink buds. Legs that were lightly muscled – she ran for a local athletics club; legs that would lock tight around my waist as I thrust into her. And thrusting into her was an oft-repeated pastime during those two days of abandon. She liked it hard and fast. 'More,' she had begged, a gasping scream at the back of her throat. 'More, more, more! Harder, harder, harder!' And her juices had flowed in torrents so that hours later the smell of her sex still hung in the room. The state of the sheets ought to have been a source of embarrassment to us, but that's the beauty of Paris: it's a city of love and lovers, and the most outlandish behaviour is not just indulged but applauded: '*L'amour, c'est tout*'

In my reminiscing I had wandered over the white line and a car coming up behind gave me a long multiple-horn blast as it overtook. A Bentley Mulsanne. I grinned at the irony and shut out the women in my life for the remainder of the journey to Fowlmere, to concentrate on getting there whole.

That evening, as I meandered through the Hertfordshire countryside, the Cabinet, I was later to learn, stayed in session all night long, debating the impending strike and its bound-to-be-catastrophic effect on the nation. The predictable outcome was the declaration of a State of Emergency from midnight on Sunday night.

*   *   *

It was five to nine and misty when I swung into the crumbling, potholed asphalt road that served the disused fighter airfield near Fowlmere in Cambridgeshire. The Rover's headlights. cut a broad white band through the dead grass and tangled brambles, silvered with frost, that bordered the road. A rut jolted the suspension and I slowed to a 10 mph crawl, my eyes straining in their sockets for a glimpse of the derelict shell of the control tower.

A small animal crossed my path in a panic-stricken scuttle and in swerving instinctively to avoid it I almost missed the flash of a torch away to my right. Reassured, I speeded up, only to plunge into another crater with a bump that rattled my teeth. I slogged on and the tower loomed at last, creepy in the thickening mist, like some modern-day Transylvanian castle. I spun the wheel to the right, followed the road that led right up to the runway apron. A figure materialized, a ghostly apparition in the headlight beam – Chadwick. Beyond him the Sierra and the insectile profile of the helicopter. It was all coming together beautifully.

I parked close to the tower and killed the engine. The subsequent quiet was an ear-splitting scream; Chadwick shattered it by opening the door.

'Almost gave you up, boss.'

'Where's the Scotsman – the pilot?'

Chadwick flicked a shaft of torchlight at the helicopter.

'Inside, keeping warm. Him and chummy both.'

I fetched my luggage from the boot and Chadwick helped me transfer it to the helicopter. Briggs climbed out of the Sierra, nodded to me, and moved across to the Rover. His rôle now was the removal and destruction of the Rover's false plates and its return to the hire company. All neat and tidy; all part of a painstakingly-woven tapestry with no loose threads for the police to unravel.

Sellar met me at the door of the copter, clad in his padded parka.

'Good evening, Mr No-name.' From his grinning exterior you'd have thought kidnapping was all in a day's work to him. Then again, maybe it was.

I handed up a suitcase. 'How's the merchandise?'

'Sleeping like a bairn.' A case in either hand, he retreated into the cabin.

I turned to Chadwick. 'Well done, Bob.'

'It's been a pleasure working with you again, boss. Make it sooner next time.'

The package that passed from me to him was about six inches by four, and an inch thick.

'In twenties as agreed.'

He smiled and it was a smile that made me glad we were on the same side.

'I don't even need to count it, Mr Richardson. Like I said – it's always a pleasure.' A half-mocking salute and he was gone, dissolving into the mist.

'Are you coming aboard?' Sellar's voice rumbled from the cabin.

'Yes. Can you fly in this muck though?'

'This is a helicopter, not Concorde,' was the warm retort. 'We go straight up. And all's clear above tree-top height, so dinna fash.'

Close by, two car engines fired almost simultaneously and headlights bounced off the tower wall. I waved an adieu and hopped up inside the cabin.

'Wind her up,' I said to Sellar, securing the rather flimsy door.

While he played with the controls, I checked out our valuable freight. He was stretched full length on the rear seat, still handcuffed and, as an additional security measure, now attached to the seat's frame. His head was still hooded, and for Sellar's protection would stay hooded the entire flight.

'Sgeir Varlish here we come,' Sellar said, jabbing here and there at the mosaic of coloured lights that constituted the control panel. There was a wicked glee about his manner that made me stare. The bastard was actually *enjoying* himself.

'Just make sure you get us there in one piece.'

For an answer he bellowed with laughter and took us up at the speed of an express lift.

Chapter Fifteen

'How's the prisoner this morning?' I asked Fiona as she completed her wary descent of the staircase, two-handedly gripping the tray containing the remains of Yeo's breakfast.

'How would you be after a week's near-solitary confinement?' she countered without venom.

'Pissed off.' This from Bull. Before him on the table was a video unit, its innards – printed circuits and suchlike – spread all around it like a starburst.

I swallowed the tepid dregs of my coffee. Tilted back my chair and feasted on Fiona's tight little buttocks. Buttocks that were becoming more and more irresistible as the days passed.

'It's a necessary part of the conditioning process, leaving him alone,' I said. 'Anyway I'll be starting on him tomorrow.'

'Really?' Fiona said, an eyebrow arching. 'Let the grilling commence, eh?'

'No grilling – honest. No steel rods, no cocktail sticks under the fingernails, no testicle squeezers.'

'Pity,' Bull grunted.

In spite of the close confinement and lack of diversions our comradeship and team spirit were holding up well. During the day each performed his or her undemanding duties, interspersed with strolls about the island – I was already intimately acquainted with every sea water-filled nook and every ordure-rich cranny – relaxing in the evening over a game of cards or chess or Risk. And the hours passed amazingly swiftly.

The lighthouse was a comfortable enough billet as century-old lighthouses on salt-encrusted, gale-battered Atlantic islands go. Fiona and more especially Bull had worked wonders between them. The kitchen/dining-room/sitting-room boasted dazzling white walls, curtains, a big square of carpet, and the best camping furniture taxpayers' money could buy. The original cooking facilities had been supplemented by an electric microwave oven, a fridge-freezer, and sundry appliances for mixing, blending, liquidising, in fact the whole culinary gamut. On the floor below were installed a washing machine and tumble dryer, together with our four generators, whose combined output of 14kw/h was more than adequate.

Upstairs, the dormitory-bedroom had become two semi-circular bedrooms, separated by a plywood screen. Even the adjacent bathroom was functioning as a bathroom should, though the modern loo flush was too efficient for the narrow outlet and messy overspills were a regular event.

Which left the top floor, the service room. Some forty per cent of the floor area had been converted into a cell, segregated from the remaining sixty per cent by a very solid partition: the wood used was an inch thick and screwed to 4 x 4 uprights themselves bolted in place. Here was where Yeo did his lonely penance.

The staircase gave direct access to the truncated service room, which could thus be entered without our prisoner being any the wiser. This was an important point, for the video camera was set into the partition and would require reloading daily with a blank casette, as well as periodic maintenance, functions that would obviously demand extreme stealth.

From the moment Yeo's incarceration began I had purposely stayed away from him. He saw only Fiona, who took his meals but, on my instructions, never spoke. This tactic was designed to increase his isolation and thus loosen his tongue when the time came to put him – metaphorically speaking – on the rack. Rather surprisingly he had made no fuss over his abduction, nor even asked where and why. He seemed resigned to his lot, one might almost say impervious to it: he was too good to be true. Was this the fire-breathing revolutionary who had daily dominated our television screens? All mouth, no man, was Fiona's characteristically caustic summing-up. I disagreed. For my money he was simply in a state of trauma.

In the late afternoon that day, before the onset of darkness, I went for a walk out onto the southern headland. I walked alone. I needed space to gather my mental forces for tomorrow's opening round. It was windy, a chill, biting west wind that stung your cheeks and chapped your lips. A wind that moaned without break – a dismal sound – and drove the sea to pit itself against our modest rock.

The sea. Boiling white in every direction. Cones of spume leaping and cavorting, dying and being born again on their perpetual journey to self-destruction. It was not often calm hereabouts.

In London they would be wondering and worrying whether I had yet made a break-through: the two ministers involved, Lord Deverill with his vitriolic hatred, Honry . . . Julia too; all of them to a lesser or greater degree mentally pacing the floor. Let them pace. No messages out until I hit pay dirt, that was the rule. And no messages in except as a matter of life and death. Our only link with the mainland was via our radio-transmitter and the more signals we sent, the greater the risk of a ham tapping into our frequency.

I felt hungry. The promise of action never failed to stimulate my appetite. I took a last look round, inflated my lungs with stingingly pure air, and trudged off along the cliff to where the lighthouse stood like a lonely picket, its mutilated top catching the sun's terminal glimmer so that for a few nostalgic seconds it appeared as if a light burned once more in the empty socket of the lantern.

On Monday morning at 9.30 am I staged my melodramatic entrance. Yeo was standing before the window, his back towards me, his shoulders slack with dejection. Gone was the strutting demagogue, the ebullient rabble-rouser. I had stripped him of his finery. Here, on Sgeir Varlish, he had no rank, no power, no troops to manipulate. The king was in the altogether.

I felt no surge of pity. Transport him back to his natural environment and the tyrant in him would be resuscitated within twenty-four hours. Dictators bounce back fast.

'Good morning,' I said with military briskness.

His head jinked puppet-fashion. Assuming Fiona had followed orders mine would be the first voice he had heard in eight days. He pivoted towards me and his surprise was near to comic.

'You!'

'Me,' I agreed pleasantly. Behind me the key turned in the lock; Bull was now my jailer too. I went over to the small square table screwed to the floor in what might be termed the centre of the room – if semi-circles can be said to have a centre. Its position was crucial: Bull's video camera was focused on it and could not readily be realigned. Hence the screws.

It was my first visit to the room since its transformation from workshop to cell. The most striking thing about it was the smell – the God-awful stink that a chemical closet gives off in any confined, badly-ventilated space. It required a major physical effort to keep my nose from wrinkling as I did an outwardly casual scan of the partition, seeking the camera lens. It should have been invisible to even the most thorough scrutiny, and it was. Along the entire length of the partition, where it met the ceiling, Bull had constructed a foot-square cornice such as might –

to the uninitiated – conceal water pipes or an electrical conduit. He had veneered it with a finely meshed grill and I knew, because he had explained it to me, that the camera lens was peeping through one of the diamond-shaped apertures in the grill. As a further precaution against Yeo poking around, Bull was only to instal the camera immediately prior to each session and to remove it immediately afterwards. It was as foolproof as ingenuity could make it.

I sat down, not with my back to the window as an experienced interrogator might be expected to do, the light then being thrown onto the subject's face, but sideways on to it; this would place Yeo in line with the camera lens.

'Won't you join me?'

Incredulity had been slow to release its hold on him.

'Is this because . . . ?' He broke off, flushed and jumpy.

'Because what?'

He made a negative gesture. 'Nothing . . . nothing. You tell me.'

'Sit down. Let's talk.'

He didn't budge. 'Why am I here?'

'Sit down. I've brought you a pipe and some tobacco.' I dumped the pipe in its original presentation box and a packet of Old Holborn on the table. 'To make life a bit more bearable.'

He sat then. Touched the presentation box with circumspect fingers as if it were a mouse trap set to go off.

'Does my wife know I'm here?'

'Don't be silly,' I chided, softening it with a slightly derisive grin. 'What do you think this is – a boy scout initiative test?'

'At least tell me why I'm here.'

I put on a look of surprise. 'Can't you guess? Can't you work it out?'

'Is it personal?'

'*Personal?*' The man was losing his marbles.

'So it's not.' Relieved. 'Then it has to be professional. What is it – a private war against the unions?'

'The strike's been called off, you know.' Actually the precise phrasing as dished up by the BBC was 'suspended pending Mr Yeo's return.' The decision had been taken the morning after Yeo's disappearance, at a hastily-convened gathering of the union clan. Without their diety to lead them to the holy grail of chaos, they had reverted to mere mortals. And frightened, confused mortals at that.

'Just goes to show how indespensible I am.' Typical Yeo vainglory and all too regrettably true. Then, the frown evaporating: 'So *that's* it. You expected the strike to fold if I wasn't around to direct it.' He seized my arm. 'That's what this is all about. I'm right, aren't I?'

It suited my book to have him think so.

'Could be.'

His triumph was fleeting as the implication took root. 'Then how long do you plan to hold me?'

'Until the issue is dead. Until the strike threat is permanently removed.'

'But that might be months!' he said, aghast.

'I'd say there's a good chance it will be.'

He groaned and his hands became fists and pounded the table softly.

Thanks to the impressive output from the wall-mounted fan heater the cell was as warm as it was fetid. Yeo was jacketless and sporting a check shirt from the generous wardrobe that came with the accommodation. The top few buttons were undone, exposing a triangle of blond chest fluff, but even so he was perspiring lightly. I peeled off my windcheater and hung it over the back of the chair.

'It doesn't make sense,' he said, his eyes tracing my every move. 'You'll be arrested as soon as you release me.'

'Don't worry about me, friend. I'm insured.'

He masticated that and clearly didn't like the taste. 'Bastard!' He prodded at me. 'The bloody Government's behind this, isn't it?'

'No comment. If I deny it, you won't believe me. If I admit it . . . so what? Nothing that's said between these walls counts as evidence.' There – seed planted: the seed of reassurance that he could speak freely, without comeback.

'Well, there it is,' I said. 'You're here and I'm here and we're stuck with each other. What would you like to do for amusement. Play chess? Dominoes? Risk? Or maybe just talk sport. Or politics.' Another seed. Sowing seeds was as far as I intended to go at this stage. It was implicit in my plan that he make all the running when it came to serious debate on subjects such as politics and economics. The conversation must be natural and be seen on video to be natural. Editing was to be a last resort – probably inevitable but to be kept to a minimum.

'Will you let my wife know I'm all right?' His priorities understandably, were different from mine. 'She'll be sick with worry . . . '

'I'll send a message.' I had a talent for lying convincingly.

'Don't say I'll be here . . . indefinitely,' he said anxiously. 'Say . . . say I'll be home in a week or two. It'll help her get used to the idea gradually.'

Considerate bastard. I promised to do as he asked.

I clapped my hands on my thighs, half-rose. 'I'll be off then . . . '

'No!' His voice shot up. 'No – wait! Just stay and . . . and talk a while.' More calmly now. 'I . . . you can't imagine how it is being on your own day after day.'

I let my backside sink slowly and with feigned reluctance. 'A few minutes then. I've things to do.'

He tapped the pipe. 'Thanks for that. Thoughtful of you.'

'Don't mention it.'

'Since it looks as if I'm going to be your guest for some time . . . what do I call you? Mr Fletcher? Fletcher without the mister?'

'That'll do. Unless you prefer to be buddy-buddy, in which case call me Vee.'

'Vee? What does that stand for? V-sign? V-neck? V-bomber?'

I allowed a small smile to creep onto my lips. 'None of these.'

'V for Victory then?'

I considered this. 'You know, David, you might have hit the nail on the head.'

The sun came out just then and threw a square of light onto the partition, like a piece of blank film projected on a screen.

'Any chance of a breath of air?' Yeo said, pathetically eager.

'Tomorrow maybe.'

'This is a lighthouse, isn't it?'

I nodded. 'On an island. Without boats or people. Except us.'

'Us, being you and the girl.'

'Plus one other. Male, ex-SAS sergeant.'

'The guard dog, eh?' He grew pensive and during the interlude I came to appreciate just how isolated it was up here on the top floor. The gulls' incessant callings could be heard, but otherwise we could easily have been on the dark side of the moon. Fiona and Bull were two levels below and no hint of their presence reached us. There was not even a panoramic view to break the tedium: the window let in light but like all the others its panes were so abraded with salt as to resembled frosted glass. No wonder Yeo was feeling the strain.

Precisely as I had meant him to.

'They say you're the Government's expert on unions.' Yeo shook the pipe out of its box. It was an unpretentious, straight-stemmed model with a plain bowl.

'Nice,' he said and sucked at it. Wet noises issued.

'Better still with tobacco in it.'

He angled a tight grin at me. 'You didn't answer my question.'

'Was it a question?' I expelled an exaggerated sigh. 'The answer is yes and no. I used to be the Government's expert on unions. Then I retired and became a businessman.'

'This is your business? Abduction?' Yeo tore off a chunk of the block of tobacco. A rich, earthy smell arose, competing with other richer, earthier smells.

'My country needed me,' I said, tongue firmly in cheek.

'To do what?'

'To do you, friend.'

He left off stuffing rags of tobacco into the pipe bowl to make puzzled eyes at me.

'My old job was to forestall strikes,' I elaborated. 'To nip them in the bud. Also, secondarily, to ferret out any inside information that might be used against the likes of you and your brethren.'

Divulging governmental secrets was at best an indiscretion, at worst a breach of Official Secrets. But a calculated indiscretion, a reasoned breach. To get a bit, I must needs give a bit. Steer him onto the tracks that would lead to the appropriate terminus.

He accepted the idea of a government-sponsored union spy with a lack of astonishment, as if long since persuaded of it. Or maybe his self-control was just very good.

'Got a match?'

I tossed over a full box of Swan Vestas.

'Stopping strikes, eh?' A match rasped. 'Did you have much success?'

'Some. And I've just stopped yours. That's my *new* job.'

He rode smoothly over that, like a skilled surfer cresting a wave. 'But you didn't go around kidnapping union leaders every time they threatened a strike, did you? In your old job, I mean.'

'You're extra-special. No responsible government could afford to let you go ahead and shut down the country.'

He peered at me through a cumulus of pipe out-pourings. 'There was an alternative.'

'The usual one, you mean? Give in?'

'Look . . . er . . . Vee, the unions have stood a lot from various governments since the days of the friendly societies.' He flapped away some of the grey haze between us. 'You do know about the friendly societies, I take it.'

'I'd be a poor union expert if I didn't,' I said. 'They were often a screen for back door union activities until they were legally recognized. In 1793,' I added, to prove I could spout facts as well as theories.

'If you're so erudite then you won't need a history lesson from me on the hostility the unions have faced ever since the legalisation of those friendly societies. Legislation only increased the hostility. Unions have borne the brunt of government anti-working class spleen and been made the whipping boys for the in-adequacies of our political masters for nearly two centuries. Take Peterloo as just a single manifestation of that spleen; thank God most of the others have been less bloody.'

The Peterloo incident, a peaceful demonstration which climaxed in the deaths of eleven Manchester weavers at the hands of the Yeomanry, was not only a gross over-reaction by the Government of the day – even I acknowledged that – but it had given the pro-union faction a hefty fillip.

'So you're carrying a chip the size of a caber on your shoulder for the whole of the union movement. What has that got to do with demanding a twenty-five per cent pay increase?'

'You obviously don't remember the immortal words of Robert Peel.' Yeo's pipe had gone out. He re-lit it, holding the matchbox to the bowl to stimulate ignition.

'Peel? The Prime Minister? Did he advocate twenty-five per cent pay rises then?'

A polite chuckle. 'Not to the exact percentage point, no. But at the time of the repeal of the Combination Act he expressed the view that men whose only property was their manual skill and strength should confer together, if they wished, for the purpose of setting a rate at which they would sell that property to their employers. Or words to that effect.'

If Peel had indeed made such a pronouncement, it was a fair and reasonable stance to take and I had no quarrel with it. 'But Peel didn't sanction strife as a means of imposing a rate on employers. He didn't suggest that those same men should be allowed to disrupt and harm and even end the lives of their fellow men.'

'Precisely. *He expressed no view.* It wasn't contemplated. No one could conceive that a manual worker would ever have that much muscle. Had they foreseen . . .'

'Had they foreseen it, Peel would have condemned it. Above all, he was a humanitarian.'

'But anyway, he's dead.' Smugly. 'And I'm not.'

I decided, in a flush of spite, to have the last word.

'Not yet,' I said with deliberate bleakness, and on that note I left him to ponder his future.

Bull was tickled when I told him about it.

'That'll have put the shits up him.'

Fiona snorted. 'He needs more than just shits putting up him.' She was crouching before the portable TV set, tuning in to the early evening news. 'A large calibre dum-dum bullet up his anal passage would be more productive.'

Bull laughed salaciously.

'You'd like to be the one to put it there too.'

'You said it.' She plonked in the vacant armchair and drew a cigarette from a crumpled pack of Peter Stuyvesant; she consumed two packs a day on average. 'But before administering the *coup de rectum* I'd have a little fun . . .'

She proceeded to amplify in mostly four-letter language. At times she could be extremely witty, albeit a wit so larded with expletives you'd never have guessed she was convent-educated – though they do say a theological upbringing is as much conducive to profanity as to piety. Bull roared until his cheeks shone with tears, and even I, less readily amused, had a chuckle or two.

'I'll bet he fucks beautifully though,' Fiona said as a postscript to her discourse.

Bull made a noise in his throat, concentrated on the TV.

'Why not try him out?' I said, and both their heads jerked round; both disbelieving, but Fiona's disbelief was tinged with excitement.

'You're kidding,' she said slowly. She had the dubious look of a child offered a sweet by a stranger.

'Not at all. We're broad-minded – aren't we, Bull?'

Bull licked his lips, cat-like.

'Provided,' I said, 'you're prepared to sell your memoirs to the appropriate publication should we need a little smut to garnish our exposé.' I wasn't entirely joking, either.

The expected outrage never materialised. She tucked a wayward strand behind her ear and her bicep flexed under the thin sweater, which for some reason brought me to a state of mild arousal. Every night I spent solo made her that bit more desirable; my libido was coming to the boil and she represented the only outlet, the only relief (apart from the hand-operated kind, which I wasn't yet desperate enough to indulge in) within range. Whereas I had once found her masculinity off-putting, it now held an erotic appeal.

'I'll think it over,' she said, looking at the TV screen with faraway eyes.

The news burst upon us with a fanfare and a fuzzy picture. Yeo's disappearance was slightly stale by now and rated only third in the line-up of sensationalism. It would have been still lower were it not for the discovery, at the bottom of the River Stour, of the car used by the 'kidnappers'. Some fibres which colour-matched the jacket worn by Yeo the day he disappeared had turned up in the boot, proving beyond doubt that this was *the* car. It gave me no cause for concern. The car had yielded no other clues and in particular no fingerprints: it was a blind alley.

The report led neatly into news item number four, the proposed resumption of talks between the AUEWE and the employers on Friday next.

'Another one in the eye for Joe Stalin,' Bull crowed.

'I'm not going to tell him though. Not yet awhile. I want him as relaxed as he can be – not fretting about his back-sliding brothers.'

'Is he going to co-operate?' Fiona asked, letting smoke filter from her nostrils. 'You can always give him a jab, if not. There's enough Pentathol in the fridge to keep him babbling for a year.'

'I know. I ordered the stuff. But only to use as a last option. If we drug him it'll show up on the video for sure.'

The rest of the news was barely worthy of the name and before it ran its course, Fiona, by tacit joint consent, returned the TV to the status of one-eyed ornament.

'Who's for cards?' she said brightly.

I paused in the act of pulling the stopper from a bottle of Glenfiddich. 'Strip poker?'

A storm had been forecast for sometime within the next twenty-four hours and it duly broke about our high-rise home that same night. It was then that I learned why the Trinity House Corporation had never been swamped with queues of applicants for the post of lighthouse-keeper. Notwithstanding the pillbox-thick walls, the rising wind roused me and I lay there listening to the fury of it, a fury that shook the tower to its mighty foundations. Remembering too, what happened to the Eddystone Lighthouse, swept away in a hurricane complete with occupants. What hope then for our humble and aged structure?

In time I lapsed back into slumber, but when I woke next morning the storm was still going full tilt, the wind blowing harder than ever and booming like distant cannon fire.

After breakfast Fiona and I ventured out to savour the elements at the height of their powers and it was an experience to chill the heart of the stoutest city-dweller. The sea raged, pure white like soap suds, violent, demented. Never had I seen the like of it, not even on the Inishowen Peninsula in Northern Ireland where the cliffs rear up to nearly a thousand feet and the waves regularly try to climb them.

We stood on the edge of the precipice in front of the lighthouse, the rain spitting in our faces, the wind threatening to upend us, and surveyed that awful panorama of water. Poor old Yeo. He had complained to Fiona of a sleepless night. The din up on the top floor, what with the lantern orchestra directly above, must have been frightful.

'It'll make him more malleable,' I said heartlessly, and I hadn't noticed her shedding any tears over his discomfort.

A gust dashed me against Fiona. We caught each other and I was instantly aware of her strength: it travelled along my arm like an electric shock. In a straight fight against the average male I wouldn't have laid odds against her.

'You're a bit of a hard case, aren't you, Vee?' she said, still holding my arm, as I was hers. 'Never get excited, never lose your temper, always civil . . . and underneath it all just a dark void. Don't you ever have emotions? Don't you *feel*?'

I grinned then. 'I feel often.' And proved it by reaching down under her parka for a fistful of crotch. It was warm down there; the swell of her pubis under her jeans fitted my cupped hand as if custom-made.

Then she went and ruined it by saying: 'It's hotter inside.'

In matters pertaining to sex I'm old-fashioned: I believe the man should not only take the initiative, but keep it too. Fiona's blatant invitation was for me an instant turn-off. My grin fading, I let my hand fall.

'Some other time then.' Her face, under its lustre of rain, was hard. She stepped back and began to pick her way around the lighthouse base. Several paces on she turned.

'Could be you've got something between your legs after all though,' she shouted, her voice thin against the baying wind and the crash of the seas.

'One day you might find out.' I replied in an undertone.

And then it was back to an altogether more humdrum form of daily grind.

Chapter Sixteen

My second session with Yeo lasted longer than its predecessor but contained, if anything, even less meat.

Our four hour symposium ranged over subjects as diverse as skin-diving – a pursuit we both engaged in – the Great Wall of China, which he'd trodden last year, and the future of South Africa (as if *anybody* could speak with authority on that).

More pertinently we debated the attitude of government towards the early trade unions, a chapter of history in which we were equally well-informed, as it transpired. We considered the Combination Laws of 1824, which gave the unions certain fundamental rights, its subsequent amendment, which grabbed many of those right back; we exchanged views on the first 'real' union – the Grand General Union of the Operative Spinners of Great Britain and Ireland – set up by John Doherty in 1829 and somewhat less than a total success since it broke up two years later after an abortive strike. We argued over Chartism – the doctrine of identity of interests of manual workers, and disagreed as to the real contribution of Francis Place, lauded as the liberator of the unions, the man who, in the early nineteenth century, agitated for the shackles to be removed.

And not a millimetre nearer to my goal did any of this ponderous pontificating bring me.

By the fifth day of the interrogation, with the wind and the rain still pounding our island home, my routine with Yeo was settling into a pattern. I would go up at about 10.30 in the morning and stay until lunch time. In the afternoon he was left to his own devices, mostly because *I* needed a break. Until the afternoon of that fifth day when Fiona challenged him to a game of chess ('Honest, that's all we did,' she insisted afterwards), and this was to become a regular feature. As for Bull, he was content to simply potter about the place, his chief function being the removal, reloading, and general maintenance of the video camera. Playback quality was first-class. Reliability of the camera was a source of constant worry to me but Bull was sanguine and had, moreover, thought to bring a back-up, just in case.

'It'll be your balls in the vice if it fails at a crucial moment,' I muttered darkly.

Outside the storm blew on.

On Sunday it was my birthday. My forty-third. No cards came. Of course – no post on Sundays. The mental image of a postman rowing over from the mainland with my birthday mail set me off giggling as I lay in bed watching daylight crawl into the room. I had decided to observe the sabbath, and take a break from pumping Yeo.

The news coming in from civilisation was brighter than it had been for many a week. Negotiations had been resumed between the AUEWE and the employers, with the moderate Stan Hanley, formerly high in the gas workers union, standing in for Yeo. Progress remained slow; Hanley would be inclined to stall, hoping – or maybe not – Yeo would reappear and relieve him of the reins. But just for the two sides to be talking again was a giant step towards sanity.

Reflecting on Hanley's position, I could almost feel sympathy for the guy. His options were limited: compromise would incur his master's wrath. Whereas to go ahead with the strike . . . Only Yeo had the nerve and the ruthlessness.

Since that first day Yeo hadn't referred to the dispute. It was as if he'd closed the shutters on that aspect of the outside world. He no longer even mentioned his family. He had become more and more laid-back, almost serene. The rapid acceptance of his circumstances was a bonus I had not expected. It boded well.

On the Wednesday of my third week on the island it snowed. Fluffy, cotton wool flakes the size of 2p pieces, the wind stirring them aimlessly so that they never actually seemed to touch down. It got colder too, though we were snug enough with our multiple gas heaters.

Yeo was restless that morning. He paced as we talked, which didn't fit the plan at all since he was off-camera except briefly when he passed the table. Consequently I didn't try to nudge the conversation in any specific direction, but simply let it drift.

At one stage, standing arms-folded in front of the window, he declared: 'At heart I'm a Luddite.'

'Smashing up machines and all that? How can you be? How can anybody be a Luddite in today's environment?'

'In the physical sense, they can't. I was referring to an attitude of mind, a philosophy, if you like.' He glanced sideways at me. 'What's the environment got to do with it anyway? Is it rock? Is it immutable?'

I made smoke signals with a cigar. 'Trotsky now, are we? If you can't change the policies, change the people. Only for people, read environment. Have I got it right?'

'Close.'

'How would you go about changing the environment?'

Sit down, I willed.

'You'd really like to know?'

I nodded. Hoping for some real red meat at last; a

succulent morsel with which to choke him. If only the bastard would sit down!

But I was chafing needlessly, because all he said was: 'It's a trade secret.' A tight, slanting smile. 'A trade *union* secret.'

By and large, provoking Yeo to discourse on a particular topic called for little effort and even less skill. It was keeping him on it that posed the main problem.

A promising dialogue on the size of pay awards died such a death. I had put it to him that excessive wage claims implied contempt for the community-at-large since the community, in the long run, would have to pick up the tab.

I reminded him that: 'Apart from the periods in the 60s and 70s when artificial pay freezes were imposed, wages have traditionally been determined by the laws of supply and demand. It's not as if you need to attract labour into the electricity and gas industries – just the opposite.'

'Forget your antediluvian economic theories,' he said snappishly. 'These are the realities of the new millennium. People have certain expectations. In some cases – the agricultural workers are a classic example – those expectations are modest and their gains correspondingly pathetic; in others, like my own union, they are high. Key jobs equal big money. That's the only equation that counts. In the end it all balances out: the highs and the lows establish a median.'

'Speaking of agricultural workers and key jobs, they arguably deserve to be at the top of the play league. Without them and the food they produce, electricity and gas would have no value whatsoever.'

'How true,' he said in that disarming way of his. 'I don't disagree at all with what you say. Let them raise their expectations, by all means. I wouldn't condemn them for it.'

'You're all heart.'

It was the sixteenth day of his interrogation, my twenty-fifth on Sgeir Varlish, and I was fraying at the edges. Losing momentum. Bereft of initiatives. The man simply would not be drawn. My policy of not leading him by the nose was proving a failure and I was becoming resigned to a change of approach.

'How much longer are you going to keep me here, Vee?' he said unexpectedly, going off on one of his damned tangents. 'It's been nearly a month . . .' He sagged, dropped his face into his hands. His shoulders shook gently.

Disconcerted by this sudden collapse I reached over to grip his shoulder. He needed some hope, that much I could understand. A tunnel with no light at the end is a tunnel of despair.

'A few weeks more,' I said, hoping this meagre crumb would suffice.

'A few weeks . . . a few weeks. How long is that? How *many* weeks?' He was talking through his hands, his voice a muffled groan.

'Look . . . it's not indefinite. I give you my word on that. It's a . . . a matter of waiting until certain political . . . er . . . objectives are achieved.' In telling him that maybe I was giving too much away, but I had to have him in a relaxed, conversational frame of mind. If he felt he was stuck in this isolated dump for ever he might close up, stop communicating altogether. I'd seen it happen to Irish terrorists, held under the internment laws with no hope of release. Some of them had become virtual zombies, refusing to speak or even to eat or drink.

'I promise you.' I said, and his face came back into view then. There were tear tracks leading from eyes that were bordered with red. The crumbling edifice. If only his adoring followers could see him now.

'Bastard,' he said slowly and deliberately, but the old Yeo vitriol was absent.

'Agreed.' I smiled to show no offence taken. 'Look,

how would you like a break from this . . . ?' I waved
vaguely around his semi-circular prison with its lavato-
rial stench. 'What would you say to a walk around the
island tomorrow morning?'

Big softie Fletcher.

'I'd . . .' His voice was hoarse. 'I'd like that very
much indeed.'

'Fine.' I got up. 'Cheer up. Think how it used to
be for those thousand of political prisoners in the old
Russia, held in conditions much worse than these and
doing forced labour twelve or more hours a day on
top of that. We Brits are too compassionate, that's our
trouble . . .' He had got over his dolour now and was
glaring, his eyes small and narrow. 'Too compassionate
and too concerned with civil rights. Wouldn't you say
so?'

For once he declined the cast-down gauntlet and for
once I was glad to leave it lie.

Around dusk, a couple of days later, Honry called me
up. Phoning from London, patched into the radio
transmitter at Holy Loch, his tone was far removed
from the urbane drawl of yesteryear.

'Do you realise it will be thirty days tomorrow?' was
his opening salvo. 'A whole month! What are you *doing*
up there? Over.'

'You really need to ask?' I snarled back. As if I didn't
have enough on my plate . . . !

'The Minister . . .'

'Sod the Minister. And screw the Government.' I was
fuming. 'I'm doing my best and I don't need the
bloody Civil Service on my back.'

He calmed, but not much – down from force ten to
eight or so.

'Better not fall down on this, old boy. The Whitehall
tomahawks are being sharpened. If it goes sour on us
they'll be out hunting for scalps. Mine probably, yours
for a cert.'

I swore at him. 'Go away, Honry. And don't break radio silence again if all you can do is whinge.'

'Look here . . .' The suppressed rage transcended distance and static.

'Give my love to Julia – over and out,' I signed off cheerfully and put paid to further chatter with a flick of the switch.

Bull tittered. 'That's telling 'em, Vee. Put the pin-striped twits in their place.'

And Fiona said: 'Three cheers for Vee. Slayer of the self-righteous, pulverisor of the pompous pricks.' She had been cuddling a bottle for the last hour and was mildly merry.

Which might have accounted for her next announcement.

'I'm going up.'

'To bed?' Bull tilted his watch towards the light. 'It's only eight-fifteen.'

'To bed, yes, but not perchance to dream, my worthy Bull.'

'Perchance to have it off with our guest?' I suggested.

Her eyes focused on me – approximately focused, I should say. It occurred to me she was quite fetchingly done up this evening: tight black skirt with a long slit up the back, medium-high heels, a white shirt-blouse, disappointingly opaque. Sex appeal at its most subtle.

'All right then.' Defiant now. 'What if I am?'

'Help yourself. But don't get so pissed and pally that you forget your name's supposed to be Helen, not Fiona. And I'm saying that for your protection, not mine.'

'Och, away and teach your grandmother.'

She stomped over to the stairs, collecting two glasses to go with the bottle. Bull and I observed her unsteady ascent, leering at her slim legs, sighing in unison when they disappeared onto the next floor.

'How's about that for charity?' I said dolefully to

Bull, popping the cork on a bottle of Château La Clotte 1982 and pouring a taster. 'Yeo gets the girl and I get the vino.'

The heavy, aromatic wine weaved a memorable course down past my palate and brought a glow to my stomach and a tingle to my skin, as such *ne plus ultra* wines are wont to do.

Bull, being of phlegmatic disposition, didn't share my anguish. He acquired a glass and, as a door slammed overhead, we pulled up a chair apiece and insulted three bottles of that marvellous wine by getting thoroughly sloshed on it.

Snow never stays long underfoot in the Hebrides and despite frequent falls over the past fortnight only vestiges of it remained the morning I let Yeo out of his cage.

It was a Tuesday. March was upon us, but no spring in the air this far north. Only clouds like shards of slate reaching across a pale sky, hinting at rain. Only wind, a nor'easter, and fresh-to-freezing.

There was just Yeo and me. Fiona was sleeping late, presumably suffering from exhaustion. Bull, miserably hung over, preferred indoors to out. I was in no less sorry a state, but a brisk walk was my choice of therapy.

'Fiona dropped in last night, I gather.' I spoke ingenuously; we were rounding the northern tip of the island at the time and the pounding inside my head was beginning to slacken.

He slowed, kicked at a grapefruit-sized chunk of loose rock. It bounded away and splashed into a crevice full of slushy water.

'You would know, of course,' he said with some bitterness. 'Did you send her?'

'No.' That much at least was the truth. 'She said she . . . rather fancied you. She went upstairs with a bottle and two glasses. She didn't return to her room until after Bull and I crashed down. Elementary reasoning, my dear David.'

We moved on.

'It was a physical need. I . . . things haven't been so marvellous between me and Carol just lately.' He glanced at me and anger bloomed. 'Why I'm pouring out my problems to you, I can't imagine.'

'Because I'm here. Anyway, so far as Fiona's concerned, feel free. I've no claim on her.'

We came to the headland. From here was an outlook towards the island of Flodday and, behind it, the cupola-shaped Sandray. On the other side of the channel Vatersay looked like two separate islands, the isthmus of low dunes barely showing above the horizon.

Closer at hand all was water, apart from two outposts of rock to the north west of the headland. Every so often a big wave would cannon into the nearer and taller rock with an audible smack, and a plume of spray like a waterspout would be thrown upwards.

'What part of the world is this?' Yeo asked.

I shook my head.

'Scotland? West Coast of Ireland?' He made signs of irritation. 'Do you need to be so bloody secretive?'

'Leave it.' I walked away from him towards Creag Vaslain, an exaggerated mull of land joined to the main island by the umbilicus of a natural arch. The sea was forced into this arch from both sides, a head-on clash that precipitated explosions of spray as fine as smoke. Roar-crash-boom-splash it went, or something akin to it. I didn't have the poetry to do it justice.

When Yeo caught up with me he seemed anxious to make amends and launched into a somewhat disjointed account of his university days with the emphasis on campus frolics. Most of it was boringly familiar. I let him blether.

Presently, as we came to the less rugged, less

weatherbeaten southern promotory, he switched to a discourse on his family.

'My elder daughter, Rowen, gives me a hard time, you know.' He said this with a short laugh that didn't ring quite true.

'Oh?' On hearing Rowen's name my conscience lurched. If he ever got wind of our affair the repercussions would be frightful.

'A bright girl,' he rambled, 'brilliant even. But you wouldn't believe the distance between our politics.'

I didn't tell him I'd watched the 'Live at Home' transmission featuring the Yeos. Or that his daughter and I had spent a weekend in Paris.

'But of course you two have met, haven't you?' This brought me out in a hot flush of guilt, until he went on to say: 'She brought you to that branch meeting in Rotherham last October.'

'It was Sheffield,' I corrected mechanically, giddy with relief. 'And it was November.'

'You passed yourself off as a journalist,' he said, then went quiet. Remembering perhaps, a certain three thugs he, or others acting for him, had set on me.

'Just a ploy. I meet subterfuge with subterfuge.'

'All's fair, is that it?'

'You follow the same dictum, don't you?'

That was when he swung at me. It was some blow, propelled as it must have been by a thirty-day build-up of resentment and animosity. He was a hefty man, in fairly good shape, and when that bunched fist connected with the side of my jaw I was hurled to the ground.

Only semi-conscious, my skull jangling, my body bruised from its contact with Sgeir Varlish, I sprawled there awhile, sky-gazing. It's not often you see pink and purple stars in broad daylight. New experiences should be savoured.

When I got around to picking myself up Yeo was nowhere to be seen. Feeling foolish as well as sore I set off towards the lighthouse, half-hidden behind the slip of the hill. In transit I came upon Fiona; she had been mussel-gathering in the island's only accessible bay and carried a bag, rattling-full. Intent on striding across a series of narrow but deep, snow-packed gullies, she didn't notice me until I called out. Then she glanced up, startled, teetering on a ridge of rock, finally over-balancing to land knee-deep in snow.

'Blast you!' She climbed out, mussels rustling and clinking, then did a double-take. 'Where's the Prisoner of Zenda?'

'Done a bunk.' Coming up to her I extended a helping hand. She knocked it away fiercely.

'Don't give me any of your gentlemanly behaviour. Where's he gone?'

'Who knows? Where *can* he go?'

She looked hard at my chin. 'He belted you, didn't he?' She gave a hiccup of laughter. 'He bloody well belted you.' The hiccup became a torrent of mirth. 'Oh, that's rich – that really is rich. Tough guy Fletcher, hero of Belfast, scourge of the unions. I hope for your sake it never gets out.'

She was still holding her sides when I pushed her off the ridge, bottom-first back into the snow, and in most ungentlemanly fashion marched off and left her cursing and floundering.

Chasing after Yeo would have been an exercise in wasted energy. There was nowhere for him to run. He was bound to this bare rock like the rest of us.

The day wore on. Fiona grew restive with the advent of dusk and proposed combing the island for him before night fell.

'He might be lying hurt somewhere,' she pointed out.

It was a possibility I didn't discount. But I was still piqued and inclined to leave him out there until the cold forced him to seek shelter.

'Let him hurt, eh, Vee?' Bull said, and I couldn't have put it better. Hurting Yeo was what this was all about.

'You're both being petty and childish.'

That was it in a nutshell. And so what?

The TV went on at the usual hour for news from the industrial front. For once it was newsworthy: Yeo's union had suspended the strike threat for three months pending an ACAS enquiry into their claim. It was hoped – a quote from Stan Hanley – that during this period of grace the union's president would be restored to his family and society. Who was really hoping? I wondered. Hanley? The union membership? Not the general public, that was for sure.

My wonderings travelled afield: had Yeo perhaps become a liability? Had the PM pressured the leaderless union executive to rat on him? These were enticing scenarios.

When midnight came with Yeo still at large, I gave in to Fiona's nth entreaty and, armed with powerful flashlights, she and I went out in heavy rain to round him up; Bull's tin foot exempted him from this particular duty.

It took us over an hour to locate him, which wasn't bad going considering the profusion of hiding places. Not that he was hiding. We came – fell, would be closer – across him sitting on a slab on the natural arch, staring out through the drizzle towards the invisible mainland. He was wet through, his hair plastered across his forehead in strands, and seemed to be in a trance of some sort.

Fiona knelt beside him, touched him tentatively. 'David?'

In the glare of the flashlight his pallor was deathly. A shudder ran through him as Fiona repeated his name. He moved then, rousing himself as though awakening from a very deep sleep, and patted Fiona's hand. 'I'm all right.'

'Then get up off your arse and let's get back indoors,'

I said in true RSM-style. Astonishingly be obeyed without demur. Exposure had knocked the stuffing out of him, I suppose.

We groped and blundered back across the island. The rain intensified as we came within sight of the lighthouse and we made a desperate dash for shelter. Yeo was too spent to climb the base unaided. We were still struggling to haul him to the top, me shoving from the rear, Fiona hauling from above, when the downpour ceased.

Bull, bless him, had hot chocolate ready to serve when we staggered into the tropical warmth of the living room. Fiona dosed Yeo liberally with aspirin and other diverse medicaments and packed him off to bed.

Whether she administered any of her distinctive brand of physiotherapy before joining us much later for a nightcap was between her, Yeo, and the mattress. I wasn't interested enough to enquire, and Bull didn't have the nerve. Apart from which, we didn't need to: some women simply can't help advertising it.

Another five days went by and I was no further forward than at the outset. I had now spent some sixty hours, spread over twenty-one sessions, closeted with Yeo. All I had to show for it was a growing stack of video tapes, every last one of which might as well have been blank for all the use it was.

The morning of session number twenty-two, Yeo was on top form and firing on all cylinders. Jovial, argumentative. We had a fine old ding-dong over the causes and failure of the miners' strike of 1844, which was directly responsible for the union's collapse during the slump of three years later. I maintained that the union's inability to rally the entire work force – only about thirty per cent were union members – diluted the impact of the strike and the miners' bargaining power was correspondingly and fatally weakened; a similar situation was ultimately contrived during the miners' strike of 1984–85. Yeo's stance was to blame the wholesale use of scab labour.

It was a lively if irrelevant debate, and my polemic as ever generated outburst after outburst.

'This Government is waging a war of vengeance against eleven million trade unionists!' was one such example.

'Save it for the cheering multitudes,' I said, yawning extravagantly.

Yeo puffed furiously at his pipe. 'History bears me out. Up until . . . what . . . 1824? Or was it '25? Whichever – unions were as good as outlawed, and even after legalisation they were persecuted and spat on by the press. Simply for staging demonstrations, union supporters were jailed, deported, even shot. Don't you think the unions have taken enough punishment from the Government, and that if anyone is due for some revenge it's *us*, not them?'

'It's a twisted ideology. What has revenge to do with trade unionism? Justice, yes; justification, why not? But revenge?' I shook my head in bewilderment. 'You can't go on bearing 19th-century grudges forever.'

'Hah!' He waggled an admonitory pipe. 'Do you think that's what motivates me? Revenge is just the icing on the cake. This whole business – our negotiations with the Boards – is much much more than a punch-swapping exercise.'

If my ears had been antennae they would have quivered. In my bones I felt the gravity pull of a breakthrough: maybe it was the tremor of excitement in his otherwise standard diction that alerted me; maybe boredom was making me think wishfully. Whatever it was, I couldn't let it pass without following through.

I made the necessary mental adjustments. Easy does it, Fletcher. Don't crowd, don't press. Play him on a long leash. Hand him the planks to build his own gallows piece by piece, and afterwards all the rope he needs to swing from them.

But softly . . . softly.

'Big deal.' The ennui came over beautifully strong and he tore into me as I hoped he would. Like all big men who are small at heart, he was hateful of derision.

'Sneer if you like. The unions are only an instrument anyway; only a means to change the country's infrastructure, and in due course its constitution.'

Go on. Go *on*. But he had withdrawn, as he occasionally did, behind a reflective portcullis. Momentum began to run down, like a clockwork toy in need of winding.

I decided to risk a half-turn of the key.

'When you speak of unions in the abstract, you're forgetting they're composed of members. People. They may not see themselves as instruments.'

There, you bastard! There's the fly – now rise to it!

The sneer was on his face now, and that on its own, videoed for the nation, was the stuff of his undoing.

'If the members are so sheep-like, so bedazzled by fighting talk, so afraid to step out of line, so blinkered they can't see they're mortgaging their own freedom, and above all so damned selfish and greedy they'll support *any* claim, no matter how preposterous . . . if they are all these things – and they are – they deserve to lose the lot. They deserve to be no more than slave-workers.'

'Is that what they would be in your rosy, revolutionary Britain?'

'Not . . . exactly.' Evasive now. Was I pushing too hard? 'Not in the sense the Poles and other defeated races were under Hitler.'

'They'll be relieved to hear that. What then? What status will they be granted?' Still I effected slightly-mocking indifference, taunting him. I was sure of my man now. I had his measure. The seeds of his doom were already sown.

'Hard to be specific, but for a start no man will be allowed to choose his own job. People will work where and at what we tell them. And pay rates will no longer be fixed by negotiation, but determined by the overall economic situation and will be unalterable for as long as the State decrees. Against that, against the loss of these . . . these freedoms, if you like . . . we will abolish unemployment – not a single individual out of work to blot the statistics. That I can certainly promise you.'

This was marvellous stuff. If only he would keep it up . . .

'With promises like those, who needs threats? Tell me . . . what will be the rôle of the unions?'

He stuck up a single finger. '*One* union. All for one and one for all. The General Workers' Union.'

The creation castrating its creators. There was a perverted morality about it.

'State-run, of course,' I murmured. 'Toeing the Government line – the Yeo Government.'

A smirk preceded his reply; I would have loved to backhand it away. His mouth was actually opening to speak when from next door came a tremendous, floor-jarring crash. Yeo and I were both startled into paralysis, though mine was fused with fury. Just when I had Yeo talking himself into oblivion . . . ! If he had the tiniest suspicion that a third party was listening in I might as well pack up and head for home right now.

As my muscles unlocked, I fairly bounded across the room and hammered on the door.

'Who's out there?' I roared.

The key scrunched in the lock and the door opened on a shamefaced Bull. I treated him to a silent roasting while saying mildly: 'Oh, it's you, is it?'

'I dropped a grindstone.'

Looking past him I saw the offending item on its side, under the workbench.

'Do your grubbing around when I'm not here in future, Bull, there's a good chap.'

I gave him another blistering glare before slamming the door.

'Bull is a compulsive tinkerer,' I said with a show of exasperation. 'Dismantling the grinder – I ask you.'

Yeo, thank God, was unperturbed. Logically, if Bull had been eavesdropping he would hardly be moving machinery around; I hoped Yeo was a logical man.

The other possible outcome of the disturbance was that he would switch to a different topic, therefore I was now obliged to take the initiative, keep him on course.

'How would a national union be prevented from going on strike?' I said, trying not to gabble in my haste. 'Think of the power they'd wield. You'd be beset with general strikes if you made their lot too unpleasant.'

He had an answer for that too, just as he had an answer for everything.

'You who profess to be so well-informed will recall that the last and only general strike in the UK was not really a *general* strike at all: it was a strike of the miners – of whom there were then about a million – plus the transport workers, some industrial workers, the printers, the builders, and the power supply workers; well under two million bodies. By the tenth day all except the miners were back at work.'

'So. What does that prove? You're simply casting doubts on the ability of unions to control their membership.'

'Not so – and I'll explain why in a minute. The General Strike failed in part because it was badly co-ordinated. It would have been successful had the negotiating committee not betrayed the members and called off the strike without obtaining a single concession or guarantee.'

'So the story goes,' I said, not bothering to hide my cynicism. There were other versions of the reason for the failure of the 1926 General Strike, but this wasn't the moment to air them. 'But nothing in your argument convinces me you'd be able to control the workers on a national basis. You're kidding yourself if you think they'd meekly fall into line.'

'Oh no, I'm not.'

My cue to respond with, 'Oh yes, you are,' of which he saw the funny side.

'Don't forget, Vee,' he went on, 'at the time of the General Strike the unions had only four million members as opposed to eleven million today. Moreover, the TUC didn't call out *all* unions, only those considered to be in key industries. And in those industries the response was one hundred per cent solid. By that yardstick there's no reason to suppose that a strike call to *all* unions, then or now, would not be equally well-subscribed. Stand that premise on its head and what do you get?'

'A no-strike call, you mean? You would expect full backing for a no-strike call--is that what you're saying?'

'Especially since it requires passive rather than active obedience.'

He certainly had it all figured out.

'Let me get this pipe dream straight: you're saying that in the unlikely event that you ever gain control of the work force of this country, unions in their present form will be disbanded. There'll be a single, state-run confederation on the old Soviet model, with, effectively, no rights and no authority.'

'You seem to have the general idea. Admittedly, imposing such a radical change on the masses may stir up resentment among the more militant factions. There may have to be further blood-letting.'

'*Further* blood-letting?'

His stare was a cold-and-frosty morning.

'Bloodless revolutions are preferable but rare. People may . . . get hurt. If they do . . .' He shrugged; no blame would attach to him. 'If they do, it will have been . . . necessary. Victory without sacrifice is not victory at all.'

'The sacrifices you're talking about are people's

lives,' I said, truly angry now. 'Wouldn't it trouble you at all if people died in bringing about your . . . what shall I call it? . . . your day of glory? Including, most probably, some of your own precious union members.'

'My members' interests don't really concern me . . .'

Oh, lovely, lovely! Did you get that, video?

'. . . I'll make use of them for as long as it suits my purpose. The AUEWE is a springboard, no more than that. As I've said, it will cease to exist once we have total control.'

'You didn't answer my question?'

'Do I care about people dying, you mean?'

'Yes. Do you?'

He laughed then, a cracked, callous shout of a laugh that revealed more of a the man inside than a million utterances. He was exposed as a man without morals.

'All I care about is control. Or power, if you prefer.' He peered inside his pipe bowl as if he expected to find his future spelled out there.

'But at *any* price? Is that your ruling commandment – power at any price?'

'You do go on, don't you? You don't make an ome-lette, etcetera.' He put a match to the pipe. 'Strictly between you and me, Vee, so long as we get control I don't give a *fuck* who gets killed.' The obscenity was a bonus; the entire session had been dynamite. My cup of manufactured dirt was full to overflowing.

Then he went and watered down that last damning statement.

'Having said that, I don't really expect much, if any violence.' He grinned disarmingly. 'Not from my people: we're too civilised.'

Another piece of humbug for Bull to censor out.

With the stuff I now had on him – the plan to instal an imitation Soviet règime; deriding the unions and their membership; laughing at the prospect of death in the streets – he was on a fast, downhill slide to extinc-tion. His destiny lay just a few feet away, in a plastic box of tricks. With judicious editing – rephrasing the questions to remove any suggestion of 'leading' – he would emerge as a potential dictator and advocate of genocide. Where once stood an upright family man would now stand a thug.

I made a half-hearted attempt to pump him for details of the *coup d'état* he prophesied with such certainty.

'You keep speaking of "we",' I said. 'Who else is committed to this takeover? Who'll be carrying the battle flags alongside you on the Great Day? And speaking of the Great Day – when is it to be? I'd like to make a note in my diary to be somewhere else.'

He squinted slyly at me and tilted back on his chair. 'Now you wouldn't expect me to name names and date dates, would you? I don't mind talking to you along hypothetical lines – it's just hot air, after all. Hard information is a different-coloured horse altogether.'

The 'hot-air' but would have to be chopped. The rest was a usable epilogue: it proved there was more to Yeo's grandiose visions than mere aspiration.

'It was worth a try.'

I let it go at that. What was already on tape would more than suffice to bring Operation Hangman to a happy conclusion.

'You won't be seeing me again; not here,' I said, and in his surprise he let his chair crash back onto all four legs. 'I've some urgent business to see to in London.'

'Where does that leave me?' No suspicion, just a natural anxiety about his own future.

'You'll be here a while yet. A week, perhaps ten days.'

'You're not having me on?'

'No. You're the reason for my trip to London.' This was pure improvisation. 'To assess the likely outcome of your return.'

We were both standing now.

'You don't need to go to London for that. I can tell you myself.'

'I dare say.'

He nodded. 'The whole pathetic exercise will prove to have been a waste of time and money. What's more, when I get back . . .' He faltered.

'When you get back – what?'

'You'll see,' he muttered, perhaps waking up to the danger of making threats while still in captivity.

The flint-chip eyes were probing mine and for an instant another face was superimposed upon his: a face a generation older, and at once familiar.

Yeo was frowning.

'What is it?'

'Nothing.' I shook off the spooky feeling. 'Nothing.'

He grunted, became absorbed in gouging out his pipe.

'I'll be off then,' I said.

He didn't offer to shake hands, which was a relief of sorts, and I left him decoking his pipe, not even looking at me. So much for a beautiful relationship.

Unusually, I went down the staircase at a plod. Seeing again the duplicated faces – one in the flesh and close enough to touch, the other in my mind yet not a fantasy; the image of a man who, even more than I, wished Yeo ill – the 5th Earl of Deverill.

The news that evening devoted several minutes to a progress review of the search for Yeo, including an interview with the co-ordinating CID officer, Detective Chief Superintendant Graham Mellow. Cheerless and overweight, with jowls that waggled when he spoke, he was not 'terribly optimistic' about the prospects of tracing Yeo.

'After five weeks the trail's cold,' he admitted morosely. 'We've run out of leads to follow.'

Did he fear for Mr Yeo's safety, the reporter asked. The lugubrious head shook. Yes and no, was Mellow's non-answer, and when pressed he confirmed that the motive behind the kidnapping still mystified him, and partly contributed to his difficulties. Did he believe it was politically inspired? Yes, he did. No ransom demand had been made, which after all these weeks tended to rule out a financial objective.

'Might it not perhaps be personal?' the reporter suggested.

'It's unlikely, we think. We have more . . . tenable theories.'

'But so far only theories. No real clues.'

The policeman, to give him his due, was abashed.

'Hardly a one – though naturally we are pursuing the case with all vigour.'

'Naturally.' The reporter's voice was as dry as a desert wind.

After the news I went out for a last walkabout with Bull. I had already radioed a request to Sellar to collect me in the morning and apart from such last-minute impedimenta as toothbrush and shaver I was all packed and raring to go. Would I miss Sgeir Varlish? Sure. Like I missed not having pointed ears.

Rough ground and Bull's artificial foot did not mix well, so we went at the most leisurely of paces. Along the low cliffs we strolled. It was warm for early March and the sun was sinking behind heaped purple clouds, throwing out golden rays in a classic fan.

'Tapes all packed?' I asked him.

'Yes – twenty-four in all. Every one marked with the date.' He sounded deflated. If I was any judge, a return to the urban treadmill was not a prospect he relished.

'You think you've done it, Vee?' he said. 'You've really nailed the bastard?'

I put my arm around those broad, meaty shoulders. 'Bull . . . if the whole fucking union movement doesn't disown him after they've seen that tape, I'll take a slow boat to Irkutsk.'

'Irkutsk? But that's in the middle of Russia. You couldn't get there by boat.'

'Well, yes . . . that's true. But you know how I like to hedge my bets.'

We burst out laughing simultaneously, followed up with a mock punch-up, then, a little breathlessly resumed our walk, descending now as we neared the headland. The sea was languid, sliding in and out of the claw of rocks that formed natural breakwaters all along this stretch of seaboard.

'You're quite clear on what to do after I've left?' I'll run through it again if you wish.'

'No need. Yeo's to leave on Sunday with Fiona. He's to be hooded, handcuffed hand and foot. The day after, I'm to remove all non-combustible equipment from the lighthouse and set fire to the place. Sellar will pick me up, with the equipment, at 15.00 hours.' He glanced at me. 'The structure itself won't burn, you do realise that? No matter how much diesel fuel I douse it with.'

'Give me credit for some intelligence.' I stumbled on the uneven terrain, and Bull grabbed my arm. 'Thanks – you'd think I was the one with the game leg.'

'What about explosives?'

'I did consider it. Flatten the place – turn it into rubble and shove the lot into the sea. But that would have meant a demolition team and still more witnesses, more mouths to gag. On balance, leaving it standing is the lesser risk. So long as all evidence of our improvements is eliminated, that's all that really matters.'

He gave a doubtful grunt.

'Remember,' I said. 'I want you in London by Monday night. As soon as Yeo surfaces he'll start yelling murder. That tape has got to be processed damn fast, even if it means working round the clock.'

'Why can't you get some government bod to do it?' he grumbled. 'You don't need me.'

'Because – again – the smaller the number of people

who know about this business the tighter we'll be able to keep the lid on it. Security, sergeant, security. Have you forgotten your Belfast tours? It won't take more than a couple of days at the most; I'll have run through it myself before you show up. All you'll have to do is go snip-snip.'

'It's not like that; this is a video-tape, not a film. Taking out the unwanted sections is a doddle – even you could do it. The art is in matching up the bits on either side to obtain a smooth transition. For instance . . .'

I made a hissing noise through my teeth. 'Spare me the technicalities, Bull. Will an extra grand cover it?'

'Nicely.' He was damn careful not to appear too satisfied. 'But that'll buy you two working days – no more.'

'You should join a union.'

'I already did,' he said, grinning broadly.

'Heretic.'

The helicopter came up over the cliff edge like a bouncing ball, its white fuselage scarring the field-grey skies, stirring up the island's winged inhabitants into a frenzy of aerobatics and vocal protest.

'I've known choppers to be brought down by birds,' Bull commented maliciously.

'Cheerful sod.' Fiona growled; she was in poor humour this morning. It could have been the thought of life on Sgeir Varlish without me. It could have been – and probably was – nothing of the kind. I mean, we hardly hit it off together. The most you could say was that we'd learned to share the same billet without coming to blows. As for sex . . . *what* sex?

The helicopter was making a controlled descent, sideways on to us. Bull threw Sellar a mock salute; the Scotsman, hands full, responded with a bare nod. Wheels met rock and I moved forward, armed with my

263

suitcases, Bull at my heels carrying the heavy metal case containing the video cassettes.

Sellar opened the door for me. 'Good morning, good morning,' he cried, as cheerful as Fiona was sober.

The engine was still running, and the rotor swishing past overhead made me duck instinctively as I went under it.

'You're late,' I accused. He had been due at ten and it was now closer to eleven.

'Aye, you're right.' No excuse was offered.

The metal case came through the door behind me, handled by Bull as if it were stuffed with rare *objets d'art*.

'See you in London,' I shouted at him, in competition with the racket from the engine. Fiona had stayed outside the wash of the rotor and thus of earshot, so I blew her a goodbye kiss, which she returned without ardour.

I was still fiddling with my seat-belt when Sellar did his usual stomach-sinking take-off, and we swept away over the hill, the island shrinking in size until it was no more than a blemish on the great, grey sweep of the Atlantic. It began to rain thinly. Outlines blurred and sea and land became as one.

I had murmured no fond farewells to Sgeir Varlish – only fervent wishes never to set foot on it again.

III
POWER MADNESS

Chapter Seventeen

The welcome home from Julia was much as Fiona's goodbye kiss – without ardour. She was uncommunicative and downright surly, and, moreover, indisposed to grant conjugal rights. An unkind cut indeed, the longest ever coitus interruptus of my adult life.

'You know I hate doing it when I'm having my period,' was her sole sop to lust and ego. I didn't push it. Sex given grudgingly was no sex at all in my book.

The vaginal door was still shut tight when Yeo's return to the bosom of family and society was announced very late on Sunday evening. A naughty French film on BBC2 was interrupted by a news flash, giving out that Yeo had walked into a police station in Tenbury Wells, a village near Ludlow, just over an hour ago. Whence, after a short interview with a senior police officer, he had been driven home. No further details available. Back to the tits and bottoms.

By midday on Monday the press were snapping at Yeo's heels. The one o'clock news on Channel 4 showed their massed ranks lined up before his house like a beseiging army. But the drawbridge was raised and several policemen patrolled between it and the white trellis fence that was bulging before the press of the press. Mr Yeo, so we were told, would be seeing the police during the afternoon and had consented to a press conference at Power Base afterwards. At that point the factual reporting ceased and Channel 4's outside reporter engaged in some fanciful speculation on Yeo's 'five week ordeal'. I was listening in amusement when Julia breezed in, accused me of crowing over 'that poor man', tartly informed me that lunch was ready, and breezed out again. Livid, I charged after her, set on a good, old-fashioned row, changed my mind in mid-hall, and quit the house instead. Undeterred by the curtain of rain, I splattered down the steps to the Bentley, which opportunely was parked close by. Spraying gravel in my wake, I took off down the drive and into Beaconsfield, to a solitary, cold table lunch at the Bellhouse Hotel.

If nothing else the interlude cooled me off, and my speed during the return to Kingscourt was but a fraction of that at which I left it. It was just as well, for, rounding the sharpish curve before the entrance to the drive I had to swerve to avoid a carelessly parked metallic blue saloon. I made the usual comments about inconsiderate drivers and was passing through the gateway when recognition sank in: barring a gargan- tuan coincidence, the blue car belonged to Rowen. I stamped on the brakes, left the Bentley blocking the drive, and met her approximately halfway between the two vehicles.

She was as comely as I remembered. Her hair was encircled by the Indian-maiden headband that suited her dark features so well, and she was wearing a short leather coat over a knee-length pleated skirt and matching leather boots. Neatly, if unsensationally pack- aged.

She had been crying recently.

As it was with Julia, so too with Rowen – I was not in favour. I quickly found out why.

'How could you, Vee?'

'Rowen!' I put my hand out to her, but she slapped it away.

'My father. How *could* you?'

Now what? Deny it and fall back on my alibi? That was fine for the police; Rowen would laugh – or spit – in my face. If her father had named me to his wife and children, she wouldn't question the truth of it. Nor would I, in her place.

So, no lies, no excuses.

'Rowen . . .' I groped for the right approach. 'Don't concern yourself with things that are none of your concern.'

'Not my concern!' she yelled, and tears mingled with the rain on her cheeks. 'What are you talking about? He's my father, you . . . you swine!'

No use reminding her of her offer to betray that same father not so very long ago – an offer I had declined.

A car came round the corner, travelling too fast, tyres hissing on the wet tarmac, at once braking and swerving to avoid Rowen's Honda. A face, flushed with near-miss fright, glared at us and I lip-read a string of rude words.

I was in no mood to be gentle with Rowen. 'I mean don't concern yourself with me and the things *I* have to do.' I wiped rain from my eyes. The drizzle was working back up to deluge strength. 'That's all.'

I turned from her and walked back to the Bentley. It had been good while it lasted, our short, spicy fling, but now it was over. Swept away by circumstances, like smoke in the breeze.

I hurled the car up the drive to the other, equally disenchanted woman in my life.

Honry phoned later on that wettest of afternoons to invite me to join him at home to watch the live telecast of Yeo's press conference, scheduled for 6.00 pm. After-wards we could discuss its implications for Operation Hangman, he suggested. Good idea, I agreed. Julia being such lousy company, any excuse to get out of the house was welcome.

I double-parked in Belgrave Square, was admitted by Honry's man and shown into the drawing-room where a smokeless fire pulsed out heat. Honry was in his favourite leather armchair, in a sea of multi-hued paperwork. His greeting was warm.

'Damn good to see you again, Vee, it really is.'

'You too, Honry. I only wish there were other members of Julia's family I could say the same to.'

'Er . . . yes, well . . .' Honry was strong on family loyalty and could never be drawn. Like Julia. *In extremis* the blood ties would be the last to be cut.

While he fixed drinks I admired the typically gloomy Van Ruisdael original over the bureau: a ruined castle throwing long evening shadows over a rushing stream. The atmosphere reached out and wrapped itself around you. Marvellous.

'A bit early for the hard stuff, I know,' Honry apologised, placing a well-charged glass in my hand. 'But it'll help us keep a sense of perspective while we listen to Yeo mouthing off. He's bound to be at his injured, self-righteous worst.'

'At least the subject matter won't be political.'

'You think? You may be sure, my dear chap, that if there's a molecule of political capital to be wrung out of this business, Yeo will wring it.'

The conference was to feature in a specially-extended version of the BBC's Evening News. For once, since the transmission was live and timed to start at 6.00 pm, the same as the news, we were spared a leisurely build-up. From the newscaster at her desk we were dumped in the back row of the stalls in the conference hall at Power Base. It was packed to standing room only, and Yeo was already speaking from the pulpit when we dropped in. The camera instantly zoomed in and treated us to a Yeo close-up. As if I hadn't had my fill of such treats lately.

'. . . I was the victim of a government or government-backed plot.' Yeo was off to a flying start. 'No more, no less.'

Uproar. Yeo was immediately peppered with questions from all corners of the hall.

'One at a time, gentlemen, please!' an aide on Yeo's flank bellowed into the mike. The tumult ebbed; a lone voice from the depths of the gathering called: 'What makes you say the Government is behind your abduction, Mr Yeo? That's . . . er . . . quite an accusation.'

Amused derision flowed across the hall.

Yeo didn't appreciate the joke.

'It's quite clear,' he snapped, 'to anyone with any IQ rating at all, that the Government saw me as a threat and wanted me out of the way in the hope of persuading the AUEWE to call off its strike. This they have achieved. Except that the issue, our claim, still has not been settled. On Monday next the union executive will meet to decide its next move. It's not for me to predict the outcome of that meeting, but I shall be surprised if my colleagues and I differ as to the appropriate course of action.'

So would I.

'He's getting back into his stride even quicker than I expected,' I said to Honry.

He tore himself away from his Scotch to grunt: 'All the more justification for Hangman.'

'And what is more,' Yeo's voice reached a rabble-rousing crescendo, 'we are going to extract every last percentage decimal point from them. That, gentlemen, is neither threat nor promise – it's a foregone conclusion.'

A thin applause was heard around the hall: representatives of the socialist press.

'Getting back to the kidnapping, Mr Yeo,' from the back of the hall, 'what actual proof have you of the Government's complicity?'

Yeo had clearly not considered it.

'Er . . . I'm sorry. I don't quite . . .'

'Proof.' It had an uncompromising ring. 'What *proof* do you have that the Government was behind it all?'

Yeo's tongue touched his lips; his discomfiture was

stark. Where he should have been content to make ripples, he had made a tidal wave.

He managed a partial recovery. 'One of the gang at least is a Government employee.'

Here and there a buzz of interest. Pens scribbled in notebooks. The camera floated over a bearded individual rattling away into a pocket dictaphone.

'Is that all?' The same voice, edged with incredulity.

'I'm afraid I'm not at liberty to add to what I've already said on the subject.'

'Mr Yeo! Mr Yeo!' Competition for the great man's ear was fierce.

He made a selection from a multitude of Nazi salutes.

'Where were you held?' A North Country accent.

'In a disused lighthouse,' Yeo said without emotion, 'on an island. The exact location was kept from me: off the coast of Scotland possibly. Almost certainly in the British Isles.'

'How can you be so certain about that?'

'In the room where I was kept someone had scribbled on the wall in English.'

That was hardly conclusive, though none of the gathering pointed out as much.

'Were you ill-treated?' This from a woman reporter.

'Not in the slightest. I could have used more exercise – that's my only real complaint.'

Unexpectedly he was passing up the opportunity for propaganda. Had he claimed to have been beaten it would have gained him sympathy. In some respects he was a man of integrity.

'How was the abduction carried out? Can you describe the events in sequence?'

'Yes, I think so . . . up to the point where I was chloroformed. We were within half-a-mile of my home, on a road called World's End Lane – it runs along the edge of the Enfield Golf Course. Tony Widdowson, my . . . er . . . associate, was driving and I was sitting beside him. We had just passed the hospital when this car, a Sierra, overtook us and forced us onto the verge. It was very skilfully done. While we sat there, collecting our wits and wondering what on earth it was all about, two men in stocking face masks jumped out of the Sierra and came at us, one on either side. Tony was going to tackle them, but I restrained him; they were both armed and any resistance would have been pointless and possibly fatal. We weren't to know what their intentions were.'

'This Tony Widdowson – would he be your minder?'

'My minder?' Yeo wouldn't want the public to learn he had a personal bodyguard. It didn't ring respectable. 'I suppose he could be called that. Officially he's employed as my driver and personal assistant, but someone in my position is bound to make a *few* enemies . . .'

An initial low-level rumble of amusement from the press grew to hysterical laughter. This was the Yeo they loved – the sardonic humour, the frank acceptance of antipathy. As a man he was not disliked by the press; and as a trade union leader he was always newsworthy, which made him popular professionally.

'What did they do to you, these masked men?' was the next question, when the commotion had subsided.

'Tony was ordered out of the car and they hit him over the head with what looked like a length of hose. Then I was forced into their car at gunpoint.'

'Was there no other traffic?'

'Not that I recall. It's a very quiet road once you get beyond the hospital; mostly used by residents. It all happened very quickly, you understand . . . a minute at the most, from start to finish. I don't mind admitting, it was a very, very slick operation.'

Bob Chadwick, if he was watching, would be warmed by such eulogy.

'Anyway . . . to continue . . . they chloroformed me

and when I came to I was in a helicopter. Handcuffed and with a hood over my head.'

'A helicopter?' Several voices spoke thus.

'Yes. With two men, but different men from the two with the masks, I'm quite sure of that. One was Scottish. The other . . .' Here he hesitated.

'What about the other?'

'I . . . he's the Government employee I mentioned. He's known to me personally.'

'*Who?*' came the roar from the pack.

I tensed, dreading the public indictment, but aware of its inevitability.

'I am advised,' Yeo replied, 'not to publicly name the person concerned. The matter is now in the hands of the police and they will presumably issue an official statement in due course.'

A disappointed rumble greeted this backsliding; a disappointment I naturally didn't share.

The camera focused on various individual reporters in turn, some scribbling frantically, others with arms stuck up like schoolboys asking to leave the classroom.

'How many were there altogether in the gang, Mr Yeo?'

'Well . . . there were the two with masks, plus two in the helicopter, and two, plus one from the helicopter, at the lighthouse: six in all. As to how many others were masterminding the operation from afar . . . I trust we shall presently learn.'

A ball of glowing clinker rolled off the top of the fire into the hearth. Honry's eyes never left the screen as he retrieved it with a pair of brass tongs.

'When did you get back to London?' A foreigner: thick, guttural pronunciation.

'The gang flew me, hooded and handcuffed again, to somewhere in Shropshire. I think it was the same helicopter; definitely the same pilot, the Scotsman.'

Sellar, unlike Chadwick, would be shitting large

bricks at this repeated reference to 'the Scotsman'.

'Didn't they extract any promises from you?' A woman.

'What sort of promises?' Yeo's puzzlement was an answer in itself.

'Not to call a strike, for a start.' The tone was mildly quizzical. 'If the motives behind your kidnapping were political, I would have thought the kidnappers would demand a no-strike agreement in exchange for your freedom. Alternatively, hung on to you a while longer. Like indefinitely.'

'That woman's got her head screwed on,' Honry remarked. 'Yeo should have asked himself that question.'

Maybe he really wasn't guileful. Maybe he really did amount to no more than a top-flight public speaker with a mesmeric style and a ruthless ambition.

In any event, he wasn't long in disposing of his latest inquisitor.

'Clearly the . . . instigators hoped for a respite; a short-term gain in the hope that once the strike had been deferred, I would never be able to reactivate it. If that *was* their motive . . .' The pulpit was thumped; we were off again, 'if they supposed the union executive and its membership to be so feeble as to let my absence have more than a passing impact on their determination to obtain justice, then they will very soon discover how wrong they were!' His voice was rising with every word uttered. 'Justice is what we demand!' The pulpit soaked up more punishment. 'And justice we shall have!'

After that the conference tended to become a bit of a free-for-all, drifting away from the kidnapping to union and quasi-political matters. By 6.20pm, when the proceedings were wound up, the lure of drinks and canapés had already exacted a toll on a large minority of the journalists in the hall.

So it was back to the studio for the rest of the news.

Honry lowered the volume remotely, but left the picture. 'Well?'

'He's given better performances,' I said, and picked up my glass to perambulate around the room with. 'Nothing there for us to worry about. He hasn't worked out what the snatch was really all in aid of. He's back in the limelight and back at the head of his legions, and that's all he cares about. Now he can prance and posture and make up for all those weeks in oblivion. The strike will be on again – just as soon as he can get his cronies to rubber-stamp it. As he sees it, nothing's changed.'

Rain beat at the window. It was apt music, symbolic of the country's economic climate. Moribund Britain. Entering its moral and industrial twilight. And no discernible means of slowing, let along stopping or – flight of fancy – reversing the process.

The State of the Nation depressed me everincreasingly of late as the decline became more absolute. Was it worth fighting for? I asked myself. Was there enough left of the old fabric to restore, or was it threadbare, beyond even the most rudimentary patching-up?

'Vee?' Honry had come to stand beside me.

'M'mm?'

'Do you still think it'll work? Are we going to win?'

I looked sideways at him. 'Ask me again tomorrow, when you've seen the video.' I knocked back the rest of my Scotch. It did me a power of good. Unasked, I took my glass to the liquor cabinet and replenished it. 'It'll work,' I said, toasting him flippantly. 'It'll work because you and your Civil Service chums will make it work. Because you don't really have any choice.'

I knocked back most of my drink, suppressed a belch. 'Do you . . . old boy?'

*   *   *

276

In the games room of Lord Deverill's mansion, within walls that groaned under the largest and most diverse collection of hunting trophies I had ever been stared at by, were congregated six people: six people privileged to be in on the secret of the disappearance of David Yeo. Honry, my arch-accomplice; Lord Deverill, my staunchest ally; Goronwy Rees, who still reckoned his way was better; Bull and Fiona. And of course, myself. No Ministers of the Crown, nor members of the committee, were privy to the cover-to-cover story, though in the case of the Ministers, ignorance was through choice: from the beginning they had adopted a wise-monkeys posture.

A largish, portable TV set had been set up on a card table and six chairs arranged in an arc before it – a makeshift cinema. While Bull wired up a video unit to the receiver, Lord Deverill fretted with impatience. I persuaded him to sit down, and sighing, he took the empty chair to my right.

'I'm looking forward to this,' he confided, offering a cigar in a tube. We both lit up and created instant smog. Fiona, on my left, coughed ostentatiously.

'Don't forget this is the unedited original,' I said to the room at large. 'Bull only arrived late last night; he'll be censoring it over the next two days.'

'All this talk of censorship,' Honry said with nervous jocularity. 'Goodness me. It's not a "nasty", is it, old boy?'

'Depends on your point of view.'

Rees sniggered. 'If it features Yeo in close-up, it'll be as nasty as they come.'

Conversation ceased as the show got on the road. There was the customary clunk, rattle, whirr, as the video unit ingested the cassette, followed by grey flickerings on the screen. Then, without title, or credits, or fanfare, the arch-villain himself stood revealed, pulling up his chair, placing pipe and tobacco on the table. No part of me was visible. Intentionally.

This was the tape of the twenty-second session: the session that rendered the other twenty-one defunct. The opening line was mine, and it came over bell-clear. As part of the editing process Bull would distort my voice – 'fuzzification' he called it – a necessary precaution against a voice-print test.

'Did you hear that rain last night?' said the invisible me. 'It kept me awake.'

'Not me,' Yeo replied. 'I haven't slept as well in weeks.'

This was typical of the small talk Yeo and I used to indulge in before the conversation turned towards politics and industrial relations.

The six of us sat through the debate over the 1844 miners' strike and Yeo's ribald dissection of the Tory Government's attitude towards trade unionism. Deverill was beginning to stir restlessly when Yeo dropped the first hint of what was to come.

'. . . negotiations with the Boards – is much much more than a punch-swapping exercise.'

'Big deal,' from me, provoking him to indiscretion.

'Sneer if you like. The unions are only an instrument anyway; only a means to change the country's infrastructure, and in due course its constitution.'

I had spent sixty or more hours plucking and trussing him. He was oven-ready. All I'd to do was stick him in, set the timer, and let him roast himself.

The air around me became electrified as the tape unwound. Deverill leaned forward, hands on knees, expression growing more rapt by the minute as Yeo hammered nail after nail into his own coffin lid. When it came to the biggest nail of all, '. . . so long as we get control I don't give a *fuck* who gets killed,' there was at least one gasp of disbelief – from Honry, I think – and a broad, gloating grin lit up Deverill's features.

The rest of the tape was anti-climactic, though Bull let it run on up to the point where I left Yeo.

There followed a silence which lasted about five

seconds. Then Deverill said quietly to me: 'Congratulations. It's a masterpiece.'

'I take back all I said against it.' Coming from Rees this was praise of the highest order.

'You mentioned editing,' Deverill said. 'What's to edit? It sounded word-perfect to me.'

'Not a lot. The odd qualification here, the odd nuance there. I especially want to eliminate comments by Yeo which tend to water down his absolute ruthlessness. I'll give you an example . . .' I had my notes on my lap; I selected a blue-pencilled section. 'Here Yeo says, "I don't give a fuck who gets killed . . ."'

'Marvellous, that,' Rees enthused.

'Quite – but he goes on: "Having said that, I don't really expect much, if any violence. Not from my people." Now that must either be changed to, "I expect violence – from my people," or, if it doesn't ring true, or can't be done without damaging the integrity of the tape, it'll have to be wiped altogether.'

'I see what you mean. Clever stuff this interrogation business.'

'On the whole though, the amount of reprocessing required will be insignificant: what we have here is stark, undiluted Yeo.' I drew on my cigar, puffed smoke at Bull, who was messing about with the video. 'Bull here will also alter my voice, make it unrecognisable.'

'With your alibi you don't need to worry about that,' Honry drawled.

'All the same, Honry, I do worry.'

'Have it your own way, old sport.'

'Sensible you,' Fiona murmured in my left ear.

We turned to the next phase of Hangman.

'How soon will the tape be ready for sending out?' Honry asked, looking from me to Bull.

'Bull?' I prompted.

'Tomorrow morning at the earliest. Safer really to say evening.'

Honry played with his moustache. 'Tomorrow evening, eh? Meaning Thursday a.m. before we get copies into circulation.'

'Say Thursday afternoon for the copies.' Bull unplugged the video lead and began to coil it.

'All right. Then the story goes to the press on Thursday morning and the tapes later on the same day.'

Deverill had moved away from Fiona and was pacing back and forth past the row of chairs.

'We are agreed that the source of the story is to be an anonymous caller supposedly representing Yeo's kidnappers who, in turn, were supposedly financed by a consortium of wealthy businessmen – forever to remain faceless and nameless. Have I got it right?'

'Spot on,' I said. 'Care to be the anonymous caller?'

His laugh was sardonic.

'You leave me out of it. I'm willing to be a faceless mogul, but I'm not doing any handkerchief-over-the-mouth telephoning to the *News of the World*.'

'*The Times*,' Honry corrected with a sniff of reproof. 'You'll liaise with me on the mechanics of the operation?' This to Rees.

The MoD man nodded, got up. 'If that's all then. Fiona and I have to be back in London by four.'

Deverill, with his olde-worlde courtesy, went to show them out.

As I was donning my coat Honry drew up alongside.

'I have it on good authority that the police will be calling on you this afternoon or tonight.'

'Thanks for the tip. Anybody I know?'

'DCS Mellow. He's been handling the case from Day 1.'

'Saw him on the box while I was . . . away. Is he Special Branch?'

Honry grimaced. 'No, but he's considered a nasty piece of work. Also a first-rate detective. Don't get on the wrong side of him, old top.' His mouth set in a downward curve. 'Your chum Hutton will be with him.'

'Wonderful. Are my witnesses well-schooled in their alibis?'

'Rest assured, dear boy, rest assured. You've got their sworn depositions, haven't you?'

'Oh yes, I've got those – for what they're worth. I'm still waiting for the balance of my pay cheque though.'

'Should be through tomorrow,' he said smoothly – too smoothly. Again Julia's warning sounded its knell.

'Well, if I go down I take the whole blooming caboodle with me. We're all passengers on the same *Titanic*.'

He took it well: a nervous throat-clearing, a vague demur.

'Ready?' I called to Bull, who was snapping the locks of the video transit case. We were driving back together.

He limped across with his equipment, gazing around at the horned heads that leered from all four walls, dead witnesses to our perfidy.

'The Deverills did a good culling job over there in Africa,' he said, speaking as if to himself.

'Not the present incumbent,' Honry said, unsmiling, not caring for the unspoken criticism of the noblesse.

The look Bull gave him was almost pitying. 'We're all responsible,' was his cutting retort. Then he hurried out, brushing past the returning Deverill.

'Animal lover,' I explained to Honry and the uncomprehending Earl.

The three of us went down the wide, marble-tiled hall and parted at the door; Deverill's handshake was warm.

'Until Saturday,' he said, this being the day set for our next conference, whose purpose was to be an appraisal of public and union reaction to the tape.

He stayed at the door until we drove away.

Chapter Eighteen

Julia and I were in the thick of an after-dinner dust-up – the why and the wherefore escape me – when Willoughby discreetly intervened to announce: 'Three gentlemen from the police to see Mr Fletcher,' which stilled Julia in mid-insult.

I hadn't warned her of the prospect of a visit from the Bill. She reacted with a triumphant 'Hah!'

'Meaning?'

'Meaning it serves you bloody well right.'

I received my callers in the study. Intros were made: Detective Chief Superintendent Mellow, big in all directions, and wearing an immaculate, belted trench-coat. Detective Inspector Dale, ratfaced, and, in contrast to Mellow, a stick insect body with narrow, hunched shoulders. And let us not forget DCI Mike Hutton, Special Branch's own. Smiles were out, a bad omen.

'Shall we sit down?' I said and set an example by doing so.

Mellow chose the only other armchair, close to the fire; Hutton and Dale sat primly side by side on the settee, like a pair of maiden aunts.

'Mr Fletcher,' Mellow began heavily; strangely for such a high ranking officer he seemed ill at ease. 'I am leading the investigation into the alleged abduction of one David John Yeo on Saturday 30th January, and his subsequent unlawful detention.'

That was some mouthful, and he hadn't stumbled over a single syllable. Anyway I nodded to show I was paying attention. Hutton had his legs crossed and was swinging the upper one from the knee. His face was plaster-cast, but his disinterest was too studied to be real.

'A complaint has been laid by the said Mr Yeo to the effect that you were a party to his abduction. Specifically that you accompanied him in the helicopter that was used to transport him from the mainland to the island and that you were with him throughout his period of detention.'

Now to test my acting ability. I avoided clichéd responses: dropping jaw, spluttered expostulations, and so on. Instead I let my expression slowly harden and my gaze pass to Hutton then on to Dale as if expecting them to refute the slander.

'Do you wish to reply to Mr Yeo's allegations?' Mellow enquired, when I offered no comment.

Outside, in the hush before I spoke, I heard the wind moan through the elms. It was a wild night. It suited my mood.

'Mr Yeo has already accused the Government of having engineered his disappearance,' I said at last. 'If he's to make the charge stick he needs a Government fall-guy: why not me?'

'I prefer to put that question differently – *why* you?'

My gaze again wandered to Hutton.

'Mr Hutton might be able to shed some light on that, Superintendent.'

'Chief Superintendent.' Mellow was as pedantic as I had expected. '*You* tell me, Mr Fletcher.'

'A few years ago I worked for the DTI. I headed a special IR unit and made a few enemies among the union bluebloods. You could say it makes me a logical scapegoat.'

Mellow was not impressed by my reasoning.

'That's a dubious hypothesis, if you don't mind me saying so, sir. This IR unit – what was your function in it?'

'Confidential,' I said with the relish of a poker player slapping a royal flush on the table.

Hutton confirmed I was bound by the Official Secrets Act.

Mellow was unimpressed. He waved Hutton aside as if he and Official Secrets were of no more consequence than a persistent wasp.

'Let me help you overcome your . . . er . . . scruples. Let me tell you what I already know.'

'Do,' I murmured.

'You were employed to infiltrate trade unions, to obtain inside information, and to generally disrupt and subvert. We have reason to believe the suicide of Eric Bottomley in 1989 arose out of your activities.'

'Eric who?'

He just glared. He wasn't fooled.

'You're still in confidential territory, Chief Superintendent. I deny nothing, I admit nothing. However, let's suppose you are right, and that I am – was – all these things; would it not explain why Yeo has singled me out as whipping boy for the Government? As an instrument of the Government's anti-union policies I would deserve to be punished, would I not? Since, in law, I have committed no crime, he's invented one for me.'

'Are you suggesting that Mr Yeo dreamed up his abduction.'

'Not at all. Only that he's dreamed me up as the culprit.'

'All right then – are you suggesting he's prepared to see you jailed for a crime you didn't commit?'

I drummed fingers on the chair arm to show my exasperation. 'If Yeo thought me guilty of plotting against the trade union movement, he would sell his mother into slavery to put his stop to it. And if you haven't deduced that much yourself, then you don't know Yeo!'

Mellow grew stern. 'That, if I may say so, sir, is an

entirely speculative view. We deal in evidence, not highly-coloured opinions.'

'You're dealing in lies at the moment,' I said with just the right measure of tartness. 'Maybe I should call my solicitor.'

Mellow bristled. 'This is an informal discussion, Mr Fletcher. When a complaint has been made and a serious crime committed, it must be checked out.' He leaned back and the sweeping wings of the chair swallowed him up. 'Can you account for your movements between 30th January and the middle of March?'

'Christ, no. Not in detail; not every day individually.'

'Quite. But where, approximately, did you spend most of this period. If not on an island with Mr Yeo.' And he came close to smiling, almost became human. Almost. He was a man who would ration his humanity.

I looked him in the eye. 'How about Taormina-Mazzarò?'

'Tor . . . Tar . . .' He gave up. 'Where?'

'Taormina-Mazzarò. Sicily. I was there for two of your six weeks.'

'Ah.'

'At the Hotel Mazzarò. I can recommend it.'

Dale, I observed, was now making frantic notes. Hutton continued to swing his leg.

'Who was with you? Your wife, I suppose.'

'Suppose again, Chief Superintendant. I went alone.'

Another 'Ah', deeper, more expressive.

'You stayed at the hotel alone then?'

'Quite, quite alone.' The folds of doubt were stacking up in his face. Then I played my trump cards. 'On the other hand, I entertained and was entertained by, a number of eminent English families who own property in the area. Now let me see . . .' I put on a memory-searching frown, 'Sir Robert and Lady Wilde – I dined with them twice, and we went sailing together in the Straits. Then there was the author, Ian Ireland – he's a

permanent resident, married to an Italian girl . . .
ravishing; we met casually half-a-dozen times at least.
Oh, and the Turnbulls . . . mustn't forget them . . .'

'The Turnbulls?' Mellow was looking as sour as cur-
dled milk by now.

'James and Sarah. He's the MP for . . .'

'Never mind.' Mellow's sourness had become acid. 'I
think I'm getting the idea, Mr Fletcher. What was the
date of your return to the UK?'

'The 14th February, I believe . . . no, sorry, the 15th.
It was a Monday. Tell you what,' I made as if to rise,
'I'm pretty sure I still have the airline ticket counterfoil.
Would you like to see it?'

'Don't trouble yourself, sir. As I say, this is off the
record.' He hadn't said, but I wasn't about to dispute
the point.

'Perhaps the hotel bill then and my Diner's Club
receipt?' Oh, I was a helpful-co-operative bastard.

'Not necessary, thank you. Perhaps . . .' His voice
tapered off. He turned to Hutton. 'Anything you wish
to contribute, Chief Inspector?'

'Not really. Except that, by the most curious of coin-
cidences, my family and I were also in Taormina-
Mazzarò at the beginning of February. Only for a
week, mind you. We stayed at the same hotel as Mr
Fletcher, too.'

Mellow must have wondered if his hearing was at
fault. Even Dale's flashing pencil was stationary. I was
equally bowled over, though I took care not to adver-
tise it. I had discounted Hutton as a reliable perjurer;
now here he was actually vouching for me without
being asked. My repeated caveats to Honry had not
fallen on deaf ears after all.

'Are you saying that you were at this hotel, the what-
ever-it's-called, when Mr Fletcher was there?' Mellow,
recovering, demanded incredulously.

'We were there from 7th to 14th February,' Hutton
said. 'You're not doubting *my* word, are you, sir?'

Dale's pencil was back in action. Dates, it seemed, acted as a spur.

Mellow got to his feet. There was a gloss of sweat on his forehead and little rivulets coursed down his temples. His investigation was exposed as a charade, his evidence as valueless. A man like him would take it hard.

'I think that will be all for now, Mr Fletcher. If we need you again, which on the face of it is unlikely, we'll be in touch.'

'You can count on my full co-operation, Chief Superintendent. I think it only fair to warn you, however, I shall be consulting my solicitor over Yeo's accusations. He can't be allowed to blacken my name and get away with it.'

Mellow dabbed at his brow with a rumpled handkerchief. 'That's your prerogative, sir, though I think you'll find Mr Yeo's testimony comes under the heading of privileged infirmation. He hasn't implicated you in public, therefore . . . ' He sounded weary, defeated. An honest cop, he was out of his depth.

'Good night, Mr Fletcher,' he said, looking straight ahead as I showed him into the hall. Dale scuttled after him. Hutton would have followed, but I restrained him.

'Good show, Mike. Is it true? Did you really stay at the Mazzarò last month?'

The frigid features unlocked.

'You don't think I'd lie to a senior police officer, do you? Certainly I was there.' One eyelid came down like a shutter. 'Weren't you?'

When in need of exercise I can strongly recommend Sir Christopher Wren's Monument to the Great Fire: three hundred and eleven stone steps, worn smooth and concave by almost as many years of masochistic sightseers.

My ascent was measured, and I reached the top with

breath to spare. It was lonely up there, two hundred feet above street level. The only other living creature was a pigeon, a refugee from Nelson's Column. Together we contemplated the city skyline, in particular the nearby Telecom Tower, jaded symbol of sixties technology. It put me in mind of a certain lighthouse.

Two days ago – on Thursday – a preview of the Yeo tape had been telephoned to the *Daily Telegraph*, and a group of non-existent industrialists thoroughly implicated. The *Telegraph*, rightly cautious, chose not to report the story in Friday's edition. No matter. The primary purpose of the call had been to divert suspicion away from the Government and towards private enterprise. So long as nothing occurred to contradict that notion, it would soon come to be accepted as fact.

Proof (the *Telegraph* had been told), in the form of copies of the videotape, was to be delivered to all leading national newspapers, to the BBC and ITN, to the TUC, and to Yeo's union, during Friday.

Delivered it duly was. Two spare copies were retained – one each by Honry and Rees, while the unedited original was safe in my safe at home, pending destruction by fire, which only the Hangman committee could authorise.

Yet the storm hadn't truly broken until that very Saturday morning, when the dailies, in varying degrees of efficacy, did their stuff. From the sensational 'BETRAYAL', occupying half a front page (*Sun*), to a diffident 'Union Leader shows true colours', heading four inches of single column text (*Guardian*). I bought a complete set of papers at the newsagents in Piccadilly Circus and went through them in the taxi that ferried me at a crawl to the Monument.

The best of the bunch was the *Express*: it was fairly splattered with quotes from the tape, presented in the form of a script for a play. Yeo's contribution was preceded by his name, mine by a faceless 'Interviewer'.

The blue pencils had been sharpened too: Yeo's ultimate expletive was reduced to 'I don't give a f***.'

There could be no going back now. No sweeping under carpets. No cover-ups. Yeo was up there, nailed to the cross just the way Lord Deverill wanted it. I hoped he was well pleased. I hoped everybody was. The Government especially should be ecstatic, though all but a select handful of their number would have no inkling of the conspiracy that lay behind it. The 'group of industrialists' fiction would be greedily seized on and promoted. Ministerial and Party noses were to be kept clean at all costs.

You could describe me as a moderately happy man that Saturday morning. Happy to have struck a modest blow for democracy; more than happy to have been so well rewarded, the balance of my fee having been tardily handed over and banked. Only my marital problems festered on. For those I had no ready solutions.

Whatever motivated other visitors to the top of the Monument, I for one was not up there for my health. At eleven I was to meet a minor AUEWE official called Sushil Saran, a young Hindu, born in Britain, and in constant need of extra funds to satisfy certain extravagant tastes, notably a Jaguar E-Type Roadster, bought on the drip. It was among the last of the E-type genre, and greater love hath no man for his car than Sushil.

Flabby and out of condition, he was snorting like a bad-tempered bull when he emerged from the stairway, two minutes overdue. A couple in their thirties were jammed up tight behind him, and had evidently propelled him faster than he cared to go, for he glared and muttered after them as they went off around the other side of the platform.

He apologised for his lateness. His English bore no ethnic trace: Oxford through and through, as was his education. He was a clever and well-qualified man. But even a BA Econ doesn't walk into a highly-paid job if he happens to be coffee-coloured. Despite the laws prohibiting it, you can't legislate racial prejudice from an interviewer's mind.

I cut short the preamble to ask what I was dying to know: 'Have they viewed the tape yet?'

'Oh yes, indeed, Mr Fletcher, sir.' He was always respectful, Sushil. 'Several times – the full executive.'

'Including Yeo?'

'Not at first. But later, yes, he was allowed to see it.'

'And?'

'You realise I am not a member of the executive. I am only a junior administrator. Policy is not decided at my level.' He ran pudgy fingers through his fine black hair that had the gloss of silk.

I moved aside for the couple who had arrived with Sushil and were making an unhurried circuit of the platform. They smiled thanks, and I dipped my head in return.

I waited until they turned the corner before resuming.

'There are five hundred pounds in my pocket, Sushil. If that's the best you can come up with they'll never see the inside of yours.'

'I did not say I had no information, Mr Fletcher,' he hissed, eyes round and fearful, ever mindful of next month's instalment on the E-Type. 'But the information I have is only hearsay. I haven't been able to verify it yet. No minutes have been issued, you see.'

'Get on with it,' I almost snarled.

He huddled up close, which I wasn't wild about, but my sensibilities were secondary to the need for security.

'Yeo has not yet been informed, but . . .' he glanced to left and right; we had this side of the platform to ourselves, 'they are going to suspend him from office under Article 67: conduct by any member of the executive council inconsistent with the aims, aspirations, and policy of the union. That's not the exact phraseology . . .'

It wasn't far out. I'd spent many a long hour browsing over the union rules of late and could recite most of the articles word for word.

'Suspend?' I analysed its purport in my mind. 'For how long?'

'A month; actually twenty-eight days. To be lifted at any time within that period if he's cleared.'

A wide-bodied jet was climbing steeply from Heathrow, trailing thin plumes of smoke as the pilot applied maximum thrust. The sun struck it as it swung away south, and it blazed with brilliance for an instant, a diamond in the sky. Then it was an aircraft once more, tail on now, a diminishing speck. In my early teens I'd had ambitions to be an airline pilot, dreaming, as children do, of flying to the faraway places with strange-sounding names of the song. Thus my private fantasy. The fact, the reality, was this treacherous, roly-poly Hindu, with the bland brown face and the moneygrabbing eyes and the facile, unctuous manner that was so distasteful to me.

But without him and his unprincipled kind I would have been unable to function.

'And what – if anything – will happen during those twenty-eight days?'

'An enquiry. Above all the authenticity of the tapes will be checked and double-checked. They are anxious to be fair to him, you understand. Meanwhile, he is to be advised to take a holiday, preferably abroad, away from the publicity. All expenses paid, needless to say. When – if – the tape is pronounced genuine and the executive is satisfied it has not been tampered with – voice-dubbing, for example – Yeo will be recalled for . . . examination.'

'Thumbscrews and hot irons, eh?'

Anglo-Saxon wit was beyond his ken.

'No, no . . . nothing like that. But if what I have

291

heard of the content of the tape is accurate, he will have a lot of explaining to do. Personally . . .' he shuffled his feet, '. . . I am certain he will be removed from office and expelled from the union. The attitude of the executive seems extremely hostile.'

'Hanley . . . is he for or against.'

If Yeo went, Hanley the moderate, was a strong contender for the throne.

'Oh, against, most decidedly. Though he may be motivated in part by his ambition to take over the presidency.'

A pair of giggling teenage girls rounded the corner and squeezed past us, conversing in whispers. Americans, from the style of their dress. Both of them flipped me an appraising glance which I didn't rise to.

'Anything else for me, Sushil?'

'Not with regard to union business, but did you hear about him and his wife?'

I hadn't.

'Go on.'

'They've split up. He moved out two days ago.'

That shook me. The papers hadn't reported it.

'Over this?'

'I'm not sure. Do you want me to make enquiries?'

'Don't go out of your way. If you gather any tit-bits though, I'd be grateful if you'd pass them on.'

I paid him. The money was in a reinforced envelope, such as solicitors use for legal documentation. He didn't look inside; he was altogether too self-effacing for that.

'There is a question I would like to ask, Mr Fletcher,' he said as he stuffed the envelope inside the pocket of his leather overcoat (his taste in clothes was an expensive as his taste in cars). He paused, seeking my consent.

'Ask, Sushil.'

'Is the tape genuine? Did he really say what he's supposed to have said?'

'If I say yes, will you believe me?'

He wriggled with embarrassment.

'If you're looking for absolution, don't look to me, my friend,' I said, then relented, so downcast and guilt-ridden did he look. Maybe the little rat did have some ethics after all. 'Yeo's words are all his own, and he was under no compulsion to speak them. On that tape is the true David Yeo – the public version is a façade.'

I left first. Descended the three hundred and eleven steps in the slipstream of some twangy American chatter laced with giggles and consisting mostly of obscenities. What were young ladies coming to? I wondered. I also mulled over Yeo's bust-up with his wife, and considered phoning Rowen for more accurate data, using commiseration as a pretext. Always supposing she would speak to me.

Let it go, the inner self counselled. Forget Yeo, forget Rowen. Sort out your own marriage – if it's not already beyond retrieval.

The Monument disgorged me through the low portal at its base. The two American girls were there, on the kerb, their joint appraisal more blatant than ever. I treated them to a stony stare, and they immediately fell about laughing. Nonplussed, my instinctive reaction was to check if my flies were undone. They weren't.

Not, at any rate, in the usual place.

Between Julia and I the rot had well and truly taken hold. Our relationship was crumbling faster than Britain's motorways.

And – *cri de coeur* – I still didn't understand *why*. Why this sudden and accelerating canker. After weeks away I had expected some improvement, if only temporary. Instead, it was continuous warfare.

That Saturday, when I returned from my meeting with Sushil, we plumbed an all-time low.

'For Christ's sake, Julia!' I seethed as we faced each other across the table, lunch behind us, coffee before us. 'What do you want from me? What have I done? Tell me – get it out of your system.'

'Done? Done?' she shrilled and slammed the coffee pot down so hard the lid shot off and rolled off the edge of the table. 'Don't you read the papers?'

'I read the papers,' I said through gritted teeth, my voice pitched low and even in the hope that she would follow suit: servants have big ears. 'What have the papers to do with you and me?'

'Everything. Aren't you just a teeny bit ashamed of what you've done? Don't you feel dirty? Destroying a man with faked evidence. You make me want to vomit!'

I was damned if I'd try and justify it to her.

'You know the score. You knew it from the beginning. Now suddenly you're brimming over with morals and conscience and all those other personality traits you never had. If you objected to what I was doing, why didn't you speak out – before the event?'

She could produce no answer. Pallid, distrait, she could only look anywhere but at me. Eyes tearful in their deep sockets, but the tears contained. Hanging on to the rags of her composure.

A lovely woman: warm, compassionate, generous. My wife. I loved her. I ached for her to love me. Yet I couldn't bring myself to go to her. To hold her, and tell her . . . what? What should I tell her? Even before I went away, our marriage had been in decline. A one-sided love is no love at all. There remained only the inevitable death-throes, a stage we were fast approaching if, indeed, we were not already there.

I felt cold and detached.

'If I hadn't been prepared to do what I did, the country would now be without electricity, without gas, and without water. People – ordinary people – would be dead and dying. Not you, not me, not all our friends and relatives. Oh no, we'd just switch on our generators, buy bottled water by the lorry-load, and carry on as usual. Or go abroad and sit in the sun until it blew over. Easy for us. Easy when you've got money.'

At least now she was meeting my eyes. With the back of her hand she smeared away an escaping tear.

'But out there,' I jabbed a finger at the window and in spite of my resolve to stay cool, my voice began to climb, 'out there, my wealthy love, where ninety-five per cent of the population only earn enough to live and might at any time be thrown out of work because business can't function without electricity and water; out there, Julia, they don't have generators to switch on. They can't afford to buy bottled water in hundred-gallon lots. They can't abscond to some tropical paradise because even if they had the wherewithal, they'd have to stay here to draw their dole money.' I shook my head in weary disgust. 'It's another world and you've never lived there. No more have I, come to that, though I've lived amongst it – Belfast is more than just a killing ground – but I'll admit I've never known hunger and cold, or wanted for basic necessities; I've only stood by and watched others suffer, salving my conscience with the occasional cheque to Oxfam. Not this time though: this time, by God, I've done something to stop it happening!'

I dried up. It was not Julia's language. Social gobbledegook, she would call it. Propaganda of and for the masses. I had hit the wrong button as usual.

So I walked out. Turned my back on her and all she stood for. If our marriage was over, so be it. I had lost the will to fight for it.

I whiled away the afternoon at my desk in the study, dreaming up and mostly discarding schemes for putting my £200,000 to work. A little before five Julia came in.

'Don't get excited – I haven't come to kiss and make up,' she said, aloof and aristocratic. She might have been addressing a servant. 'I just want some jewellery.'

Her most valuable trinkets were kept in the combination safe behind a panel in the wall. She marched across the room and I returned to my doodlings. I heard the spin of the dial, the clunk of the lock, then rustling noises. Then an 'Oh!'

I rotated my chair. She was standing before the safe holding a slab of grey plastic about the size of a paperback book – the master cassette of the Yeo interview, still in my keeping pending disposal instructions from the committee. Since it contained material that had been wiped off the circulated copies it might, if it fell into the wrong hands, be suggested that the more damaging elements had been faked.

Julia turned, wild-eyed, to look at me. 'Is this . . . ?'

'What?' I was playing for time.

'The video of you and . . . and . . . Yeo.'

'You've got the Yeo business on the brain,' I grumbled.

'But *is* it?' she persisted.

Had all been well between us I would not have denied it. Now, so far apart had we grown since my return, added to which she was daily more critical of Hangman, that I was no longer sure she could be trusted.

'It's a video of that business on the UCATT picket line,' I improvised. 'When the Chairman's car was stoned?' I padded out the fiction with an offhand air. 'Remember it? Actually, it belongs to the DTI library; I should have returned it weeks ago.'

She nodded, very slowly. 'I see.' She thrust the cassette back inside the safe and resumed her search. I sighed and the sound travelled across the room. Julia's back stiffened, but she rummaged on with no break in momentum. There was a lot of jewellery to sift through.

'Are you going out?' I asked her.

'Tonight? No. But I *am* going away.'

It wasn't unexpected, but the shock was heart-stopping nevertheless.

'On account of us?'

'Partly . . . mostly. I want to be on my own for a while. To think things out.'

'Where will you go?'

'Just away,' was her intransigent reply. 'I'll let you know when I get there.'

'Julia . . .'

Don't whine, I chided myself. Don't grovel. It won't work and you'll lose whatever sedimentary respect she has for you. Not to mention your self-respect. Tears welled like hot springs. I couldn't have borne for her to see me blubber so I spun round and bent over my papers again, seeing only a blur. Feeling a pain that was like no earthly pain.

Not long afterwards the safe door slammed shut and then the study door, and I was left alone in my misery.

By ten o'clock on Sunday morning she was gone, baggage and all. Driven by Taberner, our chauffeur, to Heathrow, though I'd had to wait until his return to extract even that much information. Whither she flew, or even *whether* she flew – it might have been a blind to throw me off her scent; she was inclined to be devious – I couldn't say. I started telephoning the airlines operating out of Heathrow, one by one, to ask if Julia had flown with them: BA, Transworld, United, Air France, Lufthansa . . . after Lufthansa I gave up. What was the point? Knowing where she landed was a long way short of knowing where she would end up.

All that day I mooched, barely glancing at the newspapers, all of which carried the Yeo story on their front pages. I saw nobody apart from the servants. Ate and didn't taste. Smoked and didn't taste. Drank and didn't care.

Went to bed very late, very drunk, and in a mood bordering on suicidal.

Monday was the same, only more so.

Tuesday, Charlotte phoned. She'd heard Julia had

'gone off somewhere' and was I all right. I told her, unpardonably, to mind her own business and regretted it even as I put the phone down on her.

Wednesday – a blank. A complete wipe-out.

Thursday – again a blank, until the evening when Honry showed up. He wasn't welcome and I said as much. I think. Especially he wasn't welcome if he had aspirations to prise me away from my newfound friend and comforter, Glenfiddich Pure Malt.

'How long has he been like this?' Honry demanded. He sounded cross.

I was sorting out an answer to this rather odd, third-person enquiry when some other party replied on my behalf: 'Since Mrs Fletcher left, sir.'

Willoughby! Snitching on me, the little creep. For that I'd send him packing, old family retainer or no. I struggled to my feet; no sooner had I done so when there was this tremendous blow at the base of my spine, followed by another to the back of my head, both of which, I duly worked out, were caused by the floor coming up to hit me. I groaned. Faces peered at me. Behind them I could make out the chandelier. Now how did the chandelier come to be sticking out at right angles from the wall, defying gravity? Back to the drawing board, Sir Isaac Newton.

Then I dimly remember shouting. I remember cursing and kicking and swinging at the owners of the hands that plucked at me and lifted me and carried me off to never-never land. Where I was content to sink into twilit amnesia, wanting nothing more than to be left alone with my bosom pal, Glenfiddich.

But the bastards were having none of that.

'Yeo,' Honry said in that throwaway tone he used when making a sensational announcement, 'is in Fuengirola.'

It was Friday. I was near to sober, and breakfasting if not quite with zest, then with a robot-like tenacity.

Doctor's orders (Honry being the doctor) were that I must eat, so eating I was.

He, Honry, had watched over me all night long like a shepherd watching over a wayward lamb, and nary a drop of alcohol did I sniff, never mind taste. When, in the small hours, the numbing effects of the booze had begun to wear off and a top-up became urgent, I had resented his calm, his solicitousness, and his steadfast, unvarying 'No'. Now, even suffering as I was from a King Kong of a hangover, I was conscious of owing him a large debt.

So I crunched away on my buttered toast like a good patient while indulging in some limited brain-work, since Honry seemed to expect some comment or other on his Yeo communiqué.

'Fuengirola,' I said, chewing and swallowing. Intelligent and witty remarks were out this morning. Then, more thoughtfully: 'Fuengirola, eh?' Was I supposed to make something of it?

'Fuengirola.' Honry, also chewing, was eyeing me. The space between us suddenly crackled with tension.

'Well, why not. Our having a villa there doesn't make it out of bounds to suspended union leaders. It's a popular holiday resort.'

'His wife and children aren't with him.'

I dug my knife deep into the butter, spread it mostly on the toast. Crunched. 'They've split up.'

'So the story goes. Did you hear why?'

'Did you hear why Julia and I split up?' I snapped back. Yeo's doings no longer interested me. I wanted my wife back and sod the rest: sod Yeo, sod the union, sod the Government, sod the universe. Sod 'em all!

'Precisely.' Honry had this smug, knowing look, which served only to feed my irritation.

'Do you want some marmalade?' I said, proffering it. Anything to shut him up. 'Or perhaps a gob-stopper?'

He smiled condescendingly. 'I realise your faculties

are not yet quite up to the mark, dear chap, but do try and engage your cerebrum. I'm painting a little picture for you. It's a bit of a jumble at the moment – rather like a Picasso – but the pieces will arrange themselves into order if you concentrate, I do assure you.'

Under my breath I consigned him to a distant place.

'Where is Julia?' he said.

I wished to God I could answer him.

'At the villa perhaps?' he murmured, and it was such a casual suggestion that it did a circuit of the room, a double somersault, and a victory roll before coming to rest in my torpid intellect.

'Julia?' The significance of Honry's picture-painting swarmed over me like an army of starving rats. 'You mean Julia and . . . you mean she's with *him*? With *Yeo*?'

'Ah.' Honry's smile grew. 'You haven't lost all your wits then. I'm so glad.'

I was out of my chair and round the table faster than a thrown knife. I grabbed Honry by the lapels of his Prince of Wales-check suit and literally hauled him upright.

'Hold on, old sport!' he whooped.

Tall and well-built as he was, I shook him so hard his teeth beat a tattoo.

'What do you know, you bastard?'

'I? Nothing.'

'You're against me like the rest of your fucking family. You want us to split up.'

He broke my hold, or maybe I just let go. We stood away from each other, me panting, hating him; he, ruffled but dignified.

'If you had watched the news last night instead of drinking yourself insensible you would have seen it for yourself.'

'Seen what, for Pete's sake?'

'Yeo. Some reporters caught up with him in Fuengirola. He refused to talk to them, but he was there all right. Apart from that I don't actually know anything. I'm just putting two and two together.'

'Then let's hope you're making five,' I said, still angry, but now starting to think rationally. Julia and Yeo. Julia and *Yeo*. Of all people. Yet it added up. That night in Brussels, dancing together, doing a disappearing act . . . Julia's frequent nights out afterwards . . . her antipathy toward me over Operation Hangman . . . over the video-tape . . .

The tape. There was something about the tape . . .

Christ!

Honry read my expression and was not reassured by it.

'Vee . . . !' His voice rang with alarm, and when I crashed out of the room, crossing the wake of a startled Willoughby, he came plunging after me. 'Vee – what is it?'

Into the study, across it in two or three desperate strides; slide back the panel to expose the safe: fourteen left, twenty-seven right, seven left, twist handle. A black jewel case slid off the untidy heap of papers and bulging envelopes. I pawed them all out, papers, jewel cases, the lot.

'Vee . . .' Honry had caught up with me and was standing helplessly by.

The safe was empty, its contents scattered across the floor. I knelt, scattered them further, seeking without hope of finding the original videotape of the Yeo interview. The box of plastic and magnetic tricks that could absolve Yeo and put me, Honry, Deverill, and others of still more exalted status in the public dock.

Governments have fallen for less.

Chapter Nineteen

The Leupold zoom binoculars brought the villa 'El Caso' – meaning 'at home' – up so close I could even pick out the two-year-old crack in the stucco above the back door and (for I was on high ground, looking down on it) the individual dead leaves lying in the bottom of the empty swimming pool where the wind stirred them fitfully. I recalled the day when Gavin, at the age of five, had swum his first width of the pool in a desperate crawl that was nine parts turbulence to one part progress. A hurtful memory; a reminder of times when he and I were still close and Julia loved me. A love that had slipped like quicksilver from my grasp as infidelity piled upon infidelity, until, finally we had come to this, the supreme treachery. Rather she had left me for my best friend than for my worst enemy.

Her other indiscretions were as pinpricks to this mortal wound. Such a monstrous betrayal was beyond my ability to grasp. Even as I had climbed the steep slope beyond the villa, out of sight of the other holiday homes dotted haphazardly across the valley, half of me was dismissing the ideas as preposterous. Jeering at my foolishness in flying a thousand miles on no more solid evidence than coincidence: the coincidence of Yeo choosing the area as a bolthole.

The coincidence, too, of his marriage break-up. It happens. All too often.

The coincidence of the missing tape. Convinced it was not as innocent as I claimed, Julia might have taken it out of curiosity.

Coincidence. How would a dictionary define it? Two or more related happenings? *Chance* related happenings was better. Yeo in Fuengirola and his separation from his wife I could just about have written off as paranoia – Honry's and mine. It was the removal of the tape that put the seal of treachery on these events.

Then, not long after I had settled down to my vigil on the hill, all doubts and with them all hopes had crumbled to dust at the sight of David Yeo, blond hair ruffled, legs bare under a short housecoat, venturing, out to deposit a bulging plastic bag of rubbish at the end of the short drive. He was barely back inside when, as if to hammer the point home, Julia brought out a basketful of washing to hang on the rotary clothes line. She was wearing her short towelling robe and as she pegged out her bits and pieces a gust of wind lifted the hem every so often to afford a glimpse of her round backside – her round, naked backside, – and kindled desire and jealous fury in approximately equal amounts.

Contrary to travel agency folklore, southern Spain in March is not invariably a balmy, blue-skied fairyland. I had landed at Torremolinos, that sprawl of concrete just south of Malaga that dispels all romantic visions of castles in Spain, in a thunderstorm accompanied by high winds – winds that howled even now, a whole day later. I had lost an hour at the airport when a pile-up of luggage jammed the carousel, and a further hour owing to a go-slow by the immigration officials (unheard of under Franco's rule). As for organizing a hire car – that was ever a procedure designed to test the most benign of temperaments. The result of all this fandango was that darkness had fallen before I edged my Ford Escort into the streaming Malaga exodus, its volume a reminder that many Spaniards toil until 7.00 pm to compensate for the three-to-four hour siesta in the middle of the day. Against my natural urge to discover the truth I decided to postpone my drive out to the villa until daylight.

Accommodation in pre-season Spain is never in short supply and my room at the Principe Sol was the best in the house, complete with sea view and a wall-to-wall sliding glass door that gave access to a balcony. Terrific in the summer, with the morning sun to greet you and the slurp of the surf an ever-present background rhythm. This particular night, with the wind coming off the sea at gale force or better, I might as well have been dossing in some dockland fleapit. What was more, the glass door that would ordinarily have been such an asset rattled incessantly all night – an extra most of us would prefer to have done without. To me, as it happened, it mattered not a jot, since I didn't sleep anyway, but lay on my back, with the lights on, staring at the blue expanse of the ceiling. Staring but not seeing, while my mind wandered down the coast to and beyond Fuengirola, to the pretty valley of the Rio de Ojén, to the villa 'El Caso' in the foothills below the mountain of Castillejos. Zeroing in on the front door, passing magically through it, tiptoeing down the short corridor to the master bedroom, the pace now slowing. Fearful of what lay on the other side of that door. A moment's hesitation then on, determinedly, boldly even, across that final frontier, stripping the sheets from the two naked forms that writhed and wrestled on the bed, flesh against flesh, moaning and gasping, the woman's breath coming in great sobs. And through it all a heartbeat, hammering inside my skull like some diabolic engine.

It was the stuff of insanity.

To follow my night of mental crucifixion, a day of physical discomfort. There were no roads as such in the valley, only a single arterial track running roughly north to south and linking up with the Marbella to Coin highway. This track came nowhere near the villa which, like most of the others thereabouts, was served by a private rutted approach. To drive up openly was to invite Yeo to do a classic Casanova bunk out of the back door, therefore I had left the car some distance away and worked my way around the lower end of the long, narrow valley on foot, through squalls of rain and in the teeth of that hellish wind; the sea on my left a dishwater grey. Sgeir Varlish all over again.

I checked my watch. Three o'clock. Should I go down now, or wait until nightfall? I had no plan – no plan at all, therefore no reason to linger. Yet my training and my subconscious both prescribed caution, and caution meant no witnesses, which meant lying low until dark. Officially I was here to recover the tape and that was all. Unofficially I wouldn't be responsible for my actions.

Julia was back indoors. I shifted my position to relieve the numbness in my legs. Between me and the wet, coarse-grassed earth was a thick sheet of black polythene, purchased along with the binoculars in Fuengirola, and I'd had the foresight to bring my parka. Even with these protections I was perished and the back of my trousers soaked. I was tempted to return to the car where I would at least be dry, but the three kilometre trudge over difficult terrain put me off.

So I stuck it out. At about 4.30 they went out in the green Seat, that had been carelessly parked with its front wheels in the flower bed. They were away an hour or more and returned loaded with cartons and carrier bags full of groceries. I spotted several melons: Julia was partial to the fruit. The mental image of the two of them sharing a melon raised a growl in my throat.

Night came abruptly and the wind intensified with it. Lights appeared below and elsewhere in the valley. By now my limbs were stiff with cold and cramp and when I finally rose the returning circulation had me leaping about like a Cossack dancer.

As the stiffness subsided and the circulation pangs

dulled to an ache, I stepped off the polythene sheet which was promptly ripped away by the wind, taking the binoculars with it. I wasn't about to grub for them in these conditions. Hood up, head hunched into shoulders, I set off down the hillside. The wind pushed at me. Twice it had me on my bottom, sliding on the slick grass, and when I stepped over the low, scalloped wall that bordered the garden and came at last under the lee of the building, it was akin to entering the windless eye of a hurricane.

In stealth I crossed the lawn and fetched up by the kitchen window. No voices, just muted pop music. I proceeded around the building, under the porch to the front door. Stood there awhile, letting the phantoms roam at will through the archives of my memory.

At last, with dry throat and throbbing pulse, I rapped on the frosted glass panel.

It was Yeo who came.

In dark slacks and the V-neck sweater he had worn for the 'Live at Home' TV session. Casually smart, well-groomed, classless. A modern man, just like our dynamic new PM. Contrast his appearance with my sodden, grubby state. Who was the under-dog now? Here I stood, on my own doorstep, like a vagrant begging shelter from the storm. Not content with stealing my wife, he occupies my property too. What next – my freedom? Since he now possessed the means to crush me as utterly as I had conspired to crush him, my freedom might well be next in line for the chop.

From his reaction I might have been no more than a dinner guest turning up on the wrong night.

'Well, well, well,' he said. Cool as an ice cube. Then of all things, he smiled, actually *smiled*.

We stared at each other for a long moment. The smile stayed in place as if engraved. I neither spoke nor – heaven forbid! – returned his smile, but let the atmosphere build until the space between us was solid with it. Then I pushed past him, through the tiny vestibule and on to the grand confrontation with Julia.

She was sprawled full length on the settee, smoking, also wearing slacks and sweater – only hers was a sweater that clung to her breasts and nipples like skin on custard. Jealousy surged once more, hot and gut-twisting, as Yeo sauntered in behind me, hands in pockets.

Julia took my entrance no less calmly than he. Slowly she swung her legs off the settee, not gladdened by the sight of me, yet equally not dismayed. Accepting the inevitability of it, I guessed. She lowered the volume of the hi-fi and the nasal chanting faded to a whisper.

'Hello, Vee,' she said after a lengthy mutual appraisal. 'You look rather damp. Would you care to take your coat off and dry out?'

Patronising bitch.

'Not necessary.' My own sangfroid amazed me. 'I shan't be staying long.'

'Oh,' from Yeo. 'What have you come for?'

'To recover stolen property,' I said, and startled glances passed between them; it occurred to me that they might equate 'property' with 'wife', so by way of clarification I added: 'No, Julia, not you. That would be rather pointless, don't you think?'

Julia's features softened. 'Be honest with yourself, Vee. Even without David . . . you and I . . .' She came to me, arms outstretched in appeal. If she had kept right on coming, into my embrace, back into my life, I would have settled for that and Yeo could have his tape. But it was not to be, and if I couldn't have Julia I wasn't leaving without the tape. I'd see him dead before I'd let him ruin *me* as well as my marriage.

'Spare me the sob stuff,' I said harshly to Julia. 'Just give me the cassette and I'll be off. You two are welcome to each other.'

Yeo moved to Julia's side, put his arm around her. I

hated him for that, especially when Julia reached across the front of her waist and laid her hand on his. Lovers' interplay. The correlation of a fresh and ripening relationship, when every word is sweet as a Sauternes and every move contains undertones of desire.

It was all too familiar.

'You are referring, of course, to the videotape of our conversation,' Yeo said, straight to the nitty-gritty. 'The *original* recording.'

'What else?'

Julia puffed nervously at her cigarette. 'You've had a wasted journey, Vee – it's not here.'

'Don't talk horse manure, lover. You took it from the safe on Saturday night. Where else would it be?'

'At Power Base,' Yeo promptly replied, and so spontaneously that I accepted it at once. 'No sense in having it here. It's being scrutinised for . . . er . . . discrepancies between it and the copies you so generously scattered all over London. Hell, Fletcher, I've got just as much as you to be mad about!'

'So we're both mad.' I spoke as an automaton: my mind was engaged with the implication of that videotape in the clutches of Yeo's union. And they must have had it since the weekend – six whole days! My gaze alighted on the phone. Alert Honry. Set Rees' dogs on the union: receiving stolen property would do for openers.

The receiver was to my ear, though I wasn't conscious of lifting it. Julia and Yeo watched me; neither made a move to intervene.

'You're too late, Fletcher,' Yeo said, and I detected a note of pity. 'The press have been informed. We're flying back on Monday for a press conference.'

'We?' I said dully. 'Both of you?' I dumped the receiver and flopped down in the nearest armchair, massaging my eyes with finger and thumb.

Julia switched on the two-bar electric fire and offered me a drink. It was then that I realised I'd had neither food nor drink since breakfast. Suddenly my tongue was sticking to the roof of my mouth.

'Beer,' I said as the heater pinged and popped.

'I'll join you,' Yeo said matily.

The beer was German, and cool and sparkling with that saccharine after-taste I rather cared for. I gulped it down and asked for seconds.

'How long?' I asked Yeo while Julia was fetching it. 'You and Julia – how long?'

'Since that reception in Brussels. That was when we first met.'

'Does your wife know?'

He nodded and picked a pipe out of the ashtray on the bamboo coffee table – a table Julia and I had wrangled over with an Arab market trader in Marbella. More memories. In fact, memories were all around, vying for my attention: the oil painting of sunset over The Rock, the marble figurine from the monastery up near Lucena, the model picador and bull we bought for Gavin that he never played with . . . Right at that moment I loathed them all.

'I told her when this business of the tape became public,' Yeo said, and stilled my reminiscing. 'I didn't *have* to; I just felt . . . ' He peered glumly into his beer. His conscience was giving him a roasting.

Julia returned with a whole pack of canned beer and some cheese and crackers on a tray. Oh, goody – we were going to have a party!

She sat, and Yeo sat next to her. I sat alone. I was the outsider.

'You didn't really think you could get away with it, did you?' Yeo said.

'The video, you mean?' Discovering a latent hunger, I made short work of a cracker.

Yeo waited for me to go on. In the interim, as I munched, the CD came to an end and a strained quiet descended on the scene.

'We did get away with it. Everyone believed it. Your

suspension is proof of that. If it hadn't been for my moonstruck wife you'd be all washed up – and deservedly. What's there on tape is what's inside your head. I didn't put it there.'

'That's not the point, and well you know it. My views are my views and I'm entitled to them. What *you* are not entitled to do is commit a felony in order to suppress those views. Why didn't you fight me out in the open? Why behave like a gangster?'

Who else had upbraided me for that? Julia? Rowen?

'You mean it's not cricket? Like submarines and germ warfare and kicking a man when he's down. Always play the game according to the rules – is that what you're saying? It's all right for *you* and your sort to use gangster tactics, but the rest of us must stiffen our upper lips and charge your defences head-on in good old Light Brigade tradition. Balls! I'm a realist: I fight unsportsmanlike conduct with unsportsmanlike methods.'

On the mantelpiece of the stone fireplace, above the now-glowing electric fire, was the rotund, wood-carved Civil Guard with the cigar-snapper in his tricorn hat. A gift from Julia the year we celebrated our eighth wedding anniversary. Even then her love was still alive; beginning to brown at the edges, but essentially intact.

I looked at it through a mist. What was one more turn of the rack among so many?

Yeo buttered a biscuit, lopped off a morsel of Gruyère. 'What'll you do now?'

'Now?' I said bitterly. 'Good question. Crawl into a hole and die, I should think. I only wish . . .'

'What, Vee?' Julia seemed almost upset, if you can believe it.

I made inroads into my second beer. Licked froth from my lips.

'I only wish, if you had to run off with somebody, that it was anybody at all rather than him.'

Yeo cackled. 'From you, Fletcher, that's a bloody big compliment.'

Inside me the last thread of self-restraint parted, severing rage from reason, and I bounced out of the chair as if from a trampoline.

'Get up,' I ordered.

He didn't budge. 'That won't solve anything.'

'Vee, sit down and don't be so juvenile,' Julia said, her dark eyes troubled.

'Get *up* or I'll hit you anyway.' I made to grab his arm, but he hacked me aside and rose up off the settee in an explosion of biscuit crumbs and other debris faster than I would have believed possible for a man his age and size. A fist crunched into the side of my face and now I know what it's like to be belted by a sledgehammer.

I crashed onto the hard tiles and slid several feet. Julia screamed. Yeo trumpeted like a charging bull elephant: 'I'll kill him . . . I'll kill him!' He sounded as if he meant business and since all I could do was roll about the floor, clutching my temples it would have been all over bar the mourning but for Julia's intervention. She gained me a respite: I was dribbling on the tiles, helpless as an upended turtle, when I became hazily aware that some kind of scrimmage was taking place. There was Julia yelling, 'No, David, no!' and Yeo grunting and growling menacingly. Talk about sleeping giants: I had awakened one all right.

I was half up, still in pain, but with most parts functional, when Yeo broke free of Julia and did an imitation of a high speed train to get at me. I gave ground and punched him hard in the belly as he swung incautiously at where my jaw would have been if I hadn't redeployed it leftwards. A second punch below the belt had him gurgling, though far from licked.

He was a big man: bigger and broader than me. But I was ablaze with fury, which gave me an abnormal strength. Plus my military training in how to disable an opponent barehanded. I slammed into him hard and fast and vicious, easily ducking his roundhouse swings. I pummelled and booted him to the floor, where he lay, curled up hedhehog-fashion, twitching and jerking under the kicks I landed on his body. Now Julia was dragging *me* away, protecting *him*.

I cast around for a weapon, a heavy object, anything at all with which to finish him. My eyes fell upon the *sable*, the Spanish cavalry sabre propped up in a corner of the fireplace. Julia followed my gaze and my thought processes, and was in motion ahead of me. We reached the fireplace neck-and-neck, but even as her fingers closed around the shrouded, embossed hilt, I threw her aside, wrenching the weapon away. Full of pluck, she came at me again, all fists and desperation. I backhanded her really hard and she pitched backwards over the coffee table with a wail and a thump.

Yeo was still on the floor where I had left him, his head lolling, his mouth slack and bloody. Probably unconscious. I held the sabre in a two-fisted dagger grip, pointing downward, my legs straddling him. All I had to do was lunge – momentum would do the rest. I pictured the curved steel entering between his ribs, the flesh parting like a lipless mouth, the blood welling, spurting, emptying his life out on the tiles.

'Vee!' Julia's voice from across the room was a racking sob. 'Don't . . . I beg you, don't. I'll come back to you . . . I promise I will. Only don't kill him . . . please . . .'

I wavered, and in wavering the dementia and with it the kill-lust fled from me, draining away like water from a tap. I cursed her – how I cursed her. I left no foul name, no oath, unsaid. When at last the torrent ran dry and my tongue lay fallow on my palate, I hurled the sabre from me, by chance towards the picture window that took up most of the front of the house. It crashed through the glass, a convulsive

312

splintering, bursting open as of a breached dam, the whole massive pane crazing over, collapsing in on itself in an avalanche of noise that went on and on and on.

And shreds of glass still tinkled musically and intermittently as I stormed from the house into a night torn by wind and rain, and simply ran – ran blindly, not knowing or caring where, just running, running, running, until my legs caved in and I could run no more.

Chapter Twenty

The TV set had been on all evening, though I was scarcely aware of its mindless outpourings, using it only as a means of contact with the outside world. Since Yeo had cast his blight over my land, my comings and goings seemed to have revolved around The Early News or the Six O'Clock News, or the Late News, or whichever, and I was glad indeed to be spared that nightly ritual. This evening, however, even the TV was preferable to a house of ghosts.

I was back at Kingscourt, but my tenure was plainly finite. Not that I intended to meekly pack my bags and hop it. Julia, I had decided, would have to order me off the premises and as yet, to the best of my knowledge, she was not even back in the country. At around 9.20 pm I had to revise this supposition when Yeo's name intruded on the rather wet detective novel I was reading.

The book was instantly forgotten as, by grace of the cathode ray tube, I joined a body of reporters at Heathrow. They were an excited bunch, waving cameras this way and that, and all was confusion and hubbub. Then came a yell: 'There he is!'

And there, indeed, he was, striding away from Passport Control, making straight for the camera. Ever classlessly smart with his overcoat draped over his shoulders, the empty sleeves flapping. Back where he belonged at the top of the tree.

No sign of Julia, for which I gave mute thanks. Flaunting a mistress would not have served Yeo's cause either. Not until the re-purification process was complete and his reinstatement officially blessed would he feel safe in diffusing his illicit romance.

The press surged forward like a pack of starving hyenas and there was the usual demand on all sides for Yeo's attention. He came to a stop and was hidden from the BBC cameras for a second; then an opening was forced and we cut a swathe through the massed journalists until the screen was glutted with those handsome features.

Cameras popped off around him, the flashes blending so as to be continuous, and he blinked, small furrows of irritation breaking out above the bridge of his nose. As if at an unspoken command, order suddenly settled on the pack and the BBC asserted its authority – after all, it was their show.

'Good evening.' Yeo greeted the Beeb's reporter tiredly. I noted, with satisfaction, the cut over his eyebrow and the bruised cheekbone; there would be other, brighter discolourations in less visible places: I hoped they hurt. He looked older too – every one of his forty-five years. Yet there was little joy for me in these superficial lesions. It was what drove him that mattered: the dynamic inner core, that nuclear reactor that generated his essential vigour, charisma, and above all his gigantic ego. I had no reason to suppose that the id of the man was at all damaged by recent events.

'Mr Yeo,' the BBC began, 'we understand there has been a new development in the matter of your suspension. Can you tell us about it?'

The gunsight eyes targeted on the TV camera.

'It has been proved that the videotape of my conversations, to which so much publicity has been given, was heavily edited.'

Heavily? I managed a wry grin.

When Yeo didn't add to this statement, the reporter said dubiously, 'Nothing more?'

'What more do you want?' The aplomb was cracking. 'The video is phoney and I expect to be reinstated at a special executive meeting tomorrow. Will that do?'

'But what was the exact nature of the proof? How was it discovered? And by whom?'

Yeo clammed up completely, which was unlike him. Usually his behaviour before the cameras was impeccable.

'Can't you tell us anything at all, sir?' the reporter wheedled.

Yeo made as if to brush him aside, then appeared to think the better of it and capitulated with a nod.

'I will tell you this much . . .'

The pack closed in around him, jostling for position.

'There will be no change in union policy. I have already spoken with my senior colleagues on the executive and we are to go ahead with the stoppage. One week tomorrow, gentlemen, will begin the most devastatingly effective strike this country has ever experienced.' Isolated groans were picked up by the microphones. This was old hat. Unpopular old hat, moreover.

'But don't worry,' Yeo said, smiling at his audience. 'It won't last more than a few days.'

'Why do you say that?' somebody asked.

'How can it, man? Everything will stop.'

'And people will die,' I said under my breath. 'And you, you shit-heap, don't care a fuck, do you?'

Yeo now made an attempt to wind the session up, but the press, having snared him, were in no hurry to turn him loose.

'Any truth in the rumour that you and your wife have separated?'

That got to him. A near-snarl tugged his mouth out of shape as he rounded on his inquisitor.

'No comment.' Which in journalese is an admission.

'Will you be going straight from here to Enfield, sir – to your home?'

Yeo was saved from a second 'no comment' by person or persons unknown, who whisked him away from his tormentors and from the screen. If there was a puff of smoke, I missed it.

That was the sum total of the BBC's Ode to the Return of David Yeo. I went back to my book. And, sometime later, with the TV still yammering, fell asleep over it.

Thursday was April Fool's Day. In the morning Julia came home. Flushed and lacking make-up, she planted her shapely legs in front of me and proposed I up sticks and away. Only it wasn't a proposition.

I was at my desk writing cheques (life goes on).

'Why the rush?' I said, mildly enough. 'The house is big enough for us to move around in without tripping over each other. I'll move into the master guest room. I'll be as quiet as a monk. You can even instal Yeo here if you like.' She never would, I was confident of that.

'There's no sense in your staying. What's dead is dead.'

I screwed the cap back on my Cross fountain pen. 'Dead for you, Julia. Not, I regret to say, for me.'

She subsided into my favourite armchair and a band of sunlight slanted across her face, making her squint. 'Don't make it so hard, blast you.' She passed a weary hand across her brow; she looked as if she hadn't been to bed. Or not to sleep, at any rate.

Stop it. *Stop* it.

'It couldn't be harder than it is. Do you have to make me homeless as well?'

She fumbled a pack of cigarettes from her handbag, had trouble lighting up, so badly was her hand shaking. I felt no sympathy. Love, yes, that still lived on: a lingering, hopeless flame that must sooner or later atrophy. But I wasn't selfless enough to smooth her path. On the contrary, the more potholes I could dig, the more obstacles I could strew across it, the happier – no, not happier, more *appeased* – I would be. It wasn't that I wanted to score cheap, petty points off her. As she said: dead is dead. If there were no embers still glowing on her side, if the fire was out and the ashes cold, why prolong the funeral? No, it was him, Yeo, I resented. Not Yeo as my wife's lover, but Yeo as Yeo. For him I would dig not mere potholes, but whacking great tiger traps, sharpened stakes and all. He might convince himself that that cuckold Fletcher was down and out of the running. Might well imagine me contemplating suicide or, less drastically, fleeing abroad before my downfall became public. Let him have his delusions. We Fletchers are at our best with our backs to the wall.

As my father had bragged before scuttling off to New Zealand.

'I want a divorce,' Julia announced. She had already smoked a good half of her cigarette and the air above her was a blue haze. 'Once the petition has been filed we wouldn't be able to live under the same roof; the solicitors wouldn't allow it.'

'Co-habitation,' I said absently, staring out towards the summer house. Bob was painting the rail with slow, measured strokes of the brush. He was a slow, measured man.

Julia was frowning at me. 'Co-habitation?'

'The legal term for living under the same roof.'

'Yes, well . . .' Julia struggled with her temper: she didn't take kindly to being sidetracked. 'Are we agreed then?'

'On a divorce? No, Julia, we are not agreed. You do your worst and I'll do mine.' I regarded her and my emotions took over. 'Julia . . . don't do this.' I went down on one knee before her. Not begging, though I was prepared to. Just rooting around in those dead ashes for a flicker, a spark, the merest glimmer to fan alive.

'Don't kill us off,' I said, and took her hands. They

318

were cold – cold and dead, like the hands of a corpse. 'I love you; I never stopped loving you . . . you know that.'

There was a break in her voice as she said, 'I can't deny it. I never really doubted it. But it's over.'

'Do you love him?' I dreaded to hear it confirmed.

She shifted restlessly. 'Love? I . . . who can say? I'm not sure I understand what love is any more. I used to think I loved you . . .' She sniffed, pulled her hands free to rummage for a handkerchief. 'Now I'm just . . . frozen inside. But it makes no difference whether or not I love David. If it hadn't been him it would have been someone else . . . almost anyone. He just happened along and I just fell for him.' She blew her nose lustily. 'Not at all crash-bang-wallop the way it was with you – just a gradual dovetailing. When you were . . . away, it was him I missed, not you. I actually hated you for taking him from me; even more, I hated what you were doing to him.'

I straightened up and stamped the pins and needles from my foot. 'I can see now why you were so opposed to Hangman. It never occurred to me that you and he . . .' I marvelled at my lack of perception. 'It was too improbable. I was pretty sure you were seeing another man . . . I just assumed it was one of your regular studs or some passing fancy.' She flinched at the bald remark. 'To think that I was confiding in you about Hangman and all along you were playing Mata Hari.'

'Not all along. Otherwise you'd never have got beyond the planning stage. It wasn't until I had that tape that I blurted out the whole story to him.'

I wasn't consoled.

'Favouring him over me.'

She bridled, the aquiline nose ascending. 'Favouring truth over lies. How could I let you ruin him, knowing I had the means to prevent it?'

'All right, Julia.' The will to fight was evaporating faster than superheated steam. 'Do what you must. Just

319

give me a few days, a week say, to sort out my affairs and find a place to doss down.'

'Of course, darling.' Now that I was cooperating she could risk the odd term of affection. 'Take as long as you need . . . within reason. I shall probably go away for a while.'

To some secret hidey-hole with *him*, I supposed. I briefly considered leaking the story to the press, but guillotined the thought at birth. Funnily enough, I wasn't keen to have it made public. To have the carrion crows of Fleet Street picking over the corpse of my marriage for giggling over and gossiping about from here to John O'Groats.

Call it pride if you like. Pride was about all I had left.

'Heads will roll fast and furious,' Honry had predicted when telephoning to summon me to an emergency war council at the Biggin Hill House. 'Be warned: it may well be your requiem.'

I did the chauffering this time, though the route was ill-suited to a car of the Bentley's proportions. Once we left the A223 south of Bromley, I made frequent use of the horn to see us safely round the recurring tight bends with their high hedgerows. The sun shone all the way and along one straight stretch we bisected a plumtree orchard just starting to blossom, while the grass around the base of the trees was studded with daffodils. It was the Garden of England at its freshest and most captivating.

It turned out to be a reduced committee, consisting only of Deverill, Rees, Sir Michael d'Abo for the Home Office, and Honry and me.

Deverill fired the opening cannonade. Did I have no concept of security? How could I have been so lax with the tape? Why hadn't I left it in the care of the Department? Thanks to me, the country now faced disruption on an unimaginable scale, and the Government was set to collapse in ignominy.

I offered no defence for there was none to offer. The brickbats he slung were well-merited. Nobody was to blame but me.

'What depresses me about the whole wasted exercise,' Deverill lamented, fifty or so aspersions later, 'is that we had him by the balls. Your plan was brilliant, both the conception and execution – a masterpiece. Then, when it's all over bar the rubber stamp, you discover your wife's having an affair with the blighter – in itself an appalling security risk – and you actually let her remove the tape *while you're in the same room.*' He slapped his hand, palm down, on the table. 'I – could – bloody – well – weep. It defies belief, it really does.'

His body drooped, his chin fell onto his chest; he looked deflated and defeated. Even the white thatch was lank and lifeless.

'When she removed the tape I wasn't aware of her association with Yeo,' I pointed out. 'Had I been, I would naturally have taken precautions . . .'

'Naturally.' The peer's voice was hollow. 'Naturally we all have the wisdom of Solomon – after the event.'

'Is there any possibility at all of retrieving the situation?' D'Abo aimed his question at a point mid-way between me and Honry.

'If we knew where the tape was we could perhaps recover it,' I said doubtfully.

'Remember Watergate,' Honry cautioned, and he was in deadly earnest.

'And if we did recover it – then what?'

Rees answered. 'Burn it.'

'Too late. Yeo's already pure as a snowflake in the eyes of the union. They'll reinstate him now, no matter what. Theft of the tape would merely confirm his innocence.'

'It wasn't Yeo I was thinking of,' Rees said quietly. 'That's a dead issue now as far as my department's concerned. The Government's integrity is our priority. This thing will spread like gangrene if we don't perform drastic surgery on it, and only two solutions can be considered efficacious: destruction of Yeo or destruction of the tape.'

'Since, much as we would all dearly love to consign him to eternal damnation, the first solution is *verboten*,' d'Abo observed, 'any debate would appear to be superfluous.'

'So all we need is a plan,' Honry grunted.

Deverill had gone quiet, withdrawing behind a stiff mask in which only his eyes were alive, glittering like wet pebbles.

'No use planning anything until our respective chiefs get their heads together,' Rees said. He was easily the least ruffled among us.

High heels clacked in the corridor outside and instinctively we all – apart from Deverill who was still sunk in his private reverie – glanced towards the door, but they clip-clopped past with no break in rhythm.

Honry opened his briefcase and tossed the now bulky Hangman dossier into it.

'The Home Secretary wishes to review the latest developments with myself and Mr Fletcher this evening – off the record. No doubt he will then consult with your department, Goronwy, as to what corrective action is to be taken, if any.'

D'Abo chuckled. 'Knowing our boss, more likely he'll pass the buck back to you, Tiverton. Deal with it, he'll say, and I don't care how. Just as long as the Government isn't compromised.' His parody of the Home Secretary was passably good both in timbre and content.

This was the first I'd heard of an informal meeting with Himself.

'Will Margaret be there?' I enquired of Honry. After all, Honry was answerable to the President of the Board of Trade, not the Home Office.

'I rather think she will have organised other commitments.' Honry's smile was grim. 'Nobody but nobody wants to be associated with this mess, dear boy.' Then, looking along the table towards Deverill: 'Shall we call it a day, my lord? There doesn't seem to be much more we can do here.'

'Can't see why we had to come in the first place,' Rees grumbled.

'Because his lordship requested it,' Honry said rather prissily.

Rees showed surprise. 'His lordship? But I thought . . .'

'No, this isn't an officially-sponsored meeting. As chairman of the committee though, Lord Deverill was entitled to hear the story first hand.'

'Anyone would think it was his private project,' Rees crabbed, while d'Abo, almost inaudibly, said: 'Seems to me he did a lot of talking and sweet bugger-all listening.'

Throughout this exchange Deverill remained in a trance-like state. Only when Honry, preceded by a polite cough, called his name did the mask fall away and the facial muscles relax.

'What?' he snapped, sitting upright.

'We assume the conference is at an end, my lord,' Honry said, unperturbed by the earl's thunderous scowl, and left his chair to head for the coat stand. The insolence implied by word and deed was not lost on Deverill.

'At an end?' he almost shouted. The room became still, apprehensive. 'No, it bloody-well isn't at an end, Mr Henry Tiverton. I don't care a bent penny for your Government. Let 'em stew. The Prime Minister will learn that a whopping majority in the House doesn't make him invincible.' He glared around, poised to savage any dissenters. 'As usual, your priorities are arse-about-face: it's Yeo we've got to go for. He's still a going concern – or hadn't you noticed? He's pointing a knife at the country's heart and this time next week he'll have plunged it in. Do you think anybody will be interested then in whether the Government has egg on its face over a touched-up videotape? *Do you?*' His colour was puce. I wondered, in alarm, if he was on the verge of a stroke.

'Lord Deverill,' I began, and started towards him.

He didn't even see me. His mouth was working, the corners flecked with spittle.

'Get Yeo – that's what we must do! Get Yeo!'

He left us then. We all stood stiff as tailors' dummies while he stalked out and away down the corridor, muttering 'Get Yeo! Get Yeo!' over and over until he passed out of earshot.

'Off his chump,' Rees said unsympathetically.

'Oh, absolutely,' Honry seconded with an equal lack of concern. 'Ready, Vee?'

And we drove back to London for our next roasting.

London is a chameleon of a city. Its daytime face is sober, drab, insipid: a colourless tundra, propped up by a handful of architectural attractions and an exhumed 'swinging' reputation that no informed person ever subscribed to the first time round.

After dark though, it does at least make an effort, donning gaudy if out-at-elbows raiment, bedaubing generous quantities of make-up over the cracks and wrinkles, and doing a few high kicks to pull in the crowds. And the crowds, because there is little else competing for their patronage, oblige, pouring into the West End like water drawn to a plughole.

I'm not knocking it. Still less analysing it. When at home I was drawn to the plughole with the rest of them, and never less than two nights a week. A sucker for a £200 (minimum) rip-off, because that's about the going rate for a meal for two plus entertainment if you aim to do it in style. One can, to be sure, do it more cheaply, and in future, lacking the cushion of Julia's million-plus, that would be my lot: doing it more cheaply. My two hundred grand – provided the

Government didn't insist on its return – was peanuts by today's inflationary criteria.

Honry and I had dined early at the Savoy Grill and thence wended through the swarming traffic to our eight o'clock appointment with HM Secretary of State for Home Affairs. Thus far Honry hadn't once mentioned Julia; now, as we lurched along choc-a-bloc Pall Mall, he said: 'Heard any more from Julia, old man?' so casually it was obvious he'd been dying to ask.

'Yes,' I said shortly. 'She came home on Monday and went away again the same day.'

'With . . . him?'

'I imagine. I didn't enquire.' I honked an accesory-laden Mini who'd had the brass neck to nip in ahead of me. Hazard lights winked a double retort.

'Cheeky bugger,' Honry grunted, following up with: 'It would be a shade . . . ah . . . tricky if she talked to the press.'

I humphed. 'You're telling me.'

Horse Guards' Parade was less busy and I managed to shift up into second gear. Tothill Street was quieter still and the remaining quarter of a mile was covered at a breathtaking 15 mph.

At the Home Office we were waved through into the car park at the merest flash of Honry's pass.

'Sloppy,' I said, letting the Bentley roll down the slope. 'There'd be ructions if Himself heard how thoroughly they vetted us.'

Honry demurred. 'They know us by sight.'

'True, but I for one am no longer on the payroll.'

The roof of the car park drew a concrete veil over the starry sky. I spun the wheel left and manoeuvered into a vacant slot by the lift. As in all underground car parks every sound was amplified and between leaving the car and entering the lift we conversed, as if by unspoken agreement, in hushed tones.

Two minutes later Drizzly Disley was hustling us along the corridor to our fate.

'Do you ever go home, Disley?' Honry enquired. The same question was in my mind.

'I'm not a clock-watcher, Mr Tiverton.' Drizzly sounded hurt.

The Home Secretary wasn't clock-watching either. He sat at his desk in shirt-sleeves and loosened tie, hair standing up in ragged clumps as if he had been tearing at it. Papers covered most of the desk surface and a multi-angle lamp cast an oval yellow splash across them. The office was otherwise unlit and the Home Secretary himself a shadowy figure. The vertical hanging blinds were closed and the atmosphere was of cosy intimacy.

What followed was neither cosy nor intimate.

Honry led, as he was given to, with his chin; understandable with a chin like his.

'Minister, on Mr Fletcher's behalf I would like to say . . .'

'Stop!' The Home Secretary rose, hand raised palm outward like a policeman directing traffic. 'I know nothing. The Government knows nothing.'

'But, Minister . . .'

'Silence!' The Home Secretary then directed a shrivelling glare at me and I was duly and thoroughly shrivelled. The Man of Straw was a Man of Steel this night. 'As for you . . . words almost fail me. Almost. You need not speak, you need only listen to what I have to say, which is this: we are faced with two separate but inter-related crises. Number one . . .' he stuck an index finger up almost under Honry's nose, 'risk of embarrassment to me, to the President of the Board of Trade, and possibly by association to the Prime Minister, the Government, and the Party. Number two . . .' the middle finger sprang up, 'a crippling strike is due to start on Monday next.'

Honry tried again: he was a glutton for punishment. 'Home Secretary . . .'

'Will *you* be quiet?'

Honry recoiled and was quiet.

'You have until Saturday, gentlemen, to resolve these two matters. Five days. Don't tell me how you propose to do it – just do it.' He looked from one to the other of us, but his gaze rested longer on me as the true architect of the disaster. 'Do it,' he repeated.

There was no 'or else', and its absence was somehow even more intimidating.

'I'm not an employee,' I objected.

His pale eyes narrowed until they were no more than slits behind the elliptical glasses.

'And I don't know anything about any £200,000.' He sat down and picked up his pen, a clear signal that the interview was over. 'Now get out and get on with it . . .'

We got out. As for getting on with it . . .

'Straight home?' I said to Honry as we swished up the car park ramp.

'M'mm. You'll stay, of course.'

'Of course not. I'm going back to Kingscourt.'

To an empty house. To a shell.

'But we must get stuck in at once. You heard . . .'

'*You* get stuck in, Honry,' I cut in. 'I need a good night's sleep. I'll call you tomorrow.'

He was inclined to protest.

'Don't nag, Honry,' I said presently, and soon after that he did actually shut up and apart from intermittent sniffs and sighs remained mute until I dropped him off at his front door.

'A night cap?' he suggested, half-in, half-out of the car.

'No thanks. Night, Honry – love to Charlotte.'

I accelerated away, leaving him at the kerb. He was still there, looking after me, when I reached the far side of the square and swung off into West Halkin Street.

Though I couldn't let him in on the secret, he had no cause to worry. I was about to deactivate both of the Home Secretary's crises at a stroke, all on my very own.

Chapter Twenty-One

It was a solution of such masterly simplicity that no plan as such was needed. Sleeping on it evoked neither refinement nor dilution of purpose. What was more, I slept dreamlessly and well, and awoke more refreshed than for many a week.

My appetite had returned too. I attacked my breakfast with an end-of-fast gusto that caused Willoughby's eyebrows to wriggle like worms on a hot plate.

'You appear to be feeling better this morning, sir,' he commented in that disinterested monotone of his.

'Much better, Willers, old top,' I said, and the eyebrows writhed again at the unwonted familiarity.

'Er . . . if it's not indiscreet to enquire . . . when might Mrs Fletcher be expected to . . . ah . . . return?'

'About the same time as I might be expected to leave.'

Which rounded the exchange off rather neatly, I felt.

From the study I made two telephone calls: Honry first.

'But can't you tell me anything?' he groused, when I advised him to take the rest of the week off.

'Not a thing. Trust me, Honry. Go on a world cruise for a few days. When you get back it'll be all over.'

I let him chunter on for a minute or so then reiterated my suggestion and hung up.

My second contact was harder to track down and arrived at the receiver wheezing.

'Only just got down from the Monument?' I cracked.

Sushil Saran vented a squeak of alarm. 'You! You mustn't ring me here! What do you want?'

'Just some harmless information. Nothing compromising.' I explained my needs and he was able to satisfy them straight off.

'Thanks, Sushil,' I said, 'and goodbye. I don't think I'll be troubling you again.'

Next, a small matter of the instrument with which to apply my solution.

I unlocked the bottom, left-hand drawer of the bureau. It contained but a single item: a plain mahogany box, about eighteen inches square by three inches deep, with brass lock, corner pieces, and a name plate bearing the inscription: W B von URACH.

It had come into my possession via my grandfather on my father's side, who had acquired it from a German army deserter while stationed in Germany immediately after World War I. For a princely 'ten bob' as he was fond of putting it, with a gap-toothed chuckle. On his death it had passed to my father, who passed it in turn to me, along with most of his other worldly goods when he did his bunk to New Zealand, slipping like wet soap through a tightening ring of creditors.

With the fancy brass key I'd had made to replace the original (presumably in New Zealand with its owner), I opened the lid on my grandfather's ten bob steal.

The Mauser C96 *Selbstladepistole* was the forerunner of all automatic pistols and good examples are becoming increasingly harder to come by. Mine was the 1915 Parabellum, chambered for 9mm, one of 150,000 or so produced for the Kaiser's army during the Great War, and having a black-stained '9' recessed into the famous broom-handle grip and all metal parts finished blue-black. Condition – mint: probably it had never seen active service. In these times of double-action automatics with ambidextrous safety-catches, rapid-fire facility, and 18-round magazines, it was beyond doubt an anachronism, yet it boasted a devastating 1425 fps muzzle velocity, half as much again as the much more successful and scarcely less venerable .45 Colt Auto.

I lifted it carefully, almost deferentially from its contoured resting place. It was a substantial weapon: over a foot long and weighing just under 3lbs. Five-and-a-half inches of barrel with six-groove rifling, right-hand twist. Accurate up to, say, a hundred and fifty yards if used in conjunction with the detachable wooden shoulder stock/holster, which occupied some two-thirds of the case. I mated the stock with the grip. Now I had me a rifle.

These early Mausers were not fitted with magazines but loaded through the top of the action by means of 'chargers' – metal clips into which the cartridges slotted. I had several such chargers, each with ten-round capacity, plus a couple of boxes of 9mm ammunition kept in the safe. My needs would not be nearly so great.

I sighted the gun, the stock nestling against my shoulder. Squeezed the trigger: *snap*. Again: *snap*. The trigger had a heavy pull, over 4lbs at a guess, but the action was velvet smooth. As it should be; though little used, I kept it well-oiled inside and out, and when last fired, over a year ago, it had performed faultlessly.

Removing the stock I re-packed the components and fetched a box of cartridges from the safe, an errand which recalled Julia's treachery and dragged an ugly word from my lips.

A tap came at the door. I composed myself, called: 'Come in,' and Willoughby entered with my mail. He deposited it on the round Queen Anne table by the door and departed, soundless as a wraith.

It was a pleasant day for an inspection tour of the estate. I changed into windcheater and a pair of old cords, and my gumboots, for it was sure to be soggy underfoot. With the Mauser case tucked under my arm and a box of cartridges making a square bulge in my windcheater pocket, I meandered past the pool, past the sculpted hedgerows, past the little orchard. A hazy sun cast pale shadows and the garden throbbed with bird life; a fly overtook me, its course unsteady, torpid still in the aftermath of winter. I followed the fly into the wood.

The path through the wood was narrow and ended in a glade where Julia and I used to spend many a summer afternoon in the early afterglow of our marriage. Before our relationship was reduced to no more than a series of coital encounters, physically explosive but emotionally sterile.

There, in that glade of bitter-sweet memory, I reassembled the Mauser. I wasn't worried about the shots being overheard; only the servants were within hearing distance, and they were paid to mind their own business.

At a range of fifty yards I fired a single round at a broad trunk on the far side of the glade. Bark flew and a green gash sprouted about five feet up: this was to be my aiming point. I squeezed off the rest of the charger, unhurriedly at first, then more rapidly as I grew accustomed to the kick and the slight lift of the barrel which, being somewhat short and light relative to the power of the weapon, absorbed virtually none of the recoil. A double-handed grip was needed whether or not the stock was used.

The marksman touch which, years before had amassed a record number of trophies for Int Corps, had not deserted me. I proved, on inspection, to have achieved a two-inch group around the aiming point, apart from two mavericks – one just outside and above the group, the other a bit higher. These would be my second and first shots respectively, before I corrected for the snatch of the muzzle.

Satisfied, I extracted the empty charger, unclipped the stock, and packed the component parts away in the box. There was purpose in my stride as I threaded back through the woods.

I had emerged from the trees and was passing the orchard when a slight figure came around the side of the house, paused, then came on towards me, walking slowly. Unrecognisably but unquestionably female. Julia! Such was my apoplectic, heart-leaping assumption – Julia was coming back to me.

But no. The walk was not Julia's, nor was the hair as dark. As the gap between us lessened, the face acquired shape and became Rowen's. We both slowed, uncertain, wary.

'Hello.' We spoke together then grinned together, which immediately thawed much of the ice.

'What are you doing here?' I asked.

She lifted her slim shoulders. Her make-up was smudged and her hair carelessly tied back with errant tendrils dangling over her cheeks.

'Shall we walk or sit?' I indicated the wooden seat under the stone archway that flanked the rear lawn. 'It's dry – the arch keeps the rain off.'

'Let's sit then. I can think better sitting.'

So we sat. I was conscious of the heavy mahogany case under my arm, but she didn't mention it. Her abstraction was total. Had she come here bent on picking up the threads of our liaison, I wondered. For her sake, I hoped not.

For a while she said nothing. Just smoked (which made me think of Julia) and stared out towards the swimming pool.

'Your gardens are beautiful,' she said at length, when the cigarette had burned down to a half-inch nub that I had to remove from her fingers lest she burn them.

'Not mine – Julia's. Nothing here is mine.'

She gazed at me and her gazelle eyes were a naked plea. Only they were the wrong eyes, alas.

'She's run away with Dad, hasn't she?'

She. To Rowen and her kin, Julia was 'she', just as Yeo was nameless to me.

'Yes.'

'Mum's so upset. It's awful – you can't imagine . . .'

Oh yes, I can, Rowen. Only too well.

'Is that what you came here to tell me?'

The tone was harder than I intended and she stiffened.

'No, it isn't,' she said frostily. 'Nor did I come to ask any favours. I came . . . because I have to tell you something about Dad. Because I'm afraid for him; whatever he's done, he's still my father.'

'I'm listening. I'm rather short on sympathy for your father right now though, so don't expect too much.'

As if at last understanding my own trauma, she touched my arm. 'Oh, Vee . . . I hadn't really thought of you being cut up about it.'

'Thanks,' I said sardonically.

'I didn't mean . . . I meant, I hoped you and I . . .' She chewed her underlip and picked at a knot on the seat. 'Anyway it's Lord Deverill I really want to talk to you about.'

'Lord Deverill? What's he got to do with your father?'

'Everything,' she said. 'Everything and, you might say, nothing at all: he's my father's real father.'

My whole body gave a puppet-like jerk. The Earl of Deverill and David Yeo? *Father and son*? It was so preposterous I genuinely believed I had misheard.

'Say it again, only very, very slowly.'

She gave me a long searching stare before complying.

'Dad is Lord Deverill's illegitimate son.'

There it was, loud and clear and unequivocal. Lord Deverill sired David Yeo. Since most adopted children are born out of wedlock, Yeo's bastardy was not much of an exposé. It was his noble status – viscount or baron, depending upon Deverill's secondary title – that was so fantastic. Yet because it was so fantastic I believed it absolutely. The physical resemblance, the eyes that were mirror images, was now explained. Yeo, the ultimate revolutionary, was a bloody lord!

But the knowledge came too late to use against him. Thanks to my slipshod conduct, Yeo was armour-plated now. Be he the direct lineal descendant of the last Tsar of Russia, nobody would hold it against him.

'Is that what you were going to tell me in exchange for . . . you know.'

'In exchange for you?' she said, forthright to the last. 'Yes, that was what I was offering, though I intended to swear you to secrecy.'

Some hope of that, my girl, I thought.

'How do you know this, Rowen? How did you find out in the first place?'

'It was a long time ago – seven, eight years. Lord Deverill came to the house on some pretext – I forget what. Mum and Dad were out with Reggie and Roger. I let him in; never heard of child molesters, you see. I made him a cup of tea and he broke down. Actually cried, there in the living-room. I can still remember the tears rolling down his cheeks and splashing into his tea. I ticked him off; said the salt would spoil the taste.'

'That was when he came out with it: that he was your . . . grandfather?'

Her nod was microscopic. 'He made me swear never to tell a soul, and especially not my parents. I kept my promise, though it wouldn't surprise me if Dad already knew.'

Me, neither.

'What happened then? After Lord Deverill unloaded his guilt on you, I mean.'

'Happened?' Her mouth trembled. 'He drank his tea, tears and all, and went away.'

'Did he ever come back?'

'Never. I never saw him again to speak to. He was on TV once, I remember, in a programme about stately homes. But, no, that was our first and only encounter.

334

Probably he had second thoughts about wanting to meet Dad.'

'Uh-huh. Calling on you was an act of impulse, I expect.' I let the vision slosh around inside my head of Deverill, looking pretty much as he did now, crying into a cup of tea in front of a pubescent Rowen as he poured out his miserable confession. And she, young yet resilient, keeping her head, taking him and his secret in her stride. Telling no one.

Until today.

'Why tell me, Rowen?'

A dumpy sparrow alighted on the nearer of the two Grecian urns that stood like sentries on either side of the arch. It hopped about, fluttering its wings, unaware or oblivious of our presence. Then Rowen uncrossed her legs and the movement startled it into a straight-up ascent, followed by a swerving rush across the lawn, cheep-cheeping as it went.

After a short, hesitant silence Rowen said: 'I saw him again this morning. He was at the end of the road, just sort of standing there. I was on my way to college, but when I saw him I naturally stopped and we ended up sitting in the car, talking. What I mean is, he talked and I mostly listened. Not that I understood a great deal – he was only semi-coherent, and in fact he behaved oddly the whole time, almost as if he were drunk. At one point . . .' A small tremor ran through her, 'at one point he said, "I'll get him, I'll get him," repeating it over and over. It was quite frightening. I'm sure he was . . . well, you know . . . ill.'

'Yes.' I didn't say he was probably half-round the twist. Coming after his irrational behaviour at yesterday's meeting, the picture was of a man on the verge of a nervous breakdown. 'Who was he going to get – did he say?'

'I asked him. "Get who?" I said. But he wouldn't answer; I'm not sure he even heard. After a while though, I realised he was talking about Dad.'

'What? He actually threatened to . . . get your father? To hurt him in some way?'

'Yes.' A frightened whisper.

It added up. And it meant that the ranting and the threats at the meeting were more than just a passing flare-up.

'In amongst all the garbage, did he say *why*?'

'Not in as many words. It was like putting together a very complicated jig-saw puzzle. Everything was out of sequence. Your name was mentioned more than once; I got the impression you had let him down, disappointed him. He was more sad about you than angry though.'

Not nearly as sad as I was.

Rowen went on: 'As I say, it was all very jumbled, but I eventually worked out that he had meant to ruin Dad through this scheme of yours, simply because he couldn't bear to have him shoved under his nose on television every night, a constant reminder of . . . of what he did when he was a young man. While Dad was only a minor union official he could tolerate it – out of sight, our of mind, and all that. It was when he suddenly became a public figure that the antagonism began to build up. And, of course, Dad being such a leftie just added to the agony.'

The sun had dimmed, losing heat, and a breeze laced with the remnants of winter funnelled through the arch and we shivered in concert. I put my arm around Rowen, the warmth of her young body seeming to flow into me like an electric current.

'Having an illegitimate child isn't such a big deal,' I said. 'Why is he so uptight about it?'

'That was what I wondered too. Until he told me the full story: how he abandoned the mother and refused to pay for the child's . . . for Dad's upbringing, for fear the connection might come out. That alone must have given him sleepless nights. What really bugs him though, is that he has no legitimate heir by his

336

marriage to Lady Deverill. No son to leave his titles and estates to. There'll be no sixth Earl. Just imagine what that must mean to someone like him.'

Imagine indeed. As he grew older and death less remote, he would more and more curse his youthful folly, the denial of his own flesh and blood. It must have eaten at him like an acid over the years, until now, with his bastard son's face cropping up at every turn, accusing him, he was poised to cross the great but hairline divide between reason and unreason.

'The upshot of all this is that you really do believe Deverill will do something . . . silly.'

'I believe it's possible. He was *so* angry, and it was all bottled up inside him like champagne.'

And Yeo, unknowingly, was shaking the bottle.

'Let's hope the cork doesn't go pop,' I said quietly.

What irony. Here she was, crying on my shoulder about Deverill, fearful of what he might do, when all along I was poised to exact a retribution of my own. My hand absently stroked the Mauser case. I may have smiled to myself.

'And what do you want me to do about all this, Rowen? Protect your father?' It was laughable. I was the last person she should ask.

The heresy of it hadn't escaped her.

'It's asking a lot, I know.' She rocked back and forth, hugging herself. 'But there's only you. I daren't tell anyone else. I . . . trust you.'

She trusted me. Dear God.

'I hoped that, if you wouldn't do it for Dad, you'd do it for Lord Deverill. Save him from himself, you might say.'

Yeah. That at least I could do: save Deverill from himself. The mahogany box was warm and smooth under my touch. And inside it the solution to all manner of problems: the Government's embarrassment, the imminent strike, my own thirst for revenge . . .

And now, on top of all this, I would save Deverill from incarceration. Such a noble cause!

For old time's sake I leaned across and touched my lips to Rowen's. She kissed back hard, her mouth moulding to mine, teeth against flesh, tongue flicking, hugging me to her as if I were a hot-air balloon about to take flight.

'I love you, Vee, my darling,' she murmured. 'I love you so very, very much.'

Wasted words, wasted emotions. I would have told her so except that it seemed kinder by far to let her love perish naturally, as perish it would when she learned of her father's death at my hands.

Chapter Twenty-Two

It was Friday. Overcast, blustery, occasional light showers. April to a 'T'.

Provided Sushil Saran's information was bona-fide, Yeo was today scheduled to address engineers and manual workers employed at Drakelow Power Station in Staffordshire. Time: 4.40 pm. Venue: the car park of The Coachmakers' Arms Inn, which lay on the road between Burton-on-Trent and the village of Walton-on-Trent, and was the 'local' for many of those same workers. Like every building in the vicinity, it enjoyed views of Drakelow's ten giant cooling towers, soulless eyesores topped with plumes of steam that rose as tall again as the towers themselves.

By telephone, I had booked accommodation at the homely, brick-built tavern for two nights, requesting a room overlooking the car park. Since the rooms on that side also overlooked the power station this stipulation was presumably thought eccentric, but the receptionist made no attempt to dissuade me.

My precautions against identification were rudimentary: I had booked under a pseudonym and travelled there by motor cycle – a second-hand BMW, big as a horse, newly acquired from a private vendor – which allowed me to hide my face inside a regulation crash helmet with a heavily-tinted visor. Checking in on Thursday evening I kept the helmet on, raising the visor no more than an inch to announce myself, and immediately fled to my room, there to while away a trogloditic twelve hours.

On reflection, my conduct must have struck the hotel staff as quirky, even suspicious, but throughout my limited contact with them I was treated only with respectful affability. Possibly they were only humouring me.

As for my getaway plan; here I had been a shade more professional. The motor cycle was parked by the external fire escape, which was reached via a conventional, bar-operated fire door down the corridor from my room. Late on Thursday evening, while last orders were being called downstairs, I had risked a discreet practice sprint from room to motor cycle, clocking a respectable 37 seconds. On the day I would assuredly improve on this – say 30 seconds, plus as many again to start up and hit the tarmac. So, one minute in total. One minute for the initial shock and confusion to be replaced by hue and cry.

On a lonely country lane, approximately four miles from The Coachmakers' Arms, I would dump my mighty machine and my riding gear and take to a public footpath which ended, a mile later, at the considerable village of Overseal, where a second-hand Vauxhall Cavalier awaited me. This, in its turn, was also due to be dumped – in Derby – in favour of a hired Metro. Beyond the Metro lay further diversions and red herrings. Hopefully, they would suffice.

On Friday morning I had ordered breakfast in my room, nipping into the loo when a knock on the door signalled its arrival. Subsequently I had spent an hour, helmet and all, under the guise of aimless meandering, pacing out distances in the car park, checking angles of fire, and so on. Of course it would have been less hazardous to kill Yeo from afar, screened by woods or bushes. But in the first place such vegetation as the surrounding countryside sported was all in the wrong place, secondly, obtaining a weapon with the required range, through the mandatory illegal channels, would have taken a week or more. The Home Secretary couldn't wait that long.

Emphatically, nor could I.

Yeo's four-strong advance guard put in an appearance around noon. From my window I watched them spill out of a glossy new Scorpio with a small trailer in tow, and rush for the entrance. I saw no more of them until after closing time, when they sauntered out, garrulous with drink, to set up the fixtures and fittings – rostrum, public address system, and suchlike. Feeling peckish, I asked for sandwiches to be sent up, together with a miniature of Dutch Courage, and used the bathroom ploy again to avoid facial contact.

Had I been capable that afternoon of standing back to consider the scenario without passion, I would have packed my bag and hopped it as fast as the motor cycle could carry me. And not merely because I was about to cold-bloodedly kill another human being, appalling though that intent was; it was my lack of heed for the consequences that would have left me aghast. Though I had indeed taken such precautions as time allowed, I was still half-resigned to being caught and to paying for my crime, according to the laws of the land. Beyond my cool, clear resolve to kill Yeo, all was blank. Every step was as if pre-ordained, every act mechanical. Thought was no longer necessary.

My door was locked, the window open just enough for my purpose, the Mauser reposing on my pillow. Stock fitted, a full charger of ten cartridges *in situ*. It was an evil-looking weapon. A villain's weapon: fictional heroes were never provided with Mausers. But villainous or not, it would have to do, since I owned no other firearm. I was truly the most ill-prepared assassin in history.

A crowd was forming in the car park; all age groups were represented, from toddler to senior citizen, and women were almost as numerous as men. The dais was in place: it was about three feet high by five square and consisted of a platform of thick chipboard supported by some sort of framework, altogether very basic. A microphone on a stand was positioned at the front, ready to broadcast the Gospel according to David Yeo. I checked my watch: 4.28, and even as I raised my head, he was rolling into the car park in another Scorpio. An expensive yet classless car to complement the classless image he strove to project. No Jags or Rovers for Yeo and Co Sybaritic tastes must not be paraded. Yet.

Cheers and applause drifted in through the window and a car horn blared a salute. I went to relieve a fretful bladder for the third time in an hour, and when I returned to the window the hullaballoo had died away and Yeo was about to speak. I perched on the edge of the bed from where I had an uninterrupted view.

Yeo saw off the welcoming address in a single sentence.

'You will be aware,' he said, his voice, carried by the speakers, ricocheting around my room, 'of the protracted talks between our union and the employers on the issues of pay, hours and recruitment . . .'

And so on. Standard Yeo introduction. Begin by emphasising how reasonable was the union's stance, and how intransigent, in contrast, were the employers; how patient and accommodating the union had been in the face of hostility. Dwell upon the major concessions agreed to by the union (in reality they had conceded next to nothing), their selfless efforts, not only to extract more momey for their members (that pitiful twenty-five per cent!), but to create jobs for less fortunate brethren.

He used no notes. He was polished and fluent and – rot him – credible. What a waste, I mused, that such a multi-talented man should be dedicated to wrecking instead of building. A prime example of abuse of ability.

'. . . though here in Burton-on-Trent,' he was saying, 'you have been relatively fortunate. Drakelow Power Station provides many jobs and the unemployment level in this area is well below the national average. Regrettably, your situation is not typical. I could tell you about other similar towns that depended on power stations for their prosperity. Until those power stations were shut down . . .'

Evoking that hoary stand-by, the unemployment spectre. Playing on a supposed vulnerability as a stimulus to collective action. Making sure that, when the moment to down tools arrived on Monday next, the downing at Drakelow was a hundred per cent solid. This was one of many such speeches Yeo had made on a whistle-stop tour of power stations across the country.

Applause swept across the car park. The crowd was still growing and now extended back to the kerb. Two helmeted bobbies appeared on the other side of the road and took up station there, arms folded. A token presence.

'. . . sacrifices must be made to achieve that end.' Yeo was still socking the same old pulpit-thumping invective to 'em. 'But believe me, brothers, this will be no long-drawn-out dispute, dragging on with no hope of an honourable settlement . . .' an oblique tilt at the recent communication workers' dispute, 'we can make our absence felt right away. Admittedly the impact would have been more severe had the strike gone ahead in the winter – which it would, but for my compulsory holiday as Her Majesty's reluctant guest . . .' break here for merriment, which was generously supplied. Would the Government dare respond to this slander? I doubted it, 'but even without the winter to reinforce our struggle, we shall win and – this I guarantee – our victory will be swift.'

Not a solitary heckle so far, which went to show how solidly his audience were behind him. Looks had a lot to do with it: the physically-attractive public speaker is off to a flying start, even before he opens his mouth. Yeo, tall, well-proportioned, a man's man yet no less a ladies man; not young, not old, therefore indentifying with no particular age group. Equally at home giving an after-dinner talk to a party of overfed industrialists or whipping up support at the roadside. His was a shifting image, the emphasis changing to suit environment and audience.

The Mauser was on my lap, the broomhandle grip, as always, alien to a hand once accustomed to the flatter, more ergonomic contours of a Browning Hi-Power military automatic. Head shot or body shot? It was a measure of my lack of preparation that I had not even decided where to place the bullet. A head shot was surer, but offered a smaller target. Was I confident enough of my marksmanship to go for it?

The range was under seventy yards, possibly as short as sixty. At sixty yards I would expect to manage, at worst, a three-inch group. A head shot then. Two bullets minimum.

'. . . without total solidarity we will either fail or, worse still, end up with half-a-strike. Not enough to force the employers' and the Government's hands, not enough to bring the country to a halt; just enough to cause inconvenience, the odd case of hardship here and there, giving the British public an excuse to indulge in that famous bulldog spirit, which the Tory press will praise to the hilt along with the usual lurid tales of suffering and deprivation; all grossly exaggerated and intended to alienate public opinion. Making us out to be evil-hearted, grasping rogues. We must not give them that opportunity, brothers. We are in this together, and we must *fight* together. We must show them . . .'

Darker clouds were forming behind the man-made clouds that issued from the cooling towers. The wind had risen in the last few minutes and my window was rattling madly against its stay. An empty, abandoned plastic bag cartwheeled down the road, and a woman in the crowd squealed when her hat blew off; it was retrieved by an unkempt, shaven-headed youth and passed back to its owner. Chivalry lingering on in isolated pockets.

I knelt by the window, settled the Mauser's stock against the soft pad of flesh next to the collar bone – man's inbuilt recoil absorber. The safety lever was off; on this model it can only be applied when the hammer is actually cocked for firing, which was my next act. Quaintly, the very first Mausers had a spur hammer designed for cocking against a horseman's saddle; mine, fortunately, was the space-age model, designed for a thumb. Much more practical.

Yeo was in full flight and, I had to admit, with the angry sky above and the wind whipping the row of poplar trees bordering the garden behind him, he cut a dramatic figure. A blond god on the threshold of deification.

A god of promises: '. . . I promise you we will *force* this Government to re-think . . .'

A god of war: '. . . we will re-shape the political face of Britain by bloody revolution, if necessary . . .'

Most of all a god of duplicity and deceit: '. . . because the only true democracy is a democracy of Government by the governed!'

Winding up on that well-trodden aphorism of all non-democrats, he stepped back from the microphone and his audience, now swelled to six or seven hundred, erupted into cheers and whistles.

I hooked my finger aound the trigger, sighting along the slim, smooth barrel, lining the tail foresight up with Yeo's head, while he lapped up the crowd's ovation, milking them blatantly for more, outstretched arms that said: *Worship me! Worship me!*

And they did. Their adulation was total and profuse. They worshipped their false god and believed he was true.

But he was about to meet the real truth: that of a bullet speeding towards him at 1000mph. An ultimate, inescapable, definitive truth.

From a section of the crowd a sudden commotion: shouting, confused noises, a woman's scream. Yeo was no longer strutting and posing but peering forward uncertainly. The crowd was in motion, undulating like a cornfield in the wind, parting before a tall, soberly-dressed man with a mane of white hair; a man whose right arm tapered to a pistol, which he used to slash at those nearest to him, machete-fashion, as if clearing a path through the jungle.

So his threat hadn't been idle, and he was here to make it good, coincidentally trespassing on my patch. He would steal my thunder yet, were I to allow it.

Yeo had spotted the pistol, was backing away, but it was an orderly withdrawal rather than a rout. Even when the interloper stood before him, the pistol no longer slashing but pointing, he declined to bolt. His nerve was awesome.

'Here it comes, Yeo,' I whispered. The Mauser was as steady as if grafted to my hand; it needed only a minuscule amount of pressure on the trigger. Nothing could deflect me from my purpose. He was mine . . . mine.

Two shots, almost blending into a single flat cough. Well below the decibel level of a car backfire, the wind shredding the report so that no resonance hung in the air, and the milling multitude in the car park becoming still as waxworks, even the children falling quiet, as if a magic spell had been cast and to move or speak would be to break it.

Epilogue

The last day of April was memorable as the day I went calling on Julia at her younger brother's house near Winterbourne Abbas, in Dorset. We hadn't met or even communicated since she left me.

She came out and met me on the steps, pale but pretty in cream jumper and matching straight skirt. It was early evening, sunny, and unusually mild, so I suggested a spin down to the coast.

'Why not?' she said, agreeably enough.

During the short journey we conversed only in laconic bursts. I mostly concentrated on my driving, she mostly on her smoking. At Abbotsbury we linked up with the Weymouth road, leaving it after a few hundred yards to head down to the sea and ultimately taking to Shank's pony to stumble – barefoot in Julia's case – over that natural phenomenon known as the Chesil Beach, a five-mile long, hundred-feet high embankment of egg-sized pebbles.

We subsided at the water's edge, tossed in a few pebbles as promenaders are compelled to do.

'What will the Government do now?' Julia said presently. 'Now that David's . . . out of it.'

David. A bare nerve twanged. I wasn't healed yet.

I shrugged. 'Heave a collective sigh of relief, I expect. One threat removed – on to the next. The Teachers are spoiling for another fight, not to mention the RMT, and the Government still doesn't know whether to stand and fight or cave in. This time though, I shan't be

347

around to pull their chestnuts out of the fire. Or foul things up, as some might suggest.'

I was tempted to tell her about the £200,000 nestling in my Zürich account, but decided against it. Best to wait until I made it work for me. Until I was doing more than just running a security outfit, earning my keep and precious little more.

'How awful,' Julia said, shuddering.

'Awful – what?'

'Classifying people as threats. Why can't we just live together in harmony. Why so much strife, strife, strife!'

The dialogue rested there for a minute, then Julia blurted: 'What about us, Vee? What's our future?'

Which implied there might still *be* a future.

'Try again?' I offered.

A shake of the head, but doubt, not rejection.

'Is that possible?'

A tiny bird of hope soared within me.

'We've each sinned against the other so the score's even. Let's pretend the last thirteen years never happened. Let's pretend we just met. Here. Today.'

Something about that off-the-cuff suggestion must have struck a chord, for she suddenly went very still.

'I don't think I could,' she said in a voice that belied it.

'Yes, you could.' I kissed her lightly at the corner of her mouth. 'And let's not forget Gavin. We owe it to him to try.' Hypocrisy, considering my non-relationship with the boy. But I'd have danced on my mother's grave to keep us together.

Julia sat in deep meditation, squeezing her knees. The sea slapped at the pebbles around our feet. It was growing dark.

A bou of about twelve came along with a young Irish setter, barely more than a puppy, and threw bits of beach flotsam into the sea for it to retrieve, urging it on with cries of, 'Fetch, Sheba, fetch! Go on, girl!' Sheba, wise beyond her years, barked and pirouetted and kept her paws dry. After all it was only April and the English Channel in April is no place for man or beast.

Eventually they wandered away along the beach and the high-pitched yip-yip of the dog faded into the dusk.

Julia and I made love – inevitably we made love. There on the pebbles and to hell with the laws of decency. It was a loving far removed from the usual cataclysm: a soft, gentle, healing experience, in which the caresses were light as thistledown and the moment of entry itself orgasmic: a parting of petals, pink and dewed, a roaring of fires, a thunder in the ears.

Away we flew, away into the night on wings of fantasy, tumbling like storm-tossed leaves, hurtling at impossible speed towards a cluster of bright stars – nearer . . . nearer . . . then, when it seemed we must plunge into their midst, the stars shivering into a billion fragments of blinding light.

And afterwards . . . drifting, enclosed in a womb of warmth, hearing only the shuffle of the sea and our own breathing. I reached out to touch her face, tracing that perfect profile, and when she turned her head towards me I saw, in the dying light, the wetness on her cheeks.

With the tips of my fingers I smoothed her tears lightly away, wondering, as I did so, who she was really crying for.